DEATH
in Pakistan

An **Alex Boyd** Thriller

Mel Harrison

Copyright Page

Written by Mel Harrison
Edited by Paula F. Howard

PRINTED IN THE UNITED STATES OF AMERICA
KDP Publishing
First Edition: August, 2019

More copies may be ordered online at Amazon.com

Testimonials

"Death in Pakistan is a fast-paced thriller by a former State Department special agent. Trust me, Harrison knows what he is talking about."

- Fred Burton, former special agent and New York Times best-selling author

"An exciting tale of a deadly plot of terrorism set in Pakistan, told by the ultimate insider...a 'must read'!"

-George Larson, author of the Dick Avery Adventure Stories

"This novel based on real-life experience will not only give you some insights into events that take place in Pakistan, but it's an exciting read as well. No one is better prepared to tell this story than Mel Harrison. His first-hand experiences during his tour as the American Embassy's Regional Security Officer (RSO), not only earned him recognition as "RSO of the Year", but also the State Department's Award for Valor.

"While the story is fiction, the account resembles events that have taken place in Pakistan and will give you a behind the scenes look into the difficulties of diplomatic life abroad. I'm confident you will enjoy this thrilling story and that it will give you an appreciation for the difficult work of an RSO.

"Excellent work Mel and congratulations on an outstanding piece of work!

-Greg Bujac, former Director of the Diplomatic Security Service and Principal Deputy Assistant Secretary of State for Diplomatic Security

ACKNOWLEDGEMENTS

I want to thank my wife, Irene, for her ceaseless efforts to improve what I wrote. Her proof-reading, her story line suggestions, and character critiques all helped to keep the novel focused and real. As a fellow career Foreign Service professional, Irene served with me in Islamabad, sharing the same risks and frustrations, as well as the excitement of living through harrowing times with many of our close friends in the American Embassy.

Two special friends need to be mentioned: Charlotte Grove and Larry Richter, who read my early manuscript, giving me their opinions on how to improve my story.

My editor, Paula Howard, deserves a special thanks for all her work reviewing my manuscript with a keen, professional eye. An extraordinary writer in her own right, she taught me how to write more effectively in order to capture the imagination of the reader.

Lastly, I want to thank The Villages Creative Writing Group for their weekly critiques of another novel I am writing. I applied their general thoughts on good writing to this book.

I hope you enjoy all of our concerted efforts!

DIPLOMATIC PERSONNEL with ACRONYMS

Ambassador **Worthington Pierce**	• Top authority at any embassy worldwide • All civilian or military agencies within the Embassy operate under the Ambassador's authority.
Defense Attaché **Colonel Walker**	• Known as the 'DATT' • Liaises with host country's military • Provides intelligence information usually obtained in a non-covert manner.
Deputy Chief of Mission **Ellen Hunt**	• Ambassador's Deputy (DCM) • Person through which all agencies at post report to the Ambassador. • Most DCMs are career former Political or Economic Officers
Diplomatic Security Service **(DSS)**	• Referred to as DS • Professional Security and Operational Counter-Terrorism arm of the U.S, State Department • Nearly every Embassy and Consulate worldwide has at least one DS officer
Emergency Action Committee **(EAC)**	• Inter-Agency Embassy committee chaired by the DCM • Regional Security Officer (RSO) is key member • Handles threats against Embassy and staff

Foreign Service Officer **(FSO)**	• Career generalists who serve at an embassy • Positions include Political Officers, Consular Officers, Economic Officers, Management Officers, and Deputy Chiefs of Mission.
Management Counselor **JC Colon**	• Senior State Department administrative officer in the Embassy.
Marine Security Guard **(MSG)**	• Marine Security Guard Detachments are assigned to embassies and consulates to provide 24-hour access control. • They are vital for the internal protection of these facilities. They are led by a senior NCO (non-commissioned officer) and supervised by the Regional Security Officer. • Marine Officers are only based regionally for occasional inspection or trouble-shooting.
Political Counselor **Winston Hargrove IV**	• The senior State Department officer under the Ambassador and DCM • Responsible for political relations between the US and Pakistan.

Press Officer **Rachel Smith**	• Monitors local media stories of importance to U.S policymakers. • Explains U.S. policies to the local media and crafts the US image to the local public. • Acts as Embassy spokesperson.
Regional Security Officers (RSO) • **Jim Riley** (Chief) • **Alex Boyd** • **Susan Witt**	• Special Agents with the Diplomatic Security Service. • In Pakistan, RSOs cover the Embassy in Islamabad, and Consulates General in Karachi, Lahore, and Peshawar. • Skilled in VIP protection, physical security, counter-terrorism, criminal investigations. • Skilled in Marine Security Guard leadership, project management, and a host of related subjects.
Station Chief (CIA) **Bill Stanton**	• Supported by numerous other CIA case officers and staff. • Responsible for covert intelligence collection and liaison with ISI.
Inter-Service Intelligence Directorate **(ISI)**	• Powerful military body within the Pakistan government • Power behind the throne, even when Pakistan has a civilian government.

Table of Contents

CHAPTER 1

THURSDAY MORNING

Islamabad, Pakistan, 1990s

Ambassador Worthington Pierce slammed a fist on his desk. Reading the classified telegram a second time, he realized the message could mean substantial long-term damage to the U.S.-Pakistani relationship.

Sitting behind his large mahogany desk on the third floor of the American Embassy in Islamabad, he was more than annoyed.

"This new policy is a frickin' disaster for us and for Pakistan! What do you both think?"

Seated in front of him were Ellen Hunt, his Deputy Chief of Mission, and Alex Boyd, Deputy Regional Security Officer.

"You're right," Ellen said. "Telling the Pakistani Prime Minister that we're significantly cutting his foreign assistance, specifically military assistance, is going to drive him nuts. It's going to be a tough meeting for you; I don't relish the idea of explaining this to him."

"When you look at the third paragraph, and see the amount of military aid we're giving India now is quite significant, the entire Pakistani establishment, as well as the man-on-the-street, will rise up in arms," Alex said. "I don't want to be an alarmist, but we could be facing anti-American riots like we did in 1979. Remember when 5,000 demonstrators attacked the Embassy and gutted it with fire?

Two of our employees were shot dead and two others were burned to death in the fire."

Ambassador Pierce slid his reading glasses down his nose and stared briefly. Alex's two prior postings as a Regional Security Officer and his background as a former Naval Intelligence Officer gave him a solid foundation to make such an assessment.

"When is Riley returning from Karachi?"

"He returns mid-morning tomorrow, Sir," Alex replied.

"Tell him to see me when he gets in," Ellen Hunt said.

Alex nodded, knowing his boss, Jim Riley, wouldn't be too pleased with such a problem upon return, but as the Embassy's Senior Regional Security officer, he wouldn't have a choice.

Pierce looked directly at Alex. "You'd better be sure the Marines are prepared for anything. I'll be damned if any bastards are going to overrun this Embassy again."

"Yes sir, I'll conduct an internal defense drill with them tonight. Good thing our Emergency Evacuation Plan was recently updated, although in a real emergency, the question remains if we'll have time to implement it."

Pierce didn't like the idea of explaining America's new foreign policy toward India to Pakistan's Prime Minister. Going over each talking point in his head, it sounded reasonable and balanced on the surface, but he knew the Pakistanis would still take an extremely dim view of reducing aid to Pakistan, while ramping up aid to their enemy.

"This new pro-India policy will really enflame relations with Pakistan. We may not have time to evacuate our people if it turns nasty," the Ambassador said.

"In the last few months, you argued it all in secret telegrams to Washington," Ellen interjected, "Look where that got us." She shook her head and shrugged.

Ambassador Pierce glared. "Damn it. All our hard work to improve relations with Pakistan is about to unravel. We've spent the better part of our assignments here balancing concerns of competing factions in both Washington and Islamabad. There are so many special interests and parochial views that maintaining a coherent policy is extremely difficult at best. And now this."

"I know," Ellen replied, "I share your disgust. Pakistan has been a great window of influence into the Muslim world for us up to now. In the past they've been a fairly stable partner in support of the United States."

"Exactly," Pierce stated. "Pakistan has nuclear weapons, for God's sake! It's not like they're some third world country without strategic importance. Now they're facing off against another nuclear power, India. Sure, Pakistan doesn't have the best human rights record, but neither does India. And there we are, trying to placate both sides. Everything in the real world is a trade-off."

Pierce glanced at his watch. It was time for him to leave for his meeting with Pakistan's Prime Minister. "Alex, thanks for coming up for this meeting, and for keeping us safe."

Alex nodded as he rose from his chair. Before he left, Pierce asked, "How's the new Assistant RSO working out? What's her name?'

"Susan Witt, sir. She seems very professional. I have her giving extra training to your bodyguards as a project."

"They seem well prepared to me," Pierce said, "Do they need extra training?"

"Well, from recent exercises on the target range, it seems they don't shoot very accurately."

"Really? I didn't know."

"It's just a matter of more practice and proper instruction," Alex stated.

"Okay, you know best," Pierce said, now looking a little worried.

"We'll take care of it, Sir," Alex said, trying to reassure him, before leaving the office.

Pierce shuffled over to his big picture window on the far side of the room. He saw the beautiful Margala Hills about a mile away. On occasion, he enjoyed walking the paths in the hills and found it a wonderful relief from pressures of his job.

Hunt noted a disturbed look on his face, and joined him by the window.

Looking outward, their view extended for miles. Straight ahead was the open and mostly undeveloped area of Islamabad's Diplomatic enclave. Close by were the Chinese and Russian embassies. The Australians were further down the road.

Pierce's eyes fell upon a section of garden at the rear of his Embassy immediately below the window. Staring in silence, he looked at two memorial grave markers belonging to Ambassador Arnold Raphael and Brigadier General Herb Wassom. They had died in 1988, along with former Pakistani President General Zia, when Zia's military aircraft had crashed shortly after take-off from a military airfield in southeast Pakistan. Their actual remains were buried in the United States.

As for the crash, even experts didn't know what caused it. Was it terrorism, a mechanical malfunction, or pilot error? Arnie, as Ambassador Raphael had been known to the American Embassy staff, was a rare statesman, an Ambassador who combined extraordinary competence with a common touch making him beloved by everyone. Pierce only hoped he could live up to that standard. He knew what people actually said about himself: "Up-tight, somewhat aloof, a man who focuses more on policy than people." Pierce decided he would make it a priority in Islamabad to remake his image.

Becoming aware that Ellen was standing next to him, Pierce said, "Thanks for listening to my concerns."

"Worthington, we're in this dilemma together," she replied.

He smiled at her and walked over to the coat-rack. Putting on his dark-blue suitjacket, he said, "Well, here goes. I guess it's now or never."

"It'll be fine. It always is. Good luck anyway," Ellen said, while still gazing out the window at the markers. Pierce wondered if she was right. Picking up a leather-bound note pad, he left the room. Passing by the desk of Joan, his trusted secretary, Pierce stopped to say goodbye.

"If Washington calls, tell them I'm delivering their damn message now." Joan knew he didn't really want her to say that, but understood his concern.

"When will you be back?"

"You've been here as long as I have," Pierce shrugged. "So you know how unpredictable such things can be."

"See you later," Joan said.

"Thanks."

Pierce walked down the stairs and out the building to his waiting black Cadillac limo. The heat and humidity hit him as if he had just walked into a steam-room. Harsh, bright sunlight attacked his eyes. August in Pakistan was almost unbearable. His Pakistani driver was standing next to a plain-clothed local police bodyguard. Both men were silent. Pierce acknowledged their presence with a wave of his hand and slid into the back seat.

The bodyguard closed the heavily armored door behind him.

An American flag was in the holder next to the right front fender. As an American Ambassador, Pierce was entitled to fly the flag at all times; but as a result of the deteriorating security situation in Pakistan, Jim Riley and Alex Boyd had asked him not to do so, except on important occasions such as visiting the Prime Minister. Both were experienced in Embassy security and had convinced him it was just too dangerous should people realize he was in the car by the presence of the flag. Pierce had reluctantly agreed for his own safety.

But, today was an important occasion, and he wanted his presence known.

For most of his local travels, the Ambassador was accompanied by an armed Pakistani Special Branch bodyguard, part of a team that rotated duty on a weekly basis. Today was no exception. The burly bodyguard was seated in the front passenger seat.

Pierce signaled the driver to go. The limo drove to the embassy's heavily fortified front gate where they waited as the gate slowly slide open.

Two local Embassy uniformed guards jumped to attention, saluting the Ambassador.

The Cadillac limousine left the 35-acre Embassy compound and proceeded toward the Prime Minister's office. Turning right onto the main, double-lane road within the Diplomatic enclave, the vehicle passed the Canadian Embassy. A few hundred yards further, they passed the British Embassy housing comprised of white-stucco bungalows with a medium height wall around them. Directly across the street was the British Embassy itself. This Embassy was an attractive modern structure raised on concrete columns for protection against attack.

Abruptly, the driver slowed down.

"Sir," the Pakistani driver said. "I am seeing a small demonstration in front of the Indian Embassy."

Pierce looked ahead. There were maybe fifty demonstrators waving bright green and red banners on the side of the road, approximately one-hundred yards in front of the car.

"Stop," he ordered. Turning to his Pakistani Special Branch bodyguard, he said, "Talwar, what do you think? Should we turn around and take the other road?"

Talwar, six-feet tall with a muscular build and a formidable black mustache, leaned forward. He had been assigned to the embassy for several years and was well respected.

"Sir, I have received no information about a demonstration at the Indian Embassy. I called only this morning. This group seems small and not violent. We should just drive past them."

Pierce looked at his watch again. Although the Prime Minister's office was only five minutes away, he would be late if he doubled back and took the alternative longer route.

"Okay, let's go ahead, slowly."

The limo crept ahead at ten miles an hour. Approaching the demonstrators, several in the gathering pointed to the Cadillac. The Ambassador's driver was now worried, but continued to follow orders at the same speed.

Pierce noticed Talwar whispering into his police radio. He overheard the large bodyguard asking for reinforcements.

"Sir, it will take about five minutes for reinforcements to arrive from the police station," Talwar said, becoming aware the Ambassador was watching him.

Pierce nodded, his eyes focused on the street mob. Ten demonstrators had moved into a line and were now blocking the road.

Ambassador Pierce's driver stopped the car.

"Call the embassy on the radio and tell the RSOs to get here fast," Pierce ordered his driver, watching anxiously as the small group of demonstrators now numbered about fifty.

The men surrounding the car were yelling obscenities. Pierce looked through the rear window, realizing it was too late to order the driver to back-up. Demonstrators were now on all sides of the vehicle.

He glanced at his bodyguard and braced himself as the furious mob stormed the car.

CHAPTER 2

THURSDAY MORNING

The Ambassador's Rescue

At the Embassy, Alex Boyd sat mulling over a small mountain of paperwork from Washington dumped upon his desk. Washington wanted endless, redundant paperwork on financial expenditures, projected five-year spending plans, guard force incident reports, and a host of other items that allowed Washington-based contractors to justify their positions and salaries. He wanted to actually be *doing* security work, not just reporting on it.

The phone rang. "Boyd," he answered in a clipped tone.

"The Ambassador's car is under attack!"

"What the hell! Are you sure?" Alex was at full alert, hearing fear in the voice of the Embassy's Pakistani motor-pool dispatcher.

"Yes slr. The driver said they are being attacked in front of the Indian Embassy."

Slamming the phone, Alex was nearly to the door when Mohammed Bhatti rushed in shouting about a demonstration and the Ambassador being trapped. His Pakistani security investigator was clearly shaken.

"Susan," Alex yelled to his fellow security officer in the next office. "We need to beat feet to the Indian Embassy. The Ambassador's car is trapped by a mob."

"Have the Mobile Reaction Team meet us there," Alex ordered Bhatti.

Alex and Susan Witt ran to the side exit of the Embassy, each wearing a 9 mm pistol holstered on their hips. Jumping into a white Toyota Land Cruiser, they rushed to the Embassy's front gate, only to be stopped by the slowness of its opening.

"Let's see if we can fix the speed of that gate," Alex said with annoyance. When clear, he impatiently gunned their vehicle at high speed to quickly cover a half mile to the Indian Embassy where a boisterous demonstration had become a riot, and the Ambassador's limo was trapped. They immediately saw a large group of Pakistanis rocking the vehicle violently from side to side, pounding on its doors and windows with fists. Some were trying to break the glass with wooden poles from their demonstration banners. A protester had removed the American flag from the Ambassador's vehicle and set it on fire. Alex worried that given enough time, the demonstrators might succeed in breaking through the ballistic-resistant glass of the armored car.

It was a full-scale assault. Despite its enormous weight, the limo was in danger of being flipped over by the sheer number of rioters. Alex reached for his pistol as he jumped out of the Land Cruiser while thinking that shooting a rioter was the last thing he wanted to do. Making a fast decision, he yelled: "Susan, grab some tear gas canisters from the back."

They each grabbed two plastic containers. Signaling to Susan, they both pulled rings from the first four and threw them into the ragging mob. Without waiting, they each hurled two more. All eight canisters exploded nearly at the same time. Thick clouds of gas formed on both sides of the besieged car. Surprised by the sudden attack, demonstrators began coughing and rubbing their eyes, not realizing they were causing more eye irritation. Soon many rioters stumbled away, some retching at the side of the road.

The first police reinforcements began arriving, to Alex's relief. Each carried a long, thick bamboo night-stick called a Lahti. Wading into the crowd, they pummeled rioters without mercy.

Alex ran to the limo driver's door and banged on the glass. The driver looked dazed.

"Go, go, go," Alex yelled, hitting the side of the door. Regaining his composure, the driver and car sped down the now-clear road.

Alex returned quickly to their vehicle, his own eyes stinging from the tear gas.

"Susan, we're staying with the Ambassador."

She hopped into the passenger seat and emptied a half bottle of water into her eyes, handing the bottle to Alex.

Racing from the scene of the riot, they were soon joined by the Embassy Guard Force's armed Mobile Reaction Team in a black SUV. The two vehicles followed the limo to the Pakistani Prime Minister's office complex, turning into the secure parking lot, surrounded by soldiers armed to the teeth.

As everyone emerged from their vehicles, Ambassador Pierce walked back to join Alex and Susan with a grim look on his face.

Sounding annoyed, Pierce commanded, "Alex, tell the DCM what just happened. I'll discuss your actions later." He then quickly turned and walked into the Prime Minister's office.

"What did he mean?" Susan asked, looking at Alex with a quizzical stare.

"I'm not sure," Alex said, although he felt relieved the incident had ended without physical injury to the Ambassador or the limo. Still, he realized that repercussions for his office could be serious.

"What I want to know is why nobody had advance knowledge

of the demonstration at the Indian Embassy. It's so damn close to us. How the hell did that happen?"

Susan simply shook her head.

Deep in thought, he walked back to the car. His own office's contacts with the local police were solid. The CIA Station also had decent relations with ISI, Pakistan's military intelligence arm. Even though CIA-ISI relations had deteriorated since the end of the Afghan-war against the Soviets, Alex still believed it should have been easy to know about a demonstration just down the street from the American Embassy.

So why didn't we know?

He'd work on these things later. Now he had some urgent calls to make. But most importantly, he didn't want a repeat of this kind of thing on the Ambassador's return trip to the Embassy. He would make sure of that.

CHAPTER 3

THURSDAY MORNING

Back to Business

With immediate danger over for now, Alex wanted Susan to accompany him to the Prime Minister's staff office and learn how these incidents were handled. He really wished they were equipped with cell phones like U.S. embassies in Europe used. But Pakistan didn't have any cellular networks installed anywhere in the country as yet, so it didn't really matter.

While somethings are advancing, he thought, other things are definitely still old-school.

Using a regular line, he called Ellen Hunt. She was hand-picked by Ambassador Pierce as his deputy; more importantly to Alex, she was a good supporter of the RSO's office.

"Why didn't we know about this demonstration?" she asked, listening to his report.

"I'm going to find out."

"Make it a priority. Was anyone hurt when you used the tear gas?"

"No, although the rioters' eyes will be sore for a good part of today," he said.

"Hmmm, okay, not a big deal. I'll call the State Department Operations Center. Be careful coming back to the Embassy." Ellen Hunt ended their call.

Next call was to Alex's immediate boss, Jim Riley, Senior Regional Security Officer (RSO), who was visiting the American Consulate General in Karachi for two days.

Normally Riley would call the Diplomatic Security's Command-Center in Washington, D.C. to report the incident, but since Alex had first-hand knowledge of what happened, Riley asked him to alert Washington immediately. The last thing the RSO needed was for the Director of Diplomatic Security in DC hearing about this incident first on CNN.

Finally, he called his secretary, Nancy Williams, to give her an update and report that everyone was all right. In the RSO's absence, Nancy held his office together. She was as valuable as having a fourth RSO in Islamabad

Then, Alex turned his attention to Susan Witt, who was standing next to him. Feeling a little less stressed now, he took an opportunity to compliment her. "Susan, you did a great job out there."

"Thanks, but I didn't do much. The question is: Are we in deep shit with the Ambassador?"

"I don't know." Alex frowned. "I definitely didn't get a warm and fuzzy feeling from him and I'm definitely not happy the demonstration took us by surprise. It's a good thing we're holding an internal defense drill tonight with the Marines. Hopefully, today's incident isn't a precursor of things to come. As soon as we get back to the Embassy, ask Bhatti why the police didn't know about the demonstration ahead of time. I'll talk to Bill Stanton, the CIA Station Chief, and get his take on why we didn't get a heads-up."

Alex and Susan left the Prime Minister's building and walked over to the limo. He took the opportunity to question both the Ambassador's driver and bodyguard in detail about how the event unfolded.

"The Ambassador ordered me to proceed and to drive past the mob," the driver told Alex. He could see the driver's hands were still shaking, and he was sweating profusely.

"That is correct," the bodyguard added.

He felt a slow anger rising inside himself that neither the driver nor bodyguard had used any initiative to avoid the mob. Alex had personally given the driver counter-terrorism training this past year. However, in fairness, he also realized it was unlikely a Pakistani driver would disregard orders from the Ambassador to make decisions on his own.

An hour later, Pierce walked out of the Prime Minister's office. He appeared morose, but silent when he entered the limo.

Alex climbed into the shotgun seat, directing the bodyguard to join Susan in the RSO's vehicle. Then, he told the driver to take a longer route to the American compound, by-passing the Indian Embassy entirely. He also asked Susan to drive ahead of their limo by a few hundred yards to ensure the route was clear.

Wondering what the Ambassador was thinking, Alex kept busy scanning the roadway for potential threats instead of initiating a conversion. Pierce sat stone-faced in the back seat.

After dropping off the Ambassador without incident, Alex and Susan returned to their offices. He wrote a telegram destined for Washington describing the entire event, then sent it to DCM Ellen Hunt for clearance, with a copy to Stanton, CIA Station Chief, for his comments.

Still upset that nobody had notified the Embassy of a possible riot, Alex decided to call Stanton, himself. After the usual niceties, Alex came right to the point.

"Bill, why didn't we know about this shit?"

"If I had known anything about the demonstration, I would

have told you first thing today."

Alex wasn't completely sure he believed him.

"I mean it, Bill, the Ambassador could have been injured or killed today. This is goddamn serious."

Stanton sounded contrite, and agreed to call the Pakistani Intelligence Service, ISI, immediately. "They're the ones who should have warned us, Alex."

Because the Ambassador, himself, was witness to the incident, he might have additional information, so Alex listed him on the telegram for approval. Riley would see a copy of the telegram in Karachi.

Within twenty minutes Ambassador Pierce called Alex and told him he approved the communique. The telegram was then sent electronically to the State Department, with copies to the White House, several federal agencies in Washington, and to a select number of U.S. embassies and consulates, as well as to U.S. military commands.

Once he knew his report had gone out, Alex sat back in his chair. His pistol was still in its holster on his hip. He had avoided using it against the rioters only because he had tear gas available. Pakistan was a dynamic powder-keg whose fuse was being lit by the most radical elements and by Washington's policies as well. There was nothing he could do to change that. Dangers were growing all around him. He only hoped they would be better prepared when another incident came the next time.

There would always be a next time.

CHAPTER 4

THURSDAY NIGHT

Practicing for Disaster

In mid-August, the outside temperature was 100 degrees Fahrenheit by 10 pm in Islamabad. One might expect it to be cooler inside the American Embassy, but it wasn't.

Alex Boyd, Susan Witt, and ten Embassy U.S. Marines were wearing heavy ballistic vests, carrying weapons with extra ammunition, and looking through gas masks. Alex's vision was limited by his mask which had partially fogged-up. In the semi-darkness, only Embassy emergency hallway and stairwell lights were turned on, making it even more difficult to see.

"Anybody warm?" he asked, attempting humor to relieve the stress.

Wiping moist hands on his black cargo pants to get a firmer grip on his Uzi sub-machine gun, sweat dripped from Alex's forehead over the eye sockets of his gas mask. His grey t shirt was now soaked.

Air conditioning in the American Embassy had been turned off an hour earlier to prevent any simulated tear gas from circulating throughout the controlled access areas. This was standard procedure for such a drill.

Low-level lighting created an eerie scene in which everything looked like shadows. The air, filled with floating particles of dust and dirt, appeared more like the set of a horror movie than the interior of an American Embassy.

The Worst-Case-Scenario drill had started an hour earlier, when Alex called the Marines to the Embassy to practice defending against a large mob supposedly forming outside the main gate. In this specific scenario, he would have the crowd turn violent and scale the perimeter wall to attack the Embassy.

He watched with satisfaction as the Marines assumed their designated observation posts within an acceptable timeline, and all posts were secured.

Now, he planned to turn up the heat, so to speak.

Using a Marine's radio at Post One in the Embassy's lobby, he reported simulated mobs trying to enter the back door and through various windows. Alex observed Gunny Sgt. Rodriguez and squad leaders moving Marines from their assigned observation posts. The idea was to throw practice tear gas canisters into the phantom crowd, maneuver around the Embassy's three floors to counter the latest threat, and test internal communications.

Thirty-two-year old Susan Witt had only arrived in Islamabad a month prior, and was getting a grasp on what needed to be done as an Assistant Regional Security Officer. She moved silently with Alex. He was impressed at her eagerness to learn whatever was needed at her new post. Earlier today, she had acted swiftly at the Ambassador's car riot, showing no fear.

She'll be a valuable asset soon, he thought to himself.

Marine Corps Gunnery Sergeant Ruben Rodriquez, a five-foot-ten-inch, hard-as-nails Marine Detachment Commander, was now standing with Boyd and Witt in the main lobby's bullet-resistant Marine Post-One. This lobby was the main entrance where visitors entered but was actually located on the second floor of the Embassy's three floors. The grounds sloped down in back so the first floor was below lobby level and only partially seen from the street.

Marine Post-One, manned 24-7, controlled a host of doors and gates that could be remotely locked. An array of camera monitors provided video coverage of the Embassy's 35-acre compound and was the communications hub for the Embassy's emergency radio system.

"Sir, I'm going to inspect the Marine's deployment," Gunny Rodriquez said, turning to leave Post-One.

"Okay. Susan, go with Gunny," Boyd ordered. He trusted Rodriquez completely. As a Gulf War veteran, and thirty-something, Gunny would be a calming influence on the young Marines in a real crisis. Alex wanted her to see how the Marines had repositioned themselves to defend the Embassy. If the Marines did not reposition themselves to handle the penetration, they would be over-run or outmaneuvered, and the Embassy could be lost with serious causalities.

Boyd remained with Sgt. Hancock, the Marine watch-stander assigned to Post-One, who was giving orders to Marines via the tactical radio system. Wiping sweat with his bare arm, Alex decided to escalate the scenario even further by telling them the mob had breached the Embassy's first floor. They had to prepare for the worst. So, he announced over the radio the unthinkable:

"All Marines withdraw to the third floor. We are vacating Post-One." He and Sgt. Hancock grabbed their weapons and ran up one flight of stairs.

He was gratified to see the more senior Marines demonstrating excellent leadership and initiative. In a real battle, Alex knew from experience that small Marine units would have to operate quickly and independently, yet in a coordinated manner. Alex made it to the location of the simulated battle on the third floor to watch first-hand how the Marines deployed tactically.

This would be where they had to make their final stand in a real attack. The Marines would need to defend the floor's three stairwells, possibly with deadly force to protect the employee safe-haven area on the third floor. This part of the drill was critical since "attackers" hadn't used firearms or explosives up to this point in the drill scenario. No one had directly endangered anyone's life, and the Marines had been able to delay the mob with tear gas.

In a real event, Alex knew he would need to ask the Ambassador, if he was present, for permission to open fire. It could cause a dangerous delay, but this step was a strict requirement of the U.S. State Department.

Alex saw all Marines had line-of-sight to each other. He knew everyone's adrenaline was flowing, even though it was a drill. The air was stagnant and the heat seemed more oppressive than on the second floor. Although in excellent shape, Alex found his ballistic vest made it difficult to breathe.

The men, though tense, appeared ready and focused. Alex decided the drill had achieved its three objectives: Evaluating command and control, effective use of communications, and coordinated movement.

"Gunny, let's end the drill," he said, turning to Rodriquez. "Have the Marines police-up their practice tear gas canisters and drop their gear in the Marine react-room."

Wiping sweat off his forehead, he added, "And turn the damn air conditioning back on ASAP. We'll meet in fifteen minutes in the lobby for a de-brief."

"Roger that, boss."

CHAPTER 5

THURSDAY ALMOST MIDNIGHT

Use of Deadly Force

Tired, but satisfied with the drill, Alex and Susan waited for the Marines to gather in the lobby while sitting in two plush tan leather visitors' chairs. He removed his ballistic vest and tear-gas mask, laying them on an empty seat. Then, he stretched out his six-foot-two-inch frame while running his hand through thick, still damp dark-brown hair.

Susan followed his lead, removing her gear as well. Her short-blond hair was disheveled, her olive t-shirt with 'Go Army' stenciled on it, was soaked. Alex studied his new assistant. Medium height, solidly built, she had moved fast with quick reflexes during the riot practice. He wondered what she thought of her new posting to Islamabad.

"So, Susan, what do you think we accomplished tonight?"

She looked thoughtful for a moment. "Well, I've conducted a lot of drills as an Army Captain, but those were usually focused on rendering-safe explosive devices in open-air environments." She paused, "I can see maneuvering a squad of Marines, in semi-darkness, over three floors of an Embassy is a lot different."

Alex nodded. "It can be, that's why we need drills like this."

"What about other civilians in the Embassy? If they're armed, would they have a role in our defensive plans?" Susan asked.

"Sort of," Alex replied. "During working hours, we can count on a handful of CIA officers, military personnel, and DEA Agents. They're all integrated into the Embassy's written Internal Defense Plan. But, in reality, we just want them to guard their own areas.

Susan leaned forward, "Do you think it's likely we could be attacked again like in '79?"

Alex was about to respond when he saw the Marines arriving in the lobby for debriefing. "We'll talk later."

With everyone gathered in the lobby, Alex stood and spoke first, complimenting them on the drill. Then, he yielded the floor to Gunny Rodriquez, who pointed out specific areas where they could improve. It was Marine Corporal Garner who asked the inevitable question.

"Sir, do you think Ambassador Pierce will allow us to use deadly force if a mob gets inside the Embassy?"

This was his greatest concern. Alex knew other Marines felt the same.

Refusal to grant permission to use deadly force had happened at several embassies in the past, including in Islamabad on November 21, 1979. In that incident, 106 American and Pakistani employees were almost roasted alive, trapped in the third-floor safe-haven communications vault during a violent attack by thousands of demonstrators. The demonstrators set fire to the building after breaching a window grill. It was a nightmare, and now over a decade later, the continued reluctance of senior State Department Officers to use deadly force in life and death situations was still a major concern.

He also knew he had to be truthful with his men or lose their trust. Glancing at Susan, Alex saw she felt the importance of the question.

"To be honest, I believe he will recognize the threat and authorize deathly force as a last option." Alex replied. "But you can never be one-hundred percent certain. It may depend on circumstances, such as whether the Pakistani Government has forces nearby."

He saw a look of concern on the face of the young Corporal and several other newer men. "Under the Vienna Convention, the host government, in this case the Government of Pakistan, is obligated to send in the police or military to rescue the Embassy staff. Our mission is to buy time until the host government acts. Our first concern is to protect our own people." Then, he looked Corporal Garner in the eye and added, "We also need to delay the enemy to allow time for shredding classified material in the Embassy, if possible."

He stopped a moment to let his words sink in."I trust Ambassador Pierce and Deputy Chief of Mission, Ellen Hunt. They've both served in the Middle East and South Asia for a long time, and they've seen how anti-American demonstrations can escalate quickly into extreme violence. Just look at what happened today with the attack on the Ambassador's limo. The question is: 'What happens if neither he nor the DCM are in communication with us, or if someone else is acting in their place?' All I can say is the Marine Detachment must remain ready for anything."

Despite what he just told the Marines, he knew in crisis, even when "ready for anything," one could never be certain.

Every RSO wondered if a Foreign Service Officer could ever be trusted to authorize killing locals, even if an embassy was violently attacked. After all, these senior FSOs spend their entire careers trying to peacefully negotiate international disputes. How could they be expected to approve taking a human life merely because the RSO thought a situation was life-threatening?

And, there was something else: Most senior FSOs never

wanted to participate in defense drills with Marines, or even read the Internal Defense Plan. Without that experience, Alex believed they were ultimately unprepared to make a life or death decision. Even so, he would never reveal his doubts about Foreign Service Officers in general. For himself, he had confidence that the Ambassador and DCM Hunt were not like the rest. Even though he'd waited all afternoon for the Ambassador to talk with him about today's attack on the limo.

Apparently, he's been tied up with results from his Prime Minister discussions, Alex was thinking. *Still, I haven't gotten a call to discuss it, and I don't like it at all.*

"I hope that answers your question, Corporal Garner," Alex said aloud, giving him a smile.

"Thank you, Sir," Corporal Garner said.

No more questions surfaced, but Alex wanted to be certain everyone, including Susan, understood the protocol needed that could save their lives.

"Just to review it one more time: Corporal Jones, please describe for us when you may use deadly force?"

"Yes, sir. According to State Department/Marine Corps Guard Orders, only if a Marine's life or the life of another employee is in imminent danger, and no other means of lesser force can resolve the threat, may Marines use deadly force. Otherwise permission is needed from the Ambassador or whoever is the senior State Department officer in the chain-of-command on the scene."

"Corporal Wilson, who's in our chain-of-command," Alex asked a tall, skinny Marine since he was yawning. "Sir, the chain-of-command is Ambassador Pierce, DCM Hunt, the Senior RSO Mr. Riley, you, and then Miss Witt."

"That's correct," Alex replied, somewhat impressed he hadn't faltered. "While there are other senior officers in the Embassy, including very senior Military Attaches, none of them is in the Internal Defense chain-of-command, unless so designated by the Ambassador." Satisfied, he turned to Gunny Rodriguez.

"Gunny, if you don't have anything else to cover, I think we're done here." After the detachment was released, Alex looked over at Susan.

"How do you like being here, as compared to your previous postings with the Army in Saudi Arabia and Kuwait during Desert Storm?"

"Are you kidding? This is great," Susan answered. "Since joining the Diplomatic Security Service, I've been assigned to the Secretary of State's Protective Detail, and Mobile Training/ Response Team. I really think my Special Agent experience so far, combined with my prior Army Explosive Ordnance Disposal assignments, is the perfect background for living and working in Pakistan. I don't have any complaints at all."

"Good to hear," Alex said.

"I think you and Jim Riley are first-class officers and excellent mentors. I'm really happy to have gotten this assignment and intend to make the most of this opportunity," she said.

Finished talking, they said goodnight.

Boyd walked out of the Embassy toward his personal Jeep Wrangler. He thought of all the drills he had run over the years and wondered whether even the best drill could simulate a real attack on an Embassy. Knowing some RSOs secretly harbored a strong desire to face such a challenge, even kill terrorists, the reality for most RSOs was that defensive measures once in place should deter such an incident from occurring. Still, he planned to keep practicing.

CHAPTER 6

FRIDAY MORNING

Life in Islamabad

Alex awoke at 6 am, still tired and slightly dehydrated from the previous night's internal defense drill. After shutting off the alarm clock, he rolled over in bed, wondering if he could catch another half-hour's snooze after tossing and turning all night.

His mind kept thinking about work, what the Ambassador would eventually say about yesterday's incident, and whether his love life, or lack of one, had any prospect of improving in Pakistan.

As much as he wanted to sleep in, he couldn't afford the luxury and needed to be at the Embassy early to read overnight classified cable traffic before the Country Team meeting. With his boss, Jim Riley not returning from Karachi until around 10 a.m. this morning, Alex would represent the Regional Security Office at the meeting.

Showering and shaving in Islamabad's semi-brown water was always a challenge not to accidentally swallow some in the shower and possibly contract an unspeakable intestinal disease. He prepared for breakfast on his veranda. Bringing out his portable short-wave radio, Alex placed it on the table and turned on the BBC's World Service.

The broadcast on this specific frequency was focused on a South Asian audience, so everyone in the Embassy got their initial daily news about Pakistan from this morning show.

Looking over the small garden in front of his house, surrounded by a high red-brick wall, always gave Alex a peaceful moment. There were flower beds with brilliant red roses, and vibrant purple bougainvillea hanging from the wall. He could almost fool himself into believing Pakistan was home.

The three-bedroom house assigned to him by the Embassy General Services Office was perfectly suitable for his needs. Other than the big picture window in the living room, all other windows had steel bars covering them for security.

Across the street was an undeveloped, area with tall trees and little vegetation. Halfway down the residential street was a small, slightly run-down mosque. One medium-height 60-foot tall minaret pointed upward with a loud-speaker on top. The building's brick was stained from years of weathering. Alex estimated the mosque could hold about 50 people.

Alex remembered walking down the street one day, early in his tour of duty, and seeing the Mullah standing outside, sweeping leaves off the walkway. He waved and the Mullah waved back. Alex had approached for a nice, albeit limited conversation in both broken English and Urdu. Ever since, Alex continued to connect with the mullah. He knew one of the great benefits of serving in the Foreign Service was an opportunity to gain first-hand knowledge about local conditions and other viewpoints. It was also a hedge against misunderstandings and potential religious strife.

"Good morning, Sahib," Samuel, his cook, said, interrupting Alex's train of thought.

"Good morning to you, Samuel. How's your daughter's leg? Did the hospital help her?"

"Oh, yes, Sahib," a grin on his face. "The doctors put a plaster on it, and bone should be healed in a month or two. I am thanking you for giving me money for the hospital. You are too much kind."

"Don't mention it, Samuel. I'm just glad her accident wasn't more serious. How's the bicycle?"

Samuel nodded. "It will be alright. It can be fixed.

While Alex ate breakfast, he thought about the way servants called American men "sahib", or "memsahib" for women. It reminded him of old British movies. When first arriving in Islamabad a year ago, he tried telling Samuel he didn't need to be called " sahib", but it was Pakistani tradition, and Samuel persisted. So, like many things in foreign countries, Alex learned he needed to respect and accept local customs. Having partially grown up abroad, first in Paris, then Cairo, Alex was adept at blending in and speaking foreign languages. He was proud to be an American, but he also loved experiencing other cultures.

Finishing breakfast, he rose from his chair, went inside and walked to his briefcase. Dialing a combination on both locks, he removed his pistol. Sliding his belt through the holster, he secured it onto his right hip. On his left hip he added two more magazines. The weapon, holster, and magazine holders were standard Diplomatic Security issue to its Special Agents. To him, it felt like normal attire.

Next, he slipped on a typical sleeveless khaki vest carried in any U.S. sporting goods store, which concealed the weapon yet allowed quick access. Alex generally carried a weapon, not so much fearing an attack on himself, but an obligation to defend anyone assigned to the U.S. Mission. The possibility of an attack on a staff member wasn't just hypothetical. Recently, he'd received increasingly worrisome reports of surveillance on Mission personnel from various sources. Yet, just who was conducting the surveillance wasn't exactly clear. Alex couldn't imagine driving to the scene of an ongoing attack without an ability to defend himself. So, the gun was always with him.

Now, only 7 a.m., it was already eighty degrees and humid with clear skies. Like every day in summertime, temperatures would eventually reach 100 degrees.

At least, I don't need to wear a suit and tie to the office, Alex thought.

Today, he chose cordovan penny-loafers, khaki dress pants and a long-sleeve blue-striped shirt, rolling the sleeves above his elbows. Not bad, he mused, adjusting his holster so it didn't show under the khaki vest.

"Samuel! I'm leaving," Alex called loudly in the direction of the kitchen.

He walked out to his Jeep, started the engine, and rolled down the front windows; then, drove to the gate at the end of the driveway. A Pakistani guard opened access out to the outer world. Alex waved as he drove by and his guard saluted smartly.

He usually rolled down the Jeep's windows despite the heat. Even though he could fire through the glass in an emergency, an open view was more enjoyable and better for accuracy, not to mention the impact a fired bullet would have upon his hearing. Discharging a gun within a closed-up car made one hell of a noise.

Driving through city streets, Alex made arbitrary direction changes. Using his rear view and side mirrors, he constantly checked for mobile surveillance. Today, no one was following.

Contrary to an image of Islamabad being a dry desert that many had, the city was actually fairly green, thanks to a moderate rainy season twice a year. The city, itself, was laid out in a logical grid system. There were several small markets, or strip malls, throughout Islamabad, in which you could usually find a pharmacy, a bookstore with English language magazines and newspapers, clothing or fabric stores, jewelry dealers, and a few shops selling pirated western video tapes.

During his drive, Alex smelled burning cow dung used by poor people as cooking fuel. While Pakistan's middle and upper classes used bottled gas with modern stoves, most Pakistanis couldn't afford such luxury. Therefore, the smell of burning dung was an ever-present feature throughout the country. Alex choose not to dwell on whether this was hygienic. Here, it was just a fact of life.

Three miles later, he saw the front of the Embassy. Noting extra guards near the front, he wondered if it was in response to yesterday's riot, or some other bad news.

At the gate, he waited while the local guard ran a mirror on a long pole under his Jeep to check for explosive devices. He made a mental note to call Iqbal Satter, owner of SMG, the Embassy's guard contract company, to thank him for posting the extra guards and for great initiative in training his 800-man force.

For the moment, it made Alex feel safe.

In Country Background

About Housing

The local housing market either had houses or shanties where poor people lived. Most houses tended to be one or two stories high, with either white stucco or red-brick exteriors. If a house had two stories, it invariably had a balcony on the front of the second floor. Many of the nearby homes had rebar protruding from the roof. Alex had once heard that if a house still appeared to be under construction, then authorities didn't tax the owner. That was one reason everything could seem to be under construction forever. In the absence of window grills and residential guards such, crime could be a serious problem.

Alex lived on a street where houses were of mixed size. His yard had a twenty-foot deep patio, or veranda, on the front of the house with a mixed pattern of grey flagstones on the ground. While the neighborhood was considered well-to-do by local standards, the overall quality of homes did not compare with those of suburban Washington, D.C. Although he preferred an apartment, these did not exist in Islamabad, other than a few on the Embassy's compound.

About Mosques

Every neighborhood had its local mosque, no doubt a throwback to the time before loud-speakers, when the mullah's voice could reach only so far from the top of the minaret. Most people who attended the mosque would normally walk there, although drivers could park nearby under surrounding trees.

Islamabad was also home to Faisal Masjid, one of the largest mosques in the Muslim world. It had been built with Saudi money several years prior and was enormous and very attractive. Five times a day the mullah would use the mosque's loudspeaker for the "call to prayers," just as every other mosque in the city did. Sometimes the cacophony from several mosques using their loudspeakers at the same time made it impossible to distinguish one voice from another. Alex never minded the noise. In fact, it reinforced his romantic notion of living in South Asia. He remembered how one irreverent Embassy political officer had called the five o'clock evening call to pray, "the call to cocktails."

About Samuel and Local Foods

Samuel, his wife, and six children lived in servant's accommodations behind Alex's house. Although this comprised only three rooms, it was considered better than average for a household servant. Moreover, it cost Samuel nothing. Although Samuel had little formal education, Alex judged that he was intelligent and had a common sense understanding of life in Islamabad. Had he been born in the west, he would have had opportunities to excel.

As Alex waited for his breakfast to be served, he took in the wonderful aromas of Samuel's cooking, especially the bacon.One couldn't buy bacon in a Pakistani market since it was a pork product, and Muslims wouldn't touch it. However, it could be purchased at the small Embassy commissary, and since Samuel was among the small number of Christians in the country, cooking bacon, thankfully, didn't present a problem. Many household servants in the western community were Christians because domestic employment was one of the few jobs open to them.

The Government of Pakistan wouldn't hire them, large companies wouldn't hire them, and they were discriminated against in most sectors of the economy.

Although the markets offered a basic selection of products one could buy in a western grocery store, the markets smelled really badly and had more than their share of flies resting on fresh produce, meats, and fish.

Without a cook, he would have to shop in the local markets himself, which he didn't have time for, nor did he want to shop there. Furthermore, without his own cook, Alex would have to clean all of the vegetables, with either an iodine or Clorox solution, to kill bacteria. Failure to do so always resulted in severe intestinal problems for westerners. Besides, if left to his own cooking, Alex thought, he would also have to learn how to make something more complicated than a tuna fish sandwich.

CHAPTER 7

FRIDAY MORNING

Attitude Problem

"Hello, Boss," the Embassy Guard Supervisor greeted Alex at the security gate.

"Any problems so far today, Ahmed?" Alex asked while waiting for his jeep to be screened for explosives.

"No, Boss."

Alex stared at Ahmed but didn't speak. After five seconds, Alex thought Ahmed seemed uncomfortable, although the guard was maintaining eye contact with him. Alex continued to wait, while Ahmed played 'who-blinks-first' with his eyes.

"Remember, I said you should always report any problems to me?" Alex said. "I'll always back you up but only if you're operating by the book."

Ahmed shifted his feet a little, then finally spoke.

"Mr. Boyd, you know I don't like to complain if I am handling a problem."

"I know, Ahmed. You're an excellent supervisor, and a fine leader of the guards, but I must know if someone isn't cooperating."

"Okay, it's Mr. Hargrove again."

As always and as expected, Alex thought. He had received

complaints about Hargrove's attitude and had spoken to him about it in the past.

Winston Hargrove IV was the Senior Embassy Political Officer, or Counselor, as he was known. He apparently thought himself too grand to have his vehicle inspected for bombs before driving into the Embassy compound. Though required for every vehicle, except the Ambassador's, Hargrove continued trying to buck the system. The Ambassador's vehicle was exempt because his driver, or bodyguard, always stayed with the car whenever outside the Embassy compound.

Alex knew that Hargrove had been born to a wealthy New York City investment banker, was a graduate of Princeton, and that he had only served in European assignments such as Paris, Vienna and Berlin since joining the Foreign Service. However, Central Personnel in the State Department finally insisted, that like all other officers, he must serve his fair share of assignments in the Third-World.

When Hargrove had arrived in Islamabad about six months ago, he immediately made it clear to Alex that he hated Pakistan. Often expressing a desire for the sophisticated ambiance and bright lights of Paris, he would say he couldn't abide the hardships other Embassy employees accepted as part of life or calling in this "exciting" Third-World country.

Alex couldn't understand anyone not wanting the stimulation of exploring such a diverse country as Pakistan. He thought of Hargrove as a typical snobbish European-area political officer whose condescending attitude didn't help America win friends abroad. He also thought of the danger his attitude could bring by refusing a car inspection, and what might happen if, one day, he was ever placed in charge of the embassy.

"Ahmed, is everything else quiet at the Agency for International Development compound, and at the American

Center?" Alex asked. Part of Ahmed's responsibilities was to coordinate guard operations at other US Mission offices in the city.

"Oh, yes, boss. It is too much early for AID people to be on their seats, and it is quiet at the American Center," Ahmed replied.

Satisfied for the moment, Alex was about to drive off when Ahmed leaned toward the driver's window.

"You should know that every day only the very tall woman arrives early at the American Center. She is always very nice to our guards."

Alex thought briefly about the 'very tall woman at the American Center.' It didn't register at first, but then he recalled it must be Rachel Smith, the Washington-based Press Officer who was temporarily assigned here recently. Because she was so new in the Embassy, Alex hadn't met her yet. He had only heard she was a rising star, and people said she was extraordinarily good-looking.

"Okay, Ahmed. Thanks for the information," he smiled, and drove into the Embassy compound.

Entering the RSO suite of offices, Alex grabbed a cup of coffee, and sat in the visitor's chair next to the office secretary, Nancy Williams. She was in her late thirties, attractive, and married with no children.

"Alex," Nancy said excitedly with pride in her voice. "You know how I've been complaining that very few of the new arrivals from other agencies know what the role of the RSO is until after you've given them your security awareness briefing?"

Alex nodded, sipping his coffee.

Nancy smiled. "Well, I drafted a handout that we can give them when they come here for their ID card on their first day. I think it will solve the problem, and I hope you and Jim approve."

Alex smiled. "Sounds like a good idea. Okay, let me see it."

Nancy gave him the document, watching nervously as he read it.

Alex drank more coffee as he leafed through both pages. Among other things, it covered the RSO's role in criminal investigations, physical security of offices, anti-terrorism training offered to local police, leadership of the Marine Security Guard detachment, and management of local guard operations.

"Pretty thorough," he said, clearly impressed. "I like this part where you conclude the RSO is responsible for security of all agencies at the post. Very clear. Very nice, Nancy. Thanks so much for taking the initiative. I'll put it in Jim's inbox with a note that we've discussed it. It will be a big help to us. Excellent work!" Nancy smiled, giving a sigh of relief. She enjoyed working with Alex and Jim because they gave her the freedom to explore new ideas and, in their absence, to manage the office. She also liked Susan Witt, although they'd known each other for only a short time.

Entering his office, first on Alex's agenda was to check overnight messages. His office was small, a ten-by-ten-foot cubby hole, but he had no complaints since the entire Embassy was dealing with a space crunch. On the wall to the side of his desk was a Meritorious Honor Award received while in Tunis. There was also a group photo of himself standing with a bunch of hard looking guys in combat camouflage uniforms, holding a fearsome assortment of weapons. Alex smiled every time he looked at the photo; his face was the only one visible in a sea of blurred-out faces, by request for anonymity. The photo was a gift from his Navy SEAL buddies at Little Creek, Virginia, where he had served as a Naval Intelligence Officer before joining the State Department. Sometimes, when the office routine became too tedious, he found himself staring at the photo and longing for his days in the Navy working with the SEALS.

Alex finished reading the morning's telegrams, leaned back in his chair, thinking about what might be raised at the Country Team Meeting later today. He was a little concerned the Ambassador hadn't spoken to him about anything since yesterday's attack on his limo. No contact was a bit unusual after such an event. Could it be Pierce was displeased? He reviewed their actions and believed he and Susan had reacted correctly to the mob violence, but from experience he also knew it wouldn't be the first time an RSO got the shaft for taking decisive action in a dangerous situation.

Picturing the mob surrounding the limo, he wondered if this was only a sign of things to come.

Background

Role of Security Contract Companies

Ahmed, and all of the U.S. Mission's approximately eight hundred unarmed guards, worked for the RSO on a contract. The local contract company was the Security Management Group, known as SMG. It was owned by Iqbal Satter, a former Lt. Colonel in the Pakistani Army, and now an accomplished and respected businessman. He hired former Pakistani Army Officers and senior NCOs to supervise an array of security functions for the RSO.

In addition to protecting various American offices and residences throughout the city, SMG had roving patrols and armed reaction teams that could respond to problems. These teams were composed of very tough and well-trained former Pakistan Army commandos. Equally important, their intimidating presence on the scene of an incident had a calming effect on any protagonist. The SMG office operated a radio system, also funded by the RSO, which helped coordinate the entire operation. These operations were identical to those in Peshawar, Lahore, and Karachi, where the U.S. Government had Consulates General.

CHAPTER 8

FRIDAY MORNING

The Country Team Meeting

In his office, Alex left his khaki vest on a chair, put his gun and extra magazines in the office safe and added a red patterned tie to his attire, feeling more up-market for the meeting. Then, taking the stairs one flight up, he walked to the end of the corridor.

Entering the Secure Conference Room, he took the seat traditionally occupied by Jim Riley, chatting a few moments while others arrived. He couldn't help but notice an attractive woman across the table, who he assumed, was Rachel Smith. Making eye contact, she smiled at him. He was about to say something to her, when Ambassador Worthington Pierce walked in promptly at 8:30 am.

The entire Country Team stood as Pierce entered. Once he sat, everyone followed suit. Wearing a white shirt with red striped tie, no jacket, Pierce was around fifty years old, brown hair flecked with gray. Taking reading glasses out of his shirt pocket and placing them on the table, he began.

"I would like to bring everyone up-to-date on a highly charged conversation I had yesterday with the Pakistani Prime Minister and Foreign Minister regarding our new policy toward India. Both are deeply upset, in fact, I can even say furious, that we have risked straining our partnership with Pakistan by the most recent decision in Washington. They want firm assurances we will maintain our commitment to Pakistan's future development and military strength. They also felt this was especially important in an era when we no longer jointly need to battle the Soviet Union in Afghanistan."

"Sir, you know we'll have to reduce military assistance if Congress has its way," Colonel Williams said, the Embassy Military Assistance Commander.

"I know, and I responded that Pakistan's welfare was still vitally important to the United States. Naturally, they listened carefully about the decision by the U.S. Congress to cut back on foreign aid. I spoke of the attempts by specific members of Congress to sanction Pakistan over its suspected nuclear weapons program. Needless-to-say, there will be difficult times ahead if we hope to maintain the closeness of our relationship."

Ambassador Pierce saw heads nodding in agreement around the conference table.

"I need not remind everyone that since Pakistan and India have already fought several wars against each other, both countries are consumed with ensuring an upper-hand in both political and military balance in the region. India accuses Pakistan of arming and supporting insurgents in Kashmir. Pakistan accuses India of creating instability inside its own borders. All of this is true. Compounding the problem of trust between India and Pakistan is that the literacy rate is low, especially here in Pakistan. Therefore, any rumor takes on a life of its own. Even the most ridiculous and impossible stories gain traction."

Heads continued to nod around the table.

"This is why elements in Pakistan's military intelligence service are supporting the emerging Taliban as a counterweight to India," Pierce quoted what the Prime Minister had told him.

As if reading Pierce's mind, the DCM, Ellen Hunt spoke up.

"Both sides see an evil foreign-hand behind every internal problem. Pakistan, in particular, can never reflect upon its own inadequate development efforts to explain why they're falling behind India. Massive amounts of corruption, the absence of a decent education system, and the pervasive influence of radical and intolerant religious leaders, with political and religious agendas, all combine to stymie economic growth and stability in this country."

"Well stated, Ellen. I thought it useful during yesterday's meeting with the Prime Minister and the Foreign Minister to review the history of our cooperation together which he agreed was substantial. At least we ended the meeting amicably."

When Ambassador Pierce finished speaking, Ellen Hunt was asked to review a critical, upcoming VIP visit to Islamabad that was planned. Hunt flipped through her notes and began.

"We have a delegation from the Senate Foreign Relations Committee, comprised of five U.S. Senators plus their wives, and Senate staff, arriving next week. They'll be traveling via a US military luxury aircraft. This Congressional delegation, known as CODEL, will call on the President, the Prime Minister, and the Foreign Minister. In view of both the current dangerous security situation, and our new foreign policy changes, we must ensure we can protect these VIPs."

Several hands went up.

The DCM waved them down and turned to Rachel Smith. "Let's start with press coverage. Rachel, as our new Press Officer, tell us what you've learned about the Senators' wishes for dealing with the media."

Alex aimed his eyes at the newcomer. She appeared poised and ready to speak, clearly experienced.

Rachel focused on DCM Hunt. "I've been in contact with the

Press Officer from the Senate Foreign Relations Committee. He said the Chairman of the Committee, who is leading the CODEL, will expect to meet with Pakistani journalists after he sees the Prime Minister and the Foreign Minister," she said, turning toward Pierce. "If you agree, Mr. Ambassador, I suggest we use your residence for at least one meeting between the CODEL and the press."

"Excellent idea, Rachel," Ambassador Pierce responded. "We can make it an informal Q and A. Let's do it as the last event in their visit. So, you're implying there will be several press conferences?"

"Yes, Mr. Ambassador," she said checking her notes. "The Pakistanis have told me they expect additional press conferences at the Prime Minister's Office and again at the Foreign Office."

Alex was impressed with Rachael's brief presentation and thought she knew her job well. He figured she was thirty-something, seemed mature and confident, and just the right type for this pressurized position. He observed her well-pressed blue pin-striped pants-suit, open in the front to a white blouse under the jacket. With her medium length, brown wavy hair, and overall athletic figure, Rachel Smith was, by anyone's definition, gorgeous.

"Thank you, Rachel," Ellen Hunt replied, interrupting the Ambassador's appraisal.

Hunt continued, "The Ambassador, and perhaps Winston Hargrove or I, will accompany the Senators to their meetings." She turned to Alex. "The RSO will ensure protection is provided by local police. Alex, are we locked-on with the police for protection?"

"Yes, we are, Ellen," Boyd nodded. "Special Branch has committed to giving us a follow car with four officers for all movements. At the Senators' hotel, I've arranged to have their floor protected by uniformed cops. The lobby will be guarded by armed Special Branch officers in plain clothes.

"Susan Witt will be with the CODEL for all movements," he continued. "I understand Diplomatic Security is considering sending two armed Special Agents on the plane with the CODEL. We'll know in a day or so if that's the plan."

Without hesitation, Ellen stated, "If Diplomatic Security is sending some Agents, I definitely want Susan or you to accompany the Senators. We can't expect the Washington-based agents to know the city like you guys. If problems arise, you'll know what to do."

"Understood," Alex replied.

"Speaking of knowing what to do," Ambassador Pierce said, "I want to thank Alex and Susan Witt for coming to my rescue yesterday in front of the Indian Embassy." He frowned. "Some of you may not have heard, but we ran into an unexpected demonstration that turned rather nasty. I had to be extracted from what became a riot."

Alex nodded in appreciation of the Ambassador's comments. He was relieved Pierce had finally supported his actions and let the rest of the Country Team know.

Winston Hargrove interrupted. "I received a call this morning from Benjamin Shapiro, the National Security Council's South Asian expert. He read our telegram reporting on yesterday's incident," the Political Counselor said, "Shapiro told me some important people in Washington questioned the wisdom, and even legality, of using Embassy tear gas on a public Pakistani street." He stared directly at Alex. "I wonder, Alex, if you couldn't have thought of a better way to handle the situation."

Alex was aware all eyes in the room were on him. Hargrove had not only challenged Alex's professional judgment, but did so right after hearing the Ambassador's support. He remained quiet for a moment, then locking eyes with Hargrove, smiled slightly.

"Perhaps you have a point, Winston." Alex saw the Ambassador cock his head.

"Although Susan and I were outnumbered by the rioters, maybe fifty to two, I considered other options," Alex noted Rachel's big green eyes aimed at him, listening intently.

"First, of course, we could have shot most of them. But it seems to me, that Shapiro, not to mention Ambassador Pierce, wouldn't have been very keen on that solution."

The Ambassador gave a small laugh and nodded.

"Or, we could have allowed the mob to turn the limo over as many times as they wanted to," Alex continued, then sighed, "We would have retained the moral high ground, and later we could have sent a threatening and harshly-worded diplomatic note to the Foreign Ministry protesting mistreatment and injury to the Ambassador. But, really, we never seriously considered that option." He aimed his darkest glare at Hargrove. "Winston, I'd love to hear your own suggestions on how we could have handled this better."

Several around the table chuckled at Hargrove's predicament. Alex saw the DCM and Ambassador each covering their mouths partially hiding smiles.

Mercifully for Winston, the Ambassador cut in before Hargrove could rebut Alex's statement and make a fool of himself. His eyes flashed between the two men.

"As I've said, I'm very grateful for the manner in which Alex and Susan handled the situation. As for the concerns of Ben Shapiro at the National Security Council, I'll give him a call. Winston, you needn't trouble yourself with this matter further. Now, let's return to our preparation for the CODEL visit, shall we?"

Alex smiled and continued, "Colonel Mushtaq of the Airport Security Force promised we'll have planeside access for our motorcade, as always. The General Services Office is now developing a list of vehicles we'll use so we can give license plate numbers and drivers' names to Colonel Mushtaq."

Realizing that by including steps the General Services Office was taking, he was infringing upon the turf of Jesus Cristobal Colon, the Management Counselor. Alex paused. He knew from experience that Colon wasn't very competent and Alex was reasonably certain, JC, as he liked to be called, would probably forget to mention this important point. But Alex was determined that nothing would be left out.

Hunt acknowledged Alex's comments with a nod and was about to continue when JC Colon interrupted her.

"Since we're talking about security," he said, "I've gotten complaints this morning from several agencies that the Marines damaged some offices last night." He glared at Alex. "Did you have a drill, again?" JC asked.

"Yes, we did." Alex said. He couldn't believe JC was complaining about the need for emergency drills and wondered how far Colon was going to pursue it.

"Drills, drills, drills. Why do we need so many? Can't the Marines just read their manuals and memorize their responsibilities?" Colon looked back and forth between Alex and the Ambassador.

Alex watched as expressions formed on the faces of several Country Team members looking at JC. It was clearly pity.

"I wish it was that easy, JC," Alex said. "But the Marines have to practice everything, so when a dangerous situation arises, they'll react instinctively in order to save the lives of everyone in this room, including yours." He smiled at the man benevolently.

"During real life and death battles, action evolves quickly and unpredictably. These drills ensure that Marines understand the overall objectives of defending the Embassy and saving lives." Alex sounded like he was JC's best friend. "In essence, these drills ensure they'll understand the Commander's intent --- that is my intent and Jim Riley's intent, and adapt accordingly based on the Embassy's Internal Defense Plan.

Winston Hargrove IV jumped into the conversation.

Not surprised, Alex believed Winston had been waiting for the right moment to take him on again.

"Let me follow-up on JC's comment," Hargrove said while pointing to Colon, his outstretched arm exposing the gold cufflinks on his well-pressed white shirt. "Should the Pakistan Government get wind of how often the Marines drill, they might conclude we don't have confidence in Pakistan's ability to protect us."

"I don't have confidence the Pakistanis will protect us, do you?" Alex exclaimed incredulously. "Remember, they didn't do it in '79, when the mobs burned down this very Embassy." He saw that salvo hit Hargrove, yet he still wasn't ready to surrender. "Winston, my friend, while things have changed a lot since then, do you really think we should abrogate our own responsibility of self-defense?" He noted Rachel was staring intently at him, her hand under her chin.

"Of course, the Pakistanis will protect us! They're our allies." Hargrove said in his most haughty voice. "It's their obligation to do so."

Before Alex could reply the Ambassador cut in.

"Enough!" he said, slapping the table. Looking at Hargrove and Colon with cold eyes, Pierce said, "Everyone here, and I mean everyone, must know that Security is an important priority of my mission. I assure you that the RSO and the Marines are doing exactly what they should be doing." Turning to Alex, he continued, with a slight grin, "Just try to limit the damage during these drills in the future. We don't want to distress Mr. Colon any further."

Alex saw Colon shrink into his seat. He almost felt sorry for him but was too aware that men like him and Hargrove were hurdles in his efforts to protect the Embassy and its staff.

The rest of the Country Team meeting went as expected until the Military Attaché, Colonel Walker, mentioned that he sensed a disturbing trend; his Pakistani counterparts were becoming less and less open with him about some of their programs.

"As you know," Colonel Walker explained, "we've exchanged information for years with the Pakistani military about what's happening in Afghanistan. Their intelligence officers are operational across the border. But lately, it's like pulling teeth to get anything from them. I am convinced ISI is holding back on us."

Alex had that feeling too, so he was especially interested in hearing the reaction of Bill Stanton, CIA Station Chief.

Stanton had been silent through most of the meeting, but now he spoke up and agreed with Colonel Walker.

Expecting more, Alex was disappointed when Stanton passed on his turn to speak further. Knowing Stanton rarely said much at the Country Team meeting, still he thought this was an opportunity he could have taken to offer a more in-depth perspective.

Bill usually had plenty to say, even though Alex knew he wasn't going to discuss sensitive operations in this forum, which Alex respected. Still, he had begun wondering just how open his "friend" was being of late.

The Ambassador stood, signaling the meeting's end, and everyone rose from their chairs. "Thank you," he said. "This was a very fruitful meeting. I think we all agree that we have our work cut out for us." He, then, exchanged a few words with Rachel Smith and left the room.

With the meeting concluded, Alex was about to welcome Rachel to Islamabad, when Bill Stanton approached him. "Alex, if you have a moment, I'd appreciate if you could stop by my office to discuss something."

"Sure, Bill, I'll be there in a minute," Alex replied, a little disappointed that Rachel was now engaged in another conversation. "I also want to talk about why we didn't have any advance info on yesterday's demonstration. I don't want to be surprised again by violent demonstrators, or anything else for that matter."

Stanton gave him a look Alex couldn't quite figure out. Perhaps Stanton's relationship with ISI wasn't as strong as people thought, went through his mind.

Background

Country Team Meetings Protocol

Country Team meetings are joint sessions where every department and agency reports news. If there is nothing of interest to say, one may pass a turn to report. Better to pass than waste people's time with trivial matters. The Country Team meeting is a time to impress others with skills, information, local knowledge, and contacts. Unfortunately, there is always the occasional Foreign Service Officer, FSO, as he or she is known, who takes this opportunity to grandstand, making much of nothing.

Background of Ambassador Pierce

An exceptionally bright career professional. He is considered an admirable breed of career Foreign Service Officer who would sacrifice much to advance America's foreign policy, such as living abroad in hostile environments, raising a family in difficult circumstances, facing health issues unknown to the average American back home, and even accepting family separation if local conditions are deemed excessively dangerous.

History of American-Pakistan Coorperation

America's relationship with Pakistan has suffered highs and lows over the years. During the cold war, the CIA worked with Pakistan's Inter-Services Intelligence Directorate to counter Soviet influence. This started in the 1950s with American U-2 flights flown from Peshawar over the Soviet Union. Then, after the Soviet invasion of Afghanistan, ISI and the CIA supported the Mujahedeen to kill Soviets and expel them from Afghanistan. These periods of cooperation were interspersed with U.S. arms embargoes, either due to wars between Pakistan and India, or to Pakistani military coup d'états.

CHAPTER 9

FRIDAY MORNING

Meeting Fallout

As everyone mingled or slowly left the conference room, Alex walked down the hall toward Bill Stanton's office. The hallway was decorated with photos of former U.S. Ambassadors to Pakistan. Recent photos were in color, older ones were in black and white. He was pleased with himself for fending off both Hargrove and Colon at the meeting. Yet, the quiet request for a meeting with Stanton left him feeling uneasy. Nearly to Bill's office, he met Ellen Hunt who stopped him.

"Alex, I share Colonel Walker's concerns regarding Pakistan's reluctance to be open to us on a number of issues," she said. "It's not only with ISI where we seem to have problems; even the Foreign Office is playing some issues too close to the vest. When Jim gets back from Karachi, ask him to see me. I want to talk to him about police cooperation, as well as blowback over changes in our foreign assistance programs to India and Pakistan."

"Okay, will do," Alex replied. "By the way, so far the cops continue to be responsive to our needs." Hunt nodded and started to turn away, but then faced Alex again.

"Oh, and another thing, Alex", she whispered. "Your witticisms at the meeting were indeed humorous but try to control your impulses to slam-dunk Hargrove. I want a smooth working, cooperative Embassy."

"You're right, I apologize, Ellen. I shouldn't take advantage of the mentally challenged."

She stared at Alex for a moment, then smiled, "Smart ass." She laughed and walked toward her office.

Alex was impressed with how well the petite, raven-haired Deputy Chief of Mission could stay on top of every issue. His previous DCMs, both males, in Tunis and Buenos Aires, confined their interests solely to the work of the Political Section. But Ellen took a broad view of her responsibilities and was an excellent manager. She also had the Ambassador's ear on all issues since she had served as his Political Counselor when they were at the embassy in Sri Lanka. Her quick grasp of complicated issues, and her ability to draft concise and well-thought-out messages to Washington, had secured her rapid rise in the State Department. He believed she deserved her reputation as a brilliant, professional officer.

Moments earlier, just as his conversation with Ellen Hunt was ending, Alex noticed Rachel Smith walk past. She wore heels which added to her considerable height, making her damn near as tall as he was. With her perfectly tailored pants suit, and carrying a leather portfolio in her right hand, she made quite a professional impression. Briefly, they made eye contact, but she continued walking toward the central stairway. Alex wished he hadn't been tied up with Ellen. Just another opportunity missed to greet his new colleague.

Finally, Alex walked further down the hall, stopping in front of the CIA Station door. He picked up the speaker-phone mounted on the wall and announced his presence. As he was buzzed in, he took one more glance at Rachel, now at the end of the hallway. To his delight, she looked back at him briefly, and he caught a hint of a smile. For a micro-second he thought of walking toward her and introducing himself, but the moment passed too quickly and then she was gone.

Alex pulled the CIA door open and entered.

"Alex, welcome to 'Camp Crowded'," Stanton said, as he met Alex. "I guess Admin can't do anything to alleviate the situation."

"You've got that right. Hell, nearly all new embassies are outdated by the time State gets funding, a contractor, and a design'."

Originally designed in the 1960s and completed in 1970, this Embassy had been gutted by fire in 1979 set by attacking mobs. Even though the current building was only a decade old and rebuilt, it was poorly designed and already showing wear and tear.

Even so, Stanton's office was large as befitted the head of one of the CIA's most important overseas stations. Alex knew, however, that most of his staff operated in ridiculously cramped quarters. Just another fact of embassy life they all had to accept.

Just then, Alan Patterson, Stanton's deputy walked into the room to give Stanton a document.

"Hi, Alex," Patterson said.

"How's it going, Alan?" Alex replied as they shook hands.

"Everything's fine here in paradise. By the way, thanks for sending me the official report of the '79 attack on the Embassy. I haven't read it yet, but I will. It's so typical that we got screwed by the Soviets when they said we were behind the takeover of the Grand Mosque in Mecca. Everyone with a brain knows that takeover really concerned the Shiite and Sunni rivalry.

"Right on the mark," Alex stated. "But you know how gullible the masses are here. The story was enough to bring five to ten thousand demonstrators to the Embassy and everything turned to shit. The assholes fire-bombed the Embassy, stole the weapons from the police at the front gate, and fired at us. One shot mortally wounded a Marine Guard who was assigned to an observation post on the Embassy roof."

Patterson shook his head in disgust. "Why didn't the Marines just shoot the bastards?"

"They never got permission. The Ambassador and DCM were out of the compound and not in communication with the RSO. The remaining senior officer in charge of the Embassy vetoed the use of force, even though there were one hundred and six employees trapped in the embassy safe-haven and struggling to survive.

"As the attack continued, the Marines repeatedly tried for a way to get all employees out of the safe-haven vault, but the hallways were still controlled by rioters, and the Marines were stymied."

"So, what happened? I know they didn't all die." Stanton asked.

Alex took a deep breath. "Finally, as the floors of the safe-haven were buckling and the paint was peeling off the walls from the intense heat, the staff forced their way onto the roof to escape the inferno. Only then did Pakistani authorities respond." He personally knew several of the officers trapped that day, and even though he wasn't there himself, their near death was still upsetting.

"When the Embassy was rebuilt, the State Department used the existing shell of the building. Now, as you can see, the office space is much too small to accommodate our expanding staff."

"Incredible! Sorry, but I have to go," Patterson said. "Nice chatting with you, Alex. I hope we never see that level of violence again here. Bill, let me know what you think about that document," Patterson said as he left the room. Stanton shook his head, and asked Alex to take a seat.

He definitely doesn't fit the Hollywood version of a spymaster, Alex thought as he sat down. Stanton stood five-feet-nine inches tall, .with thinning grey hair and a chunky, soft physique. His pale eyes were magnified by thick coke-bottle glasses making him look more like a mad-scientist than an action-figure

"Just as Colonel Walker mentioned at the Country Team meeting," Stanton began, "We've detected a certain reserve by some ISI officers. Moreover, their support for the Taliban against members of the Northern Alliance in Afghanistan has led us to believe we may have an emerging problem with religious fundamentalists in ISI's ranks. I'll discuss this with Jim Riley, but I was also wondering if you've detected anything like this in the police force."

"No, not yet. The police seem to be giving us the same cooperation as usual. That's not to say they're always competent. But they do seom to try."

"Hmm, well at least that's good news," Stanton said. "By the way, I thought your points at the meeting were right on. Hargrove and Colon are such asses. How could the State Department ever assign those two clowns here? And what a phony preppy Princeton accent Hargrove has! Holy shit! Does he think this is a country club?"

Alex laughed. "You know how the game's played, Bill. State insists all officers, like Hargrove, serve in hardship posts to 'share the burden.' As for JC, he just took advantage of his assignment in Personnel to get a bigger job. Of course, Islamabad is way beyond his experience level."

Stanton nodded. "Changing subjects, how's your father doing?" Alex was caught off-guard by the question. His father was a retired CIA Station Chief and well-known among the current upper echelons in the Agency.

"He's doing fine. Thanks for asking, Bill. He's enjoying his retirement and his health seems good."

"Really?" Stanton looked skeptical.

"Yeah, he stays busy these days writing and doing consulting for large corporations."

"That makes sense," Stanton said. "Although we never worked together since I spent large parts of my career in the Science and Technology Directorate, we did have some overlap on issues," Stanton explained. "I heard him speak several times and thought he really knew his stuff."

"Thanks, Bill. Speaking of intelligence," Alex said, "Why didn't ISI pass on any info about yesterday's demonstration at the Indian Embassy?"

"Good question," Stanton replied. "They track everything about the Indians, even more than they track us. In fact, many of the anti-Indian protest groups are simply front-groups created by ISI. Maybe they just didn't realize the Ambassador might pick that exact time to drive by. I guess they screwed-up."

Alex saw Stanton blink rapidly as soon as he had said it.

"Hold on, Bill. You're implying the demonstrators might have been working for ISI?"

"Possibly, but more likely, unwittingly."

Alex stared at Stanton for a moment, then said, "I'd like you to be perfectly clear on this point. Do you think the demonstrators were being used by ISI, or are they ISI employees?"

"It's just a theory, Alex. Something to think about. Let's keep this between us for now, Okay?"

Alex contemplated that Stanton had not really answered his question, but, overall, it made sense that ISI had screwed-up, regardless of whether the demonstrators were innocent civilians or ISI employees. The only alternative was that ISI did mention the planned demonstration ahead of time to the CIA Station, but Stanton failed to inform him. It wouldn't be the first time the CIA deliberately lied about what it knew. But that didn't seem likely here with Stanton in charge, especially in view of the good relationship between the two of them.

"Okay Bill. Maybe you can use this screw-up as leverage with ISI in future dealings." He gave Stanton a hard look. "They owe us big-time."

"I agree. By the way, don't think that I am trying to play you, but did the CIA ever try to recruit you after your service in Naval Intelligence?"

"Yes, you did. But don't get me wrong. I think the Agency is a fine place. I felt, however, I needed to make my own mark in life. Working in the Agency and being the son of a rather prominent former Station Chief, wouldn't have given me a chance to establish my own reputation. Diplomatic Security has become a great organization. They give their Special Agents lots of responsibility much earlier than the FBI or Secret Service. And the variety of tasks is challenging. Now, if only we didn't have to fight with the rest of the State Department just to accomplish our mission, it'd be heaven."

Stanton nodded his head in agreement and his face showed the irony of Alex's statement. All other agencies knew that Diplomatic Security was a high-quality organization. Their operational RSOs/Special Agents were first class. They ran protective operations as well as the Secret Service but without the large budget and resources of the latter. Their criminal investigations were also regarded as outstanding by Federal prosecutors and resulted in a very high conviction rate for passport and visa fraud. And their small numbers of threat assessment analysts in Washington were consummate professionals.

"It's a shame that within the State Department the old guard's reluctant to view DS as the wonderful asset that it truly is. I guess they see you guys as a competitor for financial and personnel resources," Stanton said.

The truth was that Congress and the White House saw DS as an important, although small, part of America's defenses. As for the rest of the State Department, their contribution was often viewed by the politicians as suspect.

Stanton nodded and stood. Was he shielding something behind his look? Alex wondered.

"All right, Alex. Thanks for stopping by. I'm glad you have a good working relationship with the cops. Although, honestly, I'm getting bad vibes about where we're headed with Pakistan."

They shook hands, but Alex still wondered if Stanton was holding back. On the other hand, he feared the CIA might not be as knowledgeable as they should be.

Background

<u>Helen Hunt, DCM</u>

Hunt served with Ambassador Pierce in Sri Lanka, where she was the Political Counselor. Although her depth of knowledge on South Asia had not been as extensive as her knowledge of Arab affairs, she learned issues rapidly and was one of the stars of the Embassy. Boyd knew Jim Riley valued her counsel and respected her management ability. As Embassy DCM, all agencies reported to Ellen rather than directly to the Ambassador. DCMs ensured that the embassy functioned as a team and fulfilled all reporting requirements to Washington, D.C. Moreover, the DCM often negotiated disputes between agencies. This might involve financial costs to be apportioned among various agency players or deciding which agency would take the lead in addressing a particular issue if it fell into a gray area. Most importantly, the DCM had to ensure that the Ambassador received accurate, balanced, and timely advice from the Embassy staff. This was often complicated because agencies had their own parochial agendas.

Bill Stanton, CIA Chief

After graduating from Purdue with a degree in Engineering, then a Masters in Engineering at Stanford, he was recruited by the Agency. It was Bill's brain power that had propelled him into the upper ranks of the CIA. Now forty-five years old and divorced, Stanton spent long hours at work. He was considered an expert on nuclear weapons development in a number of countries. It was this expertise that had resulted in his assignments to Iraq, Israel, India, and now Pakistan. Alex respected and personally liked the man, but when dealing with Stanton, he always remembered President Reagan's slogan, 'trust, but verify.'

CHAPTER **10**

FRIDAY MORNING

The Firing Range

"Okay, all you guys need to draw your revolvers faster from your shoulder holsters. And you need to increase your shooting accuracy," Susan Witt said in an authoritative voice. She had been carefully observing the Ambassador's bodyguards shooting at paper targets hung on wooden poles five yards away.

"Ideally, I want you to draw and get off two shots in two seconds. I know you can do this from the five-yard line. But you have to hit the target center mass with both shots. Let's try it again. Okay, is the line ready?" Susan commanded. "Ready, fire!"

The bodyguards drew their weapons, aimed, and fired. She looked at the targets; the results were pathetic. Susan wanted to shake her head, use sarcasm, or just plain scream. *But that would only discourage the bodyguards, after all they were trying.*

The police range was basic, just an earthen embankment, but near the Embassy and, therefore, convenient. There were four bodyguards, all of Constable rank, assigned from Special Branch. Susan thought their shooting skills were pitiful. She only hoped their personal commitment to protect the Ambassador exceeded their shooting ability.

Looking over her shoulder, she kept looking for Alex. He

said he would try to join her after his morning meeting, but hadn't arrived yet.

"All right, you can see that with eight rounds fired by four of you, only half hit the silhouette targets. Even then, not all rounds hitting the targets were center mass. Okay, watch me this time," she said.

Pointing to the targets, she was about to speak when she heard a vehicle approaching. Turning, she smiled seeing Alex's jeep. He parked behind the firing line, got out, saluted the guards who returned the salute, then joined Susan shaking her hand.

"How's it going?"

"Some improvement, but they have a long way to go."

Alex nodded. "I understand. Look, I'm here just to observe training, you're running it, so the show is all yours."

Susan nodded and turned back toward the guards.

"Okay, watch me carefully this time."

She moved in front of the spare target. With lightning speed, Susan drew her Sig Sauer 9mm pistol from her holster and fired two shots in less than two seconds. Both shots hit the silhouette in the middle of the chest. She de-cocked the weapon, holstered the gun, and then turned her attention back to the bodyguards. Their expressions showed they were impressed.

Alex stood watching from the sidelines. He was also impressed, not only with Susan's shooting, but with the way she interacted with the men. This was the real reason he was here, to observe her instructor skills. Alex needed to ensure that Susan had the temperament and expertise to train the Pakistanis.

She spoke again to the guards, "Did you notice I drew very quickly which then gave me a brief micro-second to smoothly pull the trigger without jerking it?"

"You are very fast," another guard said. "Especially for a woman."

Susan glared at him with a rather serious expression.

"Sorry, I meant no offense," the guard looked down at the ground after realizing the implication of his comment to an American woman.

"Okay, no offense taken," Susan smiled back. "Okay, not only did I draw quickly, but I shot accurately. Remember, if you don't hit the target, you can't stop the attack."

Alex smiled, it was vintage Instruction 101 from his own days as a rookie Special Agent.

Susan had noticed one bodyguard in particular, Aftab, was really slow at pulling his weapon out of his holster.

"Aftab," Susan said, "you're getting your weapon caught in your vest every time. Try using your off hand to brush the vest open and then slide your strong hand inside of the vest when you go to draw."

Aftab heard Susan speaking and turned to acknowledge her advice. Unfortunately, as he pivoted toward her, he swung the gun down the firing line at his brother officers. Susan was furious. She saw he didn't have his finger on the trigger, but this was precisely how accidents happened.

"Aftab, point the gun down-range now!" she said in her best command voice. He did so, mumbling sorry and looking sheepish. Susan walked up to Aftab and stood on his right-hand side. If he'd been a DS Agent, Susan would have reamed him out and probably said, "What the fuck are you doing dickhead?" But with a Pakistani male in his own country this would have been counter-productive. So, she directly, yet in a low-level voice, told Aftab that everyone was relying on him to be safe on the firing range; that he could be a leader if he started paying attention to every detail. She saw that his hand was shaking a little bit. But he responded by thanking her, then he re-holstered his weapon. Susan resumed her former position behind the firing line.

"Let's try some dry firing for a few minutes."

They looked confused.

"Everyone, unload your weapon." She drew her gun, popped out the magazine, pulled the slide back to empty the chamber, and then returned the slide to the carry position. She watched them dump their ammo and then holster their guns. "We'll work on speeding up your draw. Then we'll work on trigger control."

Susan gave the command to draw, then holster their handguns. She repeated this drill several times, carefully observing their progress. Most of them showed signs of mastering the skill of the quick draw.

After another ten minutes of practicing trigger control with the guns unloaded, she had them fire several rounds of ammunition at the targets, again using the double-tap method of firing two quick shots at a time.

Alex noted a clear improvement in their accuracy and decided Susan was going to be a key asset to the office.

The bodyguards' shooting ability had improved since she had started training them a month ago, but they were still way below DS standards. She thought their clothing might be the problem. The men all insisted upon wearing their native pajama-like shalwar kameez. The top was worn over baggy pants and came down almost to the knee with a slit part-way up on either side. Wearing this outfit, it was incredibly awkward to draw a weapon from a holster on their belt, as the weapon usually got caught in the fabric of the shalwar kameez.

Additionally, the Pakistanis, never being slaves to fashion, also liked to wear an open short vest over their shalwar kameez top. Alex informed her once, a while ago, that Jim Riley had decided after numerous training sessions, it was best for the bodyguards to wear a shoulder holster under the vest, rather than to carry their gun on a belt.

Although still early morning, it was near one hundred degrees. After nearly two hours on the firing range, Susan looked down at her cream-colored shirt and khaki cargo pants. They were drenched with perspiration; her hiking shoes and pant legs were covered with dirt.

"I think we've achieved all that we can this morning," she said. "Let's get back to the Embassy in case the Ambassador has to go somewhere."

With the session ended, she chatted briefly with Alex, who complimented her on the training. Then, Susan drove back to her apartment on the embassy compound to take a shower. Afterward, as she sat on her small balcony, drinking a big glass of Gatorade, she thought about her brief time in Pakistan. She really enjoyed being in Islamabad and appreciated the two men under whose command she now worked: Jim Riley and Alex Boyd.

Her thoughts roamed about how her life had evolved since college. Attending the University of Oklahoma had been fun. There'd been lots of parties, but also lots of studying. Following graduation with a major in chemistry, she decided to join the Army to see the world. Maybe it was her chemistry background, or possibly a natural attention to detail and a love of doing exciting things that led her to become an Explosive Ordnance Disposal Officer, a field dominated by men. Susan had served in the Army for four years and left with rank of Captain. She didn't exactly see the whole world, but she did see Saudi Arabia and Kuwait during the Gulf War.

But, once she joined the Diplomatic Security Service she had seen the world. She traveled on the Secretary of State's Protective Detail and probably visited fifty counties in two years. Then, as a member of the DS Mobile Deployment Team, she was deployed time and again to hot spots where U.S. embassy personnel were under extraordinary threat.

Now in Islamabad, her goal was to learn everything that she could about being an RSO.

Thirty minutes later, Susan left her apartment on the Embassy compound and walked up the hill to the embassy. Just before entering the back door, known as Marine Post Two, Susan poked her head into the SMG local guard office.

"Hi, Ahmed, how's it going?" "Tic Toc, Miss Witt," Ahmed replied. Susan chuckled because the Urdu phrase Tic Toc roughly translated into 'everything's okay.'

"I was just about to call Mr. Boyd sahib to inform him we see the same green Toyota Corolla driving in front of the Embassy gate many times."

"You mean many times this morning?" Susan asked.

"Yes. We tried to take the license plate number, but it was not possible to see it clearly because it was much covered in heavy dirt. But the plate was from the Northwest Frontier Province."

"Describe the occupants of the Toyota, Ahmed."

"There were two men, one with beard and one with only mustache. They glance at embassy each time. But still, why they drive by more than once? I have called our Mobile Patrol, but the green Toyota has not returned."

"Okay, Ahmed. Good job. I'll brief Mr. Riley and Mr. Boyd on this matter. Let me know if anything else develops."

As with all her previous days in Islamabad, Susan knew whatever was on her agenda this afternoon would be interrupted by more urgent matters. In this case, it was possible someone was conducting surveillance on the embassy. Alex had to be told.

Background
Weapons

The first thing the RSO did with any Special Branch officer assigned to the Embassy was to inspect their police-issued firearm. It was usually a .38 caliber revolver in poor condition. Moreover, the officers didn't have any speed loaders or good quality holsters. So, step one had been to replace everything issued to them by the police. After weighing the merits of using a semi-automatic pistol versus a revolver, Jim Riley decided that the bodyguards had a better chance of mastering the easy-to-operate revolver. DS Special Agents now carried a Sig-Sauer 9mm semi-automatic pistol. Years earlier, however, the agents had carried a Smith and Wesson Model 19 revolver which could shoot either .38 special or .357 magnum rounds. Because DS still had a supply of the old revolvers, Riley asked headquarters to send him some of these, including all the necessary accessories for the Special Branch bodyguards.

Bodyguard Training:

Susan Witt spent a lot of time with the bodyguards going over walking formations, exiting and entering vehicles as a unit, etc. Since she was a former Army Explosives Demolition Officer, she also created a training program to recognize improvised explosives devices. All of this training the bodyguards seemed to understand and to enjoy. She also told them how to effectively use their radios to communicate ambassadorial movements without compromising security or cluttering the airwaves with excessive chatter. After a month the bodyguards had shown significant improvement. In their world, having a woman instructor was unheard of. But they clearly recognized Susan's expertise and had great respect for her. As befitting a female embassy employee, she was treated as a normal American goddess.

Susan's thoughts about Jim Riley

Jim had an historic perspective on how the old Office of Security had evolved into the Bureau of Diplomatic Security. Now 50 years old, Riley had adapted to the new responsibilities of DS. His background was representative of his generation. Following graduation from Boston College, he joined the U.S. Air Force and served as an officer in its Office of Special Investigations (OSI), where he developed his skills in investigations and counter-intelligence. After joining DS, Riley had assignments in Bonn, Warsaw, Pretoria, and Moscow, all challenging assignments with counter-intelligence concerns. He also had Washington tours in the Office of Counter-intelligence, Office of Overseas Operations, and the Office of Physical Security Programs. His insight into how DS operated and how it related to the rest of the State Department was invaluable

Susan's thoughts about Alex Boyd

He was her direct supervisor and she thought he treated her well. Alex was more her own age and their relationship was casual, yet professional. She had heard him speak both French and Arabic and marveled at his linguistic ability. She knew that although he had been the Senior RSO in Tunis, accepting the Islamabad position as the Deputy RSO was not a come-down since this office was so large and the number of posts to cover were numerous. She had no doubt that Alex would get promoted again during his tour. She hoped that the same thing would happen to her.

CHAPTER 11

FRIDAY MID-DAY

The Clandestine Meeting

Colonel Malik sat crossed-legged on the carpet sipping mint tea and observed the others. He had met with these five Pakistani men many times before, assuring them this small, dirty hovel in the poorest section of Islamabad was completely safe. Nobody would overhear their plans. As part of Pakistan's military ISI, he carried real authority to know such things.

The dreary house was tucked away in an obscure part of Islamabad, very distant from the upscale neighborhoods where prosperous Pakistanis and foreigners lived. The inside smelled musty, although cooking odors from the kitchen helped mask some of it. The walls needed a fresh coat of paint, and the once-colorful tribal carpets on the floor were thread-bare.

Malik's penetrating stare moved from one person to the next. All were seated on the carpet in a similar cross-legged manner. Similar to Colonel Malik's attire, four wore khaki-colored shalwar kameez with brown leather sandals. Chaudhry, who used the religious title of Maulana, or "Master" or "Our Lord", wore a flowing white robe and white turban. Each man had made his way independently to this ISI-funded safe-house in Islamabad. Although they all had very different backgrounds from Colonel Malik, they shared his hatred for India and America.

"I am stating again," Malik began in Urdu, "The time

has come to show the Americans there is a price to pay for their support of India on the Kashmir issue. Moreover, I fear the Americans are considering shifting their aid from Pakistan to new programs in India. This, we cannot let happen."

All nodded in agreement around the circle.

"What is there to do about all this?" Asif Babar asked, pulling on his shaggy black beard. "How can we help change the attitude of the Americans?" He was rail thin; a twenty-four-year old who was head of the radical Students for Pakistan.

"They do not accept our concerns," Colonel Malik said. "So, we will have to push them hard in our direction. They must see that India wants control of *all* South Asia, but Pakistanis are prepared to stand up to this oppression."

"I have, myself, preached this very same message at Friday prayers," Maulana Chaudhry said. In his late thirties, he had a large following and was a known as a firebrand at one of the bigger mosques In Islamabad. A dark-complexioned Punjabi religious leader, he frequently harangued the West for their 'cultural perversions' and inappropriate influence in Pakistan. His inflammatory speeches and sermons derided the adoption of western dress and habits by Pakistani youth.

"Many good people are ready to rise up and defend Islam," he concluded.

Speaking out next was Imran Durrani of the Labor Federation, a front organization created by ISI to control unions. "We can call on a few thousand to protest against the Americans. Just tell me when and where."

Malik smiled, knowing he had the group's support for whatever action he needed to take. His plan was already formed, but he was careful with sharing too much information. Even within ISI, there were opposing factions. Some officers supported his views that westernization had gone too far; that Pakistan was becoming too compliant with America's policies. Like him, they also worried about further secularization of their country. However, others, Malik knew, did not share his complete devotion to Islam or and his vicious hatred of India.

"I will call upon you again in a few days," Malik said leaning forward. "For now, it is sufficient to know that I plan on having a big anti-American demonstration at their Embassy. I will need your support to rally our people following next Friday's prayers," he said with a smile. "This demonstration will be peaceful but should make the Americans fearful for the future."

Following a simple meal of rice, roast lamb, and naan bread, cooked by one of Colonel Malik's army minions, the group broke up for the evening. Colonel Malik stayed at the safe-house awaiting confirmation from his ISI counter-surveillance teams that all attendees had returned to their homes without being followed.

After everyone had departed, he spoke to his aide, who had been sitting discreetly in the back of the room during the meeting.

"We can never take too many precautions. Other factions in ISI or the CIA at the American Embassy may have heard about this meeting and are watching us," he said shaking his head. "One never knows for certain." Because of his precautions, however, Malik felt his operation was safe so far. Not even the attendees tonight realized the extent of Malik's violent and bloody plans.

In Malik's view, he believed there was good reason to hate the Americans. They had done nothing to support Pakistan in the 1971 Pakistan-India war. He had been posted to East Pakistan, now called Bangledesh, and when insurrection against the government had come to a boiling point, Malik's infantry battalion, was ordered to put it down, at all costs. Atrocities were committed by both sides.

India supported East Pakistan at that time, as did the Soviet Union, which sent naval forces into the Indian Ocean. The United States diplomatically supported West Pakistan as a counterweight to the Soviets. As a show of support, a powerful American carrier battle group, led by the USS Enterprise, sailed into the Bay of Bengal. On December 3, 1971, war began, but it lasted only thirteen days and was decisively won by India.

Malik had fought bravely and led his platoon into the teeth of an advancing Indian army battalion. After a day of intense fighting Malik's unit was overrun and he was captured, a fate ultimately shared by over 54,000 Pakistani Army troops. Being young, outspoken, and arrogant, Malik was dealt with harshly by his captors. His unit was not returned to West Pakistan for almost a year, during which time he was tortured whenever he irritated his Indian Army guards. As a result, Malik intensely hated India. But he also hated America because, in his view, the American naval carrier battle group did nothing to support Pakistan during the war.

As the years passed Malik was asked to join the Army's Inter-Services Intelligence Directorate. He prospered in ISI. When the Soviet Union invaded Afghanistan in 1979, he became a senior advisor and trainer to the Mujahedeen. Malik, much to his dislike, had to work closely with the CIA, who funded the war against the Soviets and poured in equipment. Malik was grateful for this material support, but it came at a price to his pride. The CIA held the purse strings and let it be known they were in charge. He resented this and swore one day he would get revenge for this humiliation.

With the Soviets now out of Afghanistan and CIA programs finished, ISI was free to support the most radical elements of the Mujahedeen. Colonel Malik, specifically, was spearheading the rise of the Taliban as a counter-weight to Indian interests in Afghanistan. He wanted the Americans to understand a tilt toward India could only result in destabilization in Pakistan, with serious damage to U.S. vital interests in the sub-continent. He vowed they would pay for their arrogance and misguided policies with blood.

CHAPTER 12

FRIDAY MID-DAY

The Bomb

Jim Riley returned from Karachi at mid-morning on Friday. He exited the airport terminal in dress slacks and blazer, carrying only a small canvas overnight bag and briefcase. An Embassy car with driver was waiting for him.

Along the route to the Embassy compound, he passed small brick factories with their tall chimneys spewing black smoke as they made thousands of bricks daily. The occasional wooden shacks dotting the landscape had small fenced in yards for cows or chickens. His driver expertly passed helmetless riders on bicycles, motorcycles, and slow-moving ox pulling wooden carts. He also drove around badly dented old pickup trucks emitting dark clouds of noxious fumes.

As always, there were five or six cars driving on the wrong side of the divided highway, sometimes heading directly into Riley's path only to veer away at the last second.

Susan Witt's predecessor called these near misses "Oles", Riley thought. *Much like a matador calls out when a bull passes within inches of his body,* Secretly, he perversely enjoyed this chaos, perhaps, because it was nothing like his prior assignments in Moscow, Warsaw, Bonn, and Pretoria.

Thirty minutes later, Riley sat comfortably behind his desk. He had called for a short staff meeting to review what had transpired during the last two days in his absence. Alex and Susan Witt, along with Nancy Williams and the Gunny, were all present. Nancy Williams recapped the recent incoming action messages.

"Washington wants info that we've already sent them, but every office wants it reported in its own unique format," she said.

Riley shook his head. He saw things as Alex did, and often complained about the difference between reporting about security and actually doing security. But Washington didn't care.

Alex reported on the Ambassador's incident with the mob at the Indian Embassy and the previous night's Marine Guard drill. He also emphasized his concerns about ISI not cooperating fully with the Embassy.

"The DCM and Station Chief would like to talk with you today about police relations, just to make sure everything is going all right," Alex said. "Since the DCM asked you to attend a two o'clock meeting this afternoon about overall security and intelligence relations between the Embassy and Pakistan, you can combine these meetings because the Station Chief will also be there."

"Okay, that's fine with me. I also want to discuss the Karachi Consul General's attitude toward security. He thinks *he's* the Ambassador, or at least a minor Greek God, not merely the Consul General." Alex smiled at Riley's comment, knowing this was a long term problem in Karachi.

Riley turned to Gunny Rueben Rodriguez. "Is everything okay with the Marine Detachment?"

"Everything's fine, sir," Rodriguez replied. "No one has gotten really sick lately with Delhi Belly or the trots, so we're at full strength. And we're getting good support from the Embassy."

"Great," Riley said. "Anything the Marines need will be a priority for us. How's morale in the Detachment?"

"It's pretty good," Gunny Rodriquez replied. "Let's face it, there isn't much to do for entertainment locally, and most of the local women aren't going to date Westerners. But the Marines party with the American community, the Canadians, the French, Aussies, and the Brits. Plus, RSO keeps us busy with drills."

Just as the meeting was ending, Riley received a phone call from his local investigator, Mohammad Bhatti.

"Hi, Bhatti, what's up?"

"The police bomb squad called to report they found an unexploded bomb in one of the shopping markets visited by Westerners. They have defused the bomb and want to know if the RSO would like to see it."

Riley put Bhatti on hold. "We have some bad news, there's a bomb incident. Susan, this is right up your alley," he continued. "I'd like you to accompany Bhatti to the bomb squad. Get any information about what they found and precisely where they found it." He picked up the phone and thanked Bhatti, telling him Susan would join him at his office.

"Nancy, please call Bill Stanton's office and tell them I'm sending Susan to check out the bomb. Tell them it's been defused and ask if they would like someone to tag along," Riley said.

"Also, I'd like to know if this bomb looks like something the CIA may have given to the mujahedeen," he said, turning to Alex, yet speaking so everyone could hear. "We should know if our own weapons programs are now coming back to bite us in the ass."

Alex nodded. How many times had he been infuriated to discover America's enemies were using US-provided weapons against its own people. He was glad to know Riley felt the same.

CHAPTER 13

FRIDAY AFTERNOON

Embassy Contacts and Outreach

At 2:00 pm, when Riley entered the reception area of the Embassy's Executive Suite located on the Embassy' third floor, he was greeted by Janet Lustig, secretary to the DCM.

"Sorry, Jim, the meeting's been moved across the hall to the conference room," she said.

In four long strides, Riley entered the conference room and saw people already seated, including Bill Stanton, Colonel Walker of the Defense Attaché Office, Marisol Lopez, who was the Deputy Political Counselor, and Colonel Bud Williams of the Military Assistance Group. Following right behind Riley, J.C. Colon, the Management Counselor entered the room. Most everyone had coffee in front of them, so Riley poured a cup for himself and took a seat next to Marisol Lopez.

He enjoyed talking with Marisol because she really knew South Asia and the Middle East. She had once told him that she studied Middle Eastern history while at Columbia University. He also knew earlier she had served in Rabat and Dacca as a Political officer, plus Karachi as the combined political and economic officer. As a native Spanish speaker of Puerto Rican heritage, she didn't want to be stereotyped, so she avoided Latin America like the plague and forged her own future in the complicated world of what used to be called the Indian sub-continent.

"How was your trip to Karachi?" Marisol asked.

"It was a good, thanks. There's a chance I'll be able to sort out some problems. But, I'm certainly glad I live here instead. Karachi is so over-crowded and, frankly, not very attractive."

"Tell me about it!" Marisol exclaimed. "I lived there for three years. While the work was good and I made excellent Pakistani contacts, the city is like an undeveloped South Asian version of New York, but without the charm."

Riley laughed, not quite certain if Marisol literally meant New York had charm. She was a native New Yorker, so upon further reflection, he assumed that's exactly what she meant. Just as he was about to switch subjects, the Ambassador and DCM entered the room and sat at the head of the table.

Riley whispered to Marisol, "Where's your boss, Winston Hargrove?"

"He couldn't attend the meeting because he's playing tennis with the Chairman of the Bank of Pakistan," Marisol said, rolling her eyes. Winston was infamous for devoting an inordinate amount of time out of the office in pursuit of his personal hobbies. But Riley had to give him credit. He did play a good game of tennis.

"Ah," Riley said quietly, "I guess he has to keep polishing his skills for the 'Twit of the Year' Award." Marisol laughed.

Unbeknownst to Riley, JC Colon, seated on the other side of Marisol, overheard Riley's comment. Since JC thought of Hargrove as a friend, he started to object. Unfortunately, this occurred precisely as JC was swallowing some coffee. As the Ambassador opened the meeting, JC choked on his coffee, spitting some of it on the conference table and dribbling the rest down the front of his shirt. In his panic, he tipped over his coffee cup onto the table.

Colon was the center of attention. The Ambassador looked irritated, but as JC continued to cough, refrained from commenting. The DCM being slightly more sensitive than the Ambassador, yet equally articulate, silently mouthed the words: 'What the shit?' Most others tried to look away, but some chuckled.

JC excused himself and ran down the hall to the bathroom with his hand covering his nose and mouth.

The DCM had also heard Riley's exchange with Marisol and stared at him. He maintained an angelic expression, opened his palms, and looked back at the DCM, as if to say: 'What did I do?'

Ellen Hunt, a small smile forming on her lips, looked into Riley's eyes, and slightly shook her head, implying Riley was a 'Bad Boy.' The Ambassador kept staring at the mess on the conference room table. Eventually, even Ambassador Pierce couldn't resist smiling. Then Bill Stanton started laughing. It was infectious. Soon the entire group was red-faced with laughter and all discipline was abandoned.

"All right, children," Ambassador Pierce finally said. "Why don't we just move into my office for this meeting?"

"Joan," the Ambassador called politely to his secretary as he entered the Executive Suite. "Could you please call GSO to have a local worker clean up the mess on the conference table."

"Yes, sir," Joan said quizzically. As the group filed into the Ambassador's office, Riley heard Joan in the conference room yell out, "Oh, Yuk!"

Once re-assembled, minus JC, the Ambassador proceeded.

"Now that the entertainment portion of the meeting is over, I want to discuss a vital issue. Several offices in the Embassy have perceived elements of the Pakistan military, and even the

Foreign Ministry, as being less than fully cooperative with us since Washington has opened a friendly dialogue with India. This attitude is not totally surprising, but we must do everything possible to keep our relationship with Pakistan from deteriorating."

"Not only is the U.S.-Pakistan bilateral relationship at stake, but our joint work in Afghanistan will be jeopardized if our relations falter," DCM Hunt elaborated.

"Of critical importance," the Ambassador added, "is that we continue to be seen as a neutral broker between India and Pakistan. Considering the long-term animosity and suspicion between India and Pakistan, not to mention the potential future threat of nuclear war in the sub-continent, our ability to keep a lid on escalating tension is paramount. But first, we must take stock of where we stand vis-a-vis our contacts. So, let's go around the room and discuss any problems."

"My contacts with the police are still excellent," Jim Riley said when it was his turn to speak. "Even earlier today the police asked us to look at a defused bomb they discovered in Jinnah Supermarket strip mall. Because we all go to Jinnah, and because of Susan Witt's explosive's expertise, I asked her to examine it along with an officer from Bill Stanton's shop. Depending on her findings," Riley continued, "the Embassy should put out a security notice informing the American community about the situation." Riley further suggested he convene an informal group of western Embassy officials that frequently met to discuss precautions.

"Excellent," Ambassador Pierce said. "Since so many foreigners go to Jinnah Supermarket, let's see if we can disseminate this information even beyond the normal 'friends' group. Ellen, would you please draw up a list of embassies beyond Jim's list so we can fax our security notice to them?"

The meeting ended shortly thereafter with the Ambassador directing all agencies to monitor further uncooperative behavior by tho Pakistanis and report it to Ellen.

When the meeting broke up, Jim asked Ellen if he could speak to her separately about his Karachi trip. After ten minutes of conversation, Ellen called Karachi and instructed the American Consul General to carry out security initiatives immediately, stating forcefully it was a Washington mandate and money was already provided. The Consul General claimed he had suggested only a delay to Riley in starting the projects. Hunt would have none of his bullshit and told him to begin work ASAP, including providing weekly updates.

Riley returned to his office with a satisfied look on his face. Yet he couldn't stop wondering whether there was a link between the attack on the Ambassador's car and the overall deteriorating relationship with the Government of Pakistan.

CHAPTER 14

FRIDAY LATE-AFTERNOON

The Swimmer

"I think your draft telegram on the unexploded bomb at Jinnah Supermarket Mall is excellent," Alex told Susan. "Your detailed description of the device and its location are right on the mark. I'm going to add a paragraph about what the Embassy is doing to alert the Western Community."

He passed the report to Jim Riley for final approval. When he heard back, he would immediately send it on to Washington.

Later that afternoon, Riley told Alex the Embassy would convene an Emergency Action Committee meeting the following day to review potential threats to the American Community. He also mentioned the Ambassador wanted to host a Town Hall meeting with Riley in the Embassy auditorium within a few days so private-sector American citizens, and other invitees, could discuss personal security measures.

At 6 pm that evening, Alex smiled and thought 'another day in paradise' had ended with the creation of yet, another 'to do' list for tomorrow. But, he figured, this sure beat a boring 9-to-5 job back home. Grabbing his gym bag, he headed to the Embassy swimming pool, deciding he needed to exercise before dinner. It was still around 90 degrees outside at 6 pm. Walking within the 35-acre Embassy compound, he passed two red brick Embassy apartment buildings, a small Club with its restaurant/bar, and the tennis courts.

Reflecting on Islamabad, he thought: *It's really nice on any given day, yet, this city could turn violent in a heartbeat. Clan rivalries, ethnic battles over jobs, intolerance over wealth, poverty, religious views, even organized terrorism from the Afghans or Iranians could set off any city in Pakistan at a moment's notice. Geez, I gotta relax.*

Changing into swim trunks in the small clubhouse, Alex noticed someone doing laps in the pool. It was a woman, judging from the bathing cap, moving quickly and efficiently through the water with strong strokes. Jumping into another lane, he swam hard for the next thirty minutes.

He'd been a good athlete at the University of Virginia, even played backup point guard on the basketball team. At six feet two inches, one hundred ninety-five pounds, he was still pretty quick, well-muscled, and strong. As a Naval Intelligence officer, he had lots of swimming practice because he was assigned to a SEAL team in Virginia, in a supportive role. While not actually a SEAL, the assignment had offered him opportunities to swim on a daily basis.

After completing 30 laps, Alex sat on a deck chair facing the pool. The woman was still cutting through the water like a fast destroyer, churning water behind her with powerful kicks. Who was she? he wondered. Another five minutes passed before she finally stopped. Oh, my God. Alex thought when he recognized her climbing out of the pool. It's Rachel Smith, the new Press Officer. Wearing a white, one piece form-fitting suit, he assessed she was close to six-feet tall. Beautiful muscles, like a fitness competitor, he noted. She took off her swim cap, shook her head, and attractive brown, wavy hair fell to her shoulders. Her arms and shoulder muscles were well-defined, legs very long, lean and tanned, and clearly very well-muscled. Amazingly, she walked in his direction.Taking the lounge chair next to Alex, she looked at him for a brief moment.

"Hi, I'm Alex," he said without hesitation. "You're really good," he nodded toward the water. "Rachel Smith, isn't it?" She turned her head toward Alex and smiled.

"Thanks for the compliment. And, yes, I'm Rachel. I, also, know who you are after hearing you speak at the Country Team meeting. Good job, by-the-way. It sounded like you've had to deal with certain Embassy luminaries before."

"Yeah, and thanks," he smiled. "There are always a few characters requiring special handling. I gather you're here until the permanent Press Officer arrives in a few months."

"That's right. I love it so far," she said, casually drying herself off with a towel. Alex wanted to volunteer helping her, but brushed aside that fantasy.

"I know you came from the Press Spokesman's Office, but where else have you served?"

"I started in Hong Kong, then went to Beijing for two years as the Assistant Press Officer," she lay back on the lounge chair and stretched out very shapely and firm, long legs. "My last partial-tour was Rome, also as Press Officer, before the Department's Press Spokesman asked me to join his office in D.C."

"That must have been quite a transition from Asia to Rome," Alex said.

"Well, it really wasn't my choice, but I'm delighted it happened. Going to Asia in the beginning of my career made sense. You see, I studied Journalism and Chinese at UCLA. Then I worked at The Los Angeles Times, where I covered Asian economic issues before joining the Foreign Service. But Central Personnel wanted me to broaden my experience by serving in a second geographic area, so they sent me to Rome. After taking five months of Italian classes, I arrived on the Via Veneto," Rachel said, with a big grin on her face. "A year later, I caught the eye of the Department's Press Spokesman during a visit by the Secretary of State. We had a lot of controversial issues with the Italians, and the Press Spokesman thought I managed them well with the local press. I hope that doesn't sound conceited. Anyway, as they say, he made me an offer I couldn't refuse. What about you? Where have you been posted?"

"Well, my first tour abroad was in Buenos Aires, my second in Tunis. Spending four years as a teenager in Cairo, I speak some Arabic, which made living in Tunis pretty stimulating and I was able to make a lot of contacts. I've also lived in Paris, so I speak French. Now, after a year in Islamabad, I'm trying to learn Urdu in my spare time. Arabic helps, but it's still difficult because Urdu draws on Hindi and Farsi, which I'm clueless about."

Rachel's eyes bore intensely into Alex's eyes. "That's damn impressive. Not too many people in the Foreign Service speak both Arabic and French."

'Thanks." Alex noticed her eyes shift to the rest of his body. He hoped she liked what she saw. He certainly was very pleased with his view and thought she had an amazing body.

"I have to tell you, you were pretty clever at the Country Team meeting," she said.

"Thanks again. And you seem to have press arrangements well in hand for the senators' visit," She smiled and winked one eye. He was enthralled, but hoped he didn't show it too soon. They continued talking for some time.

After a while they laid back, quietly absorbing the sun until it dropped too low on the horizon to get direct rays. "So, how did you become such a good swimmer," Alex asked after a long interval, regretting he didn't think of something more high-brow to ask.

"I was always a good athlete when I was young, and due to my size, a real tomboy. At UCLA, I was on a tennis scholarship but injured my shoulder. The physical therapist suggested swimming daily to help get back my range of motion. I love exercising and can sort of zone out problems while I'm in the water."

"Other than tennis and swimming, do you do any other types of exercise?" Alex asked calmly, while beginning to visualize incredibly sexual Kama Sutra positions with her.

"Just the normal gym stuff with weights and aerobics," she answered, unaware of what he was thinking. "In Hong Kong, I discovered a lot of Asians study martial arts. It was really convenient to train there, so I began training in jujitsu, although that's not considered a Chinese martial art. I was lucky to find a Brazilian guy who taught it. In Beijing I studied a local variation of jujitsu."

Yikes! I must be dreaming, Alex thought. Rachel is an intellectual Amazon with fitness and fighting skills. He couldn't make this stuff up if he tried.

Discarding his intention to go home and eat the meal his cook had probably prepared, he asked Rachel if she would join him at the Club for dinner. They agreed to meet after showers and a change of clothes. He used the pool facility changing room. Rachel walked back to her apartment, a temporary place in the Embassy compound. She showered and changed into tan shorts, sandals, and a light blue short-sleeve polo shirt; then, left to meet him at the Club. Alex was already seated in the dining room when Rachel entered. The club was two stories with a bar downstairs and restaurant on the upper floor. On the walls hung Pakistani tribal carpets in a variety of colors and patterns. Rachel walked over to Alex's table with a big smile on her face, Alex stood and returned the smile. He casually glanced at her perfectly shaped calves. *Wow*, he thought.

Conversation at dinner went smoothly since they both enjoyed exploring different countries and cultures, learning languages, and competitive sports. Alex liked Rachel's sense of humor. Her grasp of world politics and economics was impressive. Overall, she was a seriously smart press officer. Yet, Alex couldn't get over how truly beautiful she was. Not merely 'good looking,' she could be a model, albeit one with toned muscles; and her self-confidence was sexy, although he imagined many men would be intimidated by her. Clearly, whoever dated Rachel would need to be confident in his own right, or Rachel would completely dominate the relationship for as long as she decided to maintain it.

As the evening ended, they walked out of the air-conditioned Club into the hot and humid night air. "I know you don't need a ride home, so I guess I'll just say goodnight here," Alex said.

"Listen," Rachel said, "I was wondering, if you're not busy Saturday afternoon, would you come with me to a local rug shop? I want to bring home a souvenir or two. And to be honest, I will need a ride."

"Absolutely, I'd love too. In fact, I can show you one or two shops I've used in the past. Let's make it three o'clock, if that works for you."

"That's perfect."

They touched hands politely, said 'good night' again, walking off in different directions. After only a few steps, Alex turned his head to look back at Rachel.

Damn, he thought, she is magnificent. Just then she turned her head to look at him.

"Are you gawking at my legs again?" she laughed, looking beautiful in the moonlight.

"Of course, I am," Alex confidently replied smiling broadly. "Are you looking at my ass?" His comment must have caught her by surprise because at first, she was speechless. Alex worried he had just committed a massive faux-pas.

Then she burst out laughing and waved goodbye as she continued to walk back to her apartment. Alex couldn't help but wonder, *Could this be the beginning of a meaningful relationship?*

CHAPTER 15

FRIDAY EVENING

The Secret Meeting

The two-story house (1) in Rawalpindi was nondescript and blended into the neighborhood.(2) The exterior was constructed of grey concrete-block and surrounded by a twelve-foot high wall, topped with broken glass set in concrete with rusty barbed wire above the glass.

Colonel Malik arrived Friday evening dressed in a very rumpled, sweat-stained, brown *shalwar kameez,* along with brown sandals. Piled on top of his head was a dirty off-white turban, appearing more like a pile of rags than a turban, but typical of the lower economic class in Pakistan. Dressed in local attire, he didn't want to draw attention to his movements.

Stopping his bicycle at the house's rusty gate, he waited as the night watchman, or *chowkidar,* opened it from inside having seen Malik through a small slit in the metal. The chowkidar was wearing similar attire to Malik's.

"Welcome, Sahib," he said in Urdu.

"Thank you, Mahmoud." Not an ordinary chowkidar, Mahmoud was the brother of one of Malik's corporals in ISI. Malik knew Mahmoud could be trusted to keep his mouth shut about comings and goings at the house.

"Have the others arrived yet?" Malik asked.

"Yes, Sahib. They are waiting inside."

Just as Colonel Malik used the other house in Islamabad for meetings with groups of student leaders, labor organizers, and the mullah, this second safe house was dedicated to meetings with only his Frontier tribesmen.

Tonight, there were four others in attendance, all men in their early thirties. They were hard, tough, bearded men from tribal areas in either the Northwest Frontier or Baluchistan, provinces bordering Afghanistan.

All wore nondescript dirty shalwar kameez, similar to Malik's, and two wore flat, brown woolen caps, rolled up from the bottom, common among tribal men on the frontier (3). The other two wore what appeared to be rags piled on their heads.

Malik had a long history with these four men whom he had personally trained and directed in the Afghan war against the Soviets. Now, they were helping him train the Taliban. Malik knew he couldn't use active duty members of ISI for the attack they were planning. That was a precaution in case one should be captured and subsequently identified. These tribesmen were fanatically loyal to him and well-trained to accomplish the vicious upcoming mission.

"I met earlier this week with students, the religious, and labor leaders," Malik said as a way to start the meeting while he sat in one of the lumpy chairs. "Their participation as peaceful demonstrators outside the Embassy will be essential to our success. But all of you here represent the true heart of my plan."

"You are my leaders," Malik declared. "As such, you already know you will command another sixteen fighters, broken down into four groups of four men each, plus yourselves. So, our total force will be twenty men."

"Follow me over here," he said, rising. They all rose and

surrounded the table while Malik pointed out key features and objectives on a diagram. There were also photographs of the American Embassy and the Ambassador's residence taken with a long range camera lens.

"I want to emphasize that timing is vitally important. All four groups will have to act in support of one another to penetrate our targets with lightning speed," he explained. "Escape after the attack will be difficult, but I know each man is prepared to assume that risk." All four men nodded. Indeed, they were prepared and fully dedicated, because they owed much to Colonel Malik, even if their capture meant possible death.

"I am going to give each of you a copy of the target diagram and a set of photographs to bring back to your teams. You must destroy the diagram and photographs before your teams leave their safe-houses for the assault. Leave nothing behind," Malik declared. Each man agreed.

Arshad, the most senior of the tribesmen, now spoke for the three other leaders.

"Our additional sixteen men are already in the Rawalpindi/Islamabad area, spread out in the modest accommodations you have arranged. As you instructed, we have not had communication between the groups." Arshad said. He stood some five-feet ten inches tall, lean but muscular, with angry piercing dark eyes, and a slightly bent, hawk-like nose. His hair had been recently dyed with henna, giving it a red-orange tint favored by some Pakistani tribesmen.

Arshad had fought the Soviets outside of Kandahar for many years. When he wasn't fighting Soviets, he fought against other tribal groups further north in the Panshir Valley. For him, fighting and killing was merely a part of life, nothing more.

While the entire team of twenty men knew each other from

fighting in Afghanistan, they would not gather as a large group for this mission until just hours before the attack. They had brought their own weapons from the frontier and would leave them behind to facilitate escape, *if escape would be possible.*

The group began discussing Malik's plan in detail. Although photos and diagrams carried no names, the target was obvious to all: the American Embassy. Even though protected by armed Pakistani police, local guards, and U.S. Marines, the men were not worried. They had previously penetrated Soviet Army bases in Afghanistan and killed many. There was no reason to hesitate; they were ready to do the same here. Finally, after hours of review, the meeting broke up.

"Good evening, my brothers; may Allah keep you safe," he said, seeing them out the door.

As was his practice, Malik waited a short time before returning to his own house in Rawalpindi via a circuitous route. He believed his tactical plan would succeed. But he also knew no one could predict the Americans' precise reaction. Anger, of course; they would be outraged. But, he calculated, their anger would be directed against mythical rogue terrorist elements from the frontier, rather than against ISI. Indeed, Malik was staking both his career and life on swaying the blame to this element.

In the aftermath of the attack, he would have to sell his idea to the U.S. government that the terrorists were motivated by anger at America for deserting Pakistan and supporting Pakistan's hated enemy, India. This was close enough to the truth. The political success of Malik's mission was ultimately to convince the Americans that their best interests lay in giving increased support to Pakistan through both economic and military assistance. After his planned attack, Pakistan could make the case that additional assistance would help fight growing terrorism from the frontier as evidenced by the attack on the Embassy, as well as raise the overall level of education and employment in the country. If additional aid was lavished on Pakistan, Malik was not personally interested in the graft that would be skimmed off by his colleagues in the Army.

"As long as my plan succeeds, I don't care who benefits from it," he said aloud to no one.

(1) This house's value to Malik was in its obscurity. Its outside appearance had seen better days. Exterior walls were worn and stained from years of wear. Metal window frames were corroded, some window panes cracked. The concrete driveway was broken in many places and was overrun by weeds. The road outside of the house had litter everywhere. Minimally furnished, because no one actually lived there, the bedrooms had only one folding canvas Army cot apiece. The living room, with its dirty white walls of peeling paint, had two well-used lumpy sofas, covered in worn out orange striped cotton upholstery and a few old stuffed chairs with non-matching floral patterns. Everything smelled of mold and stale cigarette smoke. The dining room had a long mahogany table; its surface was well scratched and dented, was not used for eating anymore. Rather, it served as a place to spread out maps and other planning tools. The house was used by Colonel Malik for secret meetings only.

(2) Rawalpindi, with its two million inhabitants, adjoins Islamabad. But, unlike Islamabad which has broad, clean boulevards and organized street grids, Rawalpindi reflects old South Asia. Established as a Buddhist settlement roughly 1,000 years ago, it continued to grow without a central plan. Now, numerous telephone and electricity wires crisscross helter-skelter above streets and alleyways; and traffic is hopelessly congested with horns blowing constantly. Laundry hangs out windows daily as few homeowners can afford dryers, except for Pakistan's elite ruling class who live in comparative splendor elsewhere. Once one of Britain's largest Army bases in the sub-continent had been located in Rawalpindi. Now, the Pakistan Army's Headquarters are housed there with its supporting parade grounds and many military sub-units, such as the all-powerful Inter-Service Intelligence Directorate (ISI).

(3) To westerners these jokingly resembled large cloth condoms.

NEW CHAPTER 16

SATURDAY MORNING

An Arresting Personality

On Saturday morning, the sun blazed hot in a cloudless sky, same as every day in Islamabad. Yet, an ever-present haze hung over the city due to early morning cooking fires everywhere. The temperature was rising, although humidity was not high this time of day.

Alex strolled around his garden, smelling fragrant roses growing on several bushes, as everywhere else throughout the city. His own part-time mali was an average gardener, a hard worker, and Alex liked him because he got along with Samuel. Walking to the gate at the end of the driveway, he briefly chatted with the SMG guard in very broken Urdu.

"Good morning, Sahib," the guard said.

"Good morning to you. Is your family well?"

"Yes, thank you, Sahib. All is good in my home."

"Is the street quiet this morning?" Alex asked.

"It is too much quiet, Sahib."

All guards wore the same uniform: Dark green pants, a khaki military style shirt with an SMG patch on the shoulder, along with a dark green baseball cap with "SMG" in khaki thread.

Although the RSO would have preferred each guard wear dark shoes or boots, the guards all wanted to wear sandals. This latter attire prevailed because it was traditional in Pakistan. The guards also carried two-way radios and night-sticks as standard issue. Previous RSOs had tried getting permission from the Government of Pakistan for guards to carry firearms, but the government simply wouldn't allow a large private force to have weapons. However, they did agree the Mobile Reaction Teams (MRT) could carry guns.

Every home in the official American community had an unarmed SMG guard whose main function was to deter thieves from robbing the house and attacking its residents. At least that's what Diplomatic Security was paying for. However, in Pakistan, Jim Riley demanded more. He expected all guards to note suspicious activity on the street, such as possible surveillance, and report it via radio to the SMG office. The office would then send either a guard supervisor or the MRT to observe the situation. This system often resulted in numerous reports of possible surveillance.

In cases when the MRT spotted potential vehicular surveillance, the license plate number was reported to the Security Office. Jim or Alex then passed this information to local police. Half the time, the license plate was fake; not unusual in Pakistan since locals didn't want to register their cars and pay a vehicle tax, but it did leave the matter unresolved. Sometimes it simply confirmed the driver was deemed okay. Then, on rare occasions, the police never returned any information. So, the RSO assumed either the car belonged to ISI or Police Special Branch, who were doing surveillance on members of the diplomatic community. What really counted was determining whether a pattern of surveillance was occurring.

Saturdays and Sundays were considered normal days-off at the Embassy. Even so, most people had too much work to finish by close-of-business Friday. Nearly everyone worked at least half of Saturday and even a few hours on Sunday. Since Islamabad had a dearth of cultural activities, it wasn't as if working on weekends was sacrificing anything of interest. Non-work life revolved around frequent home entertainment, either within the Western community or with Pakistani friends.

The American and British Embassies offered a Darts League weekly, a pleasant excuse to drink lots of beer. The Canadians, Australians, and French also had small Embassy clubs and offered memberships to the Americans in exchange for access to the larger American Club. During cooler seasons, there were softball games at the American Embassy field, since the compound's 35-acres offered ample room for sporting activities.

After a hearty breakfast with strong coffee, Alex changed into gym clothes, then packed jeans, underpants, socks, and a polo shirt into a backpack. Heading out in his Jeep, he took an indirect route passing several strip mall markets toward Gunny Sgt. Rodriguez's house on his way to the Embassy. Rodriguez had asked Alex the previous day to hitch a ride into the office since the Gunny's wife needed their car to run errands with their two kids. Gunny was already waiting at his gate when Alex pulled up.

"Good morning, Gunny."

"Good morning to you, Boss. Thanks for the ride."

"Let's see if the police presence is heavier today since the bomb was discovered at Jinnah Supermarket," Alex said.

The city was laid out on a grid system. Other than the Diplomatic Enclave and the Blue Area, every other part of the city was designated by an alphabetic and numeric designation or the name of a neighborhood market to make it easy to find a house or business.

Both Alex and Gunny lived in Sector F 6, a 10 minute drive to the Embassy. But to pass Jinnah Supermarket, they now drove in the opposite direction before going to the Embassy. He proceeded west down Margala Road toward the Faisal Masjid, or Grand Mosque

"Every time I see the Mosque, with its four minarets and white sloping roof, I'm impressed," Gunny said, referring to the Faisal Masjid. The main road from the airport led directly to the Mosque, which had no parking lot, and nothing surrounding it, other than grassy fields.

"It was finished in 1986 and can hold about seventy thousand people within its walls," Alex explained. "Probably another two-hundred thousand can pray just outside. It's certainly the largest mosque in South Asia. I believe it's been the largest in the world for several years, although two existing mosques are being expanded in Mecca and Medina. I think Morocco is planning a huge new mosque in Casablanca as well. I heard all those will be bigger than this one."

"Uh, huh," Gunny said, nodding his head. He wasn't all that interested but wanted to be polite.

Turning south on Eighth Avenue, Alex drove a few blocks, then swung to the east so he would pass by Jinnah Supermarket, located in F-7. They were near the "Blue Area" of the city.

"Why do they call it the 'Blue Area', Boss?"

"If you look at a map of Islamabad, Gunny, you'll see this area is colored blue. That's it. Just the color on the map."

"Well what 'da ya know...who wouldda' guessed that."

"Do you see any cop build-up, Gunny?"

Police presence appeared normal at the market. Even if plainclothes Special Branch officers were around, they wouldn't be conspicuous.

"I only see two cops in the entire area, Boss. But, it's only eight in the morning, so maybe it's early for shoppers to be out," Gunny said. "Or, maybe the police feel they don't have to deploy until later today."

Alex acknowledged his point. Driving passed the large Supermarket in the F6 sector, and Melody Market in G6, they noted, again, minimal or no police presence at all.

Set back some 100 feet from the road was the Holiday Inn, the largest and best hotel in Islamabad. Half the rooms faced the road, each with a large window overlooking the Margala Hills a half mile away, rising on the horizon. A small attractive garden was planted between the driveway and its front door. Based on municipal plans encouraging other major hotel chains to come into the capitol, Alex understood Marriott was considering the purchase of the Holiday Inn.

Continuing the drive southeast toward the Diplomatic Enclave, Alex turned into the Embassy's front entrance gate. After going through the routine guard screening procedure, he drove around and parked by the swimming pool. Gunny hopped out and went directly to his office, saying he would go for a run later.

Leaving his backpack in the Jeep, Alex started his three-mile run inside the compound's perimeter wall. Early morning was a good time to work out since later in the day was too hot to run outdoors. Alex's long strides carried him at a decent clip. He noticed a few Marines, two CIA Station officers, and an Air Force Major from the Defense Attaché Office also on the path.

Half way through his time, he was about to overtake two female runners. Fairly certain the one on the left was Susan Witt, he didn't recognize her running partner at first. Then, judging from her height and spectacular legs, he knew it could only be Rachel Smith.

After all, what other girl at the Embassy is nearly six feet tall with magnificent diamond-shaped calves and beautiful muscular hamstrings? His pace slowed just enough to match their strides when he reached them.

"Good morning, Ladies," Alex said. Both gave him big smiles and returned his greeting as all three continued to run.

Alex tried small talk, but after a few minutes Rachel addressed him with a big grin on her face, "We were enjoying some 'girl talk' when you showed up; care to join us on the topic?"

Alex thought he detected a slight wince on Susan's face, even though she, too, was attempting to smile.

"Aah, a subtle hint from our new Press Officer," responded Alex. "Perhaps another time. Hoda hafez, ladies." Alex replied, using the Urdu phrase for goodbye, as he picked up his pace and accelerated away from them.

Last night at dinner, he had judged Rachel as extremely self-confident. Then, he'd marked it "an appealing quality"; now, he thought, "an arresting personality". He was definitely interested.

CHAPTER 17

SATURDAY EARLY MORNING

The Emergency Meeting

Hot and sweaty after his run, Alex headed to the locker room showers by the pool, first retrieving his gear from the back of the Jeep. Changing into casual clothes, he walked up a slight incline two-hundred yards to his office building and entered the cool lobby. The first one in, he spent the next hour reviewing last night's classified telegrams from Washington and other American embassies. He also read outgoing Embassy reports on Islamabad sent by the Ambassador, the Political, Economic, and Administrative Sections. His key to staying on top of important data was screening out routine material and not getting overwhelmed with too much information of little value.

Shortly after 10 a.m., Jim Riley entered Alex's office.

"The DCM called for an Emergency Action Committee meeting in half an hour," Riley said. "I'd like you and Susan to accompany me. The topic is the recent explosive device at Jinnah Market that Susan analyzed. Plus any words of wisdom we should tell the American community at the Town Hall meeting on Monday. Here, I've prepared some talking points," he said while handing Alex a sheet of paper. "I'd like you to take notes at this morning's meeting and prepare the telegram to Washington."

"Okay. I'll call Susan and make sure she's ready," Alex said.

The EAC meeting lasted 30 minutes and was dominated by Jim. Susan added technical details about the bomb and probable impact had it exploded. All agency heads and other invitees sat around the table in silence. Rachel listened quietly.

Finding a bomb in Islamabad wasn't unique, even finding one in a major shopping area. Their concern was to determine whether this was the beginning of a larger bomb campaign by a dissident group or a one-time event unlikely to be repeated. Whatever they decided would determine how the Embassy staff would advise the community.

Riley put the incident in perspective for the EAC:

"It's always easy for the Embassy to tell its employees they shouldn't visit markets, restaurants, and other public locations, and advise the private American sector to do the same. But the penalty paid for imposing one hundred percent security measures prematurely is great. Morale will be negatively affected if we ban personal travel off the compound. As we know, all posts in Pakistan are already in the 'High Threat' category for both terrorism and civil unrest. If the Embassy imposes even stricter security measures, then Washington will need to consider if the threat level should be raised to 'Critical'."

"That would be a very big deal," the DCM added, "Because officially raising the threat to 'Critical' means all dependents must leave the country for an indefinite period. Also, travel into and within Pakistan will be more restricted for all official Americans. What we must carefully consider is how difficult taking these steps now will make it for the State Department's South Asia Bureau to recruit good personnel for future assignments to Pakistan."

"Not only for the State Department," Colonel Walker said. "Good military officers and support staff don't want to be separated from their spouses and children if they have a choice of non-combat assignments. So, they simply won't ask to be assigned here."

Alex knew Colonel Walker was right. While State Department culture allowed families to accompany the parent/employee into what most Americans would consider "dangerous locations", their decision on raising the threat level would affect many future decisions. Currently, the majority of Middle East and African Embassies were populated with entire families, even taking into account the crime level and potential terrorism risks. Alex thought this spoke volumes about the commitment, patriotism, courage, and spirit of adventure of these Foreign Service families.

"Eventually, the Department of State will have to assign less-than desirable personnel against their wishes," JC Colon stated in his usual disparaging tone. "So, while security is something to consider, it's equally important to ensure security measures are proportionate to the real threat level." Alex listened carefully to JC's comment and actually agreed with his conclusion. After all, this was Riley's concept as well. However, he wondered if any serious threat could persuade JC to increase security since he was so reluctant to make this decision.

"Bill, do you have any info on this attempted bombing?" the DCM asked Bill Stanton.

"My office can only speculate on who planted the bomb at Jinnah Supermarket," Bill said, "I simply can't offer any concrete assessment on what's likely to happen in the near future." In the end, since no one had further comments, the EAC agreed to use Riley's talking points for the Town Hall meeting on Monday, and advise Washington that resident Americans would be urged to be vigilant, therefore, minimize, not curtail, their visits to public places.

Ellen Hunt closed the meeting and asked Riley to prepare a telegram reporting the Emergency Action Committee's decision and recommendations. Knowing Riley had already tasked him with this action, Alex hoped his report would not be the first of many concerning bombing attempts in Islamabad.

He looked over at Rachel and smiled. *She's another good reason I'm glad to be here.* Seeing her return a smile, he wondered what she was thinking.

CHAPTER 18

SATURDAY MID-DAY

The Shopping Trip

Alex thought about grabbing a quick sandwich for lunch at the Club before it closed, and after he finished the telegram on the EAC meeting. It was the only place to grab food in the Diplomatic Enclave since there were no other restaurants. People either brought their own, went to the Club, or ate nothing. Susan Witt, who lived within the compound, went to her apartment for a snack. Riley decided to stay in the office and read though some files.

Walking back to the Embassy after a quick burger, Alex glanced at the two tennis courts. He wondered what Susan and Rachel had been talking about during their run and hoped It was about him. It would be nice to know if Rachel was interested. He certainly wanted to know more about her. A lot more.

Both courts were occupied by employees from the Agency for International Development, known as USAID. Admittedly, today was Saturday, but for long periods during the work-week, USAID officers frequented the courts. Doubtlessly they work long hours into the night to compensate for such long mid-day breaks, he thought sarcastically. Back inside the Embassy, he addressed some of the endless Washington reporting requirements. For starters, it was time to conduct the annual weapons inventory for the Diplomatic Security Service. All serial numbers had to be matched with each weapon. He had already checked the DSS weapons issued to Marine Guards and their police bodyguards. These included one Remington model 870 pump shotgun per Marine, as well as their Beretta 9mm pistols. So now, he only had to double check the weapons issued to the RSOs.

In addition to a Sig Sauer 9mm pistol for each officer, the weapons locker contained several Uzi 9mm sub-machine guns with collapsible stocks and a handful of Ruger 5.56 mm rifles. While these shotguns, sub-machine guns, and rifles were all quality weapons, most RSOs wanted the shoulder weapons changed over to the M-4 carbine, which was essentially a compact version of the military's M-16 5.56 mm rifle. Since terrorists often attacked with AK-47s, the Marines and RSOs were presently outgunned by not having M-4 carbines. In any event, whenever the Islamabad RSOs took Marines to the shooting range, Alex, Jim, and Susan allowed them to fire the Ruger rifles and Uzi sub-machine guns for familiarization.

Finished taking inventory, Alex glanced at his watch and happily noted it was time to go carpet shopping with Rachel. She should be waiting for him in the Embassy lobby, if his Seiko diving watch was accurate. He smiled in anticipation of seeing her again.

"Hey, there. Ready to help me pick out a beautiful rug or two?" Rachel asked, as Alex entered the lobby. She looked at his trim, muscular physique as he walked toward her, appreciating his confident stride, then smiled as his gaze met her eyes.

"You bet. I've got two shops in mind."

"Great, I'm all for it," she said, beaming at the prospect of spending time with him.

Her loose fitting tan cotton slacks and long sleeve light-weight blouse, looked great on her trim figure. She had paired the outfit with comfortable taupe-colored sandals. Looking chic in a demure way, she had pulled her wavy brown hair back into a ponytail. Perfectly dressed for Pakistan, Alex was beyond impressed with her, well-aware that women who showed too much skin or too revealing a figure were frowned upon by locals.

Climbing into Alex's Jeep, they headed into town. He took pleasure in pointing out the more interesting sights since she was relatively new on her assignment. Their first stop was Baluch Carpets, located in a small strip mall in the Blue Area. Alex noticed two policemen roving around the parking lot and figured the cops were taking the latest bombing seriously. Waiting patiently, he watched her movements as Rachel sorted through what seemed like a million rugs. After an hour, she still hadn't selected one.

The next store, Lahore Carpet House, was located nearby. He greeted the owner and shook hands. As at the previous store, the owner insisted they have hot, aromatic mint tea, indicating where to sit while he served the steaming brew. He and Alex then continued to exchange pleasantries in Urdu, while Rachel, still seated, looked at rugs along the wall. It would have been offensive to decline the tea and not have a conversation. Alex felt a sense of relief when the owner didn't bring out two-day old mini-sandwiches with unrefrigerated mayonnaise. Alex said something in Urdu. The owner shook his head sideways, which in Pakistan's culture, meant yes. He smiled at Alex; Rachel stared in amazement.

"I didn't know you spoke such good Urdu. What did you just say?"

"I told him you are extremely hot looking, and he agreed."

"No, I don't believe you said that."

"Actually, I just said it was nice to see him again," Alex confessed, "But the other stuff is also true." They exchanged looks, appreciating each other.

Apparently, this put Rachel in a good buying mood. She picked out three carpets to examine more closely and decided on two of them. Each was about six by eight feet, which the owner folded into large, square bundles. Rachel paid in local cash and they carried both rugs out to the Jeep, placing them in the back end.

"Shukriya, thank you," both Alex and Rachel said. "Hoda hafez," Alex added.

"These rugs are going to look great in my apartment in Washington," she said. "Thanks, so much, for taking me to the shops. I really enjoyed it. Where to now?"

"There's a lookout point in the Margala Hills with great views of the city. It's about 15 minutes away. Would you like to go there?"

"Sounds perfect. I've heard about it. Let's go."

Alex drove the winding road up to the top of the hill to a particular point, then parked. They got out to admire the view.

"Wow," Rachel said. "This is beautiful. You can see the entire city. How many people live In Islamabad?"

"About one million in Islamabad, but combine it with Rawalpindi and that number jumps to over four million," Alex replied.

He gave her binoculars from the glove compartment. She

identified the roof of the Embassy, the entire Parliament, and the nearby Faisal Masjid. Rawal Lake was visible in the distance, and the outskirts of Rawalpindi; however, since it was a little hazy at this hour, she couldn't identify anything else farther away. After taking in the view for several minutes she took Alex's hand, liking the touch of his skin. She slightly squeezed it with a subtle sexiness.

"Thanks for a great day."

For a brief moment, Alex was tempted to take her in his arms, but there were too many Pakistanis around enjoying the view. So, he simply kept gazing into her eyes."Believe me, it's really been my pleasure. You have no idea how much I've enjoyed being with you, Rachel." As they continued looking at each other, Alex felt a strong connection. Rachel, still holding his hand, seemed to have no intention of letting go. Had they been in D.C., He would have planted a long, wet kiss on her lips. But not here, not in public.

People jostling by, brought them back to the present moment. Eventually they returned to the Jeep and drove back to the Embassy compound.

"Are you doing anything tomorrow?" Alex asked as he parked. What he really wanted was to touch her all over, right then, but thought she might think it a little too early in their relationship. Was it actually a relationship? he wondered. Maybe the start of a one.

"Why don't you give me a call tomorrow sometime around late morning?" Rachel replied. "I'm having dinner at the DCM's house tomorrow evening. She's hosting the Embassy junior officers as part of her mentoring responsibilities, and asked a couple of us who've been in the service a few years to casually talk with them about how the system works. But I'm free from about noon until four o'clock."

"Okay, I'll call tomorrow," Alex said. He held both her shoulders and gave a polite kiss on her left cheek. Rachel smiled and placed her hands on both sides of his face, giving him a full kiss on the mouth.

Why didn't I think of that? he joked to himself.

"See you tomorrow," she said. After a few steps she stopped, turned and smiled.

"Wait, I'm forgetting my carpets!"

He laughed as they each grabbed one and somewhat awkwardly made it up the steps to her apartment. There in the cool shadow of her hallway, they shared a long, passionate kiss.

"Tomorrow's better for me," she whispered in a sultry voice. Reluctantly, Alex said goodbye again. Then, walked to his Jeep with her aroma clearly beginning to arouse him.

CHAPTER **19**

SATURDAY NIGHT

The Dinner Party

Winston Hargrove loved his dinner parties. He reveled in "home entertaining" in a grand style which he felt he well-deserved. Instructing his servant, Ahmed, to offer all guests another round of drinks, Ahmed complied by gathering everyone's empty glasses, and returning to the kitchen to prepare Round Two.

Hargrove only regretted that his wife, Giselle and their two children, were not with him in Islamabad. Giselle was a wonderful hostess, and he missed her company. Before leaving their last assignment in Europe, he and Giselle had decided that Pakistan was no place to educate their children. So, after rigorous research, they found an excellent boarding school in Paris. Giselle's parents, who lived in Paris'16th Arrondissement, had agreed to watch over the children in their absence.

Giselle then accompanied Winston to post, but after only two months, decided she simply couldn't live in such a culture. To her, it was totally uncivilized. She knew, of course, that Pakistan had a thin upper class of Western-educated elites, but still, felt little in common with them. Moreover, she felt diplomats she'd met in other European embassies in Islamabad were hardly Foreign Office star performers. Those stars were assigned elsewhere in

Europe, America, or certain East Asian embassies.

She had looked around Islamabad and couldn't imagine what she'd do to occupy her time for the next two years. So, when she informed Winston she would be returning to Paris, she tried to soften the blow, in her way of thinking, by telling him he could visit whenever he wanted. As another small concession, she promised to bring the children to Islamabad for short visits -- possibly -- when school wasn't in session. However, there were no guarantees.

So, he was on his own to live, to entertain, to survive if he could. She wouldn't be part of it. This whole situation depressed Winston. It was one reason he was looking to get out of his assignment early. Dinner parties were meant to lighten his mood.

"Winston, I was just telling Theresa that you had season tickets to the opera in Vienna when you were assigned there," Stephan Strauss, the Austrian Ambassador, stated. In deference to other guests, Strauss spoke in English, although he knew Hargrove was fluent in German. "We also had season tickets then, in the third row. I wonder if you were nearby?"

"Yes, we did have season tickets. But we had box seats, so I doubt we would have met," Hargrove replied. He liked Stephan and his wife, Theresa, but was reasonably certain their paths hadn't crossed since Stephan had focused on Asian matters prior to his assignment to Pakistan. Hargrove, on the other hand, was deeply involved with European Union issues.

Their conversation was interrupted by Ahmed returning with the second round of drinks. He waited while his servant completely served everyone,

Hargrove noticed Marisol Lopez, his number two in the political section, having a lively discussion across the room with the Deputy Chief of Mission from the Spanish Embassy. They were laughing, although he couldn't make out the topic since they were speaking Spanish. Pleased with Marisol's work, he was glad she worked for him. He respected her knowledge of Pakistan, but couldn't fathom why she wanted to spend her career in South Asia.

In another part of the living room, JC Colon and his wife, Delores, were talking to Olaf Johansson, the Representative from the U.N. High Commission for Refugees. Ever since the Soviets invaded Afghanistan, millions of refugees fled into Pakistan's border provinces. The camps were filled with refugees awaiting their chance to return to their homelands. If one wanted to know what was happening in the Northwest Frontier Province, or in Baluchistan, then Johansson was the man with whom to speak.

Judging by the expression on Johansson's face, Hargrove realized with some surprise that Johansson wasn't all that interested in JC's conversation.

Oh well, Hargrove thought, *JC wasn't invited to this dinner party because of his intellect, nor his extraordinary gift of gab.*

Rather, Hargrove had invited JC to feel he was accepted as an equal in the World of Embassy Foreign Service Officers. But what he really needed from JC was personal: An account flexibility to provide administrative support for his social lifestyle. This included Hargrove's use of Embassy-provided china and crystal place settings for large scale entertaining and use of the Embassy's large outdoor tents, called shamyanas, for special occasions, at no charge, of course. Finally, Hargrove wanted a liberal interpretation of what was considered an 'official' expense when he filed his representational expense vouchers for reimbursement.

Tonight's remaining guests included the French Ambassador and his wife, Jacques and Monique Bertrand, and the Pakistani Chief of Protocol at the Foreign Ministry, Aftar Jalini and his wife Abida. After chatting for another thirty minutes with his guests, Hargrove announced that dinner was served.

His dining room table was immaculately set for twelve. Hargrove's chef had prepared standard European cuisine; steak with a mild pepper sauce, French-cut green beans, an eggplant dish, and a small salad without lettuce. Dessert would be lemon tarts. The only disappointment, as far as Hargrove was concerned, was the wine. The Embassy did not carry high quality European wines, so he had to suffer whatever California wines were in stock in the Embassy commissary. It barely made the semblance of an acceptable dinner party.

After the main course and dessert, they moved to the living room for a choice of digestifs. Ambassador Jacques Bertrand asked what Hargrove thought about the recent bombing attempt in Jinnah Market.

"Most unfortunate," Hargrove declared. "Of course, we're all concerned about safety. I imagine you've seen our Embassy's notice about precautions." It was a statement more than a question.

"Yes, I saw it today," Ambassador Bertrand replied. "It struck me as stating the obvious; therefore, perhaps, not really necessary."

"Interesting, I thought the same as well," Hargrove informed the group.

Olaf Johansson jumped into the conversation. "We see lots of bombing attempts on the frontier. In fact, not only attempts, but actual bombings. I have to say such things don't deter our staff from visiting local markets. So, it seemed a trifle curious the American Embassy would issue a warning to avoid these markets."

"To be accurate," Jalini said, "I believe the warning cautioned people to minimize their visits, not avoid the markets entirely."

Jalini, the Pakistani Foreign Office protocol man, had a reputation of being very detailed-oriented. He had earlier told Hargrove he appreciated such nuances in the security notice and completely understood the obligation of the Embassy to warn its employees and family members of potential danger. Having served in Pakistani embassies in Riyadh, Cairo, and London, Jalini often had occasion to interact with U.S. Embassy personnel and once exclaimed to Hargrove that, in his opinion, American security officials were first-rate.

"If you have ever seen the results of a bombing in a marketplace, you might also wish to err on the side of caution," Jalini concluded.

"Okay, fair enough, Jalini," Hargrove declared. In his heart, he didn't buy into Jalini's argument, but he wasn't going to debate the point.

Ambassador Stephan Strauss wanted to change the subject.

"We, in Austria, and indeed all countries in the EU, are aware of your country's new approach to India. Can you comment on this in some detail?"

Hargrove knew Jalini would be paying close attention to his answer. Since Marisol had actually drafted the Embassy's talking points to be used with Pakistani officials, he decided it would be best for her to respond.

"I'd be delighted to do so. However, Ms. Lopez follows this issue closer than anyone in the Embassy, I'll ask her to address your request. Marisol, would you be so kind as to describe our new balanced approach?"

"Of course," Marisol responded. For the next ten minutes she did a masterful job of outlining the issues. A series of casual questions followed, all deftly fielded by Marisol. Jalini asked the most pointed questions. It was very clear to Hargrove that

Pakistan's government did not approve of this new policy.

An hour later, the party finally broke-up. Hargrove was delighted with the evening. Apart from a diversion for the U.S.-India policy shift, he thoroughly enjoyed talking about European political and cultural matters with his counterparts.

I'll be dining at the German Political Counselor's home later this week, he thought. Considering tonight, this promises to be a good week. He smiled, while proudly standing at the door, bidding each guest a wonderful, good evening.

On the drive home, JC and Dolores Colon discussed the evening's events.

"Do you really understand everything we heard tonight," she asked him, "Especially the thing between the U.S. and India?"

"Many things were new, I'll admit," JC said, "But, still, I pretty much know what's going on. I get the big picture."

"Well, I found it all seemed complicated."

"I know," JC agreed. "To keep things straight in my head, I've come up with nicknames for all players. Here in Pakistan, for instance, everyone is called either Mohammed or Bhutto, so that's how I refer to most of them. Naturally, I need more time to understand the European issues, since I haven't worked in that part of the world. It just takes time." he told her. After arriving home, JC decided he would take time to write a letter to each of his children. They were in the U.S., about to start a new fall semester in college. Hopefully, he would be out of this wretched assignment in a little over a year, and they could be back in Washington or Latin America where he could see them more often.

Being so far away made him miss them terribly.

CHAPTER **20**

SUNDAY MORNING

The Basketball Game

By 10 a.m. on Sunday morning, Alex arrived at the Embassy basketball court for his weekly pickup game with any available Marines. Only three might show up, since others who worked the midnight shift, would probably be sleeping. Occasionally, a few Embassy employees might make it to the courts and ask to play, but since it was August, many were out-of-country on vacation or possibly deciding the heat wasn't worth it. So, Alex didn't expect too many players today. Sgt. Washington, however, was already at the court shooting jump shots.

"Hey, Washington," he greeted the big guy.

An African-American in his mid-twenties, Alex guessed he stood six feet three inches, weighed maybe 220 pounds, and was definitely solid muscle. From Chicago, he had played basketball and football, then joined the Marines right out of high school, selecting the Infantry. He was Gunnery Rodriquez's Assistant NCOIC of the detachment, otherwise known as the Assistant Non-Commissioned Officer in Charge. Gunny had told Alex that Sgt. Washington was doing a great job in Islamabad, had demonstrated solid leadership with the rest of the detachment, and was certain of promotion to Staff Sergeant at the earliest opportunity.

At courtside was Corporal Jones, sitting on a bench, not looking very well.

"Hey, Corporal, what's wrong? You look a little sick," Alex called out to him.

"It's my stomach, Sir. I've been having problems lately."

"Have you seen the nurse?"

"No, not yet."

"I'll bet he has 'Delhi belly,' " Washington called out, and shook his head.

Jones was relatively new in-country. "Uninitiated" arrivals in Pakistan often ate or drank something local resulting in an abdominal discomfort resulting in the 'Trots.' A short-term cure for the diarrhea was Lomatil, but antibiotics were needed to actually kill the bacterial bugs. Until the drugs kicked in, the infected were miserable with occasional bouts of nausea, vomiting, and diarrhea. Sometimes all at once.

"Listen, I'm afraid I can't play," Jones said, looking miserable."That's fine. I understand. I've been there myself," Alex called out, trying to be comforting. "But, be sure you see the nurse tomorrow. That's an order!" he commanded.

Watching Jones stand, then begin to walk quickly toward the Marine House, Washington turned to Alex and said, "It's his own fault. He keeps drinking sips of local water thinking it will make him immune to the Trots."

Alex let out a good belly laugh and shook his head. He was glad Cpl. Jones' specialty wasn't being a paramedic, giving medical advice to others. As Washington and Alex shot around for a while hoping others would arrive, he noticed Rachel playing tennis against Winston Hargrove. She was wearing a white tennis skirt and a light blue top with UCLA written in yellow script. Winston was wearing all whites and looked like the captain of a college tennis team. Alex let Washington shoot by himself for a few minutes as he watched the tennis match. He had no idea who was winning, but Rachel appeared to be getting the better of Hargrove. Both covered the court well and had good strokes but Rachel's shots really kept Hargrove hustling from one side to the other. Hargrove was known to be a good player, but Rachel seemed better.

Alex returned to shooting hoops with Washington for another ten minutes. It didn't look like anyone else was going to show up. Sgt. Washington said, "Sir, do you mind if I leave you on the court by yourself? I think I'll go to the weight room to work out."

"That's fine. You look like you could use some more muscle anyway. Thanks for showing up," Alex grinned back at him.

"What?" Washington exclaimed in surprise. Then realizing Alex was pulling his leg, he laughed. If there was one thing Washington had in abundance, it was muscle.

About to leave, Washington smiled and said, "I saw you noticing Miss Smith."

"Who, me?" Alex feigned innocence. "Okay, I admit it. Isn't she great-looking?"

"Yes, sir, she is. Are you ready for a funny story about her?" Washington asked.

"Sure, why not?" Alex said, although he couldn't imagine anything funny about Rachel Smith.

"Well, you can see she's got some pretty good biceps," Washington said.

"And good leg muscles, too, I might add," Alex grinned.

"And then some. Well, a few days ago, she asked if she could use the Marines' weight room to stay in shape during her temporary assignment here. Normally, we don't let too many outsiders use the equipment since we need constant access to the weights as part of our official Marine Corps fitness program. But Gunny figured since she lives next door, and is here only temporarily, it would be okay," Washington said with a big ear-to-ear smile. "Besides being a smokin' hot fox."

"As it turns out, Miss Smith can easily bench over 200 pounds for repetitions, and does a hell of a job on the rest of the equipment. But here's the best part of the story: A few days ago the Marines were practicing hand-to-hand combat in the mat room. Sgt. Monroe from the Defense Attaché's office was working out with us. He hadn't seen Miss Smith before. She came in to lift weights but when she sees us in the mat room she walks in to watch. Monroe's not doing so well against the Marines. Miss Smith smiles when Monroe gets taken down once or twice. Monroe sees her smiling and asks her if she thinks it's funny. She says, 'Yes, as a matter of fact, I do.'

"Now, none of us knows anything about Miss Smith's athletic ability, except we've seen how strong she is with the weights. On that day, she was wearing a long sleeve, loose fitting t-shirt so Monroe couldn't see her arm muscles. He could see her leg muscles because she was wearing gym shorts, but I guess he didn't put two and two together. Monroe then says something arrogant and puts down women in general. She teases him about getting his ass whipped by the Marines, so he challenges her to a friendly one-on-one, especially since she thinks his situation is so funny. To everyone's surprise, she doesn't even hesitate and says 'yes'. Bam! She just says 'let's do it.' Well, the Marines are looking at each other as if to say, 'What's going on here?'

"Now, Monroe is about five feet nine inches tall, maybe 170 pounds. Miss Smith's a little taller and I'd guess around 160 pounds. Monroe tries to grab her. She side-steps him, grabs him, and throws him over her hip onto the mat. I gotta tell ya, all the Marines were laughing their asses off and applauding. Miss Smith had a big grin on her face and Sgt. Monroe looked steamed. So, he says, 'How about two out of three falls, girlie?' She says, 'Why not?' still grinning like crazy. This time he manages to grab her shoulders, but she steps into him and trips him backward, so that he lands on his ass. Now get this, in a flash she drops behind him and gets him in a rear choke hold, at the same time locking her legs around his waist. Within ten seconds she's choked him out, and we have to wake him up. All the Marines are going crazy, whooping and hollering. They loved it."

Alex could see Sgt. Washington was really busting a gut telling the story.

"I assume Monroe was all right?" Alex smiled, then chuckled.

"Yeah, he's fine now, but he was a little wobbly for a few minutes," Washington responded. "It was the funniest thing I've ever seen. So, we asked Miss Smith how she learned to do that shit and she tells us she's a Black Belt in Jiu Jitsu, plus she knows some other martial arts warrior-shit she picked up in China." The two men enjoyed the moment, each lost in the thought of it all.

"Well, I gotta go now. Just thought you'd like to know who you're admiring. Good talking with you, Sir."

"Okay, and thanks for the story. Sounds like I better not piss her off," Alex said with a smile.

As Washington walked away, Alex heard a yelp from across the tennis courts. Hargrove was on the ground holding his ankle. Alex sprinted over to see if he was all right just as Rachel came around the net from across the court. Hargrove was cursing but, oddly enough to Alex, didn't look like he was really in much pain.

"I better go ice this ankle," Hargrove called to Rachel. "I'll need it to show you my better game which apparently isn't today."

They both watched as Hargrove made his best impression of

hobbling away toward the parking lot.

Rachel began collecting her tennis gear, but Alex didn't want her to leave just yet. "From what I saw, it looked like a pretty good match," Alex said. "Who was winning?"

"Hargrove isn't a bad player, but he lost the first set 6-3 and was losing in the second. To tell you the truth, I'm not sure he really twisted his ankle. Maybe he just didn't want to lose to 'a girl,' Rachel said with a big grin, while batting her eyelashes as if to imply she was just a soft weakling.

"Are you going back to the basketball court?" Rachel asked. "Can I join you?"

"Sure," Alex was delighted. "Have you played much basketball? I mean, you are pretty tall?"

"I've played a little," Rachel responded with an innocent smile.

"Why do I think I'm being hustled?" Alex asked. Rachel simply shrugged her shoulders.

He threw the ball to Rachel, who stood in the right corner about twenty feet from the basket. She let fly with the ball, and swish. Nothing but net! He gave it to her again. She dribbled to the top of the key and again made a jump shot right into the hoop.

"I thought you said you went to UCLA on a tennis scholarship."

"I did, but I also turned down two basketball scholarships from other California schools," Rachel answered, smiling smugly.

"Okay, do you want to play a game of 'Horse'?" Alex asked.

"How about one-on-one instead?"

"Really? I mean, *seriously*?" Alex raised his eyebrows and cocked his head to the side. He was about to say, "But you're not going to kick my ass," when he remembered the story about Sgt. Monroe and thought better of it. Rachel just stared expressionless at him and waited for his answer. Alex momentarily wondered if he had just blundered and possibly insulted her by implying playing against him was ridiculous.

"Okay, one-on-one it is. You can have the ball first," Alex said.

Rachel was very good, he estimated, but he was better. Her outside jump shot was excellent, and she drove well to her right. But she wasn't as fluid going left. Being four inches taller than Rachel, Alex always got his shot off over her out-stretched arms, except for one time she deflected it. He also blocked a few of her shots. When they got in the paint, Alex could back into her on offense and make a power move. But he could feel how surprisingly strong her upper body was for a woman. She wouldn't be backed-up easily and had no intention of willingly giving ground.

Their body-to-body contact was exciting and intense to him. Rachel tried trash talking, as if she could intimidate, which made Alex laugh every time she did it. Rachel seemed to like that Alex was unfazed by her chatter.

He won the game twenty to twelve. But if truth be told, he allowed her some open shots from the perimeter although he would never admit it.

Twenty minutes later, they were both dripping sweat and somewhat winded.

"Want to come up to my place for some iced-tea, or a cold beer?" Rachel asked.

"Yeah, thanks, that would be great," Alex responded, *and maybe something more,* was the thought that ran through his mind. He was ready for the 'next level' and wondered if she felt the same.

CHAPTER **21**

SUNDAY EARLY AFTERNOON

Love in the Afternoon

The air conditioning in Rachel's apartment felt like heaven. It must have been over 100 degrees outside, but inside it was a comfortable 75 F. The apartment was furnished in typical Embassy-style: Mahogany furniture either by Ethan Allen or a local knock-off of a type of rosewood.

Neat and clean, yet tasteful, the apartment's off-white walls were barren because this particular place was kept for temporarily-assigned people who, naturally, didn't bring furnishings or knick-knacks of their own. The floors were carpeted in a neutral beige short nap. Rachel had spread out both rugs she had purchased yesterday; one was a red Kashmir design, the other a dark brown Tabriz pattern with elegant flowers and swirls. On the coffee table he saw Friday's copies of The New York Times and the British Daily Telegraph, presuming she had bought them at the same local bookstore where he always stopped for sundries.

"Iced tea or beer?" Rachel asked.

"A beer would be nice, thanks," Alex said, making himself comfortable on the sofa.

Rachel returned from the kitchen with two beers in hand.

God, her legs look fantastic, Alex thought, Especially now they're glistening with a little sweat. Her thigh muscles rippled when she walked. He felt himself slightly aroused.

"So, I understand you've been beating up guys from the Defense Attaché's Office," Alex said casually, looking for a reaction.

She looked blank for a second, then broke out laughing as she sat next to him, propping her legs on the coffee table.

"Monroe had it coming, although I guess I shouldn't have knocked him out. But I loved it and I loved the reaction of the Marines." Alex was also laughing. Monroe was a good sergeant, but he lived in a 1950s type of world in regards to women.

"Do you do that sort of thing often?" Alex asked with mock concern in his voice.

"Now and then," she responded with a sexy deep-throated inflection and devilish expression. They continued talking for some time, learning more about each other.

After UCLA, Rachel got her master's degree in Journalism from the University of Missouri then worked at The Los Angeles_ Times which Alex already knew about her.

Rachel heard about his time at the University of Virginia and experience as a Naval Intelligence Officer. He also achieved a master's degree in Criminology from the University of Maryland's top ranked program.

Then, they spoke about prior assignments, and Alex's childhood growing up in Paris and Cairo. Although he was comfortable telling Rachel about himself, he had a strong feeling this was an evaluation and wondered if he was passing inspection.

Then, she walked to the kitchen, leaving Alex to notice

the movement of her hips. He took a long look at her legs, feeling himself getting aroused, again.

Damn. I want her.

Returning from the kitchen with second beers, Rachel walked over to Alex, still on the couch with legs propped on the table, and looked him straight in the eyes. She carefully put both beers down, swung one leg over his own, and slowly lowered herself onto his lap, clearly mounted for a ride.

He could feel himself engorge as she planted a long, wet kiss squarely on his mouth. He immediately responded, enjoying the sensation of her soft lips and smell of her skin. Finding her tongue, he ran his own around inside her mouth, then touched her breasts with both hands. They were full and soft against his fingers. His member grew harder, as hard as he'd ever felt it.

Reaching behind her, his hands slipped up under her T-shirt, and deftly felt the back of her sports bra, quickly realizing there was no clasp on the back. Rachel laughed and pulled the T-shirt up and over her head along with the sports bra. Her naked breasts bouncing with the effort and beautiful to behold. He stared at her gorgeous nipples begging to be nuzzled. Lowering her backwards onto the couch, he kissed each rosy circle until the tips became hard with delight.

Then, at last, able to feel her amazing legs, he ran both hands down and around them. Her thighs, firm yet supple, excited him even more. Rachel stroked him through his gym shorts, then slid her hand up and under one edge to feel his hardness. Her touch set him on fire. He could see her eyes closed in anticipation.

Abruptly she said, "Listen, you may like making love to sweaty women, but I like my men smelling good." Whereupon she sat up, grabbed his hand, and said "Follow me."

Alex wasn't ready for the interruption, but with a groan, and his manhood pointing the way, followed after her.

Walking into the bathroom, she turned on the shower, as they resumed pulling off the remainder of each other's clothing. Standing briefly to look at each other's bodies with obvious appreciation, they stepped under the running water. Then, taking turns, lathered each other's upper torsos, running circles over the skin and down between the legs until neither could stand it any longer.

Holding her firm buttocks in each hand, he pressed hard against her, feeling his excitement grow. She placed one leg onto the edge of the tub, spreading her legs, inviting him in. He took the invitation and effortlessly slid inside. Feeling her softness, he followed her movements. She wrapped her arms around his neck and shoulders and pressed her hips toward his own. Moving in and out, slowly at first, the feelings were indescribable. She returned his passion and their lower bodies moved in synch. Soon their rhythm increased, moving with coordination, making the sexual sensations more exciting than any Alex had ever known. For a moment he had to gasp and slow for a second to prolong the ecstasy. Then, moving again, faster, deeper, longer, their hands roamed across each other until he heard her groan in pleasure.

Feeling her powerful back muscles, he squeezed her well-muscled biceps. She slid her arms around Alex's muscular upper body and squeezed tightly, never missing a beat in their gyrations.

Then, she quieted and concentrated on the feelings he was making rise up inside her. He watched her beautiful face as an emotion of immense pleasure ran over it. His own excitement was nearing its peak, but he wanted to prolong it until she could come with him into climax. When he felt her nearing, he moved with his special thrust making sure he touched the G-spot and heard her gasp. A few more thrusts amid groans and hand groping and they climaxed together. Each crying out, as their movements began to slow. After giving Alex a long passionate kiss, Rachel said, "Alex, my God, that was wonderful."

"You're telling me? If showering was an Olympic sport, you'd get a gold medal," He replied while hugging Rachel, naked, against his soap-lathered body. Surprised at her strength, Alex figured she knew he was surprised. "Wow, you're really strong, Rachel."

"You ain't seen nothing yet, big boy," Rachel laughingly teased him, a lock of wet hair stuck to her skin over her left eye.

After partially drying off, they jumped onto Rachel's queen size bed. Now, somewhat rested, he felt desire and arousal again. She, too, was ready for more as they continued making love. He ran his hands over her long legs, squeezing her gorgeous calves, then caressing her magnificent and hard inner thigh muscles. While her legs appeared slender from a distance because of her height, her thighs were tight and well-developed. Alex already knew Rachel was strong, but when she engulfed his waist between her powerful thighs, locked her ankles, and squeezed him in a body scissors hold, he thought he might have to ask her to let up on the pressure before she broke his ribs. He groaned a little as she squeezed tighter. She laughed heartily and whispered in a sweet voice.

"Is something wrong? I'm not hurting you, am I?"

"Oh, no.," Alex replied in a constricted voice. "I just thought that you might be really strong. But I guess I was wrong."

Rachel was delighted with Alex's humor. She liked that he wasn't a wimp who pleaded for her to stop squeezing so hard. So, with delight, she constricted her thigh muscles even tighter around his waist. Alex couldn't be sure how much power she had left should she want to squeeze as hard as she could. But he guessed there was considerable strength still in reserve.

With a slight grimace on his face, he smiled and said, "Oh, thank goodness, for a moment I thought your legs were only for show."

"Good for you!" Rachel said with glee as she slowly reduced the pressure of her scissors and thrust her pelvis against his. "I wanted to see if you could take it, in case it gets really wild in a few minutes."

"You've got to be kidding? In case it gets wild? I can't wait," he replied, although he could barely catch his breath.

They made love several more times that afternoon. Each time more exciting than the last. Their athletic ability, strength, and endurance made them a perfect physical match.

Then, exhausted, they lay on their backs, Alex looked at her as she was lightly sleeping and thought he had never had such fantastic sex before. 'Size does matter,' he laughed to himself. And Rachel Smith had size. Her legs were unbelievably powerful and long; her arms were stronger than any woman he had ever known; and her abs were really hard. All that and yet, in street clothes, she seemed to have a normal build. Plus, her beauty was undeniable. In that moment, he realized, she was exceptional.

Rachel awoke, reached over, and kissed Alex lightly on the lips. "You were amazing, Alex. I haven't had so many orgasms like that in a long time."

"And I thought I was your first," Alex laughed.

She punched him on the arm, then broke into laughter.

"In a little while I'll have to clean up for the DCM's dinner. But if you're up for it, so to speak, I think I have time for one more round," she said with a huge grin on her face. Her green eyes sparkled as she spoke.

He couldn't believe her sexual appetite and was delighted. Alex smiled as he ran fingers through her thick hair.

"Ah, Rachel, I can't think of a better way to end a delightful afternoon."

CHAPTER 22

SUNDAY NIGHT

COMMAND DINNER

Rachel arrived at the Deputy Chief of Mission's house at 6:00 pm sharp. A servant opened the door and Ellen Hunt quickly slid away from a small group in conversation to greet her. Glancing around the gigantic living room, Rachel could see the house had a beautiful large garden in back accessed through several sets of French doors. While the furniture was of typical Embassy design, Ellen had a lot of her own decorations spread throughout the house, no doubt acquired from previous postings.

"Wow, Ellen, where did you get all of your treasures?" Rachel asked.

"Oh, you know, from the normal souk's over the past 20 years. That wooden screen is from a market in Amman, the gold-plated samovar is from Cairo, and some of the knick-knacks over there are from Sri Lanka."

"Well, your taste is magnificent," she declared with obvious admiration.

"Come in and meet the crowd. You'll know some of them, but the junior officers will be new to you," Ellen said.

Rachel made the rounds, greeting new faces and introducing herself as servants roamed among the crowd with drinks and hor d'oeuvres. There were two first-tour single male officers from the consular section, one from the economic section, and a female officer from political, whose husband was still in language training in Washington for an eventual slot with USAID Bangladesh. Ellen had also invited an Army Captain and his wife from the Military Assistance group, and a first-tour young married working couple from the CIA.

On the mentoring side of the equation, Marisol Lopez from Political was there, as was RSO Jim Riley and his wife, and Consul General George Wentworth and his wife. All in all, Rachel thought it was a pretty good mix of experience and variety.

Questions from the new officers were well-focused and addressed their long-term concerns over assignments, promotions, and life in general living abroad. Naturally, not all feedback applied to people from the non-State Department agencies, but nevertheless, it was a good learning experience for everyone.

Rachel, herself, had nothing to offer in terms of South Asian assignments, however, there was keen interest in her work in the Press Spokesman's office, as well as her prior assignments to Hong Kong and Beijing.

As the buffet dinner progressed, Rachel listened with interest to Ellen Hunt's description of her own background and experiences. A daughter lived with her in Islamabad, but her son was with his father back in Washington. Rachel was not clear whether this separation was permanent or merely temporary, nor whether it was personal or part of the assignment, and Ellen didn't elaborate. Rachel learned that Ellen had graduated from Bowdoin and had a master's degree from the University of Pennsylvania.

She had been the State Department's desk officer for Jordan/Syria/Iraq Affairs, and previously served in Amman, Cairo, and Colombo. In passing, Ellen mentioned she had qualified for incentive pay because of her skills in the Arabic language.

Toward the end of the evening, Rachel finally managed to capture Jim Riley's attention. Using the most subtle skills possible, she tried pumping him for information about Alex. Based upon Riley's quick smiles during their lengthy conversation, she guessed she wasn't fooling him one bit. He was too discreet, and too much a gentleman, to ask if her interest was professional or personal.

However, she did learn that Alex's oratory skills, which she had observed at the Country Team meeting, were equally matched by his writing and management skills, according to Riley. It was nice to know the man with whom she was most recently and most passionately intimate was not merely a physical beast in bed, but was intelligent, cultured, educated and an all-around nice guy. She couldn't be more pleased.

The evening drew to a close around 10 pm. Ellen graciously asked Rachel if she was settling in all right with her temporary assignment. Then, invited Rachel to have lunch with her after they finished with the CODEL visit this coming week. Returning to her apartment, Rachel was feeling very good about being in Islamabad and began having second thoughts about returning to Washington after only two months as planned. Things were beginning to get interesting.

Hmmm, I might want to stay awhile longer, she thought.

Her eyes looked at the new rugs. Then, realizing that Alex

wasn't there, felt surprised at herself that her apartment felt a bit barren. She missed him already.

CHAPTER **23**

MONDAY MORNING

Rachel Revealed

Rachel arrived at the American Center early the next morning at 7:00 am. It was part of her routine to keep an early work schedule, besides, she needed to review a variety of news stories emailed overnight from the State Department. She also needed time to summarize interesting articles that dealt with Pakistan or U.S. foreign policy in general.

Spread out around her black lacquered wood and steel art deco desk were printouts of electronic clippings from Reuters, The Associated Press, The New York Times, The Washington Post, and The Los Angeles Times. Other information would arrive during the work day. From these newspapers, Rachel prepared her morning's news summary for the Ambassador and other key officers in the Embassy. Naturally, they could read each of the complete articles in their spare time, but the first thing they needed to know every morning was which news items were hot or potentially controversial.

Finishing her last edit of the summary, she hit the send key on her computer. It would be received across town at the Embassy in seconds. Now, she could sit back to read some of the Pakistani English language newspapers, even though she knew they weren't very credible.

But first, with a moment to herself, she closed her eyes and thought of the previous afternoon with Alex. A sly smile formed on her full lips. Alex was amazingly physical and passionate. Although she told him she hadn't had as many orgasms in a long time, the fact was she had never had so many in a single sexual encounter. Most guys, in her experience, crapped out after she'd had two orgasms, if any. Alex was tops on her list of memorable occasions. Her smile turned into a full grin while remembering his considerate and unselfish side. In a flashback from their time in bed, she recalled him whispering in her ear,

"Rachel, while I need a little time to reload, let me give you a helping hand, so to speak." He had reached between her legs and delicately massaged her in just the right spot until she was pulsating with joy and reached yet another climax.

"Alex, you're unbelievable." She had responded, reaching over and hugging him tightly. While Alex may have taken her comment to refer to his physical prowess, she had really meant it about his overall sensuality. Besides, he was definitely rugged and strong, a winning combination; one she wasn't likely to let go of easily. He was definitely on her "keeper" list.

When Alex had left her apartment yesterday, not only had she continued to think about him, but to reflect on her life in general. Academic and professional accomplishments were clearly important to her. She enjoyed the recognition she had received in the State Department when winning a Superior Honor Award for her press work in Beijing. She was competitive, not only at work, but in her private life as well.

In high school she'd been a tomboy who was bigger and stronger than most of the boys. Her good looks made getting a date easy, although the immaturity of the boys made dating a giant frustration, not to mention they were all relatively weaker than she was.

At UCLA things had improved. She maintained a 3.8

grade point average while playing a busy tennis schedule with lots of road trips. Her sorority membership helped with the dating scene but, again, her expectations of finding a nice guy who could successfully compete with her brains and brawn left her unfulfilled. Working in Hong Kong and Beijing was really exciting intellectually, but the men were not up to her expectations. Rome offered great promise, but she left for Washington D.C. before having a chance to find out.

Returning to the moment she seriously wondered if Alex could be the one for her. But, it would take more than a 'roll in the hay' to decide.

"Hello Rachel, are you there?" Pete Lemon, the Public Affairs Counselor, her boss, was waving his hand in front of her face.

"Sorry, I didn't see you come in. I must have been daydreaming," she said, collecting herself.

"I'll say, you've been staring at the wall for five minutes."

Rachel blushed a little. "What's up, Pete?"

"The DCM called for a countdown meeting tomorrow regarding the CODEL visit. I'd like you to go since you'll be handling the press interview at the Ambassador's residence. Do we have a list of confirmations yet from the local press?"

"Yes, we do. In total there'll be six reporters attending. That number includes reps from both newspapers and the TV station."

"Let me see the list, please." After scanning the names Pete said, "Okay, it appears the major journalists will be present. That's great. Pass those names to Security so they can get into the compound easily."

"Will do, Pete."

He paused for a moment before saying, "Rachel, you've been here a few weeks now. I can't tell you how much we appreciate you taking this temporary assignment, especially on short notice. I'm delighted with everything you've done."

"Thanks, Pete, but the pleasure's all mine. I've never been in this part of the world before and I'm enjoying myself immensely."

"I hope we have enough quality work to keep you happy. This isn't like being in Washington, D.C."

"Don't worry about that," Rachel replied. "Some of the issues are new for me, so I like the challenge."

"Excellent. Again, thanks for being here."

Okay, back to work, Rachel thought, as Pete left her office.

CHAPTER 24

EARLY MONDAY MORNING

Getting Ready

Monday morning arrived with a quick rainstorm, cooling temperatures about ten degrees to everyone's delight. Relief, however, was short-lived before the oppressive heat returned. Dust in the air had also been eliminated by the rain, a benefit which lasted a little longer.

Jim Riley breathed in the fresh, fragrant odors after the downpour. He would have loved a walk around the Embassy compound, now that the rain had stopped. Unfortunately, he had too much to do. First, he had to prepare Ambassador Pierce's opening comments for the 'Town Hall' meeting now scheduled at ten o'clock in the Embassy auditorium. Then, he'd make a pitch for everyone to use good sense and security judgment each and every day. Thirdly, he would highlight implications of the recent bomb discovered at Jinnah Supermarket.

Attendees would include a cross-section of the American community: School teachers at the International School, American businessmen, and, of course, those officially assigned to the Embassy including Embassy contractors, along with spouses. The USAID contingent included over two hundred contractors who nominally managed or advised on projects dealing with sanitation, construction, water resources, road building, and a host of other infrastructure programs. From past experience, however, Riley knew most of the USAID contractors wouldn't be interested in the security briefing but he would include reference to them anyway. The Ambassador, Riley, and the DCM Hunt agreed that representatives of other friendly embassies should also be invited. Attendance at the meeting was always voluntary; nevertheless, a packed house was expected today.

Jim's role was to take over from the Ambassador after his opening remarks and discuss specific security measures each person could initiate on their own. He'd reinforce the idea that while the RSO and Marines could protect official government employees when they were physically present in the Embassy, it was really up to everyone in the community to be vigilant themselves when traveling in town or visiting stores, markets, and other Pakistani sites. Jim would give the audience a counter-terrorism briefing, emphasizing countermeasures on how to avoid problems in the first place. It was pretty much his standard spiel; nevertheless, he knew repetition was important in order to have the message sink in.

Following Jim's presentation, the DCM might say a few words, then the floor would be open to a question and answer period.

He expected the Town Hall meeting would last a little over an hour. After the meeting and a quick lunch, he had been invited by Bill Stanton to sit in on a meeting with a senior ISI officer. Usually the RSO didn't interface with ISI, since this was the purview of the CIA station. The topic of the meeting, however, would be a new threat to the Western community ISI had just uncovered. Therefore, Bill Stanton had asked if his Regional Security Officer,

Riley, could attend, and they agreed. Normally, meetings with ISI were held at their offices in Rawalpindi. But this time, Bill said, ISI wanted to visit the Embassy. Jim thought maybe the guy just wanted to get a break from being cooped up in his own office.

While Riley prepared for the Town Hall meeting, Alex was seated at his own desk finishing a physical security survey of the American Center. Whenever he moved to grab some item on the desk, his ribs ached from yesterday's tussle with Rachel.

God, she has strong legs, he smiled to himself. Never before had he made love to such a powerful, confident woman. He momentarily closed his eyes and recalled how passionate they had been. When she had locked her mouth over his, a shiver had coursed throughout his entire body. He recalled holding each other tightly, and hands caressing each other's bodies.

I need to focus on this survey, he thought with a sigh. But, unable to concentrate, he reached for the phone.

"Hello?"

"Rachel, hey, how's your day? I can't stop thinking about yesterday." He heard the smile in her reply.

"Yeah, me, too. Today's kind of useless. You were pretty fantastic, yourself."

Alex smiled, feeling happiness plant a seed inside his mind.

"So, how about dinner later." It was more of a statement than a question.

"Yeah, I'd like that," she answered. "I'll be done about six, I figure. Where?"

"I'll meet you at your place. We can decide from there." He really hoped they might forget dinner altogether and just repeat yesterday entirely.

The American Center had a large air-conditioned library that Pakistanis could use, either for research or as a typical lending library. The U.S. goal was to provide a wealth of books, articles, videos, magazines, and other documentation that gave Pakistanis an opportunity to explore western philosophy, politics, and culture. Some American personnel, however, wondered if the goal of Pakistani users wasn't just to escape the stifling heat by sitting in the cool air for a few hours.

Ironically, the biggest single item checked out was a video tape of the last Winter Olympics. The Center's librarian once noted Pakistanis weren't natural skiers, so perhaps the fascination with the tape had more to do with the female ice-skating competition, where plenty of firm female thighs were in evidence. Alex smiled when he first heard this and thought it amazing how much he had in common with the average Pakistani male.

While the American Center did not contain classified material, as did the Embassy, it still needed protection from terrorists and criminals. So, Alex's security survey contained a few recommendations for security upgrades. His timing was right on target and he finished just in time for the Town Hall meeting.

Susan Witt, meanwhile, was contemplating her strategy on a criminal investigation that had recently come to her attention. It involved the senior Pakistani consular assistant, Hussein Khan, and perhaps, the American Vice Consul, Sheila Winters. Allegations had been made by two Pakistani visa applicants, a married couple, saying they'd been propositioned by Hussein Khan. They alleged that in exchange for a bribe, he would ensure the Pakistanis would be issued U.S. tourist visas. They also alleged he was going to split his profit with American officer Winters. Susan wondered how they could know such a thing. Even so, such allegations of misconduct were made frequently, especially after Pakistanis were legitimately turned down for visas. Usually, the complainant used such allegations as a means of retaliating against a Consular employee for denying them, hoping to have him or her fired, along with finally obtaining the visa. Nevertheless, despite suspicions, every allegation had to be investigated.

In Pakistan, where perhaps ninety percent of visa applicants were rejected, bribery was always an option to overcome such obstacles. Being denied a visa was serious because once rejected, the applicant's chances of getting a future visa were extremely slim. Corruption was endemic in all aspects of Pakistani life, and visa fraud was only one of many types of criminal cases the RSO had on his or her plate. While fraud involving an American officer was rare, it did happen worldwide and needed to be pursued vigorously. Equally important, if the allegations proved to be false, the reputation of both the Pakistani consular assistant and the American consular officer needed to be upheld.

After reviewing the applicant's allegation letter and supporting documentation, Susan decided this case was different because the applicants in question were actually qualified to receive visas.

Normally, an unqualified applicant would offer a bribe in advance to the Consular employee. In this case, it was alleged Hussein Khan broached the subject after working-hours by visiting the applicants' home. Khan would have known, from their visa application, the applicants had money and where they lived. Susan reflected on this twist, and concluded, if the allegation was true, Khan would have correctly judged the applicants to be eligible for their visas. Knowing the American Vice Consul, Sheila Winters, would issue the visas within a few days, he might have decided to gamble that the applicants would pay a bribe rather than risk denial of their application being unaware of its imminent approval. Apparently, Khan misjudged the integrity of these applicants in wanting to acquire their visas the legitimate way.

But, why would the couple throw in the part about him splitting it with Sheila Winters? How would they suspect that? So far, she had only examined the letter with the allegation and supporting visa application documents. Now, she needed to interview the applicants in person, off the Embassy compound, and to confirm some details. After she obtained more details from the couple, she would need to interview Sheila Winters, too, watching for her reaction. Little things like that could tell big stories.

I'll discuss this case with Alex and Jim after the Town Hall meeting, she decided.

CHAPTER **25**

MONDAY MID-MORNING

TOWN HALL MEETING

The Town Hall meeting was a packed house as expected. Ambassador Pierce, DCM Hunt, and RSO Riley sat on stage, facing the audience. Alex and Susan were in the first row to provide moral support for Riley and answer any questions, if needed.

The stage, with highly polished light wood floors, contained a podium and single microphone that could be held by the speaker if he or she decided to walk around as they spoke. Audience seating was fixed in comfortable dark blue upholstered chairs stage-front in semi-circular tiers much like ones at an American movie theatre. In fact, the auditorium was used at times to present American movies to select Pakistani audiences, as well as for occasional amateur plays and musicals performed by the diplomatic community.

The meeting began on time and went well. The American civilian audience was attentive and asked meaningful questions, as did other non-American foreign embassy representatives. Much to Riley's surprise, even USAID employees turned out in pretty good numbers; but then again, only eight USAID employees could play at one time on the two Embassy tennis courts.

An hour and fifteen minutes later, the meeting ended. While in attendance, neither Winston Hargrove IV or JC Colon wanted to be there. Both had attended, not to demonstrate support for the Ambassador's agenda, but because they knew their absence would be noted.

"I thought it was overkill," Hargrove said to Colon on the way out. "In my view, there was no proof the Western community was targeted by the bomb at Jinnah Supermarket. Besides, it didn't explode."

"Maybe it was a hoax," Colon replied cynically disregarding Susan Witt's expertise in explosives. "Perhaps the RSO was hyping the incident just to get more resources and notoriety."

Before parting ways, Hargrove said, "I want to start drafting a telegram to Washington on a recent debate in the Pakistani Parliament about Pakistan's relations with the European Union. I should think the State Department's European Bureau would be especially interested in following this issue. Who knows, maybe I'll be asked to transfer to a European post to provide a South Asian perspective on the matter," Hargrove said in all sincerity, but with a gleam in his eye. He desperately wanted out of Pakistan as soon as possible.

"That's a good idea," JC responded. "In the meantime, I have to decide how next fiscal year's funding will be apportioned."

"I thought the Embassy always justified its funding request based upon specific needs," Hargrove replied.

"True," JC said "But in my opinion these requests are merely 'placeholders' in order to get funds from Washington. Once we know how much money has been granted to the Embassy and the Consulates General, I'll set some of it aside instead for projects that I want."

"Isn't that contrary to State Department regulations, which

require an official reprogramming request to Washington?" Hargrove asked.

"Nonsense," retorted JC. "It's a long-established principle such diversions of funding are the norm." *Besides,* he thought, *using the funds for specific off-the-record projects could win me some friends and benefits from other sections of the Embassy.*

Both highly pleased with themselves, JC and Hargrove separated and headed toward their respective offices to finish out the work day.

Jim, Alex, and Susan ate lunch together in the first floor Embassy cafeteria. The Pakistani special of the day was Chicken Jalfrezi with rice. This dish was cooked with the usual South Asian spices of turmeric, cumin, coriander, and chili powder, in a thick dark sauce with onions, tomatoes, garlic, and peppers. The fragrance was magnificent and one of the great aromas of South Asia. They all ordered it, along with either bottled water or green tea.

"I have to join Bill Stanton for an afternoon meeting with a senior ISI official," Jim mentioned while they were eating. "The SMG guard force owner, Iqbal Satter, will be paying a courtesy call on us in the early afternoon, but I doubt my meeting with Bill Stanton will be over early enough. So, Alex, can I ask you to meet Satter?"

"Of course," Alex responded. Both Riley and Boyd liked Satter and thought him to be an honest businessman and reliable contractor for the Embassy. More than that, Satter was a former Pakistani military officer of some renown.

"We're very fortunate Satter has maintained excellent contacts with active service Pakistani Army officers. Many are now colonels and generals," Riley said. "It just makes everything easier when some local SOB illegally tries to undermine our contract with SMG. Satter knows who to talk to and how to sort out the problem. He's a good man."

"I also understand his views on Pakistani politics and global issues are highly sought after by the Pakistani intelligentsia," Alex noted. "Lucky for the Embassy and the Consulates General, that Satter likes Americans." Alex knew he was a responsive partner in protecting the U.S. Mission. He also treated his guards fairly and paid their wages without taking kickbacks. His character was above reproach and he was well-respected by his own men.

"Susan, would you mind attending the Marine Guard School this afternoon," Riley asked. "I'm scheduled too damn tight today and I need your help." This was a weekly event where Gunny Rodriquez discussed recent Marine Corps directives or programs with the rest of the detachment. It was also a time for individual Marines to raise any concerns about Embassy security policies or note any observations or problems encountered in general.

"Sure, Boss," Susan replied. "I like racking up points with you," she smiled knowing he would understand her humor. "Besides, I also like spending time with the young Marines. They're so 'gung-ho' it makes me feel patriotic all over again."

"Like when you served in the Army, Captain?" Alex joined in.

"Yeah, something like that," she answered with a smile.

CHAPTER 26

MONDAY AFTERNOON

Malik Visits the Embassy

Colonel Malik was looking forward to his meeting at the Embassy with Bill Stanton. Not for the meeting itself, but rather one last opportunity to examine the layout of the building. Naturally, Stanton wouldn't take him into his own secure office area, but Malik could at least observe everything in general, and perhaps, gain insight into the preparedness of the American Marine Guards. Hearing that Jim Riley would be at this meeting was a blessing. Never having met him, Malik could now judge Riley for himself and decide if he seemed capable.

Malik's driver took Quaid-E-Azam Road, the main thoroughfare, and passed new office building construction. Malik felt the capital was finally becoming a major city. Noting the American Center on his left, with its huge satellite antenna on adjacent land, he wondered what American propaganda was beaming into his country today. Turning onto Constitution Road and passing the Presidency, Malik regarded the name as a joke. Since 1947, Pakistan had been ruled directly by the military at least half that time. No 'President' in power, he thought with precision. Even during periods of civilian government, the military had always been the power behind the throne, so to speak.

A quarter mile further on, his driver turned left into the Diplomatic Enclave. At the entrance, two policemen were operating a drop-bar. Their primary role was to stop vehicles if they thought occupants were not on official business. Their instructions, however, were non-specific, so anyone appearing important was routinely let through the checkpoint regardless of showing credentials. Malik was waved through without question.

Along the tree-lined street were vendors selling food. A man was giving haircuts in a beat-up old chair while stray dogs slept in the mid-day heat. They drove slowly passed modern Japanese and British Embassies on the left, across the street from the Egyptian Embassy looking like an attractive Foreign Legion fort with crenellations, or battlements, on its roof. On their right, Malik saw the British housing area, and the Indian Embassy. This road led directly to the American Embassy located about a quarter mile from the guards' post. As the road swung to the right just before the front of the American Embassy entrance, Malik could see the Canadian compound directly across the street on his right.

Getting into the American Embassy could be tedious. There were several policemen stationed outside as well as private Embassy guards. A very large, well-proportioned guard questioned Malik's driver, Syed, and noted Colonel Malik's name on the visitor's list. Malik was wearing his Army uniform, and hoped it would intimidate the guards. As they saluted in recognition of his rank, he hid a smile. They directed Syed to move forward passed the outside gate, then stop a few feet ahead.

To Malik's surprise, the guards then told Syed to open both the trunk and hood of the vehicle for inspection. At first Malik was offended, then pleased to watch the full vehicle inspection operation. He noted that his car had passed the outer gate, but here, further inside the area, there was a type of metal barrier raised out of the ground to prevent the vehicle from proceeding further. After the car was inspected, the barrier was lowered, and they were allowed to proceed to the front of the Embassy about one hundred meters away. Malik saw the entire perimeter wall topped with barbed wire, interspersed with razor ribbon. He heard this had been installed several years prior by an especially effective and aggressive RSO.

An Embassy official, presumably from Stanton's office, was at the front door to greet Malik. Since the RSO had authority to waive further inspection of VIP visitors, Malik was escorted passed the inside Marine Guard without having to go through the metal detector or have his briefcase opened. Jim Riley had arranged this courtesy in advance of their meeting.

Malik noted the Marine Guard stood behind a large glass window which Malik presumed was bullet-resistant. Both the main entrance door and an inner lobby door appear very heavy, he assessed. Likely they are bullet-resistant. The Marine was attentive, wearing combat fatigues and armed with some type of semi-automatic pistol on his hip. He also saw a shotgun in a rack on the wall behind the Marine. If this was the extent of their firepower, Malik was extremely pleased.

His escort took him passed an elevator to stairs straight ahead, and they walked up one flight. At the top, the escort punched a code to open the level's outer door, and though he tried, Malik couldn't see the numbers he used. At the end of a long hallway was a conference room they finally entered. Stanton and his deputy, Alan Patterson, were already waiting, along with another man he presumed was Jim Riley.

Malik had met with both Bill Stanton and Alan Patterson many times. Indeed, it was his job to liaise with the Americans on matters involving Afghanistan. From the chair that was offered, Malik had a magnificent view through the room's large picture window. He could see approximately two miles out in the distance. To the left, the Margala Hills dominated the landscape. Directly behind the Embassy were garden areas before reaching the perimeter wall. To the right, was a large athletic field at the bottom of a sloping hill.

Malik thought the Americans were obsessed with their sports, such as baseball and 'football,' which as everyone knew was not 'football' at all. Real football is something the Americans call 'soccer'. As for baseball, how could it compare to the manly game of cricket? Malik reflected.

"Can I offer you some tea, Colonel Malik?" Stanton asked. Malik accepted and Stanton poured from a nearby pot, while introducing Jim Riley. He motioned toward Patterson sitting in another chair. "I believe you already know Alan." They took a moment to savor the tea.

"Thank you for coming to see us, Colonel," Stanton said. "I hope you were not inconvenienced by our security measures on the compound."

"Not at all," he replied, looking directly at Riley. "I'm glad to see you're taking security seriously. In fact, this is why I have come today. We have recently been picking up intelligence that miscreants on the frontier are most unhappy with American policies of friendship toward India. Specifically, rumor has it these scoundrels may be willing to commit acts of violence to express their concerns."

"Why do improved relations with India bother these 'miscreants'?" Stanton asked.

"Ah, it is not merely that America and India might become closer; it is because some believe it will be at the expense of American-Pakistani relations," Malik replied. "As you know, Pakistan relies heavily upon U.S. aid. While these tribal leaders on the frontier don't like all of your programs, such as education and healthcare for women, they really fear a reduction of money for roads and other projects."

Stanton knew exactly what Malik was saying. Tribesmen preferred their females to be submissive village women; therefore, education programs were deeply unpopular with the uneducated men. As for healthcare, this had more to do with prohibitions on examining women who, naturally, had to undress to be examined; even when those attending the tribeswomen were female doctors.

Stanton smiled to himself. *Perhaps the tribesmen like their women smelling 'natural'.* But, actually, he knew the real reason was that without US financial aid increases, tribal leaders could not skim off their cut of the action. This applied to Pakistan Government officials as well, but Stanton wasn't about to mention this.

"So, I take it the problem is more than mere dissatisfaction with our policies," Stanton declared.

"That is correct. We have unconfirmed reports some ruffians are thinking about taking violent action to protest this matter."

"Where would this violence take place, maybe in Peshawar?" Riley asked.

"We do not know. Maybe Peshawar, maybe even Islamabad," Malik said looking him straight in the eyes.

"Bill, if you don't mind me asking another question," Riley spoke up in deference to Stanton's position in this meeting, "Malik, how often does your source contact you?"

"We can never be sure. He lives in the frontier and is not always available. But we are trying to get more information as we speak."

"Has he indicated what type of violence might be planned, or what types of targets are involved?" Riley asked. Malik paused, pretending to consider the question seriously.

"That is uncertain, but since the anger is directed against the American relationship with India, this may rule out a general bombing campaign against broader Western interests."

Stanton, Patterson, and Riley sat quietly for a moment

roflocting on what had been said.

"I am thinking I should ask the government to provide more police near your facilities," Malik said, "That is, if you want such additional protection."

"I never reject offers of additional security," Riley replied. "My real concern, however, is establishing a time frame for this threat, as well as defining a probable target. No doubt the police will say their manpower is limited."

"This is true," Malik replied. "Maybe we can review this matter again next week and hopefully I will have more information at that time."

After further discussion, the meeting eventually adjourned with Malik completely satisfied with the outcome. He was able to see the Embassy layout once again, and he believed he had deflected suspicion away from his secret element within ISI. Moreover, he could now claim the Americans had been warned in advance. However, he also assessed Riley to be a man of substance; therefore, he would have to review his plan accordingly. After Malik was escorted out of the room, Riley turned to Stanton.

"I'm not happy with the outcome of the meeting. Once again, a threat's been raised, but without sufficient details to specifically counter it. This, of course, is the nature of intelligence collection. We have enough information to create anxiety and, therefore, institute general precautions, but not enough intelligence to be really useful. I assume you'll report this meeting to Langley later today. When you do, can you ask Langley to pass it to Diplomatic Security headquarters with a note saying I was in attendance at the meeting? I'm going to send a separate telegram to Diplomatic Security telling them we are reviewing our security measures countrywide."

Riley headed back to his office and hoped Iqbal Satter would still be there talking with Alex. He wanted a conversation with him.

CHAPTER 27

MONDAY AFTERNOON

Iqbal Satter

Late afternoon in his office, Alex welcomed a visit from Iqbal Satter, owner of SMG the Embassy's guard company, and sat across from the likeable Pakistani businessman.

"It's great to see you again, Iqbal," Alex said.

"As always, it's a pleasure to come to Islamabad and talk with you, Alex," Satter replied.

Dark-complexioned with a round face, Satter was of average Pakistani height, some five-feet-eight inches tall and slightly overweight, a sign of prosperity in South Asian culture. Well-dressed in a dark business suit and medium-blue silk tie, he chose to dress in western fashion, as did many Karachi businessmen who had frequent contact with American or European counterparts.

Involved in the import-export trade, Satter also ran the largest guard force in the country. His company, SMG, had won the American contract for embassy and consulate guard protection services in a competitive bid several years earlier. The former guard contractor had cheated the Embassy and stole money from his own guards by demanding kickbacks from their salaries. In contrast, Satter was a man of sound religious convictions and led a pious lifestyle.

His passion was the welfare of his guards. To that end,

Satter set up a bank account for each guard and ensured their salaries were direct-deposited into each one's account every month; a new concept in Pakistan for low-paid guards. Most never had a bank account prior to SMG taking over, so in the beginning, they checked their accounts daily to ensure the money was still there.

He also created a special program rewarding individual guard performance and took care of their families when a guard was injured on the job. For Satter, this was merely a continuation of his Army days when officers were expected to take care of their troops as if they were family. Of particular note: He was also a part-time journalist. Moreover, he was starting to expand his business interests outside of Pakistan.

"How's your family," Alex asked. During a prior visit to Karachi, he had met the family and knew all Satter's kids were bright and well-read. Satter's wife, Parveen, was attractive and witty. College educated, she also ran her own business ventures, a rarity in Pakistan for a woman

"They're doing well. My oldest child will begin his senior year in high school next month. We have contacted several American universities who are interested in him. He thinks he may want to be a lawyer. My younger girls are busy becoming 'fashion queens'," Satter said with a laugh. "They read all of the American magazines and want to dress like the latest movie stars. It's wonderful to be young and innocent, isn't it?"

Alex smiled and nodded in agreement with Satter's personal disclosures.

"So, what brings you to Islamabad?"

"Partly because I have routine business to handle," he answered. "In addition to my regular telephone calls within the company, I try to personally visit my people every few months, whether here or in Peshawar, Lahore, or Quetta. But I also wanted to ensure that you are happy with our level of guard service," Satter said.

"Iqbal, of course we are. Your company's performance is wonderful. Equally important, when problems arise, your supervisors correct the matter instantly."

"That's good to hear. But it's not exactly what I meant," Satter said. "I am not trying to get more business from you, but I wanted to be certain you feel satisfied that our level of security is sufficient."

Alex wasn't exactly sure what Satter's was implying.

"Can you clarify what you just said?"

"Well, let me tell you a story. A week ago, I was having dinner at the Karachi Sports Club with Lt. General Haidar, the Corps Commander for Sindh Province. He mentioned that a month earlier, one of his subordinates received a general inquiry from an ISI officer about the extent of private guard coverage at the major foreign consulates in Karachi. While Haidar has only general knowledge about such things, he assumed the ISI officer was most likely thinking of leaving the Army and starting up a guard business of his own. Since the matter seemed of no urgency, Haidar only mentioned it to me at dinner last week."

"Do you know the name of the ISI officer who made the inquiry?" Alex asked.

"No, I don't. Neither did Lt. General Haidar. The query was received by a major on his staff. By the time this information worked its way up to Haidar, the name of the ISI officer was long forgotten.

"At first I tended to concur with Haider's assumption," Satter continued. "I'm not concerned at present with competition for your business since our contract will run for several years. But then I thought, what if the inquiry was more ominous, and had more to do with a potential threat to these facilities? Perhaps ISI knows something they're not sharing with anyone at present.

"So, yesterday I met with Lt. General Jamil at Army Headquarters here in Islamabad. He was not aware of any specific threat. I trust Jamil since we served together many years ago. Maybe, after all, the original inquiry was only the first step in a business venture. Who knows? So, I ask you: Are you aware of any increased risk?"

Satter looked directly into Alex's eyes, a commendable trait that gave an assurance of his honesty. At that moment, Alex was unaware of the conversation Jim Riley was having with Colonel Malik, and answered truthfully that he did not. He assured Satter that should any new information come to light, he would tell him immediately, especially since Satter's guards would be in direct line of fire.

Naturally, both men realized intelligence information had to be handled carefully, but there was always a way to protect sources and methods while enhancing security.

"Just to be on the safe side," Satter said, "I will ask our twenty-four-hour Mobile Reaction Team to stay near the Embassy unless they are called to an emergency. The same will apply in the other cities where teams will stay near your consulates."

"Sounds like a good idea." Alex responded.

He was pleased to have the services of SMG's response teams. Each Mobile Reaction Team used an SUV with a driver, supervisor, and two other members. The vehicle carried four loaded AK-47s in the back, plus extra magazines per person. Even though SMG had permits from the Pakistani government, the teams never carried their weapons openly unless absolutely neccssary. No doubt Sattor had been able to obtain these permits because each member of his response teams was a well-qualified former army commando. He was a responsible businessman who ran an excellent company.

Alex and Iqbal chatted a while longer. Iqbal mentioned he would be in Islamabad a few more days. Alex knew he could reach Satter through the SMG office if needed.

Then, just as Satter rose to leave, Riley arrived. They exchanged firm handshakes, and Jim asked him if he had a little more time to talk. Satter welcomed the opportunity to speak with Riley and sat down again.

Silent a moment, Riley then explained he had just received new threat information. Not mentioning ISI might be involved, he simply stated the information had not been confirmed, nor details provided. Nevertheless, he wanted Alex and Satter to know where things stood.

Alex described Satter's suggestion of keeping the Mobile Reaction Team near the Embassy, and in other cities, near consulates when not responding to incidents. Riley liked this idea.

"If you agree," Satter said. "I will brief the Guard Force Supervisors on the need to pay special attention to visitors and packages they may be carrying. Also, they must be vigilant and inspect every vehicle closely for explosives," Satter concluded as he rose to bid them good evening.

At that moment, none of the three could know the extent of Colonel Malik's plans to do something about the perceived imbalance of power wrought by the new American-Indian alliance. They could never imagine his burning desire for revenge, nor the vicious steps he was about to take.

They only knew it was, mercifully, the end of a very long day.

Chapter 28

MONDAY EVENING

Meeting with Khan

Hussein Khan left work at the American Consular Section at six-thirty Monday evening. He headed for his old battered red Toyota Corolla in the local employee parking lot, outside the compound walls. Feeling unhappy about driving 36 miles north to Murree, a town outside the city, he knew it would take an hour requiring slow speeds on the windy unlit road. Adding to that was the lack of side barriers which kept drivers from plummeting down the mountain side. He also feared on-coming trucks usually driven much too fast for such road conditions. But he had to go. He had a secret appointment to keep.

Leaving the flat plain surrounding Islamabad, the road climbed steeply into hill country. Khan's Toyota was ten years old and showing its age. He knew Murree's elevation of some 7,500 feet meant its engine would be straining to keep up speed during the long ascent to the hill town. Khan also owned a second-hand Mercedes, which might have traveled the road better, but he never brought it to the Embassy for fear someone would question how he could afford such luxury. Although he disliked Tahir, the man he was reluctantly meeting, he did like the area of Murree. It was 15 to 20 degrees cooler than Islamabad in August and even had substantial snow in winter. From the town's summit, Khan had often seen the lush green forests and hills surrounding it. On a clear day, he once viewed the snow-capped Nanga Parbat in faraway Kashmir, with its awe-inspiring elevation of over 26,000 feet.

Murree had been established in the 1850s by Sir Henry Lawrence and originally conceived as a sanatorium for British troops needing rest and a change of climate from the harsh Indian summers.

Now, having to go there for a clandestine meeting, he cursed the traffic coming towards him, forcing him closer to the precipice to avoid a head-on collision.

He had been driving awhile and from time to time, observed areas along the roadside where vehicles must have swerved off the highway. Only skid marks remained as evidence that a car had been there, leading off the pavement toward the cliff. It must have meant certain death as evidenced by a few crushed trees hundreds of feet below. Khan down-shifted frequently to keep his old car from stalling on the hilly road.

Finally, after an arduous drive, he saw the spire of Murree's Holy Trinity church in the town center. Looking over the nearby parking lot for a silver Toyota four-door sedan, Khan spotted one with Tahir sitting in the driver's seat. Luck was with Khan as he found an open space next to Tahir's vehicle. He parked and exited his own car, then slid into Tahir's passenger seat.

"You made excellent time getting here," Tahir said in greeting. He was dressed, as always, wearing a long sleeve white shirt, dark pants, and black shoes. His black hair was cut short and his general appearance was of a man who kept very fit.

"The consulate was less busy than usual, so I had no trouble leaving precisely at six-thirty, as you requested."

"I don't have any new demands today," Tahir said. "But I want to know if there have been any changes in the Embassy's security since we last met."

Khan felt distaste for Tahir welling up in his throat. If that is even his real name, he thought, realizing he hardly knew the man.

Six months earlier, Khan had been approached by Tahir at home. Tahir had informed him that he knew all about Khan's visa fraud activities. Introducing himself as part of the all-powerful ISI, he claimed to be a Pakistani army officer. Khan wasn't exactly sure how Tahir found out about his scams, but suspected one of his victims must have known Tahir and complained to him. Tahir then must have followed him home that night from the victim's house.

Now, in exchange for not telling the Embassy, and the police, about Khan's criminality, Tahir demanded information about the American Embassy compound and security activities of the American staff. Khan was terrified at this turn of events but knew he could never tell anyone at the Embassy about this development. If Tahir really was from ISI, Khan's failure to cooperate would mean harassment at a minimum, and imprisonment at worst.

"I'm not aware of any changes," Khan responded. "The SMG guard force operates as usual, the Marines practice often in the evenings, I am told. I know this from friends in other parts of the Embassy. What else can I say?"

"What about the number of police officers around the Embassy? Are there any more lately?"

"Everything seems as usual,"

"Is any additional security training going on?"

"No, not that I've seen or heard about from others. There is only the normal testing of the Embassy's alarm system," Khan said. "But again, the Consular section is not in the same building on the compound as the main part of the Embassy."

Months before, Tahir had pumped Khan for details of guard force schedules, maps of the Embassy compound, and weaponry carried by security forces. Now, he only needed to know last-minute changes that may have occurred.

"The guards, police, and Marines carry the same weapons as before?" Tahir asked.

"Yes, as far as I can tell. But I am not a weapons expert."

Tahir thought for a moment, contemplating whether he had all the information Khan could reasonably provide.

"Okay, you've done well. I may call upon you in the future, but for now, we are done."

Khan got out of the car and walked to a nearby restaurant, where he intended to enjoy a pleasant meal in their outside garden before leaving for home, glad his meeting was over. He detested Tahir and hated the control Tahir had over him. Hopefully, he would never have to see him again.

As he sat at a table in the restaurant, he picked up a folded Urdu language newspaper the previous customer had left, and read the headline: "Army denies supporting freedom fighters in Kashmir." Khan shook his head and thought to himself, Who could believe such a denial? Obviously, ISI was behind the violence in Kashmir. He knew democracy in Pakistan was only a veneer that covered the true power structure which was the Army, more specifically, ISI, controlling the country.

Tahir watched Khan enter the restaurant, then leaned back in the driver's seat and lit a cigarette. He rolled down the window and watched the smoke curl into the air until it was sucked outside. The pleasant aroma of nearby pine trees filled his nostrils. Using Khan had been child's play. The man's greed and minor visa fraud scam trapped him. While Khan had not provided much new information over the last six months, his access was useful in double-checking facts. Once Tahir's friends had told him of Khan's plan to extort them in exchange for issuing visas to their families, Tahir instantly saw the possibility of turning Khan into an informant inside the American Embassy.

He also took care that Khan would never know his real name, even though it was extremely unlikely Khan would ever reveal his own actions as a source of information for ISI. Any disclosure would mean immediate loss of his job, his pension from the Americans, and imprisonment by ISI. So, for the time being, he was certain his fictional persona of "Tahir" would be the only way Khan would know him.

Colonel Malik started the engine of his silver Toyota, took one more look at Khan in the restaurant window, and drove out of Murree toward Rawalpindi to have dinner with his own family on this very dark night.

CHAPTER **29**

MONDAY EVENING

Dinner for Two

It was dusk, and the city looked almost beautiful in the twilight. Alex left the office at 7 pm to pick up Rachel at the American Center. They had dinner reservations at the Holiday Inn's Chinese restaurant which had remarkably good food.

First, however, he stopped at the SMG office to talk with Ahmed, the guard supervisor before going to his Jeep parked in the Embassy lot.

"Have you seen that green Toyota driving past the Embassy any more?"

"No, Boss. But the guards are watching for it, or for any other suspicious misadventures," Ahmed said, shaking his head from side to side.

"Misadventures, huh?" Alex smiled to himself. He loved Pakistani English. "Okay, Ahmed, Miss Witt and Mr. Riley are also aware of this matter. Call us on the radio if anything looks suspicious."

"I will, boss. Be assured the Mobile Patrol is waiting to pounce on any miscreants."

"That's excellent, Ahmed," Alex smiled again. "Miscreants need a good pouncing every now and then."

Driving out of the compound toward Constitution Avenue, he found traffic was light. Occasionally, he passed a truck or lorry decorated in the most gaudy paint job imaginable. Colorful portraits of the Prime Minister or local movie stars were among them, as well as depictions of F-16s. He wondered who the artists were, and why this was such a custom in Pakistan. As if the paintings weren't enough, shiny aluminum strips of metal were added all over each lorry to 'enhance' the beauty of the vehicle. Alex thought if there was an 'Ugly Truck of the Year Award,' among nations, Pakistan would undoubtedly take top honors in all categories.

Parking in the American Center's lot, he walked past the SMG guard, nodding in recognition, then headed toward the main double-glass doors. The guard saluted Alex sharply. Alex returned the salute, entered the building and headed upstairs to Rachel's office on the second floor.

Approaching her doorway, he saw her saying goodbye to a distinguished-looking oriental man dressed in a dark blue suit, light blue shirt, with red tie. Their conversation was in Chinese. Rachel saw him approaching and waved him to enter. Continuing her conversation with the gentleman, she pointed at Alex. He assumed he was being introduced. The man looked in Alex's direction and laughed, then extended his hand in greeting as he entered the room. Alex shook hands cordially while nodding. Following a moment of pleasantries still in Chinese, the man bid them both good evening and left.

"Who was that?"

"Oh, that's the Cultural Attaché from the Chinese Embassy."

"Wow, your Chinese must be pretty good, since you weren't hesitating at all in conversation."

"Yeah, it's not bad."

"Why did he laugh when we were introduced?" Alex asked.

"Oh, I told him you're extremely hot-looking, and great in the sack."

"Well, good," he said with a laugh, while thinking: Now, that's exactly how I would introduce her. He also guessed he would never really know what Rachel had said to the Chinese visitor.

"Ready?"

"As ever, and hungry."

They left the American Center as night settled-in and drove to the Holiday Inn. The restaurant was attractive with typical Chinese dark-lacquered furniture and red-flocked wallpaper showing scenes of dragons, trees, and bridges. Colorful red and blue Chinese lanterns hung from the ceiling transporting guests into an Asian atmosphere. Since alcohol wasn't allowed in restaurants in Pakistan, they ordered hot green tea.

Being brewed at a high temperature, tea in Pakistan is safe to drink without danger of dysentery or other uncomfortable intestinal problems. Usually, Westerners are savvy enough never to ask for plain water unless the water is brought in a sealed bottle and opened in front of the patron. Another precaution involving ice: It's never a smart option.

Looking over the menus for a few moments, they made small talk.

"I'll have the beef with garlic sauce," Alex told the waiter.

"The ginger chicken with steamed vegetables looks good to me. Let's get both and share," Rachel suggested.

During the first course of Hot and Sour soup, Alex asked, "How's your job going?"

"Usually it's routine, but lately every journalist in town wants to know about our relationship with India. Someone, probably in the Pakistan government, is spinning tales of America screwing Pakistan in exchange for cooperation with India."

"Pakistan is obsessed with India, no doubt for some valid reasons," Alex replied. "Even though we've sold Pakistan some of our latest weapons, like F-16s, not to mention all the economic aid we give them, they still question why we should be improving our relationship with India. I guess they don't quite understand the concept of 'cooperation'."

"No kidding," replied Rachel. "When the Congressional delegation visits in a few days they'll get an earful from the Prime Minister, and others, on Pakistan's views regarding maintaining balance in South Asia."

The main courses arrived at the table. As they ate, Alex was pleased with the flavors, but Rachel differed.

"This is marginal compared to eating in Beijing or Hong Kong," she said.

"Then again, I imagine Chicken Vindaloo isn't so good in Shanghai," Alex retorted.

"Good point. At least this has some flavor."

As they continued eating, Alex gently probed her for personal information.

"So. Are you an only child?"

"No, I have a sister, Ellie, and a brother, Joe. Ellie is younger than I am by two years and Joe is older by three years."

"What do they do?"

"Ellie's a lawyer in Los Angeles and single. Joe handles marketing for a company in San Francisco; he's married with two kids." Anticipating Alex's next question, she said, "Yes, they're both tall and athletic."

"What a mind reader you are. Do you know what I'm thinking now?" he asked with a sly smile on his face. Rachel laughed.

"I certainly do. I speak that language very well."

It was Alex's turn to laugh.

"What about you? Any siblings?" she asked, turning the spotlight on him.

"I have one brother, Sam. He's a year younger than me and works in project management for a defense contractor outside D.C.," Alex explained. "He's divorced with no kids."

"You said you moved around a lot while growing up," Rachel said. "That must have been tough when you were young." She had really meant it as a question, but said it more like a statement, then continued. "I pretty much lived in the same California neighborhood until I went to college."

"I wouldn't call my growing up years 'tough'," Alex clarified. "Maybe 'challenging'. Obviously, it often meant changing schools and making new friends. But it seemed natural to us at the time. My dad worked long hours, but he and my mom always tried to be there for Sam and me. She worked as well, just not as much as Dad. Sam and I learned to be very independent and resourceful. We would link up with kids who knew the local city, whether in Paris or Cairo. That's how we really learned French and Arabic, from other street kids."

"Sounds like you were lucky to turn out all right."

"That's what my shrink says. In another few years I'll finally be normal," Alex stated with a deadpan expression.

"Stop it," Rachel laughed grabbing his hand. "I just meant your upbringing was different from what most of us had."

"Maybe. But not much different than many Foreign Service or

military kids."

Their conversation was light and enjoyable as they discussed family life growing up, and how overseas assignments in the Foreign Service made it hard to stay abreast of family developments back in the States. The dinner was pleasant to the end. Leaving the hotel, they took a short walk outside, stopping to look at the night sky.

"I know a great place for a nightcap." He said, giving her a long lingering look as he touched her shoulder.

"Why do I feel I'm about to be dessert?

"God, I hope so. After all, this meal cost me all of fifty rupees."

"Oka, I'll tell you what, why don't I grant you fifty rupees worth of pleasure."

"Crap," Alex replied. "If I had known that, I would have picked a more expensive meal."

"Hmm, maybe I'll pick the place next time," Rachel chuckled.

They drove to Alex's house where he served vodkas on the rocks. Then moved to the window where they could look at a full moon peaking over the rooftops.

"Given the right company, even this post seems lovely," Rachel said looking into his face, emotions playing with her heart.

"Now, my dear, let me show you my 'art collection', Alex said, slipping a hand down her back, encircling her firm buttocks.

"Only if I can show you mine," she answered seductively.

They embraced passionately, finding excitement in the feel of their kisses and the mutual arousals both felt. Then, moving into Alex's bedroom, they began an unforgettable night of pleasure. Without trying, they surpassed the All-Pakistan record of sexual positions in a single night; however, only tied the alleged All-Indian record rumored to be set in 1934. They did surpass the record, set by Reginald Chalmers, a British District Officer of the Indian Civil Service in Meerut, who had an affair with his boss's wife, the charming, but sex-starved Caroline Goodbottom.

At least that was their agreed upon story.

CHAPTER 30

TUESDAY MORNING

Catching Up

Early Tuesday morning, Jim Riley began briefing everyone in the Regional Security Office about the previous day's developments. He needed to advise Nancy Williams, Susan Witt, and Gunny Rodriquez on the latest threat information, as well as measures SMG was taking to enhance security around the Embassy compound perimeter.

Riley's office was reasonably spacious with a sofa, upholstered in a neutral tan cotton weave, and two matching stuffed chairs. On one wall hung a huge map of Islamabad, with blue and red colored pins to indicate locations of Mission offices and residences. Another wall had a map of Pakistan, showing all major cities and moderate-sized towns. Naturally, Riley also had on display a few of his State Department awards. Nearby was a bookcase filled with State Department manuals, including Diplomatic Security guidelines on physical security, investigations, and firearms.

Resting his arms on his desk, Riley turned to Gunny Rodriquez. "Let's hold another intruder or riot drill tonight. Gunny, I'd like you to create the scenario this time. Make it especially challenging. Perhaps have one or two Marines injured or out of action in your scenario. I want everyone to think outside the box."

"Okay, Boss, will all the RSOs be here this evening?"

"I think so, unless you guys have other commitments," Riley said, turning to look at Alex and Susan.

This was Riley's 'polite' way of saying they were expected to be there, and to acknowledge that they would be. Everyone nodded.

"Great! In a moment I need to use the secure phone and call the consulates about this vague threat from tribesmen along the border with Afghanistan," Riley said. "Then I'll send a short telegram to Washington about my meeting with Stanton and Colonel Malik. Also, I need to check with Bill to see how he wants to handle the briefing of the Ambassador and DCM on this threat.

"Nancy, would you please draft a security notice to all Mission personnel that we'll conduct handheld radio checks with Post One tomorrow? I want to ensure that everyone's radio is operational and employees know how to use them."

She answered in the affirmative, as he looked around the room.

"Gunny, I know you'll do this anyway, but I want to ensure that the Post One Marine notes who calls in, and who doesn't call, when we test radio procedures. Nancy, follow up with anyone who fails to call in. I know we do this monthly, but we might as well exercise the radio net in view of this new threat information."

"The DCM is chairing a countdown meeting this morning in advance of the CODEL visit,"

"We're set on the security side," Alex spoke up. "The GSO told me the hotel and motor pool are locked on. Susan and I will go to the meeting. Jim, it's at ten o'clock if you want to go."

"No, you handle it, Alex. I'll be making those phone calls and sending the telegram to Washington. I guess that's about it. Anything else?"

"I need to talk to you and Alex about an investigation," Susan said.

As Gunny and Nancy left Riley's office, Susan began describing the visa fraud case she had just begun working on. They all agreed the allegation against Hussein Khan and Sheila Winters was worth pursuing. They also agreed it didn't fit the normal pattern of such fraud.

"Here's what I'd like to do," Riley said. "With the CODEL arriving in two days, we really don't have time to do justice to this case now. I suggest you call the Pakistani couple back and tell them you can meet with them next week. Either Alex or I will accompany you to the meeting as backup, but you will be in the lead on this case."

"Thanks," Susan replied. "I'll make the call today."

CHAPTER 31

TUESDAY MORNING

Countdown Meeting

Opening the 10 am countdown meeting, DCM Ellen Hunt made an announcement to the employees.

"The CODEL will arrive early Thursday morning at 0600, after their usual two-day rest stop in London. Let's go around the room and update everyone on your area's preparations for this visit."

Rachel, wearing a beige pants suit with pale blue blouse, was seated to Ellen's left. Ellen nodded at her to begin. Squirming slightly in her seat, her thoughts were on the previous evening's antics in bed with Alex. As she focused on all the faces looking her way, she hoped no one had noticed. Glancing briefly at Alex, she smiled, then began.

"All the invited journalists have confirmed they'll attend the press conference and lunch at the Ambassador's residence on Friday. There should also be a few journalists attending the Prime Minister's meeting at his office, but the number and actual selection is up to the Prime Minister. I suspect we'll see some of the same faces at both events. We've also arranged for the overnight stateside news reports to be delivered to the CODEL in their hotel rooms. My staff will distribute the material."

"Excellent, Rachel," Ellen said. Then, looking at General Services Officer John Sherrill, she questioned: "Did we get the entire floor at the Holiday Inn?"

"Yes, we did," responded John taking off his reading glasses and putting down a note pad. Balding at forty-eight-years old, the former U.S. Navy Seabee was enjoying a second career. "We have rooms for all Senators and their staff. Additionally, we'll set up the normal Control Room and Hospitality Suite on the same floor. The Control Room will be manned by Embassy staff from 0600 in the morning until 2200 at night. They will be provided updated schedule information, extra newspapers provided by Rachel, office supplies, and other administrative support items. Naturally, the Hospitality Suite will also be manned by Embassy volunteers. Soft drinks and snacks will be on sale, while the Senators' free booze from their military flight will be transferred in. Clean, filtered embassy bottled water will also be placed in every room."

Alex listened to John's presentation, variations of which he had heard, perhaps, ten times before. A professional who paid great attention to detail, John had served as a former Navy Chief Petty Officer, and Alex expected no less of him. His comment about providing clean, filtered bottled water was no joke. Even staying at an upscale western hotel like the Holiday Inn, it was essential visitors used only filtered bottled water, even to brush their teeth. If they didn't, they'd become best buddies with the hotel toilet.

"We also have rooms on the floor for the two DS Special Agents accompanying the CODEL, and we have a 'down room' for the police bodyguards," Sherrill finished.

"Great, I'm impressed you managed to get the entire floor on such relatively short notice," the DCM stated.

"I'll let Alex describe how that happened," Sherrill chuckled.

The DCM raised an eyebrow at Alex who took the cue.

"The hotel was very accommodating in moving people

around," Alex explained, "But there was one long-term USAID contractor who told the hotel he'd no intention of moving off the floor selected for the CODEL. The hotel then offered him a better room on a different floor, but he still said 'No Deal'. Apparently, he's been living there for two months and has another six months to go on his USAID contract."

"You gotta to be kidding! How did you resolve it?" queried the DCM.

"I called the USAID Administrative Officer, who told him he would move, or his contract would be terminated. He took the deal."

Ellen Hunt laughed. "So, we are all set at the hotel. What about the airport and movements around the city, Alex?"

"Yeah, the hotel is all set. We've got the uniformed policemen we wanted to be posted on the Senators' floor. Special Branch will be present in the hotel lobby every morning from six until around midnight. Of course, there are always uniformed cops in front of the hotel twenty-four hours a day. Colonel Mushtaq, with Airport Security, reconfirmed we'll have planeside access for the Embassy motorcade."

"What about bodyguards?" Hunt asked.

Alex took a deep breath before answering. Suddenly, he felt a twinge of pain in his ribs on the right side. He grimaced, but was unaware he had done so.

"Alex. Are you all right?" the DCM asked.

"Oh, I'm fine. I think I pulled something in the gym."

Rachel placed a hand over her mouth and smiled, remembering the previous evening. Got him, she thought. Yes, I'm still the Queen of Wrestling and reigning World Champion, she said to herself. A juvenile thought, she knew, but once a competitive jock, always one, she reasoned.

"The cops will provide a follow car with four armed policemen," Alex continued. "Susan will ride with the two accompanying Diplomatic Security Agents in the Embassy lead car. Since the Ambassador will be using his armored limo for all movements with CODEL, we'll have his bodyguard riding with him."

"What vehicles are we using for the CODEL?" asked the DCM.

"We're renting a luxury mid-sized bus," John Sherrill answered. "We'll also have a couple Embassy sedans available for separate staff movements or in the likely event that spouses want to go shopping."

"What about protection for the spouses if they go off on their own?" the DCM asked.

"The cops wouldn't give us anyone for spouses," Alex replied. "So, I've arranged for the SMG Mobile Reaction Team to be nearby when they go to the markets. It's not ideal, but it's the best we can do."

Winston Hargrove IV and Marisol Lopez then took turns describing issues that would be discussed at the Prime Minister's Office and at the Parliament. They also mentioned a possible meeting with the Army Chief of Staff in Rawalpindi. Colonel Walker elaborated on how this might happen, but no one could account for who would be attending at this point.

Just when everyone thought the meeting was about to end, JC Colon proposed an idea.

"As a means of mentoring our young junior officers in the Embassy, why don't we let them be site advance officers at each location the CODEL will visit?"

Alex and John Sherrill frowned, shaking their heads. They knew the DCM was a strong advocate of mentoring newly minted Foreign Service Officers, but allowing untested and inexperienced junior officers to participate at the last moment as site advance officers would be courting disaster. In the past, only someone from RSO, GSO, or an experienced officer from the political or economic sections handled site advances. These people were known to their Pakistani counterparts, so the system worked well. But unknown new officers would not work at all.

"Hmmm, maybe," the DCM said cautiously.

"It will be a great opportunity for them to feel part of the team and learn the ropes," countered JC. "I've drawn up a list of those who are available, if you'll agree." He slid the list directly over to Ellen.

Unbeknownst to everyone at the countdown meeting, JC had a long conversation the prior week with the Executive Director of the South Asia Bureau in Washington, D.C. In response to JC's pathetic complaints about not being among inside power players at the Embassy, the Executive Director had urged him to show leadership at every opportunity, telling him to demonstrate initiative and creativity. JC had reached a conclusion that he would start improving his image with this idea of mentoring junior officers. Obviously, timing wasn't his concern.

Ellen looked over the list. Somewhat unorthodox, yet, each officer listed was doing a fine job in his or her respective field. The list included two young AID Rural Affairs Officers, two brand new Consular Officers, a newly arrived junior Economics Officer, and a few others.

"Have you spoken to them about this?" Hunt asked.

"Yes, I have and their enthused with it. I hope you like the idea."

"JC, it's a little late to introduce first timers into a CODEL visit," stated Hunt. She wanted to scream and shake her head 'no'. But, now that JC had made the mistake of already talking to each officer on the list, she had to anticipate how they would feel if she rejected the notion.

"JC, let's do it this way," she said, trying for an end run. "Have each officer you've selected hook up with existing site officers who've already been designated to handle each location. You can pick which junior officer goes to which site so they can learn the ropes."

JC's face lit up. He was delighted with her response. Unfortunately, in his excitement, he misunderstood, and thought the DCM had authorized him to have his junior officer cadre replace, not assist, the previously designated site advance officers. He couldn't wait to tell his junior officers as much. He believed they would consider him the most visionary officer in Islamabad.

He was totally blind to the disaster that loomed ahead.

CHAPTER 32

TUESDAY MORNING

Pitching the CODEL

While the DCM was chairing the countdown meeting, Ambassador Pierce was in his office turning the last page of Colonel Bud Williams' thick report entitled, "U.S. Military Assistance Forecast for Pakistan in the Next Fiscal Year."

Colonel Williams and Colonel Walker, the Defense Attaché, both sat before him.

"This doesn't look very promising, Bud," Pierce frowned, looking at Williams.

"No, sir, it doesn't," Colonel Williams answered. "The Pentagon has cut one hundred million dollars out of next year's plan. Part of the cutback is a result of getting less money from Congress. But another part is based upon a decision by the White House to shift some financial resources to India. Of course, it's too soon to know specifically what programs we'll offer India, but whatever it is, Pakistan won't like it."

Williams had been in charge of the Military Assistance Group in Islamabad for over two years and had excellent contacts with Pakistan's military leadership. He knew how they would receive the information about cutbacks in assistance.

"Can we appeal these decisions?" Pierce asked.

"At this stage, you'd have to make a direct appeal to the Secretary of Defense, the Secretary of State, and The National Security Advisor regarding reprogramming of funds to India."

"That's just great," Pierce said. "I imagine my counterpart, Ambassador Gallagher in New Delhi, will weigh in with an opposing view. Since he's a personal friend of the President, the odds are already stacked against us."

"There is one other possibility," Williams said, "Can you convince our CODEL visitors that the overall foreign assistance budget needs to be restored to its previous level?"

"I agree with Bud," offered Colonel Walker, who had been invited to sit in on the meeting. Ambassador Pierce valued his input, even though military assistance was not his area of expertise.

"Okay, prepare a pitch to the CODEL," Pierce said "I'll lead the discussions with them, but I need both of you to discuss the importance of each program. Some of the senators may be disposed to our position. But others have been waiting to cut foreign assistance to Pakistan for years," he projected.

"It doesn't really matter whether they're Democrats or Republicans. Some don't like Pakistan because of human rights issues, and others don't like foreign assistance, in principle, unless vital national security interests are involved," he paused.

"Hopefully we can make a case everyone will find acceptable. But keep in mind, the CODEL represents just one committee in the Senate. We may not get very far, but we can try. Let's talk again on Wednesday afternoon about our pitch to the CODEL."

They discussed small details before Walker and Williams

left his office together.

Pierce leaned back in his chair to reflect: Most people thought an American Ambassador was a powerful figure. Worthington Pierce understood the reality as something less grand. Everyone had a boss, or certainly should have. In this case, Congress controlled the purse strings, and the White House determined overall strategy. His prior input, advocating caution on Washington's proposed policy tilt toward India, had been well-received, but in the end, the Administration chose to disregard his cautions and head in this new direction.

Pierce knew he was the U.S, Ambassador to Pakistan, not Pakistan's representative to the United States. So, he would be a loyal soldier and support the new U.S. policy in general. Nevertheless, he reasoned if he could convince Congress to re-establish the prior foreign assistance budget to Pakistan, in addition to supporting India, then all sides would be satisfied.

"I can't believe it's already noon," Pierce said to Joan in his reception area. "I think I'll walk over to the Residence for lunch."

"Yes, sir. But remember your wife is at a Women's Club luncheon, hosted by the Foreign Minister's wife."

"Thanks, I forgot, but I think I'll still eat at home. Would you please call the cook and tell him I'm on my way?"

"Will do, sir."

As Pierce walked through the Embassy lobby, he saw Alex and Rachel talking together. On impulse he stopped and said, "I'm on my way to lunch at the Residence. Would you both like to join me?"

"What a nice offer," Rachel replied. "Thank you, I'd love to join you."

"That makes two of us," Alex said. "Thank you very much."

Alex had been to the Ambassador's residence many times for official functions or social gatherings and always enjoyed the atmosphere there. Worthington Pierce was very pleasant toward his entire staff whether at home or at work. It was one reason so many officers were now volunteering for assignment to Pakistan. Reputation. It went a long way.

The three made small talk while walking one hundred yards to the Residence together. Entering the foyer, Rachel looked around appreciatively.

"When was the Residence built? It's looks very modern."

"I'm not exactly sure," Pierce replied. "It was completed in late 1979 or early 1980. I know it was under construction when mobs burned the Embassy in late '79, but they never touched the Residence." Pierce then turned to his Pakistani bearer, who appeared out of nowhere.

"Please let the cook know I have two guests for lunch," he said. "And would you mind bringing us three iced teas?" the bearer bowed slightly, disappearing into another room.

The Residence was ideal for entertaining large groups, but as a Regional Security Officer, Alex disliked the large expanse of glass windows on the ground floor that looked out over lush gardens and the swimming pool. Security risks were always on his mind. Of course, the State Department never built residences or embassies with security as a main concern. He sadly reasoned, perhaps if enough of them were attacked, the architects would finally get the message.

"Rachel, I believe this is your first time at the Residence," Ambassador Pierce said. She nodded in agreement. "Let me give you a tour. As you can see from the foyer, I've got an extremely large living room to the right." Six sofas, all covered in white upholstery, with numerous stuffed chairs in a variety of muted stripes were all well-placed around the interior.

"The living room wraps around the stairs, which leads to the second floor," Pierce continued. "Upstairs I have an office, the master bedroom and five guest bedrooms."

Walking behind the stairs, Pierce pointed to the huge rectangular dining room with an equally expansive table. Beyond it was a large kitchen. Continuing around to the other side of the stairs, Pierce pointed out handsome double wooden doors that led into his study.

Modern paintings hung on all walls. Not exactly Alex's taste, but every ambassador selected art for their official residence from among the State Department's cache of paintings through the Arts-in-Embassy Program. On-loan, all art in the program was from world class American artists, museums, or wealthy patrons. No doubt they were expensive. But then, why not, Alex thought, an ambassador is representing the United States of America. So, why shouldn't they represent the best?

"Looks like lunch is served," Pierce said, noting the bearer waiting for them. "I'll show you the gardens later."

As they seated themselves in the dining room, they were next to windows overlooking the gardens. It was relaxing as they enjoyed a well-seasoned lentil soup. The entrée was a goat's cheese-stuffed chicken breast and green beans from the Ambassador's garden. "So, Alex, are you enjoying Pakistan?"

"Yes, sir, you bet. It's still as exciting as when I first arrived. The amount and quality of work is wonderful, and the support we get from you and Ellen is greatly appreciated."

"Well, you guys have earned my support. In fact, Diplomatic Security in general has evolved into a strong, well-managed and professional operation. I've served in a lot of embassies, so I can tell you not every place I've served in the past had the quality of

RSOs like here in Islamabad." Alex slightly colored at the praise.

"I'll tell you what, since we're just here casually eating, why don't you both call me Worthington?"

Listening to the exchange with great interest, Rachel was delighted Alex was perceived by the Ambassador as a good officer. Although she hadn't been close to the RSOs in Hong Kong, Beijing, or Rome, so couldn't make direct comparisons, she had a feeling Alex, Jim, and Susan were truly good at their jobs.

"Rachel," said Ambassador Piece, "I guess you'll return to Washington in maybe two months."

"That's right, Sir, I mean Worthington."

"I don't suppose I can entice you to stay longer?"

"I'd love to work here. But a full-time replacement is already picked, and the Department's Press Spokesman wouldn't be happy at all if I didn't return. I couldn't do that to him without an extraordinary reason. He's been really supportive of me."

"Well, you can't blame me for trying to keep you here," Pierce laughed. "I know the Spokesman and he's a good man. Linking up with the right people in your career is as equally important as doing a great job. With our 'selection out' personnel system, a lot of good officers are forced to leave the Service because they don't get promoted in a timely fashion. So, knowing people who can get you the right assignments will give you that chance to shine in an Embassy or in a job that really matters."

"That's exactly what we were discussing at the DCM's house during the mentoring session for junior officers," Rachel replied.

"Alex, I believe you have just under a year to go here. Where would you like to be assigned next?"

"Well, I'm of two minds. I'd love to serve in Europe and soak in the culture, but I've learned from my tours in Tunis and here, that the

Middlo East is where the greater challenges are in security."

"You're right about that. Let me know when you find out what's available and where you want to serve. I'll see what I can do to help."

"I'd really appreciate that," replied Alex, pleased at the offer. Such support was invaluable.

Rachel smiled at Alex, *Oh my God, I may be dating a superstar.*

CHAPTER **33**

TUESDAY NOONTIME

First Demonstration News

Riley grabbed a grilled cheese sandwich at the cafeteria for lunch and brought it back to his desk. Just as he was about to take a bite, Nancy Williams, his secretary, appeared in the doorway. "You have Bill Stanton on the line."

"Okay, thanks," he said, putting down the sandwich and picking up the phone.

"Bill, what's up?"

"I have a report you need to see right away."

Jim knew not to ask the CIA Station Chief what it contained over a non-secure line. He simply said, "I'm on my way."

Taking the stairs one flight up to Stanton's office, he knocked on the outer office door. Stanton's secretary buzzed him in via her remote.

"Bill wanted to see me," he told her as he entered.

"Can you wait a minute?" she asked. "He's just taken a call from the British Embassy."

"Okay, I'll look at the reading file while I wait," Jim said, reaching for the top folder off a pile. Stanton had granted access to RSOs to see the Station's daily reading file, or part of it. Some items would always be withheld from those outside the CIA even if on the same Embassy team. But for classified information intended to be shared with the State Department in Washington, Stanton had authority to share it with Embassy RSOs, so he did. The information in the file helped provide the big picture in Pakistan, and the region. Occasionally, there was specific information the RSO needed to act upon in order to protect the Embassy or broader American community.

After five minutes, Stanton emerged from his office and invited Jim inside.

"Sorry about the wait, but that call will be of interest to you as well. We'll talk about it in a moment. I asked you to come up because our sources are saying a big demonstration is planned at the Embassy after Friday prayers, three days from now. We're hearing this from the mosques, the university, and now from the labor unions."

Riley didn't have to ask Stanton who his sources were because they were invariably reliable. Besides, Stanton wouldn't tell him in any event.

"How big is 'big'?"

"We can't be sure, but probably over a thousand people. That's just an estimate. We'll know more tomorrow."

"Does the Pakistani Government know about this?"

"Yeah, they do. So, you should be able to get more police support for Friday,"

"Are there any other details known to you at this time?" queried Jim

"No, that's it."

"Okay, thanks. Can I mention anything to the cops right now, or even say something to SMG?"

"I'd like you to wait until tomorrow. Obviously, some of my

information is coming from ISI, so I'd like to give them time to talk to the cops themselves."

"All right, but let's brief the Ambassador and DCM this afternoon," Jim said.

"Sure enough, Jim. Now, about that call I was on from the British Embassy. They've been asked by the Pakistani Ministry of the Interior about anti-terrorism training. My contact at the Brit Embassy, Geoffrey Ainsworth, knows that Diplomatic Security is already providing such training to the Pakistanis, so he'd like to coordinate with you rather than waste money on duplicative training."

"Smart idea. Want me to talk to him...and when?"

"I have a better idea," Stanton replied. "How about we go over there now?"

"Okay, I was just about to bite into my lunch, but since I won't be able to eat my grilled cheese, I'll go only if he gives us tea and crumpets with jam."

Stanton couldn't help but laugh. He liked Riley a lot. A serious and competent officer, yet he kept a sharp sense of humor.

"Your car or mine?" Stanton asked.

"Let's take mine," responded Jim slyly. "This way no one will think I'm a spook."

"Fine," said Stanton returning Jim's smile. "I need to tone down my image and slum it a little, so we'll take your car," he paused. "Oh, was that insulting?" They both laughed.

Driving a short distance, they arrived at the British Embassy within minutes. It was also known formally as the High Commission since Pakistan was a Commonwealth country.

Both men waited for Ainsworth to return from down the hall

before being shown to his office. He offered them a choice of seats.

Minimally furnished, his office walls were painted a neutral off-white color. Visitors' chairs were metal-framed with black leather seats. His desk was an industrial gray color much like those Jim had seen in British police stations. A brown blotter with frayed leather edges covered half his desk. Off to one side was an empty in-box, cleared of any secret papers in advance of their meeting, and a vintage-looking fountain pen resting nearby. In the corner of the room were two four-drawer safe cabinets. On the wall hung a few prints of traditional Middle East scenes, probably done by the famous Scottish artist David Roberts in the 1840s. Jim guessed these were Geoffrey Ainsworth's personal additions to this dreary enclosure.

"Please, call me Geoff," he said with a smile.

Riley guessed the ginger-haired Geoff was in his mid-forties and spent a lot of time outdoors, judging by his ruddy complexion. He looked reasonably fit, certainly his handshake was firm. Riley noticed Geoff wore a signet ring on his right pinky, but couldn't see if the ring had Geoff's initials on it, or some type of family crest.

"I understand from Bill you've actually lived in the U.K."

"Yeah, that's right," Jim responded. "In the Air Force, I served three years at RAF Lakenheath with the Office of Special Investigations. We did a lot of joint work with the Cambridgeshire Police Constabulary, as well as with the Metropolitan Police's Special Branch, and with MI-5."

"Excellent," Ainsworth said, adjusting the knot of his striped tie as he spoke.

He couldn't be sure, but Riley thought the stripes might represent some British Army regiment, perhaps indicating Ainsworth was a former officer. He knew Ainsworth was MI-6, the British equivalent to America's CIA, but since he hadn't offered this up, Riley decided not to ask. He also knew no other foreign country had an organization such as the State Department's Diplomatic Security Service, so most foreign embassies handled security and counterterrorism matters in their own unique way. This was the way the British did it.

"As Bill may have told you, the Ministry of Interior asked us for anti-terrorism training to augment what they're getting from you Yanks. If it's not a secret, can you tell me what you have been providing?"

Jim thought about demanding tea and crumpets before divulging anything, or maybe fish and chips with a pint of beer. Reflecting further, Jim thought, Perhaps this is not the time to joke.

"I can do better than that," he offered. "You see, our training isn't classified. Congress wanted the program to be open and transparent to their committees. We report our training to Congress annually. I picked up a copy of our annual report in my office just before coming over here. You can keep this one," Jim said, handing it to Geoff.

Ainsworth was amazed "And none of this is classified?" he asked. "I'm gobsmacked." Everything in British training was considered very sensitive.

Riley laughed at the Brit's use of gobsmacked, or "astonished" in American vernacular. "That's right," stated Jim "One reason is because we train only police. We don't train intelligence or military personnel, unless they're doing a job equivalent to civilian police in America."

Ainsworth quickly glanced over the document, entitled 'DS/ATA Program for Pakistan,' and reviewed the list of courses the Americans had already provided to the Pakistanis.

"Bloody hell, you've given them about twenty courses over the last three years. How are they doing?" Ainsworth said.

"Geoff, let me put it this way Some of them do all right, but the real issue is the selection process. Because our training is done in the States, our first problem is to screen out any senior officers only interested in getting an all-expense paid trip to America for a few weeks. Unless, that is, the course is actually designed for senior officers. I can't tell you how much time I've spent at the Ministry of Interior battling with them over their proposed candidates. Some they want to send shouldn't even be working here in Pakistan."

"I see," said Geoff rubbing his chin. "Well, all our training will be given here, so we'll at least avoid the mass stampede for visas to the UK."

"Who are you going to train?" Jim asked.

"We're not sure yet, or even whether we will agree to provide training at all."

The answer seemed reasonable on the surface, but Jim had worked with Brits long enough to know his new best friend Geoff might just not want to say.

"I see you've provided a single Airport Security Course a year ago, but haven't given any follow-up training since then," Geoff stated, still glancing at the report.

"Very clever of you to notice," said Jim. "Yes. Our view is that while the Pakistanis don't use much security technology at airports, their security screening is probably more thorough than ours in the States. Of course, the weak link is that their screening personnel can be easily bribed because of their low salaries."

"Hold on, Jim. Are you saying that American airport security is deficient?"

"Yes, I am. We've tried to get the FAA to train at a higher security standard in our DS/ATA Program than what ICAO requires. I think you know that ICAO is the International Civil Aviation Organization, and its security standards are bare minimum. Even though the FAA knows it, they just won't raise the bar. We've suggested they adopt Israeli screening procedures, but they constantly fall back and teach ICAO standards once they're in the classroom with our students. I'm afraid until we have a major aviation terrorist incident in America, the FAA just won't come on-board."

"Fascinating," said Ainsworth, taking notes.

Riley figured Bill and Geoff would coordinate their joint program details later, so he simply asked Geoff if he needed more information.

"No, thanks very much, Jim. You've been extremely helpful."

Jim rose from his seat, preparing to leave.

"If you need any details on who attended which course, just drop by our Embassy. We can discuss it over tea and crumpets."

Stanton laughed so hard he actually snorted a few times. Geoff laughed too, but Jim guessed he didn't have the foggiest idea what the laughter was about.

Chapter 34

TUESDAY AFTERNOON

Clueless JC Colon

Marisol Lopez was in her office reading the latest batch of incoming classified telegrams. She had been in the position as Deputy Political Counselor for the past year and was very comfortable with her duties at the Embassy. Now she stretched, rubbed her eyes, and decided on another a cup of coffee.

Walking to the common area next to her office, she reached for the communal coffee pot and reflected upon Hargrove's miraculous recovery from his weekend's ankle injury on the tennis courts. It had improved enough for him to play tennis again today, against a member of Pakistan's Parliament. He hadn't yet returned to the office from his morning game, but that was fine with Marisol. Hargrove was actually an impediment to accomplishing the Political Section's work. Clearly, he didn't know South Asia or the Middle East very well, nor had he made a decent effort to grasp nuances of the culture, since he didn't intend to serve here for long.

As she spooned coffee creamer into her hot beverage, she contemplated the probability of getting a job as a political counselor in a medium-sized embassy after Islamabad. She had the contacts in Washington, but it really depended more on the type of performance report she would receive from Hargrove. Just then, Ellen Hunt walked past, stopping when she saw Marisol in the coffee area."Hey, Marisol, do you have a minute to talk about our political reporting plan for the end of the fiscal year?"

"Sure," Marisol replied. She always enjoyed talking with Ellen.

"Okay. Let me get a cup of coffee; we can talk in my office."

Meanwhile, JC Colon was meeting with his hand-picked junior officers to discuss the upcoming CODEL visit. He was about to make the mistake of telling them something false, although he had convinced himself it was true.

"The DCM agreed that all of you can be Site Advance Officers for this CODEL visit," JC said. "I've written down your individual assignments."

He passed papers to each man and woman in the room. After a few moments of looking them over, one new consular officer, spoke up.

"What exactly are we expected to do? None of us have any idea. Is there a check sheet or some list of duties?"

JC had no idea if there was a check sheet or not. In his experience in Latin America, the local embassy employees took care of details and the Americans were mostly around to 'Meet and Greet'.

"I'll see if I can get a check sheet for you," JC responded, somewhat annoyed with these details. "I've noted on your list who the Embassy had initially assigned to each site. Talk to them about what they've done so far, then take over. You can call me with any questions."

The young Consular Officer spoke again. "I assume we should pick up radios from someone. Who has these radios?"

"Just use the radio you've been issued by the Embassy," answered JC.

"What about transportation to each site?" another officer

from USAID said.

"You'd better check with local employees in the motor pool to find out which car and driver you should use," declared JC, not at all certain.

Everyone in the room was ill-at-ease. A tension began building within the group along with a common feeling they lacked experience for these new tasks. No one wanted to blow this important meeting assignment in front of the Ambassador or visiting Senators. Surely JC wouldn't let them fall on their faces, nor embarrass the Embassy. He must know what he is doing, right?

After JC left, the group talked amongst themselves for ten minutes, then decided that in addition to speaking to the initial site advance officers, they should first talk to Jim Riley, John Sherrill in GSO, or Marisol Lopez. Dividing up their tasks, they went in search of advice.

Finding neither Jim nor Marisol available, the only person some junior officers encountered was John Sherrill. He was stunned when he heard that JC had told them they would be replacing the initial Site Advance Officers.

"That's not my understanding," John said to the junior officers. "I thought the DCM told JC you're to accompany the experienced officers to learn the ropes. But if the DCM has changed her mind, so be it."

After a pause, Sherrill added, "No, wait, this doesn't sound right. I'll speak with her and get this clarified."

With noticeable relief, the junior officers returned to their regular jobs to await word about further guidance. But a seed had been planted regarding their trust in JC Colon's ability to lead them. Their confidence in his ability to manage the Embassy had just taken a severe blow.

CHAPTER 35

TUESDAY MID-AFTERNOON

Emergency Action Committee

Ellen Hunt called an Emergency Action Committee meeting for mid-afternoon Tuesday based upon the briefing she'd received from Stanton and Riley on the serious nature of Friday's demonstration. Not wanting to be an alarmist, but needing to be fully aware, she alerted the Ambassador who decided to attend the meeting as well.

The EAC began with Bill's threat analysis from his sources.

"Well, for starters, we expect at least 1,000 demonstrators," he began, "And they won't all be happy. My sources say they're mood is going to be ugly because they're mad, really angry about the changes we're making in our relationship with India."

He continued for a while laying out every detail of which his sources had made him aware. Notes were being taken around the table. After some minutes, he asked for questions, gave answers he knew, then indicated to Ellen that his report was finished

"Thanks, Bill," Helen said, taking over the meeting again. "Now, we'll have a few things to decide. Jim, I assume you'll request a greater police presence around the Embassy."

"Absolutely," he replied.

"So, Worthington, next we'll need to focus on our plan to have the Senators hold a press conference at the Residence," Hunt continued.

"Right. That's certainly a concern" Pierce said. "We could move it to their hotel, but I rather like the informal setting at the Residence. That venue might be more calming on the journalists, whom, I'm assuming, will already be hyped over the issue of our new relations with India. Let's wait until Thursday night to finally decide if we need to make that change. A demonstration with one thousand protestors is larger than usual, but the police should be able to handle them. The protestors probably won't even be able to enter the Diplomatic Enclave, much less reach the front of the Embassy. Rachel, will waiting until Thursday night work for you in terms of contacting the press?"

"That won't be a problem," she responded. "Some of them will already be with us for the two morning press conferences at the Prime Minister and Foreign Service offices. But I'll see what I can do about spreading an 'either here or there' type concern about location so they'll at least be aware there could be a change."

"Good. Thanks, Rachel. Next for consideration," Ellen stated, "is whether we need to reduce the number of employees on the compound in advance of the demonstration. Jim, what do you think?"

All eyes in the room turned to listen to Jim's counsel. Alex and Susan, sitting in the back row, knew what Jim was going to say.

"I think we should do the prudent thing and send people home Friday morning before lunch time, around eleven or eleven-thirty. There's no point in putting them at risk simply for another few hours of work."

"Hold on," JC objected. "I don't agree. We're talking about losing at least half-a-day's work, if not longer for some. We shouldn't let people go home every time there's a possible demonstration. If that were the case, we'd never get anything done."

"There's a huge difference between 'possible' and 'probable', JC. Seriously, how much work is really going to be done on a Friday afternoon, especially if the demonstrators make a lot of noise?" Riley retorted.

"Well, can't you keep the demonstrators away from the Embassy by stopping them at the entrance to the Diplomatic Enclave?" JC asked.

"In theory, it's possible. But that's up to the police to handle the crowd," Riley stated. "We can't be sure how effective they'll be with a large crowd like this. Besides, we must plan on what we can control, not others."

Winston Hargrove IV entered the room at that moment and caught the tail end of this conversation having just returned from three invigorating sets of tennis.

"So sorry I'm late, but look, this doesn't seem to be that serious. In Europe, we have demonstrations all the time, and no one is sent home early. Perhaps we can make it a voluntary half-day off."

"I don't like the notion some employees can choose to stay while others can go home," the DCM countered. "I'd prefer we make a clear decision based upon facts and our best judgment."

"I agree with Ellen," said the Ambassador. "As I've said earlier: Let's wait until Thursday night to decide on both issues. First, whether to let people go home early, and secondly, whether to hold the Senators' press conference at my Residence.

"Alright. Perhaps, we'll know more about the size of the

demonstration by Thursday. In the meantime, ISI is looking for the organizer of the demonstration, a guy named Pandit Baba." Stanton said, looking directly at JC when he said it, with an irresistible urge to poke a little fun at him.

The Ambassador, Ellen, and Jim wanted to laugh, but barely showed even the hint of a smile. No one else in the room seemed to get the joke.

"Pandit Baba, who's that?" JC asked, staring at Stanton.

"That's the point, no one knows for sure," replied Bill with a straight face.

Pandit Baba was a fictional character in a Paul Scott series of novels known as the 'Raj Quartet,' in which Pandit Baba was the secret organizer of anti-British demonstrations. The novels were made into a British TV mini-series, set in 1940s India in the waning days of the British Raj.

Worthington Pierce watched the exchange and thought to himself, 'I can't believe Bill just said that.' Jim Riley looked at Bill and discreetly shook his head; finally, he couldn't resist a little smile.

"Okay, the meeting's adjourned," Ellen said. On the way out she whispered to Stanton, "You're naughty today." A minute later everyone within ear shot heard Ellen laughing as she walked down the hall.

CHAPTER 36

TUESDAY LATE AFTERNOON

Demonstration Preparations

As Tuesday drew to a close, Riley was feeling more concern. His anxiety level was beginning to climb about this impending demonstration. It was just a feeling he couldn't put a finger on. Still, he decided he needed one more meeting with his team.

"Nancy, would you please call everyone to have a quick meeting in about fifteen minutes in my office."

"Sure, Jim. Shall I call Bhatti and Gunny Rodriquez as well?"

"Yes," he replied. Since Bhatti was his local investigator, hired directly by the RSO to assist with police liaison, and maintained important police contacts year after year, Riley wanted to ensure that Bhatii remained in the loop, especially when Riley needed to call on police backup.

Once everyone was assembled, Riley quickly covered a few points.

"Bhatti, could you please call Inspector General Qasim and ask if we can meet tomorrow? Whatever time he has available will be fine with me. I'll need about fifteen to thirty minutes."

"Okay, Jim. What can I tell him you want to talk about?" Bhatti asked. "He'll ask me for sure."

"I believe we'll need more police protection on Friday.

I've heard there will be an anti-American demonstration at the Embassy and the numbers seem to be climbing. I'm getting a bad feeling and want us to be prepared."

"Yes, of course. But just so you know, only this afternoon Inspector Nasim from the Diplomatic Enclave Police Station rang me up to say he has instructions to add police around our compound," Bhatti replied. "I was going to tell you."

"Interesting," Riley. "Who gave him those instructions? I wonder if they've heard more about this demonstration than we know. Alex, I believe you've met IG Qasim several times. When was the last time?"

"A little over a month ago, when we were planning the July Fourth celebration," Alex responded.

He had met Qasim only a few times but found him hard to forget. Qasim stood over six feet tall, distinguished, yet rugged looking, with black hair tinged with a bit of grey. Clean shaven, he could easily be mistaken for a senior civilian official or diplomat. Clearly, an individual didn't rise to be the IG of Police in the Capitol unless he was very sharp and knew how to negotiate the minefield of Pakistan's politics.

"Okay. In that case, since you're already well-acquainted with Qasim, I think Susan should also meet him by coming along with Bhatti and me," Riley said, as he looked at Susan. "Does that work for you?"

"Absolutely," Susan enthusiastically replied.

"Good. You'll like Qasim. He's charming and bright. We should also thank him for giving us cops at the hotel for the CODEL, as well as the extra Special Branch bodyguards," Riley said.

"Okay, Bhatti. Go make your call to Qasim and let me know when we have an appointment."

"Yes, Jim," said Bhatti as he left the room.

Riley turned to the remaining group. "I find it interesting that some of the information about the demonstration was apparently given to Bill Stanton by ISI. Yet at the same time, everyone, including Bill, is worried about lack of cooperation by the Pakistanis. Don't forget Colonel Malik of ISI has also just given us some threat information about potential attacks on Western interests in either Islamabad or Peshawar."

"I suppose the Government of Pakistan is no different than any other government," Alex interjected. "There are always factions with competing agendas. So, when cooperation among those factions does happen, should we be surprised? Are we missing something?"

Riley nodded in agreement. "Well said, Alex. In the U.S. the FBI and CIA often fail to share important information. The White House views events through a political prism; they'll all play their cards close to the vest. Hell, even within the State Department the various bureaus sometimes withhold information from each other. I can't tell you how many times Diplomatic Security would have been blindsided by some incompetent element in State if we hadn't anticipated every scenario and had secret friends in other agencies as well as in Congress."

"Damn," said Gunny. "I never appreciated how simple life is in the Marine Corps." Everyone laughed.

"That's because everyone in the Corps has a unified commitment to accomplishing a particular mission," Riley clarified. "You might have different ideas on how to accomplish that mission, but once given a task, you guys get onboard."

"Unfortunately, in State, once a decision is made, that merely begins another round of in-fighting and back-stabbing. It isn't pretty, and it isn't loyal either," Alex added.

"Okay, enough politics," declared Riley. "Gunny, let's kick off tonight's drill at eight o'clock."

"Roger that, sir. I've decided to leave you out of the scenario, pretending you're traveling to Lahore. So, Mr. Boyd will be in charge. Since I'll be running the drill, I'll have Sgt. Washington in charge of the detachment. The drill will simulate having two armed intruders taking hostages in the Budget and Finance Office on the second floor."

"Why are the intruders doing that?" Riley asked.

"Because the embassy is refusing to pay them for some contract work, sir. I also rounded up two DEA agents to play the bad guys, and some others volunteered to play the local employees who will be taken hostage."

Riley, Alex, and Susan smiled in admiration for Gunny's ability to get role players whenever he created a drill.

"Okay, I guess that wraps up the meeting, unless anyone has something else to add," concluded Riley. "Keep your eyes and ears sharp. This thing could be bigger than we realize." No one said anything more, so the meeting ended.

Returning to his office, Alex called Rachel. When she answered, he felt a stir of happiness, and greeted her.

"Hi there, beautiful."

"Hi, yourself, Alex," her voice was soft and silky. "I'm just about to leave the office. Thought I'd swim at the Embassy for half an hour."

"Great, I'll join you, if you're going to swim nude," Alex kidded.

Rachel laughed. "Fat chance of that, big boy."

"Okay, I guess not. Actually, I have a drill at eight tonight. Before that, I thought I'd grab a sandwich next to the pool and watch the darts league. Why don't you stop by after your swim? There will be some Canadians and Brits there, as well as our Embassy crowd."

"Okay, I'll see ya there," Rachel said. She put down the phone, glad he had called.

CHAPTER 37

EARLY TUESDAY EVENING

Two Days Before CODEL Arrives

Alex was relaxing at the Embassy pool sitting at a table near the snack bar under the covered patio area. Before him was a hamburger and Coke. Next to him was John Sherrill from GSO. Across the table from them were two U.S. Embassy communicators, Bob Boudreaux and Carrie Sherman. The three of them were waiting for their darts match to begin.

Embassy communicators didn't have a high rank in the Foreign Service, yet they were an important cog in the Embassy wheel. They handled all the secure electronic messages sent to and from American embassies and consulates. They also administered an embassy or consulate radio program, ensuring employees had emergency communications from home. Alex served with Boudreaux in Buenos Aires, and he really liked him. He knew Boudreaux had a sharp technical understanding of his communications equipment and its capabilities, even though he loved to emphasize his Louisiana Cajun roots and pretend he was just a country bumpkin.

Watching as Boudreaux pulled out a small bottle of Tabasco hot sauce from his pocket, he counted about ten shakes Boudreaux plastered onto his plate of chicken and rice.

"You don't go anywhere without your Tabasco, do you, Bob?" Alex said, smiling.

"Absolutely not," Boudreaux replied. "If it wasn't for this hot sauce, I'd starve to death for lack of flavor. Plus, I reckon it kills all them local amoebas. Can't nothin stand up against Louisiana hot sauce."

John Sherrill chuckled. A Texan native, he was used to spicy food, yet he knew nobody could handle the heat like the Cajuns.

"What's this I heard about your uncle introducing the world to Tabasco sauce?" Sherrill asked.

"That's right," replied Boudreaux. "You see, fifteen to twenty years ago my uncle Louie from Lafayette, Louisiana, was a courier for the State Department. Wherever he went with his diplomatic pouches, he'd carry some small Tabasco bottles. He'd usually always leave one behind in each hotel he stayed in. Claims he eventually was the reason those hotels bought their own Tabasco. That's how it became popular all around the world."

Carrie Sherman, who was in her early forties and had been in the Foreign Service for twenty years, had heard this story many times. Working daily with Bob Boudreaux was a delight, since listening to him was like hearing Mark Twain spinning tales of adventure and intrigue.

"Bob, I'm going to miss your stories when I leave here next month," she said.

"Carrie, although I imagine my uncle Louie dropped off Tabasco in Ecuador many years ago," Bob smiled, "I better send you some regular shipments when you get to your next assignment, so you'll remember me."

"Ha, believe me, remembering you won't be a problem," she answered as everyone laughed.

While listening to their conversation, Alex saw Rachel at one end of the pool ready to begin her laps. She noticed him, and gave a small wave of her hand. He returned the wave. She was wearing a light blue bikini.

God, her body's amazing, Alex thought. Her abs are great, her weight is perfectly proportionate to her height, and her lean muscle definition is the sexist thing I've ever seen. And, she's smart and really good at her job.' Alex laughed. *Okay, maybe those last two qualities aren't as equally important as the others,* he thought in jest. She dove into the pool, and Alex knew he wouldn't see her for another thirty minutes.

Loud voices coming from the end of the patio indicated a darts match between the Brits and another American team had begun. Alex looked over and saw everyone in the group had a beer and was having a good time. Carrie, Bob, and John excused themselves from the table and joined their group about to begin a game at another area of the patio. They were joined by Sgt. Monroe from the Defense Attaché Office. Squaring off against them would be a team from the Canadian Embassy. In total, there were about ten teams in the darts league, although not every team played each night.

Alex watched the two matches, half bored while thinking of Rachel. He wasn't happy that she would only be assigned here for another two months before returning to Washington. Crap! he thought. She's incredible, but she'll be out of Islamabad in no time. He had never bonded so quickly with a woman before. Suddenly, he felt a hand on his shoulder. It was her. Alex looked at his watch and realized that 30 minutes had passed quickly.

She had changed into khaki shorts that showed off her long legs and had on a short-sleeve yellow t-shirt, highlighting shapely biceps. On her feet, she wore sandals.

"Can a girl get a drink around here?" she asked. Alex waved to the waiter who came over immediately. "I'll have a beer and a hamburger, please," Rachel told the waiter.

Turning to Alex, she noted he had a Coke in front of him. "You're not drinking tonight?"

"I'd love a beer in this heat, but since I have a drill with the Marines later, I thought it best to stick with Coke."

Rachel understood and agreed with a nod of her head.

"That was a good lunch at the Ambassador's house. He certainly seems like a nice guy."

"He is a nice guy, and great to work for," Alex replied. "It's too bad not all Ambassadors are like Worthington."

"Can he really help influence where you're assigned next?" Rachel asked.

"Depends. If it's an onward assignment in the Middle East, then perhaps, yes. But if it's out of the area, then I doubt it. In any event, Diplomatic Security has the final say in these matters, although it never hurts if the Ambassador talks with the Assistant Secretary of DS."

Sgt. Monroe walked by their table carrying a few beers back to the darts match.

"Hey, Monroe," Rachel said. "It's good to see you again."

Monroe nodded his head but kept walking without a comment. Alex grinned broadly and gave a low laugh. He looked into Rachel's gleaming green eyes.

"You really love intimidating people, don't you?" Alex said.

"What do you mean? It's been about a week since I choked out Monroe at the Marine House. I just wanted to show him he's still a friend."

Alex shook his head and smiled. "Rachel Smith," he said,

"you are a piece of work. But, I like it "

Rachel smiled, blew him an air kiss, and put her hand on his. "We might make a great team," said Rachel with a huge smile. "With your brawn and my brains who knows what might happen?"

"Actually," Alex replied with a sly grin, "I was thinking it could be my brains and your brawn."

"Hey," Rachel said as she punched him hard in the arm.

"Ouch! See what I mean," Alex said, pretending injury. "You are the brawn on this team." Actually, she packed a hell of a punch, but he wasn't going to admit to it.

They talked a while longer, then Alex looked at his watch. Time for the evening drill with the Marines.

"Kisses," he said to Rachel rising up from the table.

"Have fun," she answered him back.

CHAPTER **38**

WEDNESDAY MORNING

One Day Before the CODEL Visit

Wednesday mornings were busy for most Embassy staff. However, this particular weekday was busier than usual. The CODEL was arriving in less than twenty-four hours, plus a large anti-American demonstration was anticipated on Friday. Key sections in the Embassy were either busy confirming arrangements for the visit, or figuring how to avoid the demonstration. Such events should never be taken for granted in Pakistan.

"Hi, Jim," Alex said when Riley answered his home phone. "Sorry to call you during breakfast, but I had an idea. I should go to the airport and see Colonel Mushtaq to ensure he's received our access list for the CODEL's arrival."

"Sounds like a good idea. Try to get back by ten o'clock to cover the office. Bhatti called me last night and confirmed that Susan and I can see Inspector General Qasim at ten-thirty."

"No problem. I'll be at the airport from eight to nine and will return right after that."

"Okay, give my regards to Mushtaq."

Alex didn't really want to drive to the airport this morning, but experience had shown him to double-check everything in Pakistan, or inevitably something would go wrong. He dialed the airport security number direct to the Colonel's desk.

"Hello, Colonel Mushtaq, this is Alex Boyd," he said when Mushtaq answered. "I hope you're well. If you're available, I'd like to come see you in about thirty minutes."

"Alex, how are you? Yes, I'll be free then. We're almost done clearing the morning's international flights. I'll be too much delighted to see you."

The drive to the airport would take him some twenty minutes in morning traffic, unless he hit a goat crossing the road. Halfway there, Alex pulled into the right lane to pass a slow-moving truck, then saw a huge pile of rocks blocking his lane ahead.

"Shit!" Alex yelled as he slammed on the brakes and swerved his Jeep back into the lane behind the truck.

"God damn it!" Alex said emphatically as he regained his composure. Some asshole put a pile of rocks on the road when his car broke down, and didn't have the courtesy to remove them when his car was either fixed or towed away. Rocks piled on the road seemed to be the Pakistani equivalent of flares or reflective triangles. Naturally, at night the rocks couldn't be seen until someone ran into them. He couldn't count the times that had happened to Embassy personnel.

Twenty minutes later, Alex pulled into the airport parking lot and found a space in the section reserved for diplomats. Congested at this time of the morning, the airport was brimming with life. Families of arriving passengers filled the outside waiting area, not allowed inside the terminal unless they were a VIP. Small yellow dilapidated taxis with no air conditioning were lined up outside the terminal; drivers standing next to their vehicles, hawking for business. All fares were negotiable, and all rides were cramped and uncomfortable.

The terminal itself was an unattractive one-story gray cement building. For a departing passenger to get into the building, it was necessary to show an airline ticket, pass through a metal detector, then endure a pat-down search. Once inside, there were no concessions until passing the immigration control point and a second security screening area. When finally arriving at the passenger waiting area, passengers would find a small snack bar, rows of dirty plastic seats, and one small bathroom. The latter was thoroughly disgusting and smelled as bad as a French Quarter street the morning after Mardi Gras.

Well-off, or very lucky travelers, could enter the Business Class lounge of an airline, or go to the VIP lounge. A really important or well-connected individual could use the V-VIP lounge. Alex always laughed at the concept of a V-VIP lounge for Very, Very Important People. Today, however, Alex didn't need to enter the terminal at all.

As he walked toward the adjacent Airport Security Office, he pulled out his VIP pass issued by one of the Ministries in the Pakistan Government. The pass worked at all Pakistani airports and would got him beyond the guards outside Colonel Mushtaq's office. Additionally, it would allow him access to all VIP lounges, arrival and departure areas, even onto the tarmac. He prized his special pass dearly.

After being announced by the receptionist, Alex entered Mushtaq's office.

"Hello Alex," Mushtaq said, rising from his desk chair and coming around to embrace him. "Please have a seat. Would you like some tea?"

"Yes, thank you, I would."

Mushtaq waved to a private, who brought a tray of tea, biscuits, and milk for them. "How have you been, Alex?"

"I'm fine. How are you and your family?"

He had actually met Colonel Mushtaq's wife and two children about a year before when they came to the Embassy for an appointment with the Vice-Consul to pick up their tourist visas which Alex had arranged. At that time, Mushtaq had been scheduled to attend an Airport Security course in the States, arranged by the Diplomatic Security Service's Anti-terrorism Assistance Program. His wife and children decided to join him at the end of the course for a few days' vacation stateside. Mushtaq's wife was an attractive woman in her early thirties, and their two children were adorable. Mushtaq, himself, was a handsome man, standing just less than six feet tall, sporting a slim mustache and trim physique..

"My family is fine, thank you for asking, Alex."

After exchanging pleasantries for fifteen minutes, as was customary, Alex came to the point of his visit.

"Have you received our access list of personnel and vehicles for the arrival of the U.S. Senators tomorrow morning?"

The official list was not sent directly to the Airport Security Office but was first sent to the Foreign Ministry for approval. This was a formality all foreign embassies in Pakistan followed. In reality, each embassy also faxed an unofficial copy to the Airport Security Office, which they could later compare against the official one received from the Foreign Ministry.

"Yes, I have it here," said Mushtaq reaching for a brown file on his desk. "Everything seems in order."

"Do you mind if I take a look at the list?"

"Not at all," said Mushtaq.

Alex noted the Embassy GSO vehicles were listed, along with names of local drivers and Americans who would welcome the CODEL. Also noted on the access list were the Defense

Attaché Office personnel who would take care of the U.S. Air Force crew members. However, the name of the experienced Site Advance Officer was not on the list, although the name of a USAID junior officer did appear. Rather than discuss this with Colonel Mushtaq, Alex made a mental note to talk to Jim Riley when he returned to the Embassy.

"Okay, thank you," Alex said, returning the folder to Mushtaq. "It seems everything is fine, indeed. As always, it's been great to see you again. Let's try to have dinner soon." Mushtaq nodded agreement and walked Alex to the door. It was just 9:00 a.m.

Meanwhile, at the Embassy, Winston Hargrove and Rachel Smith were reviewing the schedule for the CODEL in Hargrove's Office.

"As you can see, Winston, the Senators will have to answer questions from the press at several locations," Rachel pointed out. "First, following the meeting at the Parliament with the Speaker and all party leaders, the Pakistanis have set aside only fifteen minutes for the press. We can expect a lot of posturing from the Pakistani parliamentarians during the Q and A."

"Gee, what a surprise," responded Winston haughtily.

"Then, following a meeting at the Foreign Ministry, there'll be a photo opportunity, along with microphones set up in the lobby of the Ministry to handle more press questions. That should also last about fifteen minutes," Rachel continued. "At the Prime Minister's office, the press will be invited into the session room for a meeting lasting thirty minutes. You and the Ambassador, or DCM, will be at every event and may have to address the press, if asked direct questions."

Winston nodded his head in acknowledgement.

"Of course, we'll have our own press conference at the Ambassador's residence. I expect the same journalists will be at each venue," Rachel concluded.

"So, tell me, why are we having so many press conferences?" Hargrove asked.

Rachel thought the answer was obvious, but if Hargrove didn't understand, she'd explain it. "These are really good opportunities for the Pakistanis to go on record demonstrating their concern over our India policy. Each politician wants to be photographed and quoted as showing objection to our policy shift."

"But we're not calling it a 'policy shift'!" Hargrove exclaimed.

"Of course not. But it's a shift, nevertheless, from the Pakistani point of view."

"Okay. I'll be ready to help any senator who looks like they're in trouble," Hargrove said.

Thank God, Rachel thought to herself sarcastically, Winston has it under control, so I can take the day off.

"Here's a list of journalists who'll attend the press conferences," she said, handing Hargrove a piece of paper.

He studied the list for a moment. "Are there no European journalists attending any events?"

"No."

"Why not?"

"Well, first, Winston, these are press events arranged by the Pakistani Government and they decide who to invite. Secondly, the European journalists are focused on news along the border and inside Afghanistan and aren't interested in this event. And thirdly, they don't really care about the U.S. Senators' visit."

This only reminded Hargrove of why he hated being in Pakistan. If this was Paris or Vienna, sophisticated journalists would be knocking on the Embassy's door for background material. There would be civilized lunches as well, where Hargrove could show off his intellectual prowess, language skills, and dine on foie gras or pork schnitzel smothered in a creamy mushroom sauce.

"So, I guess that wraps it up, unless you have other questions," Rachel said.

"No, that's it. I'll see you tomorrow morning at the airport," concluded Hargrove, as he pretended to look at some papers on his desk.

Rachel stared at him for a few seconds.

"You're welcome. Oh, and by the way, how's your ankle? I hope it's better," deliberately reminding him of his failed tennis efforts. She left his office, not waiting for a reply. She had a pleased smirk on her face as she walked down the hall.

CHAPTER 39

WEDNESDAY MORNING

Meeting with the Chief of Police

From the airport, Alex went directly to Jim Riley's office. He found Jim looking over stateside reports in preparation for the CODEL visit.

"I checked the airport access list as you asked, Jim. Strange thing: The original Site Advance Officer's name wasn't on the list, yet surprisingly the list did included the USAID Junior Officer's name along with a few other names. What do make of it?"

"This sounds like JC is doing his best to screw up well-laid plans," said Riley. "JC was the last person to sign off on the list before it went to the Foreign Ministry. I'll bet he deleted the name of the original officer and put in the USAID name instead."

"Of course," Alex said. "Now, I remember how he argued at the countdown meeting for a cadre of junior officers to replace our normal cast of experienced players. But the DCM didn't authorize him to replace the original group. She only said the junior officers could tag along and learn the ropes."

"I'll bet he did it anyway," replied Riley. Susan Witt came to the doorway in time to hear the last part of their conversation.

"Look, I'll be at the airport tomorrow morning with the motorcade," she said, "So, we don't really need a Site Advance Officer. I could just tell the USAID guy he's not needed."

"We could do that," said Riley. "But I'd like to correct the problem at the source, since I think JC might have done the same thing at all the other CODEL stops."

"Good point," Susan replied.

"Here's what we'll do," Riley decided, "I'll mention it to JC now. Then, you and I will go see Inspector General Qaism about Friday's demonstration. If JC hasn't corrected the situation by the time we get back, I'll speak to the DCM."

Riley walked down the hall to JC Colon's office. On the wooden door was a large sign with gold letters that said, Counselor for Management. He entered and saw JC's back as he was bending over his briefcase set on a credenza behind his desk.

"Hey, JC, do you have a minute?"

"Just barely," he replied. "I have a management staff meeting shortly."

"I only need a minute of your time," Riley stated. "We just saw the access list for the arrival of the CODEL at the airport tomorrow. There seems to be some confusion as to who the Site Advance Officer is. Do you know anything about it?"

"Confusion? There's no confusion as far as I know. We replaced the Embassy Maintenance Officer with a young USAID officer."

"Really?" Riley replied. "Did the DCM authorize changing our routine group of people?"

"She sure did. So, I've substituted replacements at all sites; the Parliament, the Foreign Ministry, and the Prime Minister's Office." JC was obviously proud of his accomplishment and believed he was now part of the team.

"Well, JC, I believe you've got it wrong," Jim said. JC stopped all movement. "I understood that Ellen agreed to have your group tag along with the experienced officers to learn the ropes. They were most definitely not to be the point of contact at each site."

"No", retorted JC swinging around to face Jim, his face flushed with anger. "You've got it wrong." Jim's eyes opened wide at the upset look in the other man's eyes. Then, he collected himself and responded quietly.

"Look, I don't have time to debate this with you, I'm on my way to a meeting, myself. I want you to double-check this with the DCM."

"Yes, I'll do that," JC said. In truth, this had him rattled and he was becoming a little less confident in his position.

Susan Witt sat in the passenger seat of Riley's silver colored Toyota sedan as they drove to the Inspector General's office. Looking over the cream-colored leather upholstery and brown faux wood paneling, she thought, His car is really nice.

"This is certainly more comfortable than my old Chevy Blazer," said Susan, adjusting the seatbelt over her left shoulder.

Riley laughed. "Before I came here, I wanted to reward myself with a comfortable car to handle the bad Pakistani roads. So, I ordered this directly from Japan with right-hand drive for driving on the 'British' side of the road." She acknowledged his comment, then changed the subject.

"So, what did JC say about the Site Advance Officer at the airport?"

"He admitted making the change, as I suspected, and at every location to boot. But he doesn't really think he's got it wrong. While our security arrangements won't be affected, I just hate to see the Embassy look stupid if his junior officer replacements can't gain access, don't know where to go, or what to do when they get there! It's great for them to get experience, but not at the expense of an important visit. They shouldn't be expected to carry a full load without being coached by someone experienced. It'll make us look bad in everyone's eyes. I'll speak to the DCM later today."

Susan thought for a moment about Jim's concern for the big picture, as well as the Embassy's reputation. His concern impressed her.

"What are we going to ask from IG Qasim?" she asked, breaking the silence.

"If we're really going to face a thousand demonstrators on Friday, we better have as many cops as they can spare. I don't have an exact number in mind, so I'll let him tell me what he plans to do."

They drove west on the main thoroughfare called Khyaban–E–Quaid–E–Azam. Susan looked out the window at the surrounding area. There were many half-finished gray concrete office buildings, mostly two or three stories high with the usual rebar sticking out of the roofs. They continued passing small shopping areas with cheap jewelry stores, clothing shops, and furniture merchants. They passed people walking on the road or on the dirt shoulder. There were no sidewalks anywhere in Islamabad. Some shopping areas had paved parking lots, others had only packed dirt lots. Numerous signs were posted about future development, announcing new hotels or office complexes soon to be built. Considering Islamabad was an artificial city, created only thirty years ago, much like Brasilia in South America had been, she understood why the city's infrastructure was a work in progress.

"I know you've been to one or two local police stations, so this won't look much different, but it is bigger," Riley said to Susan as they finally pulled up to the Headquarters of the Islamabad Police.

The four-story building had numerous large antennas on the roof. Most of the windows were open, indicating a lack of air conditioning. However, the IG's own office had two window air conditioning units in place. Susan saw policemen at the entrance, armed with bolt action Lee-Enfield rifles. Presumably, she thought, these were in .303 caliber. She wasn't sure about their magazine capacity but figured they could hold ten rounds. Great in their day, these rifles were a staple of the British Army for several decades until the post-WWII period.

The policemen looked sharp in their pressed khaki uniforms with wide colorful belts that indicated unit affiliation. They wore turbans with a colorful, starched cloth fan-like object protruding from the tops.

Each man stood at attention as Susan and Riley entered the building. No doubt they had been expected, not to mention Riley's car had Diplomatic license plate numbers. She assumed the function of the both cops was to react to an attack rather than simply screen visitors.

"Mr. Riley and Miss Witt to see IG Qasim," Riley said to the receptionist. Riley straightened his blue striped tie and adjusted his white shirt sleeves under his blue blazer, while he waited for a response.

"Yes, Mr. Riley, you are expected. One moment, please," the charming female receptionist replied.

Within a few moments, a police constable escorted Riley and Witt up the stairs to Qasim's second floor office. The Inspector General's suite had an outer area with two metal desks. Assistant Inspectors were seated at each desk, sorting through a huge numbers of files. Across the room was a three-seat leather sofa and two leather chairs. The room was painted cream and the floors were black and white tile. Since Qasim's office door was open, the constable motioned for Riley and Witt to enter.

Rising from his chair to greet them, Qasim enthusiastically shook first Riley's, then Susan's hand, saying to her, "I understand you are new to Pakistan. I hope you are happy here in my country."

"I'm really enjoying it. Your city is lovely, and I look forward to seeing as much of the countryside as I can."

Qasim, beamed with pride as he directed them to the seating area where the RSO Local Investigator, Mohamned Bhatti, was already seated. Susan knew Bhatti had driven to the meeting separately, which also gave him a chance to stay behind afterwards and schmooze with old police friends. Networking was always essential in their business.

Scanning Qasim's large office, Susan noted that he had two, three-seat brown leather sofas and four leather chairs. At the end of the room was a wooden conference table surrounded by eight chairs. Qasim's own desk, made from dark wood, perhaps mahogany, had inlaid leather on the top, and was enormous. The walls were covered with maps of Islamabad, lines on the map dividing the city into districts. The floor was tile, but covered with several colorful Pakistani tribal carpets, each about six by eight feet.

As soon as they were seated, two constables brought in the requisite trays of tea and cookies. Susan didn't really like tea; she preferred strong, black coffee, but understood what was expected in the culture. She forced herself to sip at least some of her tea. Riley did most of the talking.

What she had heard about Qasim seemed right on the mark. He was diplomatic, sounded intelligent, and appeared distinguished. His English was perfect, with a British inflection. He was wearing his police khaki uniform, which was immaculately pressed. He had several service pins or bars on his shirt but she couldn't place the awards. Glancing at the credenza behind Qasim's desk, she saw plaques apparently given to him by various police departments from around the world, and smiled when she recognized the Diplomatic Security plaque with the DS badge in the center

"Susan," Qasim said, "I understand you are a bomb disposal expert."

"Yes," she responded. Her attention snapped back into focus as him addressed her. "That was my specialty when I was a Captain in the U.S. Army."

"I've also heard you served in Saudi Arabia and Kuwait."

"I did," she said, "Although it was during and immediately after the Gulf War, so I was kept pretty busy and didn't get to see much of either country."

"I, myself, have visited Riyadh twice to consult with the Royal Family," Qasim said. "You may know we have thousands of Pakistani workers in The Kingdom. Sometimes, they get into trouble, and the Saudi's are always looking for ideas on how to head off these problems. Did you get to see Riyadh at all?"

"No, I'm afraid I only saw the desert and the border areas with Kuwait. Maybe in the future I'll have a chance."

"Jim, perhaps you can lend us Susan from time to time to help instruct our young police officers on how to handle improvised explosive devices," Qasim asked. "We seem to find more of them every month."

"That would be a very good idea," Riley replied. "Let me know in advance and we can set up some training."

"I'd be delighted to help in any way I can," Susan said, pleased at the appreciation. They continued the tea and cookies and small talk until an appropriate amount of time had passed.

"Now, about this demonstration on Friday," Qasim said. "We have also heard it may grow to be about one thousand people. At least, that is their plan. So far, no one is talking about violence, only peaceful protesting. Naturally, there are many groups involved in the protest with different agendas. So, we can never be sure of any specific protestor's intentions. I will send an extra one hundred armed officers to the Embassy. Of course, we will have reserve units available should the demonstration grow larger."

"Thank you, Qasim," Riley said. "As you know, we have a big compound with a long perimeter wall. Do you think one-hundred officers can secure such a large area? Would you also block the entrance to the Diplomatic Enclave, so the demonstrators can be held nearly a mile away from us?"

"If we think they will be violent, we can do this," stated Qasim. "But the problem is that many other embassies require access to the Diplomatic Enclave as well. They complain loudly to the Foreign Ministry whenever they cannot get through. Moreover, if the crowd is stopped at the entrance to the Diplomatic Enclave, they will be demonstrating in front of the Japanese and French Embassies located there, so we'll get more complaints from them."

"I understand," replied Riley. "We don't want to intentionally irritate the Japanese."

Qasim hesitated, then smiled at Riley's intended dig at the French by omission.

"Okay, I know your concern, so let's see what we can do on that day. By the way, how is Alex doing? He's a nice chap and has been very helpful."

"Alex is fine. He loves being in Pakistan. I'll send him your regards."

Everyone rose from the couches, shook hands, and prepared to leave."Thank you for your hospitality, I especially enjoyed the tea," Susan lied.

CHAPTER 40

WEDNESDAY MORNING

Last Minute Instructions

Colonel Malik told his boss he needed Wednesday morning off to go to the dentist. This was a lie. He was meeting his frontier tribesmen for their final plans before Friday's planned demonstration at the American Embassy.

Pulling his entire twenty-man team together increased risk of detection by either the CIA or those in ISI who would oppose his plan. But Malik needed to be absolutely sure he had total coordination for this important operation.

His wife's car, a beige Nissan, was safer to take than the silver Toyota he had used to meet Hussein Khan in Murree. It wasn't impossible to trace this vehicle, but why make it easy in the event someone was watching his movements. He drove through the congested roads of Rawalpindi toward Islamabad. The streets were filled with fast-moving motorcycles, an occasional broken-down truck, and buses spewing noxious and visible clouds of gases and fumes from their tailpipes. Every year the traffic worsened and air pollution thickened, choking the city more than the prior year.

Malik was dressed in a white shalwar kameez and brown sandals. He glanced at his round stainless steel watch realizing if the traffic didn't clear up, he would arrive late. This was not really a problem, however, because the meeting was his to control.

Horns were blowing everywhere on the street as drivers tried to improve their chances of getting ahead. Each time a bus accelerated away from the curb huge clouds of smoke enveloped the vehicle behind it.

Slowly, Malik began to make progress. He looked at the endless rows of small shops around him. Dilapidated buildings, one story brick or stucco structures with corrugated metal roofs that had rusted with age; occasionally a two or three story building appeared. Most had their double doors wide open to catch a rare breeze. Every shop had whirling overhead fans. The businesses were a mixture of brass shops, tire repair places, food markets, even the odd antique merchant. Finally, after several long blocks, the traffic opened and Malik, shifting gears, sped away.

The safe house in Islamabad that Malik had chosen for today's meeting was actually used by one of his five-man teams. Two stories high, it was like every other house in the area and surrounded by a high gray concrete wall with a solid metal gate at the end of the driveway. Since he was late, he knew the long driveway would be crowded with vehicles from the other teams, so he parked fifty meters down the street and walked to the house.

All twenty of his men were in the living room when Malik entered. As a sign of respect, they stood to acknowledge his arrival. He shook everyone's hand, embracing some, and engaging in small talk; then he motioned for them all to sit.

"I have already asked much of you on past occasions. This Friday, I will ask even more," Malik said in his crisp military command voice.

"On this day, you will have a chance to make a big difference in how Pakistan will be treated by the Americans in the future. Many bad things will be said of you as a result of your actions.

Even the Army will condemn you. But know in your hearts that such condemnation will be said without conviction. Those who make it back to the Frontier need to know we will protect you and your families. For those who may not survive, know your families will be taken care of, and you will be honored as a hero of Pakistan, a martyr in the struggle against India and America."

Malik looked at the strong faces around the room; men committed to serve. *Not a man here will flinch from doing his duty,* he proudly thought. *These men fought against the Soviet Army in the rugged mountains of Afghanistan. They braved death from Soviet helicopters and bombers. Now, they will deal with a much softer target.* Malik believed success was certain.

"Let us review the entire plan," he said. "Ask any questions, if you are unsure of your tasks." Malik and the men spent the next hour going over every detail.

When he was satisfied that all understood their mission, he ended the meeting with a prayer, then wished them good luck.

Driving back to his house in Rawalpindi, he changed into his uniform, and calmly went to work. No one could suspect the raging storm beneath his calm exterior.

CHAPTER **41**

WEDNESDAY LATE MORNING

Mistaken Instructions

True to his word, on Wednesday morning, John Sherrill, General Services Officer, spoke to DCM Hunt about JC Colon's instructions replacing the experienced Site Advanced Officers with untried junior officers.

"I confirmed with all of the young officers they were told by JC to handle each site for the CODEL visit on their own," John said to an astonished Hunt. "As you can imagine, none seemed comfortable with the prospect, although they all wanted to help out,"

She shook her head and wondered if JC had been born an idiot, or simply had never been trained at his prior embassies.

I'm really tired of babysitting him, Ellen thought. *I'm tired of using precious time to constantly override his poor management of the Embassy. I've counseled him on several occasions, but it never seems to have a positive impact on changing his actions.* Outwardly, she smiled at her visitor.

"Okay John. Thanks for bringing this to my attention. Since JC is your boss, I'll protect you and just say the matter was raised by one of the original Site Advance Officers. Then I'll call the original group and tell them they're still tasked with their assignments for the visit, and all junior officers are there to tag along and get experience. I'll also ask JC to personally explain the situation to the junior officers; maybe that will deflate his ego some."

"Sorry to bring this to your attention, Ellen, but I didn't have a choice."

"You did the right thing, John."

Sherrill left the office and Ellen sat at her desk for a moment. *Hell, and damn it. Just glad we caught that disaster in time.*

"Janet," she called her secretary in the next room, "Get messages to all Site Advance Officers to keep their assigned duties for the CODEL visit. Tell them they're still in charge and the junior officers are there to learn." She also told Janet to have JC report to her office ASAP for a discussion on CODEL visit assignments.

Around mid-day, Riley returned from his meeting with Qasim. He called Ellen Hunt's office and asked her secretary if he could see Ellen.

"Jim, if it's about the Site Advance Officers, I don't think it'll be necessary."

"It is. What's up?"

"John Sherrill spoke to Ellen this morning and told her. She has JC in her office now. Well, you know how mild-mannered Ellen is with everyone, but from the decibel level coming through the walls, I can tell you she's giving JC an attitude adjustment."

"Okay Janet. Thanks. But what I think JC really needs is a brain transplant." Jim said, hearing Janet laugh before hanging up.

As a veteran of the Foreign Service, Janet never understood the logic behind the State Department's Central Personnel Office having senior officers, such as JC, with no experience in particular geographic regions, being stationed at embassies around the world. Surely, ability, effectiveness, and willingness to serve should outweigh vague notions of fairness in the assignment process.

Oh well, she reflected, it wouldn't matter much longer. Unless Ellen Hunt was selected to be an Ambassador somewhere and wanted to bring her along, she was planning on retiring to sunny South Florida at the end of her assignment. Today's events just made her more committed to retiring as soon as possible.

CHAPTER 42

WEDNESDAY EVENING

Night Before the CODEL Visit

It was nearly 7:30 pm. Alex and Rachel were both finishing paperwork in their respective offices. Because she had to be at the airport very early the next morning to meet the CODEL, they agreed on having a quick meal together that evening. Dinner at the American Embassy Club seemed like the easiest thing to do.

"All set for the press conferences with the CODEL?" asked Alex as they were seated at the Club restaurant.

"As best as I can be. I've even met most of the journalists personally or spoken to them on the phone."

"What about the Senators' staff members, do you know any of them?"

"I've met three of the guys when I worked in Washington. They're a pretty conceited bunch, not to mention horny as hell and apparently not getting enough sex," she said with disgust.

"Did they try to hit on you?"

"You bet."

"Can you blame them?" Alex said with a smile.

Rachel grinned, then turned serious. "Look, business is business. If I'm briefing them on some aspect of foreign policy, I don't expect them to gawk at my legs."

"Ah, the curse of being a 'Foreign Policy Goddess'," Alex replied. He assumed he was pressing the envelope of Rachel's tolerance for mixing business and pleasure, but it worked.

"Okay" she smiled. "You can get away with saying that because I know you take what I do seriously."

"Indeed, I do. Of course, not everyone can multi-task like I can."

Rachel looked quizzically at Alex, her head tilted sideways, unsure of his meaning.

"I can not only absorb and appreciate everything you say about US-China relations," he explained, "But I can gawk at your legs at the same time."

"Men!" Rachel said in mock exasperation, but with a smile on her face.

The waiter arrived with menus. The special of the day was steak in a pepper sauce with French fries. Then, there was the usual offerings of pizza or pasta, hamburgers, grilled chicken, club sandwich, with an assortment of vegetables. Alex opted for the pepper steak, Rachel selected grilled chicken.

"So, Alex, I guess I won't be seeing much of you for the next day or two."

"Probably not. Susan will take care of the CODEL's security. "I 'baby-sat' the last CODEL, so it's her turn."

"Just as well," Rachel said, "I'll be pretty busy." She didn't need his presence to be a distraction while she should be focusing her attention on the CODEL visit, but internally, she realized his attraction was becoming a serious thing for her.

"I know you'll be beat after Thursday and Friday, but give me a call if you want to get together," Alex said as he reached out and held her hand.

She liked the feel of his skin on hers and responded by squeezing his hand tightly and smiling.

"Maybe Friday night. Let's see how things go with the visit."

Dinner was enjoyable, as much for the company as for the fact that the 'good' chef must have been on duty. Everything tasted great.

Walking Rachel to her apartment, he kept the mood light. "Good luck with your stuff."

Then, before leaving, he took her face in his hands and slowly and passionately kissed her good night.

CHAPTER 43

THURSDAY MORNING

Motorcade and Airport Passes

At 4:00 a.m. Thursday morning, cars for the official motorcade were lined up in the Embassy parking lot. It was well lit, so getting the vehicles in order wasn't difficult to do for GSO John Sherrill; it was generally the same as he had done for many previous CODEL visits. Even though the U.S. Air Force plane carrying the CODEL was not officially due until 6:00 a.m., one could never take a chance on not being at the airport on time, should the plane arrive early. As pre-arranged, a police escort would meet the motorcade on the airport tarmac.

Susan Witt was already enroute with an embassy driver. She would check with airport authorities, and radio Sherrill with a status report on the CODEL's arrival time. Once the CODEL was firmly on ground, she'd find the two Diplomatic Security Special Agents on board who would ride with her to the hotel. Everyone else would trail behind in the official motorcade.

Back at the Embassy compound, all cars were ready to depart. The Ambassador's black Cadillac sedan was at the head of the motorcade, although he would not be present. This vehicle was for Ellen Hunt to accompany the Chairman of the Senate Foreign Relations Committee and his wife, to the hotel. Next in line was a large bus with a 44-seat capacity that the Embassy had rented for the rest of the CODEL, their wives, and staff. Winston Hargrove would ride with this group and handle any political questions that arose. Rachel Smith would also be on the bus to talk with the committee staffer responsible for press events. John Sherrill would be with them to address any logistical questions.

Following behind the bus would be the baggage truck, overseen by an Embassy officer from Sherrill's section, plus local Embassy warehouse staff who would unload the CODEL's luggage from the aircraft and take everything to the hotel. A final car in the outbound motorcade held an Embassy Consular Officer and driver. The Consular Officer would take all of the CODEL's passports, have them stamped by Pakistani Immigration after the CODEL had departed the airport, and return them to all members of the CODEL later at the hotel.

A separate group from the Defense Attaché Office would handle all arrangements for the Air Force pilots and crew.

John Sherrill reached into his jacket and pulled out a pack of cigarettes and grey Zippo lighter. Igniting the unfiltered end of his first for the day, he sucked smoke deeply into his lungs. Although the lighter only cost ten bucks from some post exchange, or PX in military slang, it was one of John's treasures because it had the Navy Seabee insignia on it.

Taking another drag, he thought awhile. Though he was glad to help ensure every VIP visit went smoothly as part of his job, he shook his head in disgust at the waste of U.S. taxpayers' money associated with most congressional trips overseas.

"John, what are you thinking about? Is there a problem?" asked Ellen Hunt when she saw him deep in thought.

"Oh, I was dwelling on all the overtime money we spend for these visits."

"Well, at least this CODEL is going to actually talk to

Pakistani leadership, so they'll honestly be working," Ellen said. "We may even get some benefit from this group."

"I know some CODELS are useful," John replied, accepting the inevitable. "But I also know each trip is a fortune in fuel costs for the U.S. Air Force and its manpower. Plus, I can't tell you how many carpets and pieces of brass my section has packed for CODELS in the past. Shopping seems more important than working to most of these D.C. types."

Ellen couldn't disagree. She had seen it at every embassy where she'd been assigned. Few members of Congress had a real understanding of foreign issues. Perhaps they were too busy sightseeing to grasp details of their assignments; perhaps the congressional staff was too biased to brief them properly, or, no doubt, some members were just too dense.

"As a junior officer in London at the beginning of my career, we had a CODEL visit almost every week," Ellen stated. "They were usually passing through on their way to Africa, the Middle East, or wherever. Leaving Washington on Friday night so as not to miss any votes in Congress, they'd arrive in London on Saturday morning. To 'justify' their stopover, each CODEL would ask to see the Prime Minister or some other official. Naturally, the Brits would never agree to meetings on weekends for rank and file senators and congressmen. All British Parliamentarians return to their districts on weekends to see constituents and weren't even in London," she stared out into the distance, remembering.

"Members of the CODEL knew this full well. So, with no meetings scheduled, they would shop at Harrods, see a play, have dinner at an expensive restaurant, and generally waste our time. As usual, this involved four or five embassy officers spending their weekend setting up the hotel control room, meeting and greeting them at the airport, overseeing their transportation, arranging for their per diem to be paid to them in cash, etc. All at the U.S.

taxpayer's expense, as you know. Then, the CODELS wouldn't leave until Sunday night or even Monday morning. Naturally, they never flew a commercial airline, only U.S. Air Force VIP planes."

Ellen and John looked at each other, bonding for a moment at their mutual distaste of how some people take advantage of their positions.

"By the way, John, I assume we have everyone's clearances back from the Foreign Office for tarmac access in the motorcade, right?" She meant for the lower level workers from GSO.

"Oh, yeah, Ellen. Everything's in order. Besides, you'll recall, some of us have permanent individual airport passes as well, just in case the larger group has a problem. But we're set in any event." Hunt nodded in satisfaction.

Sherrill briefly turned away from Ellen Hunt, smiling. What she didn't know was that six months earlier, he and Alex had pulled off a major coup.

At that time, the Pakistani Government had sent out renewals for individual airport passes to every embassy in Islamabad. When the new passes arrived at Sherrill's office, he was horrified to find they had restricted full access at all airports for everyone except Ambassadors or DCMs. It was the government's way of trying to control the total number of foreign embassy staff with full access to all the country's airports. Others, such as himself and the RSOs, only had access to the VIP lounge and the arrivals/departures areas. Such limitations were relatively useless for CODEL visits or for other VIP visits such as Secretary of State. When he showed the new passes to Alex, an idea struck them.

The original passes issued by the Pakistani Foreign Office were crude. Each had a photo of the pass-holder, his or her name, and a grid off to one side of the pass listing airports and access levels. The grid had X's marking the level of access, such as tarmac, VIP lounge, etc. The pass was laminated to prevent tampering.

Alex suggested they could probably find matching colored-paper at a stationary store in town. All they had to do was put the new paper on top of the old grid, carefully draw the lines of the grid, and use a pen that matched the original ink to mark X's granting full access at all airports. Alex suggested John Sherrill's shop could laminate the newly altered passes over the existing lamination.

John loved the idea. Alex found matching paper easily enough, and John's people did the detailed work. When all was said and done, about ten embassy staffers were magically allowed full access nationwide, as had previously been the case.

One twist, however: John intentionally didn't upgrade JC Colon's airport pass and left it with its limited access. Ironically, JC subsequently accused John of never requesting full access for him in the first place. Hiding a smile, John truthfully denied this and suggested that, perhaps, the Foreign Office probably didn't think JC was important enough to warrant full access.

As far as the Ambassador and DCM were concerned, they were happy with their passes and could see that other officers, who needed full access, had it. End of discussion. Over the next six months Alex successfully used his modified pass at all airports in Islamabad, Karachi, Lahore, Peshawar, and Quetta. His access was never challenged, and he made valuable security contacts at each of those airports.

Coming back to the moment, John looked at his watch.

"Well, time to roll." Everyone started their motors, and the motorcade departed for the twenty-minute trip to the airport just as the sun peeked over the horizon.

CHAPTER 44

THURSDAY MORNING

The CODEL Arrives

Susan arrived at the airport early and was drinking tea with Colonel Mushtaq in his office.

"I'll call the Control Tower to check on the flight's arrival," Mushtaq said. Susan nodded. Mushtaq was on the phone only briefly, and after a few pleasantries, had his answer.

"They report the aircraft is on time and will arrive as scheduled at six am."

"Great, that's good to know." She radioed John Sherrill who was enroute to the airport in the motorcade. "Hi, John. It looks like the plane's on time."

Everything seemed to be going as planned, except she hadn't seen the USAID Site Advance Officer yet. JC had insisted the officer should be at the airport, even though Susan told him she would handle the arrival. 'Oh well,' she thought, 'so be it.'

Fifteen minutes, and a second cup of tea later, Susan heard her radio squawk, "Eagle Three, Eagle Three, this is Seabee One", Sherrill said, using Susan's call sign. "We are ten minutes out from your location."

"Seabee One, Seabee One, Eagle Three, I copy. Meet you as arranged."

Susan excused herself, walked out of Mushtaq's office

to her waiting car and told the driver to pull around to the VIP Gate entrance where they would wait for the motorcade. Upon arrival, she led the line of vehicles inside the secure tarmac area, ensuring each one was correctly lined up. Now, they simply had to wait for the aircraft's arrival.

"John, I'm going back to Mushtaq's office to monitor the plane's arrival status," Susan said to Sherrill. He knew she would rejoin the motorcade when the plane touched down.

Mushtaq offered her more tea, which she accepted, although she still preferred black coffee. Wearing her Sig-Sauer 9mm pistol in a shoulder holster under her left arm, she felt on her right side for the holster rig which held extra magazines. On her right hip, her Embassy radio was secured by her belt. Since this CODEL visit would not be the same as working a protective detail for the Secretary of State, she dispensed with the concealed microphone wires and earpiece that were so necessary to communicate every movement with the other Agents when on the Secretary's Detail.

Today, she had worn a dark blue pants suit to conceal all this gear. Like many DS Special Agents, she bought a jacket one size bigger than normal to comfortably cover the added bulk of the necessary equipment.

At least it's still cool outside, she thought. Susan knew later in the day, when the temperature rose to over 100 degrees, she'd be sweating.

This time, she spent considerable time talking with Colonel Mushtaq about his experience visiting the United States, before his phone rang. He answered and was told the CODEL aircraft was ten minutes from landing. Susan radioed Sherrill with the latest information. Everyone else on the team were monitoring Susan's transmission via their own radios. As per protocol, the motorcade would not actually move until the aircraft came to a complete stop and cut its engines.

"Wheels Down," Susan radioed Sherrill.

She thanked Mushtaq for his hospitality and walked out to the motorcade. Everyone was in their vehicle and ready to move. However, she also noted Defense Attaché Office personnel were there, and guessed Sgt. Monroe had been in the control tower, communicating with the pilot. Susan entered her lead vehicle to wait. Within minutes the big long-haul aircraft came into view. On the side of the plane, written in large letters, was "United States of America". A large American flag was painted on the tail. No matter how many times she saw that, it always choked her up a little and made her proud of her country.

After a near perfect landing, the heavy bird taxied onto a runway toward the terminal and was directed into one of the few parking spots before shutting down its engines. Pakistani authorities drove a small open truck with mobile stairs up to its side so passengers could deplane. Islamabad, unlike most modern airports, was considerably smaller and had no jetways for aircraft. A second mobile platform needed to be brought alongside the plane to the baggage compartment.

The motorcade, meanwhile, slowly edged up to the side of the plane, and the Embassy arrival group exited their vehicles to greet the CODEL. As Deputy Chief of Mission and official greeter, Ellen Hunt and Hargrove shook hands with each of the senators, their wives, and all staff members. Susan found the two Diplomatic Security agents without a problem. She had worked with them both before on the Secretary of State's Protective Detail and thought highly of them. After ten minutes of exchanging pleasantries and directing the CODEL visitors to their correct vehicles, the motorcade finally departed, heading back into Islamabad toward the hotel. At this moment, no one could know this quiet arrival would be the best memory of the entire trip.

Passing in front of the airport terminal, Susan saw the USAID junior officer standing at the terminal entrance, gaping at the motorcade as it passed by. Susan felt sorry for him. It was obvious he had no idea what he should have been doing.

"Look at that poor guy," Susan said to the two DS Agents. "He works for USAID, and the Management Counselor, JC Colon, told him to come to the airport for the CODEL's arrival, even though I told Colon I was handling the advance. Well, we can't stop the motorcade. He should have called me on the radio, but I suppose no one briefed him. I wonder if the DCM saw him standing there."

"I don't get it," said one of the DS agents. "Why was that guy in front of the terminal at all? You had the entire motorcade at planeside as usual."

"Hard to explain," Susan responded. "I heard Colon has never been involved in any of the VIP visits here. Then, at the last minute, he wanted a bunch of newbies to handle each site. To top that, he didn't coordinate anything."

Ellen Hunt didn't see the USAID Officer watching the motorcade leave the area, being too busy talking with the senators, but John Sherrill saw him. He also felt sorry for the guy, but was secretly pleased to realize JC would, again, be recognized as a totally incompetent management counselor. He chuckled at the thought.

CHAPTER 45

THURSDAY MORNING

The Senators are Briefed

The driver of the lead police car could see slow-moving oxcarts ahead in the early morning light, and changed lanes in time to keep the motorcade moving at a good clip.

As always, smoke rose from chimneys of nearby brick factories, filling the air with low-level haze. The police car had flashing lights on, which seemed to have no bearing on traffic. No other drivers moved over to let the motorcade pass. So, the lead car handled the matter by weaving from one lane to the next giving the appearance of a large serpent moving forward.

Waiting at the hotel was John Sherrill's deputy, Keith Robinson, the assistant general services officer. His job was to set up the Embassy Control Room on the Senators' floor, and that's where he had been since 5:00 am. After the motorcade arrived at the hotel, Susan Witt and one of the DS agents led the first group up the elevators. The second DS Special agent went with the next group. Susan directed the CODEL to the Embassy Control room.

"Good morning, Senators," Keith greeted them. "We've pre-registered you into the hotel, so if you look on the adjoining table, you'll find labeled packets with your room key, Islamabad information, and Embassy contact lists. You'll find coffee and pastries in the Hospitality Suite after you settle into your rooms."

Susan watched the operation, now familiar to her, as each

visitor entered the Control Room. From her experience traveling with the Secretary of State, she knew all this preparation was routinely done worldwide by State Department officers. Since Congress controlled the purse strings, the care and feeding of these Congressional potentates by the State Department was as important as doing their substantive work.

Ellen Hunt chatted with the Chairman of the Committee. Not unexpectedly, he said, "I think we'll rest up until eleven o'clock. I won't be at breakfast."

"Okay, we'll pick you up then, in time to take everyone to the Embassy for a briefing. Ambassador Pierce will meet you there. The spouses are welcome to attend the briefing, although we'll have transportation for them if they want to do something else."

"Thanks, Ellen," said the Chairman. "I imagine they'll want to go shopping."

"All right, Senator. As you can see from the itinerary, the Ambassador is hosting a luncheon for the group. Your first appointment is at 3:00 p.m. this afternoon at the Parliament with the Speaker and other senior Parliamentarians. Details of each event are in the packets."

Susan took the two DS special agents into the corridor for a quiet little chat.

"As you've seen, there are two Pakistani police officers with rifles posted in front of the elevators on this floor. They'll stop anyone they don't think belongs here. We have two more Special Branch officers in plain clothes in the lobby. Mostly likely, they'll be carrying .38 caliber revolvers. We don't have any known threats against the CODEL. So, I recommend you get some sleep, if you can. I'll be back here at 10:30 a.m. to organize the CODEL leaving for the Embassy at 11:00 a.m."

"Okay, thanks for your support, Susan," said one of the agents. "I could really use the sleep."

Since Susan had everything well in hand, Alex Boyd and Jim Riley were working at the Embassy. They each had radios turned to Susan's frequency. Jim was writing his monthly RSO status report for Washington, one of about thirty annual reports cabled to headquarters as demanded from the field. That didn't include investigations or other ad hoc terrorism reports.

It was Alex's turn to give the 'new arrival' briefing to the employees. He was in the conference room with about fifteen of them from different parts of the Mission. His briefing was expected to last about two hours and end just in time to clear the room before the CODEL arrived from the Holiday Inn.

By close to 11:15 a.m. fifteen of the senators had arrived and were seated in the Embassy's conference room. The Ambassador took his seat at the end of the conference table, flanked on either side by Ellen Hunt and Bill Stanton.

Pierce was wearing a dark gray chalk-stripe suit with white shirt and blue tie. Ellen wore a navy dress with matching high heels. She had added a gold Egyptian pendant with her name written in hieroglyphics at the last minute. It was a favorite piece of jewelry she had purchased in Cairo. Stanton was wearing his best blazer from J.C. Penny and a wrinkled striped tie of unknown origin, clearly not spending much time worrying about the fashion police. Next to Stanton sat Winston Hargrove, attired in the latest haute couture from Paris.

Senators and senior staff were clustered around the middle of the table; lesser senior staff members sat in a row of chairs against the wall. Colonel Williams of the Military Assistance Group sat at the other end of the table, flanked by Rachel Smith and Colonel Walker from the Defense Attaché Office. The main subject of the briefing would be the Pakistani reaction to America's proposed increased assistance to India and decreased aid program for Pakistan. Ambassador Pierce opened the meeting.

"Senators, the reaction of the Pakistani Government to our proposal in assisting India has been severe, to say the least. If projected aid to India were only economic assistance, then the Pakistanis would probably be less concerned. But since the White House has mentioned the possibility of military aid, albeit unspecified, the Pakistanis want us to understand very clearly such an outcome would seriously harm our relationship." Ambassador Pierce removed his glasses and pretended to clean them off, creating a pause to let his message sink in with the assembled group.

"We have been allies of Pakistan since its creation in the late 1940s. Along with China, we've been Pakistan's largest provider of military assistance, thanks in large part to Congress' bipartisan support. During the early Cold War, Pakistan allowed us to fly U-2 planes from Peshawar over the Soviet Union. Later, we joined them in supporting and arming the mujahedeen against the Soviets. Naturally, there have been times when, due to their internal politics, we have withheld our military and economic assistance.

"Clearly for Pakistan, India is their mortal enemy. They have fought three wars against India, and Kashmir remains a potential flashpoint in their relationship. This is what you'll hear when you visit the Prime Minister, the Foreign Minister, and the Parliament. They simply can not understand why – as they see it - we would turn our back on them, our long-term ally, and give military assistance to their enemy, not to mention we will be making actual cuts in our military aid to Pakistan."

Senator Desmond, official chairman of the group, spoke in his New England accent.

"We appreciate your perspective on this matter,

Worthington. I might add, we won't be surprised by what the Pakistanis tell us during our visit. Their embassy in Washington has been very busy lobbying us." All senators and staff nodded their heads in agreement. "I know this Embassy believes it's looking out for America's best interests, but it won't come as a shock to hear that others in Congress, and in the Administration, believe our long-term interests would be better served by balancing our relationships in South Asia."

Rachel listened with great concern. She didn't personally care about the outcome of the issue; rather, she was focused on how it would be handled in the press. She judged that Senator Desmond was implying the switch away from the present level of aid to Pakistan toward a more balanced aid to India was a done deal in Washington. What remained, therefore, was trying to emphasize continued positive aspects of the relationship with Pakistan, or perhaps offering something to them not yet on the table.

"Let me continue, if I may?" asked Senator Desmond with a certain mock politeness. "America not only has a vested interest in supporting a long-term democracy like India, but we also need to send a signal to Pakistan that their efforts in developing a nuclear arsenal are not acceptable."

"That's exactly what Pakistan says about India," interrupted Bill Stanton.

"We know they do," replied Senator Desmond. "But I think we have some degree of confidence that India's nukes will only be used in defense against either a Chinese or Pakistani attack. Can we say the same thing about a future Pakistani nuclear arsenal? The newspapers don't call it 'The Islamic Bomb' for nothing."

"I think the questions are not whether Pakistan develops a nuclear arsenal," Ambassador Pierce said, jumping into the discussion with an appeal to the opposite side of the argument.

"They will. But what type of government will control those nukes, and secondly, what will their relationship with the United States be in the future? We have a better chance of keeping those nukes out of the hands of terrorists by staying close to Pakistan. I believe this looming estrangement increases the likelihood of them acquiring such devices?"

"You have a good point," declared Senator Desmond.

"I believe the less conventional military capability Pakistan has, the more motivated they'll become to acquire a large nuclear arsenal," said Pierce. "I know we like to reward our friends and punish those who don't always agree with us, but sometimes we have to accept the realities of the world. Perhaps giving some military assistance to India is inevitable, but do we have to directly cut conventional military aid to Pakistan at the same time?"

"Ah, now we're talking about overall spending, but I take your point," replied Senator Desmond.

"Here's what I propose," continued Ambassador Pierce. "I'd like Bill Stanton to give you a briefing on what's happening in Afghanistan, and what Pakistan is doing to support specific undesirable elements there. Then, I'd like Colonel Williams to talk about the specific cuts Congress has proposed in military assistance to Pakistan. By examining both matters in some detail, maybe we can see a way to influence Pakistan against supporting radical groups across the border."

"Sounds like a good idea," said Senator Desmond. "But I have to say, Worthington, many believe Pakistan is just playing us like a fool. They take our money and equipment, then do exactly what they want, regardless of our interests."

"That's one perspective, I'll admit, Senator," Pierce said. "But we should never lose sight of the fact that every country has internal factions, all battling for the upper hand. We just want to make sure our political actions don't inadvertently reinforce the hostile Pakistani faction against us."

Senator Desmond nodded his head in agreement.

"Bill, if you could please start your briefing," said Ambassador Pierce.

Stanton rose, walking over to a large map his staff had hung on the wall shortly before the CODEL arrived.

"Senators, as you can see, this map covers both Afghanistan and Pakistan. The areas in light blue are controlled by Amad Shah Massoud's Northern Alliance in Afghanistan, the light green in the south by the Taliban, led by Mohammed Omar. Other colors represent control by Gulbuddin Hekmatyer, and smaller groups. I won't go into detail about the history of the Afghan war, rather, let's focus on more recent events."

"As recently as 1992, when the Communist Afghan Government of Mohammad Najibullah fell, the various groups fighting against him crafted an agreement called the Peshawar Accord," explained Stanton. "However, rival militia groups failed to abide by the accord, and civil war erupted in Afghanistan. After severe fighting and widespread destruction, the Northern Alliance forces gained control, with President Rabbani now running the government and with Ahmad Shah Massoud as the Minister of Defense.

"Nothing, however, is ever stable in Afghanistan," he continued. "Then Gulbuddin Hekmatyer fell out of favor with Pakistan, because he failed to take control of the Afghan government. He had received a huge amount of Pakistani support in both the fight against the Soviets, as well as during the subsequent Afghan civil war. Hekmatyer is a dangerous demagogue and religious fundamentalist. It's worth mentioning that Massoud, known as the 'Lion of the Panjshir Valley', received very little support from the CIA, in large part because our aid was channeled through Pakistan's ISI and Massoud, an ethnic Tajik, was not supported by ISI." Bill Stanton continued, "Now replacing Hekmatyer, as the flavor of the month in the eyes of ISI, is the recently emerging Mohammed Omar, often called Mullah Omar and leader in the map's light green area. He is an ignorant peasant from the Kandahar region, who seldom travels outside of Kandahar. He's an extreme religious fanatic, an ethnic Pashtun, and missing one eye, although very little else is known about him. I believe this nut-job needs to be stopped, or one day we may live to regret his existence.

"By comparison, Massoud is both a devout Muslim and well-educated. He was an engineering student when the Soviets invaded Afghanistan. He also speaks between five to seven languages."

Senator Desmond interrupted, "So, Pakistan's ISI has always sided with the most fundamentalist elements in what used to be called the mujahedeon. Are these fundamentalists all anti-American?"

"I think it's fairer to say they're anti-Western," Stanton replied. "They don't tolerate diversity; they don't want modernization unless it furthers their cause; and they have an extreme view of religious teachings. But let's continue. Pakistan, like any country, has different domestic factions. I'm sure you've heard this before. In the case of the Taliban, however, they seem to be united in granting them support, because the Taliban can potentially stand up to any influence from India."

"India?" asked Senator Desmond, somewhat confused. "Yes, India," Stanton replied. "India would like nothing more than to have a friendly government established in Afghanistan. What used to be called 'The Great Game' during the British colonial period, when the Brits and Russians were vying for influence in the larger region, is now continued by Pakistan and India. Pakistan wants an ultraconservative Islamic government in Afghanistan, and India wants a moderate Islamic government there. On top of this, there are probably some religious fundamentalists within ISI who would want a Taliban controlled Afghanistan, regardless of India's presence."

"Worthington," Senator Desmond said as he turned to Ambassador Pierce. "You mentioned earlier how this would tie in with a change of military assistance to both Pakistan and India."

"Yes, I did. Basically, we want to reinforce the mainline factions in the Pakistani government who could tone down ISI's support for the Taliban and other fundamentalist groups in Afghanistan. But, we must use a carrot to entice them to see things our way. Hitting them with a stick by cutting their aid will only strengthen their hand to support ISI, who can then say it is America who is deserting them. I think now is a good time for Colonel Bud Williams to explain how these cuts to Pakistan's military will damage our position. Even if we can't, or shouldn't change our new initiative toward India, perhaps you will at least find a way to maintain the current programs with Pakistan."

Colonel Williams spoke next for some twenty minutes, using handouts as references for each program. He addressed aircraft and parts sales, naval vessel transfers, armor and infantry equipment upgrades, and a host of information sharing and training programs. The senatorial staff, more than the Senators themselves, asked detailed questions.

"I want to thank all of you for your clarification of the issues," Senator Desmond said at the end of Colonel Williams' presentation. "I think we all see your perspective now. I can't guarantee we can restore the cuts to Pakistan's programs, because we have to deal with the Senate Armed Services and Appropriations Committees. Not to mention, the House committees will have their own views. But let's see what we can do. The question is how can we handle this during our meetings here and what do we say to the press."

"Rachel, could you comment on the press?" Ambassador Pierce asked.

Rachel had been taking notes during the entire meeting. She put down her Italian Aurora fountain pen, straightened the sleeves of her fuchsia Giorgio Armani jacket, and spoke for ten minutes, outlining a strategy to be used at each of the press conferences.

"As you can see," she said in conclusion, "I believe you'll need to demonstrate a positive understanding of Pakistan's concerns if you want them to accept our policy direction. It's probably best to hold out some hope of restoring at least some of the cuts, while at the same time demonstrating the reality of needing to deal with other committees and the House."

"I might add," Ambassador Pierce said, "When we meet with the Prime Minister and the Foreign Minister, we should be explicit in linking our aid to reining in ISI's support for the Taliban. They won't like us interfering in their decision-making, but we have as much at stake as they do in this matter."

Judging by the heads nodding around the table, everyone seemed to be in agreement and to understand the issues.

"Gentlemen, ladies, shall we go to my residence for lunch?" Ambassador Pierce led the way out of the room. It remained to be seen if the briefing had really been a success.

CHAPTER **46**

THURSDAY AFTERNOON

DS Special Agents

While the CODEL was being briefed, Susan Witt had taken the two visiting Diplomatic Service special agents to the Regional Security Office for coffee.

"Jim," Susan said, "I'd like you to meet Walt Lennon and Charley Matthews. Guys, this is Jim Riley, our Senior RSO." Turning to the open door, Susan said, "This is Alex Boyd, Jim's Deputy."

'Good to meet you guys," said Alex, entering and firmly shaking their hands. He'd been serving overseas when these two men had joined DS and hadn't met them stateside. "Is this your first time in Pakistan?"

"First time for both of us," replied Walt.

"I guess you'll be in town until Sunday, right?"

"Yeah, until Sunday," said Charley.

"I worked with both Walt and Charley on the Detail," said Susan, using the normal verbal shortcut for the Secretary of State's Protective Detail. "Look, why don't you take off your coats, get comfortable and grab some coffee."

Riley said, "You can hang out in my office; it's the biggest that we have."

Both Walt and Charley were wearing dark suits, since they would be accompanying the CODEL to the Parliament in the afternoon. They each had a Sig-Sauer 9mm pistol secured on their right hips in holsters, plus extra magazines. Since their Washington-issued radios worked on a different frequency band than in Pakistan, neither had bothered to bring their own radios on the trip. Following coffee, Susan would arrange for the Embassy's Communications Section to issue them. Walt and Charley returned to Riley's office with Susan as Alex returned to his own.

"How long have you been with DS?" asked Riley.

"I joined three years ago," stated Walt. "First, I was on the Secretary's Detail, now I'm in Overseas Operations." Walt was a little over six feet tall and looked like he spent a lot of time in the gym.

"I've been on almost four years," Charley said. "I worked with Walt and Susan on The Detail, and then was assigned to the Washington Field Office." Standing about five foot, ten inches, he appeared fit and looked a few years older than Walt.

"So, what did you guys do before joining DS?" asked Riley.

"After college at the University of Illinois, I joined the Army and was an infantry officer for four years," replied Walt.

Charley chimed in, "I was a cop for two years in Newark, and then went back to college at Rutgers. After graduation, I was a State Trooper for about six years."

"Well, I'm glad you're here to help us support the CODEL

visit." said Riley.

"Now, make yourselves at home. The CODEL probably won't finish their briefing for at least an hour. Susan told me she'll take you over to the Ambassador's Residence in a little while, just to see the place."

"Yes, and afterward I'll take Walt and Charley back to the cafeteria for lunch," said Susan. "The CODEL will be eating with the Ambassador and the others, but that's really a continuation of the briefing."

"Good plan," said Riley. "What are you guys doing for dinner later?"

"Well, some of the CODEL staff may go to a restaurant called Usmania in the Blue Area," Charley said.

"Excellent Pakistani food," Riley commented.

"We're not sure if some of the senators are going. If so, we should accompany them. If not, we'll probably eat at the hotel," Walt said.

"I know how it is when you're traveling and doing protection, even when there isn't a specific threat, like this trip. But if you've got any free time, call me and I'll have you over to my house. My wife, Jill, and I like to offer our hospitality to visiting agents."

"That's very kind of you," said Charley. He saw Walt nodding in agreement.

"Okay, guys, are you ready to see the Residence?" Susan asked while standing and moving toward the door.

"Let's stop first in Communications to pick up your radios." They walked up to the third floor. Susan led them to the vault, opened the outer daytime access door by tapping in the code on the pad, and rang the bell once she was inside. Bob Boudreaux opened the inner door.

"Hey, Susan, how've ya been?"

"I'm fine, Bob. Meet Walt Lennon and Charley Matthews. They're here to pick up the two radios we talked about."

"Glad to meet you boys. I'm Bob Boudreaux." They shook hands. Bob brought the group into the core area of the communications center. He prepared paperwork to issue the radios while Walt and Charley waited.

"Boudreaux, huh? Are you from Louisiana?" asked Walt.

"I sure am."

"I have a cousin who went to Tulane," stated Walt.

"My condolences," responded Bob. "Good school, but they should drop their football program or replace it with flag football. My family is all LSU Tiger fans."

"Wow, talk about rivalries," said Walt. "You guys take football seriously."

"Only four things important in life," responded Bob. "Faith, fishing, food, and football. Not necessarily in that order. Ain't that right, Susan?"

"More or less, Bob. Except I don't fish," she smiled.

"Hi, Susan," said Carrie Sherman, as she walked by the doorway. She was the second of four Communicators. Stopping, she stuck her head in and said, "I see you've just met our resident Cajun philosopher." Both Walt and Charley nodded their heads.

"How was darts the other night, Carrie?" asked Susan.

"Oh, we didn't win, but we got close. In any event, it was lots of fun."

Bob finished the paperwork and handed Walt and Charley their radios. "Enjoy your visit, boys. And remember, always bet on purple and gold."

Susan couldn't resist jumping in. "I think that my Sooners might have something to say about that."

"In their dreams, Susan," said Bob, "In their dreams."

CHAPTER 47

LATE THURSDAY AFTERNOON

Various Conversations

Lunch at the Ambassador's Residence had high points and low ones. On one hand, the Embassy team was delighted to continue educating the visitors on complexities of foreign relations in the sub-continent. On the other hand, Winston Hargrove was having a hard time with two of the committee staffers.

Rachel overheard one of them tell Hargrove, "That's what you believe, but you just told us you've never served in South Asia before."

Rachel didn't have to worry for long; Ellen Hunt joined the conversation and redirected it toward key talking points of the Embassy's arguments. Rachel tried to listen further while still speaking at length to the committee press staffer seated next to her. She smiled to herself and thought Alex would be proud of her multi-tasking ability. She wanted him to be impressed.

Rachel was never certain whether or not to be grateful that congressional staffers existed. On one hand, they helped clarify issues for the senators, most of whom either didn't know much about policy issues, or didn't have any intellectual interest in them. On the other hand, many staffers took the opportunity to subject senators to their own biases. She had even met a few staffers who had admittedly failed the Foreign Service Entrance Exam. She wondered whether they held a grudge against the Service, resulting in negative talk on their part. She had also met one or two staffers who had been selected out of the Foreign Service for failure to perform. From experience, she knew this same situation of bias and intellectual dishonesty existed in the House of Representatives, although it was probably worse in the House because a congressman's constituency was less diverse than a senator's, and, therefore, allowed a congressman to pander to a smaller, more homogenous audience.

"Rachel, I was just telling Senator Desmond that you're our resident China expert," said Ambassador Pierce, clearly looking for Rachel to respond.

"Thank you for the compliment, sir, but I wouldn't go so far as to call myself an expert," Rachel replied.

"You're being too modest," Pierce said. "Senator, Rachel served in both Hong Kong and Beijing, speaks Chinese, and covered Asian economic issues when she worked for The Los Angeles Times."

"I was just saying to Worthington, I'll be leading a Senate delegation to Beijing next month. If we have some time during this visit, perhaps we can discuss current affairs in China,' Senator Desmond said.

"I'd be glad to, Senator. Although I imagine your staff has probably kept you up-to-date already." Judging from the lack of reaction by the staff seated around the table, Rachel didn't get a warm and fuzzy feeling.

To no one's surprise, the wives of three Senators declined to attend either the briefing or the lunch at the Residence. So Caroline Pierce, Worthington's wife, volunteered to take them shopping. Caroline called upon her good friend, Nasreen Hasan, a published writer of fiction, to help her host the women.

Nasreen was an attractive, and well-educated woman of about forty. She had raised two children while becoming a successful writer of a best-selling novel in Pakistan. In addition to being happily married to a well-known Pakistani architect, she was very independent, witty, and a pleasure to be with. Since Nasreen had a van to shuttle her kids and their friends around town, she offered to drive the group.

Worthington Pierce and the DCM had been briefed earlier by Jim Riley about using the SMG Mobile Reaction Team in support of the wives' shopping trips. As Nasreen and Caroline departed the hotel with the Senator's wives, the SMG vehicle followed at a discreet distance. Altogether, the group visited three jewelry stores, two rug merchants, and two brass shops. Four hours later, after much shopping and even better conversation, they were exhausted.

"Nasreen and Caroline, I can't tell you how grateful we are that you've taken the time to show us Islamabad," Natalie Desmond said. The other two Senator's wives added their gratitude.

The five women returned to the Holiday Inn, and sat in the rear of the lobby lounge for High Tea. As they sipped mint tea and ate scones with butter and strawberry jam, they were watched from a distance by the two Police Special Branch officers assigned to the lobby. The SMG guards remained outside the hotel entrance should they be needed. At that moment, no one could know they would be needed very soon.

CHAPTER **48**

THURSDAY AFTERNOON

Meeting at the Parliament

After lunch at the Ambassador's residence, everyone returned to the motorcade for a short drive to Parliament, the Congressional Delegation's first appointment.

"Mr. Chairman," Ambassador Pierce said to Senator Desmond, "Why don't you ride with me in my limo?"

"Thank you, Worthington," Desmond replied, "I'd be absolutely delighted."

The other four senators and ten staff members, plus Winston Hargrove, Rachel Smith, and John Sherrill, boarded the rental bus. In the lead car was Susan Witt, Walt Lennon, and Charley Matthews in an Embassy vehicle. In last position was a Pakistani police SUV with four armed cops.

Ellen Hunt, as Deputy Chief of Mission, could have chosen to participate, but she'd been to the Parliament many times and knew all the players. Additionally, she wanted to accompany the group on Friday to their more important visits meeting the Prime Minister and Foreign Minister. So, today, Winston Hargrove was given the honor of chaperoning the CODEL.

As the motorcade departed the Embassy compound,

Hargrove saw about ten protestors holding signs across the street from the Embassy's front gate. Positioned between them and the gate were about twenty uniformed Pakistani police. "Unbelievable!" he said, turning to Rachel. "I doubt tomorrow's demonstration will be anything to worry about. Look at that; it's pathetic. Once again, Security is the tail wagging the dog."

"Let's hope tomorrow's protestors don't bring their own dog with big teeth," she replied. Disgusted with Hargrove's attitude, she still didn't want to get into an argument in front of the CODEL.

Susan Witt called the Site Advance Officer, Marisol Lopez now at the Parliament, on the radio from her lead car. "Pol. Two, Pol. Two, this is Eagle Three, we have departed and are en-route to your location."

"Eagle Three from Pol. Two, I copy," responded Marisol from the office of the Speaker of the Parliament. Upon receiving her response, Marisol informed the Speaker of their impending arrival. He accompanied her down to the main VIP entrance of the building to greet the CODEL.

Any number of Embassy officers could have been picked as the Site Advance Officer, but Marisol was chosen because she would also act as the official 'note-taker' for the meeting. This was a traditional function for State Department Officers. Since the Ambassador and Senator Desmond would be primary American interlocutors during the meeting, they couldn't be expected to also write down details of conversations while fully engaged with the Speaker of the Parliament. Normally, the Political Counselor, Winston Hargrove, would be tasked with the note-taking chore, but since Marisol had a superior understanding of the issues, the Ambassador and Ellen Hunt preferred Marisol to handle the job. After the meeting, Marisol would translate her notes into a report telegram to be sent to Washington and other U.S. embassies on their progress. The brief 10-minute ride was uneventful. The motorcade pulled up to the entrance, pleasantries were expressed by everyone with their greeter, then everyone walked to the Speaker's office. Susan Witt and the two accompanying DS special agents waited on alert just outside the Speaker's door. Additional chairs had already been brought into the meeting room for the American senate staffers.

The office had a very high ceiling, with large windows overlooking the Blue Area in central Islamabad. The Speaker had a substantial dark mahogany wooden desk set to one side of the room. There were several large sofas, as well as numerous leather chairs. Behind the desk hung a large flag of Pakistan: A white crescent moon and white star on a green background, with a white stripe on one end. A giant oil painting of the country's founder and first Governor General, Muhammed Ali Jinnah, hung on one side of the room.

Marisol turned her attention back to the meeting in time to hear the Speaker of the Parliament address the visitors.

"Senator Desmond, Ambassador Pierce, gentlemen, and ladies, it is a pleasure to host you today in our Parliament," he said.

"We appreciate your invitation, Mr. Speaker. It is our pleasure to be here as well," replied Senator Desmond.

With several other leading Parliamentarians, U.S. Senators, and the Ambassador beginning to jump into the conversation, general chit-chat lasted for about fifteen minutes. Culturally, social time needed to preceed the serious nature of business. It was a Pakistani tradition.

Finally, the Pakistanis got to the point.

"While our democracy is not as old as yours," the Speaker of the Parliament intoned, "Our culture and our society extend back for a millennium."

Senator Desmond found this statement condescending. He knew Pakistan had been ruled for half its existence since 1947 by one military dictatorship or another. When not ruled by the Army, it was basically a country ruled by clans, tribes, and ruthless landowners, most of whom were thoroughly corrupt. India, of course, had its own problems, but Pakistan seemed to be constantly slipping considerably behind India in the race for modernization and growth.

Today, however, Desmond wouldn't comment on such matters. Rather, he wanted to hear the Pakistani perspective on the problem at hand.

The Speaker continued, "We believe Pakistan is at a crucial moment in its history. Although the Soviet threat next door has just been eliminated, mainly because of our joint efforts to cooperate with the Mujahedeen, we find that instability still exists in the region. The outcome in Afghanistan is uncertain, with foreign elements trying to influence the political mix there. Our continuing dispute with India over Kashmir also remains a point of contention, as it has since 1947. India's armed forces are much larger and better equipped than ours, and they continue to add to their military capability."

"I'm not aware India has made any recent threatening gestures toward Pakistan," commented Senator Desmond out loud.

"Not lately, no. But we are concerned with the long term," the Speaker said. "Now we see America intends to provide military aid to India and it seems our own aid programs will be cut. We are very grateful for America's past assistance. Your expertise and your generosity have been critical for many years." He seemed ready to go on at length.

"There are two things I should clarify," Senator Desmond

interrupted again. "First, with the Cold War against the Soviets over, and specifically with the end of the war in Afghanistan, popular sentiment in America is calling for a reduction of Foreign Assistance and defense spending in general. Secondly, we are still continuing aid programs to Pakistan, although many feel it's time to recognize that India, as a friendly neutral country, also needs our assistance."

"India may be neutral for the United States, but certainly is not for us," responded the Speaker. "Is not the contemporary American view more about lobbying from U.S. defense companies for increased sales abroad? We believe that political elements in America also constantly favor India over Pakistan!"

Desmond knew he'd be on a slippery slope if he addressed the Speaker's points. His hesitation gave Ambassador Pierce an opportunity to speak.

"Mr. Speaker, I think we can all agree that each country has a variety of internal forces with differing ideas and differing solutions to problems. This comes as no surprise. But I can assure you, however, of America's continuing support for Pakistan. What aid eventually may be provided to India is, as yet, unknown. We haven't had any detailed consultations with India in this regard. The White House has not presented specific programs nor has the Congress held hearings. We're cognizant of the need to maintain a reasonable balance between India and Pakistan. Pakistan is a long-time friend and valued ally."

Although somewhat reassured by Ambassador's Pierce's comments, the Speaker wanted more assurance.

"Senator Desmond, I take the Ambassador's point that things have not yet been decided, but what reassurance can you give us that sufficient assistance will continue to be provided to Pakistan?"

"I can only say that this matter will be thoroughly examined very carefully with a view toward helping Pakistan," Desmond responded. "My Committee, however, does not totally control the issue. We have to deal with the Appropriations Committees in the House and the Senate, as well as with both Armed Services Committees. Naturally, the White House is a key player. I share your concern and understand the problem. You have my personal support."

After another five minutes of closing comments, the meeting ended and the CODEL members returned to their hotel. Ambassador Pierce, Winston Hargrove, Rachel Smith, and Marisol Lopez spoke with the Senators in the Hotel's Embassy control room for twenty minutes about the rest of the schedule, before departing for the Embassy.

No one could say if any real progress had been made. But, as always, tomorrow would be another day.

CHAPTER 49

THURSDAY EVENING

Evaluating the Threat

All Thursday afternoon, Stanton and Riley had been talking to their contacts about tomorrow's scheduled demonstration at the Embassy. Now at 6:00 pm, the Emergency Action Committee was assembled in the Secure Conference Room to lay out known facts and propose a course of action.

"At this point, the police have told us they now expect less than 1,000 demonstrators to march on the Embassy after Friday prayers," Riley stated. "They may arrive about 1:00 pm.. The cops will reinforce their normal number of police around the compound, and have more on standby. In any event, I've asked them to block the demonstrators at the entrance to the Diplomatic Enclave. Whether that works is another matter."

"Bill, what do you have from your intelligence sources?" Ellen Hunt asked.

"They're saying the same thing as the police," Stanton responded. "They believe the cops may be able to contain some of the rowdier elements before they get to the Embassy."

"Does that mean the police know who the key organizers are and where to find them?" she asked.

"More or less," Riley replied. "But even accounting for known labor organizers, student groups, and religious leaders, they still believe there'll be large groups who are presently unknown."

"I agree with that assessment," Bill Stanton confirmed.

"What about Pandit Baba?" interjected JC Colon.

Ellen Hunt started chuckling, but JC didn't notice since he was looking at Stanton. Ellen realized, once again, Stanton would pull JC's leg about the mythical TV series instigator from the Raj Quartet.

"He's still hasn't been located," Stanton said with a straight face, shaking his head in mock despair.

Ambassador Pierce had remained silent so far, content to let Ellen run the meeting. But now he said, "Okay so what are the odds of this becoming violent, Jim?"

"I can't give you odds, but I believe we should try to reduce our exposure. Specifically, since Friday is a normal workday for us, I think we should release all local employees and non-essential American staff at noon. The Consular Section should put out a notice that they'll not be open for business after lunch. We should also use the Embassy warden network to advise the American community to stay away from the Embassy from mid-day tomorrow because of the demonstration. That also means closing the commissary and the Club."

"How long will the demonstration last?" asked JC. "Why should we shut down our operations if it only lasts for an hour or two?"

"We can't project when the demonstrators will leave," Riley replied. "Besides, the real point is not when they leave, but if they will become violent."

"Oh, come on," Hargrove declared arrogantly. "You're just speculating. We can't give in to protestors. If we did that, we'd be out of business. Just look at that ridiculously small group in front of the Embassy today."

Alex had been sitting in the back row since Riley was seated at the main table. He now decided to jump into the fray.

"In 1979, a small demonstration started at the Embassy front gate at mid-day." All eyes in the room shifted to Alex.

"After a relatively brief period, it broke-up, the original group left the area, and everyone thought it was over. Within an hour, massive crowds, numbering between five thousand to ten thousand rioters, showed up and attacked the Embassy. As I think everyone knows, we lost four employees and fires set by the mob destroyed the Embassy. No one anticipated either the size of the mob or the level of violence that ensued. Once the mob was at the Embassy, it was too late to send people home. I think it would be prudent to err on the side of caution this time."

He finished speaking and looked at Riley, who had a small smile on his face. Riley dropped his hand below table level and gave Alex a thumbs-up sign, indicating he agreed with his points.

Rachel was also seated in the back row and listened carefully to what Alex had said. She was impressed with his explanation and his logic as were the others. JC and Hargrove shook their heads in obvious disagreement.

"Ellen, what do you recommend," Ambassador Pierce asked.

"Since this isn't clear cut, let's do the following: First, put out the notice through the warden network that people shouldn't visit the Embassy tomorrow afternoon. Secondly, we'll close the Consular Section to the public at noon. Third, let's allow employees to come to work in the morning, but reserve the right to let them go at mid-day if we have more information about the demonstration possibly turning violent. And lastly, regarding the Senators' Press Conference at the Residence, we'll also reconsider this, if necessary."

Worthington Pierce thought about this proposal for a

moment. "I'm concerned both Ellen and I will be with the CODEL for much of tomorrow morning. Therefore, we'll be out of touch should Bill or Jim get new information."

"That's true," agreed Ellen. She knew this would leave Winston Hargrove as the acting officer-in-charge. He'd already expressed his view that employees shouldn't be sent home early, so she challenged him.

"Winston, you'll be the Senior Officer in the Embassy, if the Ambassador or I can't be reached. Should Jim or Bill come up with new threat information, I want you to consider very seriously getting people out of harm's way."

"I agree," said Pierce.

"Understood," responded Hargrove. What else could he say?

Ellen, on the other hand, seriously wondered if he would do anything at all.

CHAPTER 50

THURSDAY EVENING

Night Before the Demonstration

Because the CODEL had traveled overnight to Pakistan, then worked the entire day of arrival, the schedule allowed them free time on Thursday evening. This decision proved to be a lifesaver for several. The five senators and their wives all agreed either to get room service or eat at one of the hotel restaurants before calling it an evening. Some of the staff wanted to go into town, but most decided to stay in the hotel that night.

"Walt and Charley, what do you guys want to do about dinner?" asked Susan Witt as she spoke to the two DS special agents in the hotel's Embassy Control Room. It was 7:00 p.m.

"We agree that one of us should stay here with the CODEL," Charley Matthews replied.

"Sounds right to me," Susan replied. "I'll be glad to take one of you to a local restaurant or the Embassy Club."

"Is the restaurant close by?" Walt asked. "And do we have to worry about getting sick if we eat there?"

"Nothing is far away in Islamabad. So far, no one I know has gotten sick after eating at the restaurant I have in mind."

"Okay," Charley said. "Let's flip." He pulled out a coin,

tossed it in the air. Walt called heads. It was tails.

"Well, Susan, looks like I get to go with you," Charley said. "Great. We'll have our radios, so if you need us, Walt, give us a call."

"Will do, Susan. I think I'll order room service."

"Let's go, Charley," she said. "We're headed to Usmania, which is not far at all. It's a Pakistani restaurant with pretty good food." They left the hotel and drove to the restaurant in Susan's Chevy Blazer.

Meanwhile, Rachel was talking to the CODEL Press Officer, Brewster Walcott, and another committee staffer, Abigail Wythe, in the hotel lobby. They were all having coffee in the lounge.

"Were either of you surprised by what was said at the Parliament today?" Rachel asked.

"Not really," Abigail answered. She followed South Asian issues for the committee on a regular basis and was the most knowledgeable staff member on Pakistan-India issues. "I would have been surprised had they not made a pitch to retain their foreign assistance."

Abigail Wythe had been on the committee staff for eight years. Prior to that, she served in Senator Desmond's own senate office for five years. Rachel thought Abigail looked vintage prep school all the way. She was wearing a pearl necklace over a blue cotton blouse, matching pearl earrings, a grey/blue plaid mid-calf length skirt, and sensible dark blue pumps. Her long, straight blond hair, held in place with a tortoise shell beret, belonged to someone who easily could be named Muffy, and her accent was unmistakable for having attended exclusive New England schools, very exclusive schools. She wore rimless small round glasses that didn't detract from an otherwise attractive, yet somewhat severe-looking face.

"Tomorrow's meetings should be a rerun of today's exchanges," Rachel declared.

"What should we expect from the press tomorrow at the Prime Minister's Office and at the Foreign Office?" Brewster Walcott asked.

"I think they'll contain themselves for the most part," Rachel replied. "Those mini-press conferences will really be a chance for the Prime Minister and the Foreign Minister to go on-the-record to press Pakistan's interests with the United States Government. Since these same journalists will be at the Ambassador's residence in the afternoon, they all know there will be another opportunity to probe further on the senators' views."

Rachel felt she could work with Brewster. He seemed the most concerned of all the staffers with accomplishing a specific task. Indeed, it was his responsibility to craft Senator Desmond's remarks to the American press upon their return to the States. He was also a long-term senior staffer on the Foreign Relations committee, one who had managed to survive the last change of the committee's chairmanship.

"If you need office space during your visit,' Rachel offered, "you can use the Embassy Conference Room, where you had today's briefing. Remember, it's big enough to hold all the staff."

Abigail snickered. "Oh, I don't think most of the staff will want to do extensive work. They're just along for the ride." She had one of those smiles where the ends of her mouth actually went down rather than up. "After being 'seen' tomorrow at the meetings, they'll be content to read Brewster's press release and my Committee Report."

"Okay," responded Rachel. Why should I have assumed anything else? she thought. Being well aware that congressional staff members viewed overseas trips as perks of the job, not really work assignments, still, she was a bit surprised. Abigail's attitude toward her colleagues demonstrated both her utter distain for them and a self-confidence in her own ability to withstand criticism.

Brewster spoke up, "I'm pretty tired and hungry. Do you know of a good restaurant in the neighborhood?"

"I'm still new here," Rachel replied, "but I've eaten at a place called Usmania, not far away."

"What type of food does it have?" Abigail asked.

"Pakistani."

"Hmmm, I love a good curry," said Abigail.

"Okay let's take an Embassy car. Are you ready to go now?" Rachel asked.

"Yeah, let's do it," they both agreed, looking forward to seeing downtown.

CHAPTER 51

THURSDAY EVENING

Meeting at Ghulam's Pharmacy

Colonel Malik looked at his watch and saw it was 8:00 pm, time to call Hussein Khan at his home. They needed to meet.

"Hello, Khan, this is Tahir," Malik said on the phone using his fake name. "I need to see you immediately. It is very important."

"So late, Tahir. Can't it wait until tomorrow? We are closing the Consular Section at noon, so I'll have plenty of time after that."

"No, it can't wait. If you can make it tonight, then I probably won't have to bother you again."

That got Khan's attention. Could it be possible he would finally be out from under Tahir's boot?

"Very well, where shall we meet?" Khan asked.

"Go west out of Islamabad and take the Grand Truck Road toward Peshawar," Malik replied. "After exactly ten miles you will see a building on your right with the name of Ghulam's Pharmacy. You can't miss it. It is a one-story building with nothing else around it. I'll meet you in the parking lot behind the pharmacy."

"That is pretty far. Why don't we meet in Islamabad?" protested Khan.

"It's not convenient for me," Tahir replied tersely. "You must go where I say."

"Okay I'm leaving now," Khan said very reluctantly.

When Malik arrived early at Ghulam's Pharmacy, he walked over to Arshad, one of his tribal team leaders, who had driven in another vehicle with three more tribesmen. "You know what must be done."

"Park your vehicle around the corner, then all of you should wait behind the bushes and trees, until I walk Khan over to you."

Originally, Malik thought he could keep Khan as a long-term asset well beyond Friday's event. But after some consideration, he realized Khan was of no further use. Moreover, should he decide to cooperate with the Americans at some future date, Khan could prove to be a threat to Malik.

It was dark when Khan arrived at Ghulam's Pharmacy. There were no vehicles in sight. He drove around the back of the building and spotted another vehicle, a silver Toyota sedan. It was too dark to make out the exact model. Parking near the Toyota, he exited his car. Looking around, Khan saw there were no other buildings immediately nearby just as Tahir had said. Beyond the parking lot were dense bushes and trees. At that moment, Malik walked around from behind the Toyota and greeted him.

"I am glad you could make it, Khan."

"You said this might be your last request for information, Tahir, so how could I refuse?"

"That is very true. Tell me, has anyone in the Embassy questioned you about our meetings?"

Khan looked puzzled. "Why would anyone even know about us?"

"Exactly. I assume you've been totally discreet in never mentioning our relationship," Colonel Malik stated.

"Absolutely, I have never said anything to anyone."

Malik put his arm over Khan's shoulder as he slowly guided him toward the bushes. Malik was smiling. "Good. You've been most helpful, and I appreciate all you have done."

Malik gently turned Khan so his back was toward the bushes. Then he stepped backward and away from Malik. Suddenly, Arshad and all three tribesmen burst from the undergrowth. Their dark clothing had hidden them especially well.

With his right hand, Arshad plunged a long knife into Khan's back. Khan screamed and arched backwards in excruciating pain, slightly turning his body to see what was happening. Two tribesmen grabbed each of his arms. Arshad stepped closer behind Khan and pulled his head back with his left hand, using his right hand to slit Khan's throat with the long, sharp serrated blade.

Blood spurted in an arc over the parking lot and into the bushes. The tribesmen continued holding Khan until Arshad finished beheading him. Then they dragged his headless corpse into the dense foliage and took off all of Khan's clothes and his watch. The body was covered with dirt and leaves, easy for animals to find.

Arshad placed Khan's head, his clothes, watch, and wallet into a large dark plastic bag and wrapped it well. He would dispose of these in a pit two miles away that they had dug the night before. Once the pit was filled with dirt and rocks, it might be months or years before it was found, if ever. With any luck, it would take a long time for the police to link a headless body in the foliage to Khan's disappearance, should the wild animals fail to do their part.

One of the tribesmen then got into Khan's car and drove it away to another remote location. He would remove the license plates and any personal items from inside before dumping it away from the nearest road.

"Thank you, Arshad," Malik said. "May God be with you tomorrow."

Everyone quietly left the scene. It was during such outings that

that these men bonded. Not so much in friendship, but in fear of what could happen to any one of them should they cross Malik.

CHAPTER **52**

THURSDAY EVENING

At Dinner and Unaware

When Rachel, Brewster, and Abigail arrived at Usmania's, they saw Susan and Charley were already seated and asked to join them. The easiest thing to do was to share several dishes, so Rachel and Susan ordered for the group. Waiters brought lentil soup, Chicken Tandoori, Lamb Dopiaza, Basmati Rice, Baigan Bharta, and Chicken Madras along with an assortment of condiments such as chutney, achar, and raita, plus Peshawari Naan.

"Wow, this smells incredible," Abigail said with delight. What are we having?"

Rachel gave a gastronomical lesson by describing each dish. "First, you have to know that most Pakistani or Indian dishes have the same basic spices but used in different proportions. You'll also find that garam masala, onions, garlic, cayenne pepper, and ginger are used in all of these dishes. The Chicken Tandoori also uses cilantro and is baked in a tandoori oven. While it should be moist, it does not have a thick sauce like most of the other dishes."

"The Lamb Dopiaza," she continued, "Which translates as lamb with two onions, also includes cardamom, cumin, and coriander." Then she pointed to a mid-size circular dish in the center of the table. "This dish, Baigan Bharta is an eggplant curry dish, also with cumin and some curry powder."

"What are these things in the small bowls?" Charley asked.

"Those are condiments," Rachel replied. She pointed to each bowl as she spoke. "The chutney is made from mango. The achar is either lemon or lime that's pickled. It has cardamom, peppercorns, cumin, and dry red chilies in it and has a wonderful, powerful flavor that you probably have never experienced. Finally, the raita is basically yogurt with cucumbers. The raita will soften the burn of the spicier foods."

"Gosh, this bread is delicious," Brewster declared as he munched on a small brown piece.

"That's Peshawari Naan," Rachel said. It has raisins and nuts in it."

"Damn," Susan Witt said, addressing Rachel. "You've only been here a few weeks. How did you learn that stuff so fast?" Susan's idea of a great meal, until she arrived in Pakistan, was a large Oklahoma steak grilled well-done, with an Idaho baked potato.

"My Pakistani journalist buddies have taken me to lunch a few times, and I always want to know what I'm eating," Rachel explained with a pleased grin on her face.

Thirty minutes of small talk later, Rachel used the dinner as an opportunity to guide Brewster in the nuances of what eventually would be the committee's press statements. She also thought even Abigail had loosened up a little and appeared to be enjoying herself. Charley and Susan, she noted, were telling stories of past Secretary of State trips around the world.

"I insist that everyone share two desserts," Rachel said as their meal was nearly over. "The first you'll recognize as Rice Pudding. It's delicious here. The second is called Gulab Jamun. It's made with milk and flour, then deep fried. Finally, sugar syrup, cardamom, and saffron are poured over it. It's really special."

After finishing their last course and splitting the bill, everyone effusively praised Rachel and Susan for taking them to their first authentic Pakistani restaurant and introducing them to its splendid cuisine.

At this moment, only a few of them vaguely remembered that tomorrow there would be a demonstration at the American Embassy. No one could possibly know this would be the last good meal they would enjoy for a while.

CHAPTER **53**

FRIDAY MORNING

Calm Before the Storm

Rachel felt Alex's hand caressing her shoulder, she felt the warmth of his body next to hers. She even thought he whispered something in her ear and leaned closer to hear his words.

'Damn!' she cried out, reaching to shut off her screaming alarm clock. The dials read 5:00 am. Laying back in bed, she slowly turned her head to the side confirming Alex's presence had only been a dream. What a restless night. It was probably the spicy food at Usmania's. Then, she smiled at the thought of dreaming Alex was in bed with her. She missed him.

Rachel walked into the kitchen and turned on the electric coffee pot which she had filled before going to bed last night. In the bathroom, she splashed water on her face, patted it dry, then went into the living room. With no time for a quick run, she decided on some exercises to work off last night's dinner. Laying on her back on the carpeted floor, she stretched. Then did five sets of twenty sit-ups, followed by an equal number of pelvic lifts. Rolling onto her stomach, she did three sets of twenty push-ups. Finally, she moved to her side and did some side planks, balancing on an elbow while keeping her body in a perfectly straight position, other than her leg which she raised off the ground.

Lightly sweating, but otherwise feeling good, she drank coffee, and ate a small yogurt before showering and putting on make-up. Being only temporarily assigned to Islamabad, she had an Embassy driver and car available to take her to the American Center. Arriving early gave her time to put together press clippings for the CODEL and email copies of the same to the usual

Embassy players.

Across town, Alex had slept like a hibernating bear. After finishing one of Samuel's light meals the night before, he'd continued reading Professor Paul Kennedy's 'The Rise and Fall of the Great Powers,' which had been written only a few years prior. He enjoyed studying the interaction of economics and strategy. This book focused on the period from the 16th century to the present. After reading a few hours, he'd gone to bed early and awoke refreshed at 5:30 am this morning. For a brief moment, the thought of Rachel ran through his mind.

Not feeling he had time to work out at the Embassy, which he preferred, he opted instead for a two-mile run along the edge of the Margala Road. Throwing on some jogging shorts and a University of Maryland T-shirt, he quickly stretched and went outside. The sun was rising, so he figured he was visible to cars driving by. Heading west toward the Faisal Grand Mosque, he ran passed houses on his left with walls and tall, leafy trees surrounding them for privacy. Across the street on his right was a lightly wooded area not yet developed.

As he ran, Rachel entered his thoughts, again. Because she was busy with the CODEL he probably wouldn't see her until tonight, or maybe even Saturday. She was the most impressive woman he had ever met. Their interests meshed; their humor was good. He just liked everything about her. Admittedly, he was totally smitten.

While running, stray dogs could sometimes be a problem. He carried a three foot long stick that had a sharp pointed end. For defense against stray bandits or 'brigands', as the Pakistanis called them, he wore a fanny pack containing a small .38 caliber Smith and Wesson revolver which held five rounds. Not a lot of bullets, but a hell of a lot better than merely pointing his finger at an armed bad guy and yelling, 'Bang!'

Near eighty degrees outside, Alex returned drenched in sweat. He left his stick by the front door and put the fanny pack and gun away in a locked desk drawer. In the bedroom, he dropped to the floor for a series of push-ups and sit-ups. Then, showered and devoured Samuel's breakfast of French toast with maple syrup, coffee, and orange juice. Knowing the planned demonstration was this afternoon, it promised to be a reasonably busy day.

Nancy Williams reminisced over breakfast about her assignment in Islamabad as the RSO's secretary. It was turning out to be a great decision on her part. Over breakfast with her husband in their small kitchen, she talked about yesterday at the Embassy. Her husband, Bill, worked as an English teacher at the International School. No children, this was their second overseas tour of duty.

Her first assignment had been to Jakarta, Indonesia, where she worked in the Political Section. She loved Jakarta but had hated her job there.

Her Jakarta Memories:

It was beyond boring and she had little to do. The political officers had no sense of timing and came in an hour late every morning, unless there was an early scheduled staff meeting. Then, they would read a few newspapers to stay abreast of current events. At mid-day the officers would go to lunch with some Indonesian politician and return two to three hours later. Finally, around closing time they would begin drafting a telegram concerning their lunch conversation or newspaper articles for the day. Then, at five in the afternoon when she was ready to go home, that's when her bosses wanted her stay around and help format their telegrams. Naturally, each telegram needed to be seen by the DCM or Ambassador. The entire process lasted until seven o'clock nearly every evening. She couldn't wait to leave that assignment.

Her secretarial friends in Jakarta told her all Political Sections worked the same way, but Administrative and Security sections offered real satisfying work. So, when her Career Counselor in Washington offered a 'plum' assignment to the Political Section in Embassy Tokyo she turned it down, opting instead for the

Islamabad tour. The Jakarta political officers were baffled by her decision. After all, they thought of themselves as the elite arm of the Foreign Service.

However, she knew her decision had been correct. The RSO Section was busy all day, often handling serious issues of counterterrorism, criminal fraud investigations, emergency planning, and terrorism incident reporting. She loved it. Most important was that Jim, Alex, and Susan treated her as an equal. Frequently out of the office, they relied on her and she became the de-facto office manager, answering questions from concerned employees, and making decisions in line with Jim's security philosophy. She was a vital cog in monitoring the office budget, which included the huge local guard contract. Now halfway through her tour of duty in Islamabad, she looked forward to every new day.

After finishing breakfast, Nancy and Bill gave each other a kiss and small hug, then drove off in opposite directions for work.

"Good morning, Nancy," Jim Riley greeted her as she entered the office. Riley had arrived about thirty minutes prior and was busy reviewing overnight telegraphic traffic.

"Hey, Jim, how are you this morning?"

"I'm fine; it looks like we'll have a 'spot of bother' today, as my new British friend would say."

"You mean the demonstration?" she asked.

"Yep, that's right. Listen, after you have a chance to get your morning cup of tea, I want you to help organize an impromptu shredding drill today with the other sections that store classified material. We can talk about it in a few minutes."

"Sounds good to me," replied Nancy before walking off to the cafeteria.

Alex entered Jim's office, holding his completed copy of the

American Center Physical Security Survey. "If you have time to look at this today, I'll send it out in this evening's diplomatic pouch to Washington," Alex explained.

"Are there any physical changes since the last survey?"

"No, none."

"Okay, then I'll focus on your recommendations," Riley said.

Alex left the office and stopped by Bill Stanton's shop to read the morning intelligence summaries. The reading file usually contained material about current Middle East events and information about internal Pakistani affairs. Nothing earth-shattering in the material. The one piece that did have a bearing on this afternoon's demonstration contained nothing new. As Alex read, Stanton's deputy, Bill Patterson stopped by to talk to him.

"Our sources haven't come up with any additional information about the Demonstration beyond what we already know," said Patterson.

"So, I noticed. Let's just hope it's really a peaceful protest," Alex said. "In any event, the Marines will be ready, if needed."

"We'll be in touch with ISI throughout the day and let you know of any developments."

"Thanks," replied Alex.

He finished the file and walked down to Gunny Sgt. Rodriquez's office. Knowing Riley would be contacting Inspector General of Police Qasim during the morning, Alex decided ensuring the Marines and local guards were ready was his most useful pursuit.

No one could possibly predict this morning was the quiet before the storm.

CHAPTER 54

FRIDAY MORNING

The Storm Approaches

As Alex left Stanton's office, Susan Witt, Charley Matthews, and Walt Lennon were finishing breakfast at the Holiday Inn. Several senators were sitting at nearby tables with their wives and a few members of the committee staff. It was still over an hour before they were due to call on the Prime Minister.

"I can't wait to get permanently assigned overseas," Walt said. "At this point I'd consider any assignment. Washington, D.C. is all right, but it's not why I joined DS."

"What about you, Charley? Where do you want to go next?" Susan asked.

"I'm really interested in criminal investigative work," replied Charley. "I'm looking at embassies with a high volume of visa or passport fraud. I guess that means some place like Mexico City, Manila, or Santo Domingo. But it also needs to have a good school for my kids and, hopefully, where my wife can find work."

"By next year, you'll probably both be overseas," Susan stated. "I hope you get whatever embassy assignment you want."

She knew, however, that being able to select a specific assignment was extremely difficult and seldom worked out, but at least the Career Counselors took note of the desired geographic preference.

"Switching to business-at-hand," she said, "Today's visits shouldn't be difficult. The Prime Minister's Office is well-protected and has good access controls. The Foreign Ministry is not as tight, but again, they have access controls."

"Any problems carrying our guns into these places?" asked Charley.

"No. They know we're carrying, so it's not an issue," Susan responded. "The bad news is that a huge number of Pakistanis are armed throughout the country. In Tribal areas and the Northwest Frontier, everyone has an AK-47. In Peshawar, for example, it's like the Wild West. Tribesmen even wear crossed bandoliers of ammunition, like in 'spaghetti westerns.' The good news is the government doesn't really care about diplomats carrying guns."

"Great," said Walt with a note of sarcasm.

"Yeah, well…" Susan's voice trailed off. "Jim and Alex once told me about a town called Dara in the Tribal Area outside of Peshawar. Every type of weapon and ammunition imaginable is made and sold there. They told me the town has a main dirt road lined with one or two-story buildings. Some are constructed of cinder-block, others of wood. The shops sell either weapons, ammunition, or drugs. A drug store has the head of a dead animal above the front door," she said.

"I don't understand it all, but that's the way it is. And in the back rooms of the gun shops, you can watch tribesmen making 'new' World War Two-era Lee-Enfield bolt-action rifles, Colt .45s, old British Webley .38 caliber revolvers, even recoilless rifles, and other stuff. Alex claims he saw one shop fixing a damaged Soviet 37mm anti-aircraft gun. I'm not sure how well these guns function, but they do fire." The two men just looked at her and shook their heads.

"Jim says there's nothing more satisfying than to watch a CODEL full of liberal, gun-control congressmen or senators firing AK-47s into the air on Dara's main street," she continued, "Or fondling some handgun as if they were a long-term advocate of the right to armed self-defense."

"What about the CODELS? Do they take home souvenirs from Dara since they're flying on U.S. Military aircraft and can bypass Pakistani airport screening?" asked Walt.

"Geez, imagine that!" Susan said in mock surprise without really answering him. "I'm shocked that a member of Congress might do such a thing."

They talked another thirty minutes before Susan stood up and brushed crumbs off her clothing.

"I'm going to the parking lot to see if the motorcade is lined up."

It was actually John Sherrill's responsibility, but she wanted to start moving and figured it wouldn't hurt to double check. It was never smart to just assume all was well.

"I'll see you guys up at the Embassy Control Room in a few minutes."

CHAPTER 55

FRIDAY MORNING

Demonstration Preparation

It was close to 8:30 am when Alex walked down the hallway toward Gunny's office. He saw Riley coming from the other direction.

"Apparently great minds think alike," Riley said. "I want to speak with Gunny about the prep for today's demonstration."

"We're on the same wavelength," Alex replied.

"Ah, gentlemen," said Gunny Rodriguez, greeting both men as Alex and Jim entered his office. "I was just thinking about today's demo."

"We're all ears," Riley responded.

"I'll get my Marines up to the Embassy by noon in their utilities with side arms, plus shotguns ready and loaded. They can hang out in the react room in case they're needed."

"Oh, I think we can do better than that," Riley said. "How many civilians do you think have ever seen Marines in full battle gear and deployed throughout the Embassy?"

"Not many," Gunny replied. "I see your point."

"Great idea, Jim," Alex said.

"So, we're agreed," continued Riley. "The Marines will be assigned their normal observation and internal defense posts. They should take their standard gear, including ballistic vests and load-bearing web-gear. If the demonstration drags on but seems peaceful, the Marines can take off the vests and web-gear but keep them nearby."

"Roger that, Sir. I'll tell each Marine to prepare for questions from civilians about Marines' responsibilities and their gear. What about passing out the RSO weapons to the Marines, I mean the Ruger Mini-14s and the Uzis?"

"Let's decide once we see what's happening with the demonstration," responded Riley.

"Okay. I haven't had so much fun since the Gulf War," Gunny said with a broad smile on his face.

"Wow, a regular Arnold Schwarzenegger," Alex said with a knowing nod of his head.

The CODELS' motorcade left the Holiday Inn at 9:20 am precisely. The drive to the Prime Minister's Office would take only five minutes. Allowing time for the security check, they would be greeting the Prime Minister at exactly 9:30 am. Again, Marisol Lopez was tasked with being the Site Advance Officer, although she would share note-taking responsibilities with Ellen Hunt.

As the motorcade passed through the outer gates of the Prime Minister's office, Susan noted the Pakistan Army's presence. In addition to the usual ceremonial Army guards with turban and wafer-style head-dress, she saw three armored personnel carriers spread out around the grounds. She knew the Prime Minister had personal close-in protection from the Special Branch of Islamabad Police, but, their professionalism left a lot to be desired.

The meeting went as expected, with the Prime Minister focusing on the new aid program to India, and the CODEL countering with need for a balanced relationship among Pakistan, India and the United States. Senator Desmond again described complexities of the U.S. Congressional process, as well as Congress's relationship with the White House. As during the CODEL'S stop at Parliament, the Senator reiterated his commitment to review what could be done to continue support to Pakistan at the current level.

The first press conference followed in a room adjacent to the Prime Minister's office. Its wooden floor was covered with a huge red-patterned Pakistani Tribal carpet. At the head of the room, sat the Prime Minister in a large splendid chair covered in light-colored silk fabric. On both sides were several long sofas. The Pakistan delegation sat on his right side, including the Foreign Minister and other senior advisors. On his left were the Americans. Behind each set of sofas were rows of chairs. Rachel sat on a chair behind Senator Desmond, and identified each questioner to him. Brewster Walcott sat next to Rachel and Abigail Wythe next to him. Ambassador Pierce sat on the sofa next to Senator Desmond. The rest of the senators aligned themselves on the sofas in no particular order. At the end of the room the press clustered to ask questions. Several television cameras were set up to capture the moment, with arrays of bright lights that partially blinded nearly all participants.

The press conference lasted thirty minutes. In addition to the Prime Minister, Senator Desmond and the Ambassador addressed the group with several of the U.S. senators making comments.

"I want to thank Senator Desmond and the rest of the American delegation for listening to our concerns about the balance of power in the region," the Prime Minister said in his concluding remarks. "Pakistan has a history of working with the United States in deterring aggression in South Asia. We want that relationship to continue strongly in the future. As the world grows more complex with each decade, we think it is wise to remember who our allies have been and to continually reinforce those relationships."

"I also want to thank the Prime Minister for his hospitality and for affording us an opportunity to discuss issues of mutual concern," replied Senator Desmond.

Rachel listened very carefully, hoping the senators would not commit a faux pas by criticizing either Pakistan or India. She knew India would be scrutinizing every word from these press conferences. Using the term "to discuss issues of mutual concern" normally meant nothing was agreed upon and differences remained. The phrase really signaled little or no progress and didn't fool anyone.

Overall, she thought, the press conference went as well as could be expected.

Following the press conference, the Foreign Minister departed ahead of the others. The CODEL and accompanying Embassy officers then departed and drove to the Foreign Ministry, five minutes away.

The Demonstration – and everyone's future -- was just a few hours away.

CHAPTER 56

MONDAY MORNING

The Body

The burning question on their minds: Were demonstrations planned elsewhere? Jim Riley and Alex Boyd were calling consulates in Peshawar, Lahore, and Karachi as a follow-up to earlier conversations. Meanwhile the CODEL was holding its meetings with Pakistani officials.

"Hello, Will," said Jim as he spoke on the secure phone to Will Bannister, the RSO in Karachi. "I'll get right to the point: Are any anti-American demonstrations planned today at the Consulate? Have you heard anything along those lines?"

"Hi, Jim. Nothing so far. We've checked with the cops, and Stanton's people have checked with ISI. But, if that changes, you'll be my first call."

"That's great," Jim said. "By the way, is Consul General Leighton behaving himself?"

Will Bannister laughed. "Yeah, since the DCM spoke to him, he's been quiet about security upgrades at our residences. But he never gives up completely on controlling security. Yesterday I told him about next month's trip to Quetta I'll take to support a visit by the Ambassador to the American library there. He doesn't think I should go, but rather that the Embassy RSOs should cover the visit. For God's sake, Quetta is the provincial capital of Baluchistan, and that's in Karachi's Consular District."

"It sounds like he's still fighting for his turf against the Embassy," Jim replied. "I'll send a telegram to Karachi next week, telling them I need you to advance the visit."

"Thanks," stated Will. "Are you still expecting a sizable demonstration today in Islamabad?"

"Yes, we are. Plus, with the CODEL in town, we have to worry about their safety."

"Good luck, Jim," Will Bannister concluded. "Talk with you soon."

"Hello, Brian," Alex said, as he called the RSO in Peshawar. He had just hung up from calling Lahore who reported plans for a small demonstration there.

"Alex! I thought you might be calling today," replied Brian. "If you want to know about any demonstrations in Peshawar, it looks like we'll be entertaining a crowd that might reach two hundred people. Our police here plan to keep them about three blocks away from the Consulate General. We're sending our employees home at noon."

"Geez, it seems like your Consul General is pretty supportive," Alex said.

"He is," Brian replied. "Word is that you had a battle with your Management and Political Counselors over early release of personnel."

"Yeah, we did. But at least we were able to put out a warden notice for everyone else to stay away from the Embassy. So, I take it you're happy with the support from the cops in Peshawar."

"Yeah, I think we'll be fine," replied Brian.

"Okay give me a call if you have any trouble," Alex said

before hanging up.

Conferring on their calls, Alex and Jim decided they could focus on upcoming events in Islamabad without diverting attention toward the Consulates General. Jim's next call was to Inspector General Qasim to see if the cops had more information. He was told that nothing had changed. Alex called Bill Stanton, and was told the same thing.

"At least the predicted size of the demonstration hasn't gotten any bigger," Jim stated.

"True, but, still, one thousand people is a large demo for Islamabad, and we can't rule out it could still turn violent," Alex replied. "What are you going to tell the Ambassador and DCM about sending people home early?"

"It's tricky. Nothing's changed for the worse since our last meeting. So, I don't have any new info to support a change of policy. But, I'm equally concerned about the CODEL press conference at the Residence."

"So, we wait and see what develops."

"I'm afraid so," Riley added.

The telephone rang at Nancy's desk. She listened for a moment, then called to Jim.

"It's Sam Wentworth for you, Jim. He has a problem with a missing employee."

"Hi, Sam," Jim said greeting the Embassy's Senior Consular Officer. "What's up? Nancy tells me you have a missing employee."

"That's right. Do you know Hussein Khan?"

"Sure, he's your senior local guy."

"Yeah. Well, he didn't come to work today, which is not like him. Normally, I wouldn't think much of It, assume he was sick and would call us later. Except his wife just called, and said he went out last night, and never returned home."

"Usually reliable?" Jim responded.

"Extremely so, "said Wentworth.

Alex could hear the conversation since he was sitting next to Jim's desk. He whispered, "Why don't we send Bhatti to check it out with Khan's wife?"

Jim nodded his head in agreement. "Sam, I'll send our local investigator to Khan's house to speak to his wife and get more information from her. He can also check with the police and hospitals."

"Okay, thanks, Jim," Wentworth said.

After getting briefed by Jim, Mohammad Bhatti left his office mid-morning and drove to Hussein Khan's home in Islamabad. Mrs. Khan told him of the phone call yesterday evening that came in around 8:00 pm. While she didn't know who called, she managed to hear her husband say the phrase "Ghulam's Pharmacy". Bhatti vaguely remembered once seeing a sign for the name, but couldn't recall its location. Driving to the nearby market, he stopped at the D. Watson Pharmacy, well-known to Embassy personnel, and inquired.

"I hope you can help me," Bhatti addressed the pharmacist. "I'm looking for Ghulam's Pharmacy. Do you know it? I'm not familiar with its location."

The pharmacist thought briefly before answering, "I have never heard of it. But let me check my reference book of all pharmacies in the area."

Bhatti watched him thumb through a booklet until he found it. "Ah, here it is," said the pharmacist. "It's located on the Grand

Trunk Road. But why do you want to go all the way there? I'm sure I can help you with whatever it is you require."

"Thanks, but I need to meet someone there," replied Bhatti. Now he remembered Ghulam's Pharmacy. He'd seen it several times while driving to Peshawar. But as the pharmacist just stated, why would Hussein Khan go there, especially so late at night? Bhatti got back into his small Nissan deciding he must drive to Ghulam's Pharmacy to make any progress on Khan's disappearance.

The drive would take him at least thirty minutes, perhaps longer, because he would look along the way for signs of an accident involving Khan's car.

There was nothing suspicious along the Grand Trunk Road, as Bhatti drove. Parking in Ghulam's lot, he looked around. No sign of Khan's car. He walked inside and spoke to the pharmacist, who didn't know Hussein Khan, nor did he stay open past seven on any evening. Bhatti thanked him and went outside. Resting against the side of his own car, he lit a local brand cigarette to help himself think.

Prior to 10 years with the RSOs office, he had been a police deputy assistant superintendent. Now in his forties, the dark haired, medium-built Bhatti had investigated a lot of crimes. His experience told him this disappearance seemed very suspicious, mainly because of the strange phone call so late last night. Adding to this, Khan's wife knew nothing about the caller. Even if Khan was having an affair, thought Bhatti, he never would have gone to Ghulam's Pharmacy thirty minutes away from the city. So, it must be for another reason.

Getting back into his car, Bhatti started to drive out of the parking lot. Then his police instincts kicked in and he had a second thought. Driving behind the pharmacy, he carefully scanned the area. There were no cars parked at all. Getting out, he walked the edge of the lot by the tree line. Nothing could be seen through the dense foliage. About to leave, his eyes fell upon a dark splotch that looked like blood splatter near the back end. Walking over, he carefully examined the stain. It appeared relatively new since there were no tire marks on top of it, no footprints, and no real dirt to speak of. Touching it, he felt it had already dried. Deciding to call Riley with an update, he would also call his police contacts for help with the investigation. Bhatti returned to the pharmacy and borrowed their phone to make his calls.

Forty-five minutes later, the police finally arrived. Bhatti had waited in his car and now greeted one of his long-time friends, Inspector Mansoor.

"Mansoor, it is good to see you again," said Bhatti with a big grin on his face, placing his hand over his heart in the Pakistani custom.

Mansoor embraced Bhatti. "I think it's been maybe two months since I saw you last. Just now I received a briefing before I left the police station but tell me again what this is all about."

Bhatti noted Mansoor had brought two other police officers with him, a sergeant and a constable. He repeated to all three the story he told to Inspector Mansoor's boss.

"I agree, this seems very suspicious," Inspector Mansoor said while examining the blood stains on the parking lot. "Something tragic may have happened to Khan and it may have happened right here."

The parking lot held no other clues, but when the team started examining the edge of the lot, they noticed grass and bushes had been crushed by something. Moreover, there appeared to be dried blood on the bushes. Following the trail into the already trampled foliage, it wasn't long before they uncovered a headless, naked body. While internal decomposition had begun shortly after the body's last breath, it wasn't visible on the outside, but rigor mortis was. Even without a head, Bhatti could only believe it was Khan. However, without identification, there was nothing at the scene to confirm it.

"I guess you'll bring this body to the Islamabad morgue," Bhatti said. "I'd like to take the body's fingerprints there. If it does belong to Hussein Khan, we'll be able to match the prints against those we took when he started working at the Embassy."

"Good idea," replied Mansoor. The killers probably never thought about the hands since almost no employers took fingerprints of employees in Pakistan, he thought. I'm glad the Americans are so thorough.

"Let me make a phone call back to the Embassy before we leave," Bhatti said. He needed to tell Riley about the body. Riley could decide whether to wait for final identification or call Sam Wentworth about his employee.

While Bhatti made his call, Mansoor radioed his office for a special morgue vehicle to carry the body back. Bhatti decided to wait at Ghulam's Pharmacy for the morgue vehicle to arrive. It would give him a chance to talk further with Mansoor and the two other police officers.

Because of this, he would not return to Islamabad until mid-afternoon, too late to help at the demonstration. He would be sorely missed.

CHAPTER 57

FRIDAY JUST BEFORE NOON

Counting Down the Minutes

The CODEL's meeting at the Foreign Ministry was more strained than the morning session had been with the Prime Minister. Senior Pakistani Foreign Office officials were less diplomatic and expressed clear irritation with America's new-found "love affair" with India. During the press conference following the meeting, the CODEL's second one this morning, journalists' questions were more pointed and emotional.

"I tell you, Worthington," Senator Desmond said to Ambassador Pierce as they rode back to the Embassy. "I'm not looking forward to the last press event at your residence." Desmond looked at his watch and saw it was almost noon.

"You have legitimate cause for concern, Senator," Pierce responded. "Both the Government officials and journalists are fanning the flames to whip up public sentiment against us. The Pakistan-India relationship is merely one aspect of our foreign policy. But the Pakistanis see it as central to their very existence as a nation. Let's finish this discussion when we get back to the Residence."

Before leaving the Foreign Ministry, Susan Witt radioed for an update on the demonstration. She received word that barely anyone was there. Based on this info, she decided the motorcade could use the front entrance. The trip was short and uneventful.

Since the journalists wouldn't arrive for the visit's final press conference until shortly before 1:00 pm, they had an hour yet. Susan and the DCM decided to go into the Embassy for a brief discussion with Jim and Alex. Abigail Wythe, senior CODEL staffer for South Asia, decided to join them, find a quiet desk area, and begin writing her trip report; with any luck she could get most of it done before the CODEL even left Islamabad. She wasn't needed at the press conference because Brewster Walcott and Rachel Smith would be there.

Ellen and Susan entered the RSO suite together and greeted both Jim and Alex who were in the midst of a discussion.

"So, Jim, no action in front of the Embassy, yet. Do you still want to send people home early?"

"I'd like to, but honestly, Ellen, original estimates on crowd-size are holding so far and there's no word on any planned violent actions. Even though our phones have been ringing off the hook with employees wanting to know if they'll be released at noon, I have to say, it's still early. We don't really expect the crowd for another hour. I know everyone is feeling a lot of concern about the demonstration."

Ellen nodded at the perpetual problem of decision-making. Never having enough information on which to base decisions with one hundred percent confidence.

"Okay, it looks like we'll hold the press conference at the Residence and also keep people working," she said. "We all agree no one wants to risk people needlessly, but in the absence of a concrete threat, I guess, it's my decision."

"You're the boss, Ellen." *And a damn good one,* he thought.

"All right, I'm going back to the Residence," she said.

"Jim, I think we should mention the latest on Hussein Khan," Alex spoke up.

Both Ellen and Susan looked at Alex, then at Jim. "If it's important, I have the time," Ellen said, looking at both men.

"Well, it may be nothing, but a few days ago, Susan

received information from a complainant that Hussein Khan, who works here in the Consular section, was taking bribes in exchange for issuing, or I should say, *influencing* the visa process. The allegation further mentioned Vice-Consul Sheila Winters. But with the CODEL about to arrive, and a demonstration planned, I thought it best to start an investigation immediately afterward, when we'll have more time. Nothing has been confirmed yet about the allegations."

"All right, that sounds fine," Ellen said, turning again toward the door, about to leave.

"But, that's not all," Alex jumped in. "While you were with the CODEL, Sam Wentworth reported to us that Hussein Khan didn't show up for work this morning. Also, that his wife called to say he failed to return home last night after receiving a phone call and leaving for a mysterious meeting on the Grand Trunk Road. Jim sent Bhatti to interview Khan's wife. She gave him a lead regarding a place called 'Ghulam's Pharmacy'. Then, a short while ago Bhatti called to report they'd discovered a headless body near the pharmacy. It may be Khan's; we'll check the body's fingerprints against our records."

Ellen put her hand to her mouth in a reflex reaction. Susan silently mouthed, "Whoa!" Clearly, both were concerned with the news.

"We're not certain it is Khan's body, yet. But if it is, it may be related to the visa fraud allegation," Jim said.

"Does Sam Wentworth know?" Ellen asked.

"Yes, I told him a few minutes ago."

"What about Khan's wife, does she know yet?"

"I'd rather not say anything until we confirm the fingerprints."

Riley thought Ellen looked like she had just been hit with a sledgehammer. Rubbing her chin, she shook her head.

"God, I hope it's not Khan. If it's not, I know you'll continue searching for his whereabouts."

"You bet," Riley replied.

As Ellen and Susan walked back to the Residence, Ellen asked her to describe the allegations against Khan in full detail.

Elsewhere, Nancy Williams, Jim's secretary, was busily shredding documents on Jim's orders. A short time before the demonstration was set to begin, Jim and Alex had decided that Embassy employees should get rid of classified documents that were not critically needed. Since all memoranda and telegrams were now backed up on the Embassy's computer system, retaining paper copies was no longer essential.

This lesson had been painfully learned in Tehran in 1979 when mobs seized the American Embassy and gained access to thousands of classified papers. Even though they had been shredded, the attackers were able to patch together many of the classified documents. Today's more sophisticated shredders cut-up documents so fine that reconstruction of material is impossible.

Nancy had been tasked with coordinating this document destruction since the Marines were fully engaged in preparing to defend the Embassy. She was located on the third floor within the safe-haven vaulted area, and just outside of the actual Communications Center.

"Hi, Nancy," said one of the junior officers from the Political Section bringing her a large bag filled with sensitive documents. She and two other staffers were continuously feeding sheets of papers into a giant shredder. The noise of the machine was so loud that Nancy and the others were wearing ear protection.

"Thanks," Nancy said, nodding in recognition. "If you'll put that material on top of this pile, I'll get them next."

Shortly after the Political Section employee left, another staffer entered with a full bag from the Economic Section. In a high threat post such as Islamabad, full emergency destruction should normally take less than twenty minutes because of regular classified material destruction drills. But this wasn't a drill, so all docs needed to be shredded. Nancy expected to be busy with this task for a while longer.

Meanwhile, Alex asked Gunny to go with him to check on each Marine and confirm they were correctly situated in their defensive positions throughout the Embassy. All observation posts were being manned and several Marines had direct line of sight to the front of the Embassy. Each Marine was wearing his helmet, body armor, load bearing vest with sidearm and shotgun. Each carried a gas mask with his gear, but it wasn't necessary to put it on now.

"Nothing to do now except wait," Alex said. "Let's see what happens."

CHAPTER **58**

FRIDAY NOON

NEW THREAT INFORMATION

The Army X Corps Commander in Rawalpindi, Lt. General Jamil, was listening with total focus to the briefing being given in his office by one of his senior division commanders, Major General Liaqat. Jamil was in his fifties, yet had the bearing and posture of a much younger man. Standing six feet tall, he kept in shape by regular exercise. Jamil was a decorated veteran of the infantry and had commanded troops with distinction against Indian forces.

Following a recent discussion with Iqbal Satter of SMG regarding ISI's concerns on private guard protection for foreign embassies and consulates, Jamil thought he'd better make some discreet inquiries into the matter. He had tasked Major General Liaqat with doing so. Jamil didn't have any particular opinion regarding ISI's inquiries, but because all of the foreign embassies were in the area of responsibility, he thought he should at least find out if there was a cause for concern.

Liaqat now glanced at his watch and saw it was almost noon. He realized Lt. General Jamil had a busy schedule, so he would be as brief as possible.

"Sir," said Liaqat, "I've contacted some old friends of mine in ISI about the matter. No one is aware of any *official* inquiry being made by ISI into private guard services at embassies."

Lt. General Jamil raised his eyebrows and tilted his head slightly to the side. "Really, no *official* inquiry, you say?"

"Yes, sir. However, the rumor is that Colonel Malik has sources who claim to have knowledge of a potential attack on western facilities in Pakistan, perhaps even on an embassy. Maybe that's why there have been some informal inquiries about private guard services."

"I assume you didn't speak with Colonel Malik directly," said Lt. General Jamil.

"That is correct. I confined my conversations only with former colleagues," replied Major General Liaqat. "There is another piece of the puzzle, Sir. I contacted the Commander of the 7th Infantry Division, based in Peshawar, who I have known for years. He said there are also vague and unconfirmed rumors of a special group of tribesmen who are talking about making attacks against Americans within Islamabad. Of note is that these tribesmen allegedly have links to the Army."

"To the Army? But only vague rumors?" asked Jamil.

"Yes, according to my friend. Others may have more information."

"If these rumors are true and ISI knows about it, I wonder why ISI hasn't shared this with us in X Corps?" stated Jamil.

"My view exactly, sir. Unless, of course, they believe there is little substance to the rumors."

Lt. General Jamil leaned back in his chair and thought for a moment. "Unless not everyone in ISI Headquarters is aware of those recent rumors, or alternatively, unless they are true and something very dark is going on."

"Possibly, but do you think that is likely?" replied Liaqat.

"I don't know, Liaqat, I don't know."

"Do you want me to pursue this matter further?" asked Major General Liaqat.

"No, but I think I need to speak with Colonel Walker at the American Embassy immediately. And as a precaution, until we can clear this up, I'd like a company of infantry from your division to be kept on alert to respond to an incident, if necessary. You can rotate the company as you desire. Make up a story about why they are on alert, but let's not mention anything yet about western targets."

"Yes, Sir," said Liaqat and he left the office.

When Lt. General Jamil spoke on the phone with Colonel Walker he mentioned the possibility of a threat to the Embassy. Walker agreed to come to his headquarters and suggested he bring Jim Riley, even though Jamil did not know him. Jamil thought this a good idea and agreed.

"Josh, thanks for including me in the meeting," said Riley after speaking with Walker. But before we go, we better let the Ambassador know about Lt. General Jamil's phone call and what we're doing."

"OK, but let's hustle, because I told Jamil we would be leaving right away."

As they briskly walked out of Riley's office, Riley called out to Alex, "I need you to come with us while we walk to the Residence." During the walk, Riley and Walker explained what they knew to Alex. At the Residence, they asked both the

Ambassador and the DCM for a private moment without the CODEL; they went into the Ambassador's study for privacy.

"This sounds serious," said Pierce after receiving their briefing. "I'd like to go with you to speak with Jamil, if you don't mind." After a brief pause, Pierce said, "I know him; we've met at several functions," He felt he should put their minds at rest, since it wasn't as if Jamil would be talking to a total stranger. "Besides, I've been with the CODEL for two days and I need a break from them."

Neither Riley nor Walker were in any position to disagree, although Jamil would be surprised to see the American Ambassador as part of the group.

Ambassador Pierce turned to Ellen Hunt. "I guess you'll have to give my apology to the CODEL and just tell them I'll be back around two o'clock or maybe a little later." Pierce picked up the phone and called the motor-pool number. He was in luck, his driver was about to go to lunch, but he was available instead to drive them to Rawalpindi. They left the Embassy compound at twelve-twenty and headed to Army Headquarters in Rawalpindi.

CHAPTER 59

FRIDAY 12:40 pm

Demonstation Minus 20 Minutes

The Ambassador's black limo entered the gates of X Corps Headquarters and stopped in front of a red brick entrance. Ambassador Pierce, Colonel Walker, and Jim Riley quickly exited the big car.

A Pakistani Army Colonel, standing in front of the entrance, came to attention and executed a smart salute in British style with his palm open to the visitors. All three Americans returned the salute, American style, then shook hands with the Colonel. He led them up ten steps into the building. Walking up another flight of stairs, they reached Lt. General Jamil's office.

Riley noticed the walls adorned with portraits of senior Pakistani officers, presumably former X Corps Commanders. The oldest portraits were of British Officers. Uniformed office personnel stood to attention as the Americans, led by Colonel Walker, passed by and entered Jamil's office.

"Ah, Ambassador Pierce. This is an unexpected pleasure," beamed Lt. General Jamil as they shook hands. Then he shook Walker's hand and was introduced to Riley.

"Gentlemen, please be seated," Jamil said, directing them to a group of brown leather sofas and armchairs. His office was spacious. In addition to the casual seating area and Jamil's desk, there was a long wooden conference table and twelve brown leather chairs off to one side. Walls were covered in maps of the X Corps, which included all of the northern territories up to the border with India in Kashmir.

"Normally, I would have gone through channels to pass on this information, but that may have taken weeks to get to you. Moreover, there are unresolved issues with ISI; the entire matter is quite sensitive."

In fact, I am already having second thoughts about whether I should be talking with the Americans directly, Jamil thought. Regardless of ISI's knowledge, or lack thereof, about the threats, should it emerge later that I have spoken to the Americans without official clearance, it could be a career-ending move for me.

"Mr. Ambassador, did you drive here in your limo?" Jamil asked.

"I did; why do you ask?"

"Just curious," Jamil replied. *Well, that settles it. Word will spread that the American Ambassador has called on me. So, I might as well give them the full story.*

Lt. General Jamil liked the Americans. While it seemed true that some American officers he had met were brash and a trifle conceited, he could not argue with their success on the battlefield. Their dynamic approach to problem solving, as well as ability to coordinate the actions of various battlefield and support elements was unrivaled. As a less senior officer, he had been sent to the U.S. Army's Command and General Staff College at Fort Leavenworth, Kansas, to study their methods. He found the academic program stimulating, but carried away an even greater appreciation for the willingness of up-and-coming officers to challenge the status quo thinking on doctrine and strategy.

Lt. General Jamil began his briefing, then halted when two corporals brought in green tea and wafer cookies for the group. He picked up again when the corporals left the room, out of earshot.

"First, I want to emphasize that this threat information is not confirmed. Had it been, we probably would all have known about it already. Secondly, this puzzle has been assembled from diverse sources which only reinforces my view that something strange is going on."

Jamil began reviewing the information he had received from Iqbal Satter without mentioning his name. The Ambassador interrupted him,

"Don't worry about protecting Satter, if that's who you mean." Jamil nodded his head. Pierce continued, "Satter briefed Jim a few days ago on an unusual inquiry about the guard services. As a result, we began reviewing our security."

"Excellent," Jamil said. He then divulged his inquiries into ISI. After listening, Riley mentioned an ISI Officer named Colonel Malik who had called at the Embassy to discuss potential threats from the tribal area.

"I see," Jamil said. He was now uncertain whether he could provide any new pieces of the puzzle, but decided to continue and let them know everything he had.

"All right, finally, I want to tell you about our information from sources in the Northwest Frontier Province. We have discreetly heard that some tribesmen were talking about violence against Americans in Islamabad, perhaps the same ones connected to the ISI information we have just mentioned. Furthermore, these tribesmen may also have links to elements in the Army, specifically to ISI."

It was as if Jamil had thrown a lightning bolt into the room. Everyone stiffened in alarm. "Are you certain?" the Ambassador asked urgently.

"I cannot confirm it, but I am sure this was said to my colleagues in Peshawar," replied Jamil.

"I should add, these senior Army officers near the tribal areas are known to me, and they could not possibly have anything to do with supporting such actions against you."

Jamil laid out further options concerning credibility of the information. "I'm afraid we can see fingerprints of ISI on this matter. Either they are well on top of the situation, or to the contrary, someone within ISI is at the root of the problem."

Ambassador Piece knew Lt. General Jamil had just done the unthinkable. He, a serving Pakistani Army officer, had raised the possibility of ISI involvement in a plot against the United States.

"General, I cannot thank you enough for your courage in bringing this to our attention. We will take this information very seriously. You can count on our total discretion if we are asked who provided this information," Ambassador Pierce stated.

"Thank you. As I said earlier, I fear the diversity of pieces in this puzzle does not bode well for us. But maybe it is only a case of circuitous information being repeated over and over again," Jamil said.

The Americans rose and shook Jamil's hand. Hurrying down the stairs to the Ambassador's waiting limo, they knew time was of the essence. They needed to return to the Embassy as quickly as possible. This information could be explosive and the demonstration was about to begin.

CHAPTER **60**

FRIDAY 1:00 pm

The Demonstration Begins

The limo driver raced down the road as fast as he could safely drive.

"Josh, it looks like you've been right all along about ISI," whispered Ambassador Pierce in the back seat so the driver and police bodyguard couldn't hear. "When we get to the Embassy, let's call in Stanton and get his take on this allegation. I'll have Ellen join us."

"Sounds like it's more than an allegation, sir," Walker responded in an equally soft voice.

"I agree," Riley interjected. "It's extraordinary that a senior general in the Pakistan Army would come to us on his own with such information."

"What do you recommend?" the Ambassador asked.

"After we talk with Bill, we should cable Washington with the info. You make a secure call to the Secretary. I'll call the Assistant Secretary of DS at the same time."

"We'd better be prepared with immediate action steps," Pierce stated.

"If the threat is from a powerful element inside Pakistan's

Government, but doesn't actually represent the *view* of the Government, I believe we should show support for the pro-U.S. faction," whispered Colonel Walker. "It could entail direct and covert DOD intelligence support to the Army, but not to ISI."

"That sounds like more of a long-term strategy," Pierce stated. "We need something to help us now. As soon as we get back, let's draw up a specific list of things to discuss with Washington and recommend actions we can put into effect immediately."

"Jim, what can Diplomatic Security do for us?" the Ambassador asked Riley.

"They can dispatch one or two Mobile Deployment Teams within a day or two to help protect the Mission. But what we really need do is cut our Embassy personnel staffing by perhaps fifty percent. That decision will take approval from the Undersecretary for Management and probably take a week, but we don't have that much time. However, should we ask, and if it's approved, Washington will want to withdraw all dependents and non-essential employees. We already have a draw-down list developed for emergencies. Morale will suffer, but I believe it needs to be done."

The traffic was unusually heavy since Friday midday prayers had just ended. People were free for the weekend, so the ride back to the Embassy would take another twenty minutes.

At the Residence, the final press conference was winding down. It had been difficult since some of the senators had trouble understanding journalists' accents, and their questions demanded detailed answers the senators weren't accustomed to providing without prompting from their staffs.

On top of that, the increasingly loud noise from the demonstration outside the Embassy Compound was becoming a real distraction.

When Rachel called a finish to the press conference, all groups thanked each other politely and moved to the dining room for light snacks and casual conversations. Mrs. Pierce hosted the group in her ever-gracious style.

Meanwhile, outside, the storm was brewing.

Shortly after the Ambassador, Riley, and Colonel Walker had left the embassy to see Lt. General Jamil, the demonstrators started showing up at the entrance to the Diplomatic Enclave, roughly a half-mile from the American Embassy.

By one o'clock around two thousand had arrived on buses. There were only a few squads of policemen to handle the crowd. For fifteen minutes the protestors shouted their anti-American chants, waved their placards, and blocked traffic.

Then two of the lead buses, one at each street entrance to the Diplomatic Enclave, slowly nudged the drop-bars manned by the policemen. Without using much force, the buses snapped the drop-bars off their retaining holders. Then all the buses, thirty in total and loaded with demonstrators, drove to the front of the U.S. Embassy. The police stood watching.

During the next twenty minutes, an additional three thousand demonstrators came to the Embassy, most arriving in buses arranged secretly by Colonel Malik. These numbers were thousands in excess of what the Embassy had expected. Malik's people had done a superb job of providing transportation and organizing the attendance of different groups within the Rawalpindi-Islamabad area. The crowd blocked the entire road in front of the Embassy yet maintained a small degree of discipline. Nevertheless, groups started infringing on Embassy property outside of the perimeter wall.

As the decibel level from the demonstration increased, Ellen Hunt, inside the Residence, glanced at Susan Witt. Susan acknowledged the glance with a nod, and said to the two DS Special Agents," I'm going outside to assess what's going on." The two Agents remained inside the foyer. Susan had to walk fifty yards from the Residence to the front gate in order to see the crowd behind the wall.

God, she thought, this is really huge.

"Eagle Two from Eagle Three," called Susan on the radio for Alex. "I'm sure you must be monitoring the crowd size."

"Eagle Three, this is Eagle Two. Roger that. We estimate there are several thousand demonstrators and about one hundred cops spread out in front of the Embassy."

"Eagle Two from Eagle Three, any chance of sending one or two Marines to support us at the Residence?"

Alex turned to Gunny Rodriquez and said, "I think we should. Who do you want to send?"

Even though he knew the State Department-Marine Corps Memorandum of Agreement stated Marines were assigned for the sole purpose of protecting the Embassy and its classified material, Gunny didn't hesitate in answering.

"Sir, I'll send Sgt. Hancock and Corporal Jones."

"Make sure they bring their shotguns and all their issued ammo," ordered Alex.

"Eagle Three from Eagle Two, Hancock and Jones are on their way," Alex reported.

"Eagle Two from Eagle Three, roger that, and thanks," Susan replied.

Susan walked back to the Residence and briefed the DCM. Hunt looked worried but was satisfied the RSO was taking reasonable steps to beef up protection of the CODEL.

"Eagle One from Eagle Two, did you copy last transmissions?"

"This is Eagle One," Jim Riley replied. "I copied. We have departed Rawalpindi and will use the side entrance to the Compound if there are no demonstrators there. We'll be at your location in fifteen minutes."

"Eagle One from Eagle Two, I'm looking at a camera monitor and there are no demonstrators at the side entrance now, but call again when you are two minutes out," Alex instructed.

"Copy that, Eagle One out."

Standing in Post One, Alex continued watching the crowd through the CCTV monitors. He turned to Gunny Rodriguez and asked, "How are the Marines doing?"

"Fine. Everyone's set, in case something happens."

Every few minutes a radio situation report was received from individual Marines with a view of the demonstration. These updates were essential, providing useful information to Marines without a line of sight to the crowd.

"Now, it's too late to send employees home," Alex cursed to himself. The crowd had blocked the streets, as he feared. He knew if the demonstration ended peacefully, JC Colon would claim he was vindicated by not letting people go early. On the other hand, if it turned violent, he would try to blame security for not pushing the issue.

"It looks like the crowd has a few instigators," Gunny said, pointing to the CCTV monitor as he zoomed in the camera for a tighter shot of the front gate. "See the guy with the turban and a beard?" Gunny asked.

"Yeah, I see him," responded Alex. He watched further as the turban-headed man waved his arms about and urged on the crowd to cheer. Just then, Bill Stanton knocked on the ballistic door at Post One, and Alex let him into the control center.

"My guys have been watching the demonstration from our office upstairs," Stanton pointed at the CCTV screen. "That guy with the turban is Maulana Chaudhry. He's a badass religious fanatic. The guy's nothing but trouble. You might want to keep an eye on him."

"Thanks, Bill, we were just watching him. Is there anything else you can tell me?"

"Unfortunately, no, I can't. We don't have our people in the crowd. ISI just told us they were taken by surprise at the size of the demo."

"No shit," Alex replied. "Does ISI have anyone in the crowd?"

"Sort of," Stanton replied. "They have a small presence to monitor what's being said, but they're letting the police take care of the situation. Sorry, I've got to get back upstairs."

"OK, Bill. Thanks for your help."

"Look at this other guy," Corporal Wilson said, standing next to Alex and viewing another monitor. Alex switched his focus to Wilson's monitor and saw another man passing out signs. He couldn't make out what was written on the sign since they were too far away.

A nervousness began to invade Alex since the police hadn't contained the crowd at the entrance to the Diplomatic Enclave. He thought the crowd could easily become an out-of-control mob if something wasn't done soon to contain their enthusiasm.

"Gunny, I'm going up to the third floor and check on how the employees are reacting," Alex said. "I've got my radio with me." He left Post One and quickly took the center stairwell up one flight, two steps at a time. Walking past offices with doors open, he saw many employees looking out windows at the crowd. The employees seemed on edge. He didn't blame them; he felt the same.

CHAPTER 61

FRIDAY AFTERNOON

Turning Violent

Maulana Chaudhry was preaching through the bullhorn to the crowd gathered in the front of the U.S. Embassy, imploring them to continue their chants against the Americans. Chaudhry had organized their transport to the Embassy and paid many of them to be there. Earlier, he had assigned key followers to make large signs with bright red letters protesting American corruption of Pakistani values. The crowd waved these signs back and forth and shook their fists at the Embassy's front gate.

"Stop your attacks on Islam," Chaudhry yelled into the bullhorn as he pointed to the Embassy. "Stop sending your movies and pornography into our country."

Nearby, Asif Babar stood on a makeshift platform, more of a wooden box than a proper stage. He yelled at his Radical Students for Pakistan to scream their demands that the Americans end their support for India.

"India is the devil," called out Babar. "America must stop helping our oppressors."

Imran Durrani, the Labor Federation leader, was not to be outdone as he called for his Labor Federation cohorts to demand an end to American quotas on Pakistan textile imports and other products. "Jobs for Pakistanis, not Americans," he yelled.

In a short time, the crowd had grown alarmingly large. There were now about five thousand demonstrators outside the Embassy compound. They blocked the road in front of the Embassy just by their large presence. Alex continued watching the demonstration on the CCTV monitors in Post One. He saw a few in the crowd carrying effigies of what he assumed was 'Uncle Sam.'

As he watched, the crowd set fire to two of the effigies. Then, an American flag was burned. The actions of the crowd were ramping up.

Earlier, when Alex and Gunny had checked on each Marine, they had confirmed all were situated correctly in defensive positions throughout the Embassy. By dispatching two Marines to the Ambassador's residence, the detachment was now down two men, who would have served as backups at the entrance to the third-floor safe haven. Nevertheless, all observation posts were manned, with several Marines having a direct line of sight to the crowd.

As the crowd outside continued growing in size and ferocity, Alex authorized the RSO-issued shoulder weapons be taken out of the weapons locker. As a last-minute thought, before Hancock and Jones had left for the Residence, he had given Hancock an UZI sub-machine gun, concealed in a briefcase, to bring to Susan Witt. The case contained three loaded magazines of twenty rounds each of 9mm ammunition. Alex kept the two remaining Uzis at Post One for himself and Gunny Rodriquez. As always, Alex was armed with his Sig-Sauer 9mm pistol and Gunny had a Beretta 9mm pistol. Alex distributed the Ruger Mini-14 rifles to three of the Marines on the embassy's third floor. Each Marine also had his assigned shotgun.

"Corporal Wilson," Alex said. "Do an all-call on the radio net and tell everyone the demonstration has grown to at least five thousand. Tell them that under no circumstances should anyone come to the Embassy compound."

"Okay, boss," Wilson answered. The all-call would broadcast to every radio on the U.S. Mission network, including AID offices, the American Center, the International School Principal's Office, and every American employee residence, where, hopefully, spouses would be monitoring the net.

Alex picked up the phone at Post One and called the Inspector General of Police.

"Hello, sir," said Alex when IG Qasim answered. "Thank you for sending the extra police to the Embassy, but it appears the demonstration has grown to around five thousand people. They're burning effigies, as well as an American flag. Would it be possible for you to send additional men immediately?"

"I was told the demonstration is peaceful. I didn't realize it had grown so large," replied IG Qasim. "Perhaps I should send reinforcements as you request. I will see that it is done."

"Thank you, sir" Alex said and hung up.

Alex then called Ahmed, the SMG Embassy guard supervisor. "Do you have anything to report from the MRT?" The Mobile Reaction Team was parked down the street from the Embassy, just beyond the crowd. Before noon the men had switched to an unmarked SUV and had taken off their SMG baseball hats while sitting in their vehicle. Although not really undercover, these small changes had made them less conspicuous. The team was monitoring the crowd from a distance and had already reported to Ahmed.

"The crowd is very agitated with too much anger," Ahmed told Alex. "Also, the Team can see four vehicles parked across the street from the Embassy with men just sitting inside doing nothing. I am thinking this is strange since they are on their seats in the car, and not participating in the demonstration at all."

"Okay. The MRT should continue to monitor and report

immediately if there are serious changes in the situation."

"Yes, boss, I will see to it."

As the demonstration raged outside, Winston Hargrove IV was working in his office when the phone rang. It was Joan, the Ambassador's secretary, transferring a call on a non-secure line from the White House National Security Advisor's Office in D.C.

"Winston, I have Benjamin Shapiro on the phone for you," Joan said. "He wanted to speak with the Ambassador or the DCM, but I told him they're out of the Embassy. He asked to speak to you."

"Okay, thanks," Hargrove replied.

He knew Shapiro from his student days at Princeton. Hargrove always thought of him as a somewhat geeky policy nerd. Being short, non-athletic, and not a WASP, Shapiro just didn't fit in with Hargrove's crowd. Now he was one of the senior officials at the NSC, having worked in a variety of Washington think tanks over the years and associating himself with powerful foreign policy gurus. As a result, Hargrove was forced to speak with him from time to time.

"Ben, how are you, my old friend?" as if he cared.

"I'm fine, Winston. I was just calling to find out how the senators' trip is going."

"Well, to be honest, the Pakistanis have been exceedingly blunt and negative about our relations with the Indians. I think the senators are a bit surprised at the intensity of the local reaction."

"I was hoping the embassy could smooth over the impact of our policy shift while the senators are in town," Shapiro said.

"I'm afraid it won't be as easy as you may wish."

Suddenly, the noise level from the crowd dramatically escalated. Hysterical shouts and screams could be heard through Hargrove's closed window.

"Just a second," he told Shapiro while putting down the phone. He opened the window to get a better sense of the action, then picked up the phone again. "Good heavens," exclaimed a clearly panicked Hargrove. "There are thousands of demonstrators outside the Embassy and they're throwing fire bombs and rocks at the Embassy perimeter wall. It looks like some of the demonstrators themselves are on fire!"

Shapiro replied, "Oh, hell, whatever happens, try to keep the Embassy from over-reacting. We have enough trouble with Pakistan already. It's better to send employees home, than to fight it out with a wild mob and have us accused of killing Pakistani civilians."

"It's too late to send people home," Hargrove said. *Damn,* he thought, *Why did I ever listen to JC about keeping all the employees working in the Embassy?* But, he rationalized, he had never been in such a situation in his career.

"Again, don't let Security over-react," cautioned Shapiro as Hargrove hung up on him.

CHAPTER 62

FRIDAY EARLY AFTERNOON

FIREBOMBS and RPGs

Alex watched in horror at the Post One camera monitors. In what seemed a coordinated action, at least twenty men in the crowd took Molotov cocktails out from brown cloth shoulder bags each carried. They lit the gasoline bombs, then hurled the flaming objects at walls of the guard house compound. Searing heat and flames erupted when the bombs exploded against the building.

The guard house withstood the attack and was not seriously damaged due to reinforced construction and ballistic glass. Nevertheless, Alex picked up Post One's direct-phone to reassure the guards they'd be all right.

"This is Alex Boyd. I can see firebombs just hit your guardhouse. Remain calm. The guard house is too strong to be damaged. Just stay inside and observe."

"Thank you, boss. We are doing much observing."

Despite the strength of the guard house, once the bottles broke against it or against nearby walls, the gas and flames reached out like tentacles engulfing demonstrators and police nearby.

Another round of Molotov cocktails was immediately hurled by the same men indiscriminately. Alex could see the crowd scattering, some running with their clothes on fire. The Pakistani cops were converging on the area where the firebombs had hit. It was the perfect diversion.

Down the street, the SMG Mobile Reaction Team also observed the fire-bomb attack with alarm. The MRT leader radioed to Ahmed, the SMG compound Guard Supervisor.

"Even some of the policemen have been set on fire," he reported. Now, all four of the SMG guards exited their vehicle, but were holding their positions as instructed.

Again, the MRT leader spoke to Ahmed, "All the men that we were observing in four vehicles across the street from the Embassy are getting out of their SUVs. There must be about twenty of them. Four are running toward the Embassy perimeter wall with smoking satchel charges."

The men with the satchel charges were separate from the demonstrators. They were part of Colonel Malik's secret attack group of frontier tribesmen. Two of the tribesmen threw their charges against the perimeter wall; the other two threw theirs over the wall into the compound. Ten seconds later, after the men had run back to their vehicle for protection, the bombs exploded, sending bricks and mortar in all directions, creating a hole in the wall itself. Screams of anguish could be heard from the injured outside the compound. Demonstrators and police lay on the ground writhing in pain, many with serious injuries and bleeding out. The four MRT guards retrieved their AK-47s from the back of their own SUV and prepared to engage the terrorists.

On the camera monitors, Alex saw the attackers throwing the satchel charges. "Hit the Duck-and-Cover alarm, now!" He yelled to Corporal Wilson in Post One.

Wilson hit the switch and instantly an extremely loud wailing sound assaulted everyone's eardrums in the Embassy. Because Jim Riley had installed external speakers on the Embassy roof the year prior, the alarm signal could be heard throughout the compound.

In their offices, most employees dove for the floor or crouched under desks, as they had been trained to do by the RSO. Unfortunately, a few American and Pakistani employees, against all training, couldn't resist looking out the window to see what was happening just as an explosion shattered most of the windows in the front of the Embassy, sending shards of glass flying into offices at lightning speed. The Mylar protective film installed on each window seriously degraded the overall impact of the explosions; but not all broken windows would remain intact. Several people standing in front of the windows were instantly impaled by jagged glass, bleeding profusely as they dropped to the floor screaming in agony.

After the blast, Alex hit the off-button on the alarm and grabbed the public address speaker. "All employees immediately move to the safe-haven on the third floor. I repeat, all employees immediately move to the safe-haven on the third floor." Then, he turned the wailing alarm back on.

Just then, Jim Riley called in on the radio. "Eagle Two from Eagle One. The Ambassador's bodyguard heard on his police radio net the Embassy is under attack. What's happening?"

"A bomb just went off against the front perimeter wall," Alex replied. "Some demonstrators have been using firebombs against their own crowd. Do not, repeat, do not come to the Embassy until we figure out where this is all headed."

Just then, Winston Hargrove and JC Colon converged on Post One. Banging on the clear bullet resistant door, Hargrove screamed, "What the hell's going on?"

As Alex opened the heavy ballistic door a crack, he said, "Obviously the Embassy is under attack. Get up to the safe-haven, now!"

"Listen to me," yelled Hargrove. "I am the Senior Officer in the Embassy now and I don't want you to use force against the demonstrators. We must stay defensive only and not over-react."

"You're not in the chain of command, and I'll decide what we do," Alex said in a controlled yet forceful commanding voice. "I don't have time for you now. Get upstairs!"

"I'm in the chain of command because the Ambassador and DCM are not here," Hargrove yelled.

"Wrong, Hargrove. We have radio communication with them and I'm following our standing orders," Alex replied, even though he hadn't yet spoken to either Ambassador Pierce or DCM Hunt.

"If you so much as hurt even one demonstrator, I'll have your ass for this," Hargrove screamed, his face a beet-red.

Jim Riley's voice came over the radio again. "Can you give me more details?"

Alex began to reply but was cut off mid-sentence when a huge explosion rocked the Embassy with a deafening roar. While Alex was dealing with Hargrove, fifteen of Colonel Malik's tribesmen had rushed from their SUVs across the street and darted through the newly created opening in the wall, using the smoke from the perimeter wall explosions as cover. As soon as they were inside, one aimed his RPG at the Embassy's third floor. It had just penetrated into the building and detonated as it hit the Communications Center vault. It couldn't have struck a more vital area.

The Center was currently designated a safehaven. Fires now broke out around and within the vaulted area with thick smoke billowing out through a gaping hole in the wall. Employees from the military, DEA and CIA from adjoining offices who were not injured in the blast grabbed hallway fire extinguishers and fought their way through smoke and the smell of burning material to battle small fires before they grew into infernos.

Fortunately, the blast occurred before all employees had made their way up to the third floor. When the RPG made contact with the vault's outer wall, the warhead sent super-heated molten lead into the vault as it exploded. Bob Boudreaux and Carrie Sherman, Alex's good friends, were working at desks precisely where the rocket impacted. Instantly, their bodies were ripped apart and burned nearly beyond recognition. Two other communicators on the other side of the room, both suffered such extensive head and organ injuries they died within minutes.

Nancy Williams had just finished shredding and was standing a few feet outside the safe-haven when the RPG hit the vault. The force of the blast threw her across the hallway into a wall, breaking her right arm. Although in pain, bruised down her right side, and somewhat dazed, she survived the initial impact of the blast. Somehow, she managed to pull herself up from the floor and lean against the wall, fighting off a wave of dizziness and nausea.

"Nancy! Are you all right?" a young CIA officer called to her as he came out of his office. He placed his hand on her broken arm to give her support, causing her to scream in agony.

"I think my arm's broken," She said with tears streaming down her face. "Shit, it really hurts."

After a few more seconds, she regained her equilibrium and, despite her trauma, bravely directed two more arriving employees to use fire extinguishers to battle fires at the entrance to the communications vault. Only after ensuring that several more seriously injured employees were taken care of did she agree to be escorted down the hall and taken into an office to lie down on a sofa.

The blast damaged all antennas and transponders on the roof needed for the Embassy radio net, as well as destroying the rooftop satellite dishes for secure communications with the outside world. Now Alex and the Marines had no radio communications at all.

Corporal Wilson yelled to Alex in order to be heard over the wailing alarm signal, "Sir, that was an RPG! I saw the guy fire it on the camera monitor."

As Corporal Wilson was describing the attack, a second tribesman, already inside the compound, stopped seventy meters from the Embassy and aimed his own RPG at the ground floor. The RPG warhead streaked away from him and blasted the cafeteria, leaving a massive hole in the wall for the tribesmen to gain entrance. Numerous small fires started, as after the blast in the Comms Center, and smoke poured out of the hole. Two of the Embassy Pakistani cooks, who had not understood the order to move to the third floor safehaven, were killed in the explosion.

"Sir, I still have a visual on the attackers," Corporal Wilson said to Alex. "I see five of them breaking off and running toward The Residence. Looks like ten are heading toward us."

Alex tried to raise Susan on the radio, but there was only silence.

"Shit," he said. Alex worried that without a warning, Susan wouldn't be fully prepared to deal with the assault. "God damn it," he said. Taking a deep breath, he thought: *Susan is a trained DS Agent and has two more Agents with her, plus two Marines. They'll have to make do.*

A vision of Rachel momentarily flashed in his mind. He wanted to protect her, hold her in his arms and comfort her, but there was nothing he could do now.

Chapter 63

FRIDAY AFTERNOON

TERRORISTS ATTACK

Immediately after the blast at the perimeter wall, the four Mobile Reaction Team members from SMG sprang into action. Three rushed the attackers carrying their AK-47s, trying to stop them before they could enter the compound. The fourth man reported the attack via a separate SMG radio net to SMG headquarters in Islamabad, then he raced to join the other three.

But before the MRT men had run even twenty meters, the last five tribesmen opened fire on the police. They had stayed in front of the Embassy to act as a rear protection element for the fifteen–man assault force. Now, several demonstrators were killed, along with several policemen who were also about to pursue the attackers through the opening in the perimeter wall.

The four MRT members were taken by surprise having lost sight of these remaining five tribesmen opening up with their AK-47s. Now as the closest, and greatest threat, they engaged this 5-man rear protective element of attackers based on years of training with Pakistan Army Special Forces.

Two MRT commandoes stopped at fifty meters and opened fire in short bursts while the other two flanked the terrorists to the left, across the road from the Embassy. One MRT commando scored a direct hit; the tribesman flew into the air from the impact of several well-placed rounds to his chest and was dead before his body hit the ground.

Now it was the terrorists turn to be surprised. They had expected only light and ineffective resistance from the ill-trained police. Recognizing the MRT guards' uniforms once they had been fired upon, the tribesmen now realized they had been under observation while waiting in their SUVs. Cornered, the remaining four tribesmen knelt next to their beige Toyota Land Cruiser, returning fire with the MRT men.

The blast at the perimeter wall near the entrance gate was felt and heard throughout the Ambassador's residence. All senators and journalists froze in terror. While Susan Witt was unsure what had happened, she spoke rapidly to the DCM and Corporal Jones.

"Help me get these people upstairs." Susan said. "The Residence's safehaven is much too small to hold a group this size, but they are too vulnerable to stay on the ground floor."

"I'll spread everyone out into the upstairs bedrooms," Ellen Hunt responded. Turning to the assembled group of Americans and Pakistani journalists, including the Chairman of the Senate Committee and Mrs. Pierce, Ellen Hunt called out to them.

"The Embassy's under attack! Come upstairs with me," Ellen instructed. "Spread out into separate rooms, lock your doors, stay away from the windows, place furniture against the door, and get on the floor. Each door is reinforced, but probably won't stop bullets. Stay as calm as you can. The security agents and Marines will protect us." She then knelt next to Rachel in the second-floor hallway to ensure that none of the visitors left their rooms. Rachel was remaining calm under the circumstances. Thoughts of Alex ran through her mind.

Susan knew the Embassy was under attack having been

monitoring Alex's last radio transmission with Jim Riley but didn't know any details. She saw the two visiting DS special agents take up positions in ground floor rooms overlooking the entrance, thereby covering the front door as well as a few of the ground floor windows. Each had his Sig-Sauer 9mm pistol with spare magazines. Sgt. Hancock stood adjacent to the front door, using a side glass panel for observation down the long driveway. He carried his Beretta 9mm pistol with one spare magazine, plus his Remington 870 shotgun with double 00 buck shells. Five rounds were loaded in the shotgun and he had another twenty shotgun rounds available in his load-bearing vest.

Susan and Corporal Jones positioned themselves at the top of the stairs after trailing the CODEL, the journalists, and Mrs. Pierce upstairs to ensure that they were out of any direct line of fire. Susan opened her briefcase and snatched the Uzi. Slapping the back of the collapsible stock, she pulled and extended it so it rested against her shoulder. Inserting a twenty-round magazine, she put two other magazines in her pants pockets. Feeling for her own Sig Sauer on her hip, she knew it was already loaded with a 9mm round chambered.

Susan tried, again, to raise Alex on her radio, but nothing. Corporal Jones took up a position against the wall opposite from Susan, then aimed his shotgun down the stairs into the void.

Chapter **64**

FRIDAY AFTERNOON

KILLING THE ENEMY

Employees throughout the Embassy were using the stairwells to reach the third floor, many unaware of the destruction from the RPG blast. Marines were helping move American and Pakistani staff from the lower floors upwards, trying to cram them into the undamaged portion of the third floor hallway, but the area just wasn't large enough.

Some were taking cover in offices and lying on floors. The air was filled with smoke and debris from the explosion; people were gagging and coughing. Many had the presence of mind to bring their State Department-issued gas masks from their own offices, others did not. All Marines had put on their own gas masks after the first RPG hit the building. The hallways looked like a real war zone.

Alex was about to leave Post One to view the damage first-hand when Sgt. Washington appeared at his side with the Gunny.

"We have a huge hole in the outer cafeteria wall," reported Washington. His adrenalin was kicking in, yet his voice was controlled and professional. "Also, the commo-center is destroyed and all communicators are dead. We have people stacked up in the third-floor hallway with nowhere to go."

"All communicators are dead?" repeated Alex, hardly believing what he had heard.

"Yeah, all of them, Sir" Sgt. Washington said.

"What about Nancy? Is she all right?" His throat tightening up, but he was almost afraid to hear the answer.

"Broken arm, maybe a mild concussion, but okay," Sgt. Washington replied. "Despite her arm, she's telling everyone else what to do."

Alex smiled briefly at Nancy's courage and tenacity, but had to fight back tears when he thought of his good friends, Bob and Carrie, being dead along with the other two communicators. He knew the Marines would now have to defend every inch of ground including the first and second floors since the third floor safe haven was partially destroyed.

"All right, Washington, come with me to the cafeteria. Gunny, go to Stanton's office, DEA, Defense Attaché's Office, and Military Assistance Group. Tell them I need help defending each of the stairwells to the third floor, or whatever is left of them. I don't want anyone coming down into a potential firefight. Then find me on the ground floor. Move all other Marines to protect the ground and second floor stairwells, and send one Marine to support Corporal Wilson in Post One. Finally, have the Marines drop teargas all over the ground floor hallway."

Alex knew that Corporal Wilson would have already remotely locked-down the Embassy elevator.

"Roger that, Boss," Gunny replied.

As Alex started leaving for the cafeteria, Hargrove and Colon, who had waited outside of Post One, stopped him, still wanting to argue. Hargrove grabbed Alex by the arm and tried to hold him.

"Boyd, I ordered you to take no action against the crowd!" he screamed.

"This isn't a crowd problem anymore, you *stupid fuck*! It's an armed attack!" Alex yelled directly into Hargrove's face. The Embassy's wailing Duck-and-Cover alarm still screamed in their ears. Colon backed up in fear, but Hargrove stood his ground.

"Boyd, you're out of line! You've received a direct order from me, the Senior Officer."

He wouldn't let go of Alex's arm, so Alex pushed Hargrove with full force into the wall, grabbed his throat with his left hand and dragged him along the wall. Hargrove winced in pain, momentarily slumping before regaining his balance, face purple from the vice-like grip.

Then, Alex released his hold on Hargrove and pushed Colon out of the way. Coughing as he spoke in a shaky voice, Hargrove looked at Colon.

"Let's get upstairs," he said, then screamed at Alex's departing figure: "I'll see that you're thrown out of the Service!"

Alex gave him "the finger" as he ran toward battle.

Pausing in the center stairwell, Alex tightened the straps on his gas mask, ensuring a snug fit over his face. Next, he pulled the bolt back on his Uzi. Turning to Sgt. Washington, he said, "Let's get those assholes."

Cautiously, they moved down the center stairwell to the ground floor. Approaching the entrance to the cafeteria, Sgt. Washington threw his four tear gas canisters into the dining room, then both men positioned themselves on either side of the double doors leading into the cafeteria.

The glass panes from the doors were now lying on the floor in slivers from the RPG blast. Dense smoke from the tear gas and fires obscured their view. Refracted rays of sunshine streamed into the cafeteria through the hole in the wall and mixed with airborne debris and smoke, creating a vision of Armageddon for Alex.

Aware of his own breathing into the gas mask, he felt his shirt sticking to his body from sweat.

Suddenly, two men armed with AK-47s, ran through the hole in the wall and headed directly for Alex and Washington, screaming "Allahu Akbar."

Alex opened up first, firing a three-round burst from his Uzi into the first attacker's chest; the man fell to the side and died within seconds. The blast from Washington's shotgun sent the second man flying backward through the hole in the wall.

Two more attackers immediately ran through the opening, but dove onto the floor behind some overturned tables for protection. Since neither man was wearing a gas mask, they started coughing uncontrollably from the tear gas, eyes watering and burning profusely.

Sgt. Washington pumped two shotgun rounds through one overturned table. The rounds penetrated the cheap wood, devastating the attacker's head, turning it into something akin to strawberry jam. Alex fired two separate three-round bursts through the other table immediately killing the second attacker.

As Washington started to reload, he saw a round object fly through the hole in the wall and crash onto the floor.

"Grenade!" he shouted.

The remaining attackers outside, realizing what was happening inside, had tossed a grenade into the cafeteria before entering. Since the internal Embassy walls were flimsy and offered no protection, both Alex and Washington took off sprinting in opposite directions, diving onto the floor after a few strides. When the grenade exploded, neither was near enough to be injured. Scrambling to their feet, Washington now stood guard at the base of the center stairwell. Alex did the same at the north end stairwell.

"I'm with you, Boss," Gunny yelled into Alex's ear. "Corporal Garner should be with Washington now in the center stairwell." Both Gunny and Garner had brought more tear gas with them and threw the canisters into the ground floor corridor.

While the attack raged on inside the American Embassy, the Ambassador, still in his fully armored limo, decided his group couldn't return to the Embassy after all. Rather, they should drive to the British Embassy down the road and call the State Department from there. As they drove within the Diplomatic Enclave, they saw thousands of protesters milling about and smoke arising from the Embassy compound. This route would not take them in front of the U.S. Embassy, but was still close enough to run into possible major trouble.

"Drive quickly," Riley instructed the driver. "But don't spook the protestors. Just don't stop the vehicle under any circumstances."

"I hope you're armed," Ambassador Pierce said to Riley.

"I am. I have my Sig with me. And your bodyguard has his gun."

"I also have a Beretta in my briefcase," Colonel Walker added.

Worthington Pierce had never been a big fan of guns, but he appreciated the fact he was among professionals who knew how to use them. As they drove, he worried about the safety of his wife, the CODEL back at The Residence, and the safety of everyone in the compound.

Arriving at the British Embassy, the guard allowed them to park in a secure lot in the building courtyard while he called the British Embassy Security Chief. Within minutes, the British Ambassador, Nigel Farnsworth-Smythe, came to the lobby with a look of total amazement on his face.

"Worthington, I'm glad you're safe! But how in blazes did you even get here from your compound?"

Farnsworth-Smythe, who spoke fluent Urdu and Hindi, was an old South Asian hand and a good friend of Worthington Pierce. His grandfather had been in the British Colonial Service, or Indian Civil Service, as it was called then, so his own background was steeped in South Asian history.

"I'm afraid I need to impose upon you, Nigel. We were returning from Rawalpindi when this attack occurred. In fact, I'm still not certain exactly what's going on. Our communications are completely down. Could I borrow a phone to call Washington?"

"But, of course. My chaps tell me there's a major shootout going on at your place, and, indeed, we can all hear explosions," Farnsworth-Smythe said.

The British Ambassador led Pierce to his private office and left him alone in the room. After ten minutes, Pierce emerged and spoke to the group, including Farnsworth-Smythe, "I called the State Department Operations Center and described what we know is happening. The OPS center then transferred me to the Secretary of State, who will call the Pakistani Prime Minister and demand immediate help. Josh, you better call Lt. General Jamil. Jim, would you call the Inspector General of Police. We need help, now!"

"We've already made those calls while you were talking to Washington," Riley replied. "Look, you're safe here, but I need to get closer to the Embassy and find out what's going on. So, unless you object, I'm going to work my way to the Embassy."

"I'm coming with you," Colonel Walker said.

"You guys don't have to do this. Are you frickin' nuts?" Ambassador Pierce said. "The mob is all over the place outside."

"I afraid we do, sir," Riley responded.

Everyone stared at each other for a moment. Finally, Pierce

contact with the Residence!"

"Here," the British Security Chief said. "Take one of our handheld radios so you can stay in contact with us."

"Thanks," Riley said, as both men left the British Embassy on the run.

Chapter 65

FRIDAY AFTERNOON

Rachel Fights for her Life

Sgt. Hancock looked down the driveway toward the Embassy while standing inside the Residence, next to its front door. Everyone inside the Ambassador's home had heard the RPG explosions and knew the Embassy was under attack. He couldn't directly see the building because of his angle of view, but he could see black smoke rising in the distance.

"Eagle Two from Eagle Three, do you copy? Repeat, Eagle Two, do you copy?" Susan called into her radio. Receiving no answer, she yelled down the stairs to Hancock and both DS special agents. "The radio net is down."

Hancock's eyes widened. "Take cover, some asshole's gonna fire an RPG at us!" he yelled, diving away from the foyer and landing under the nearest table.

Both agents dove for the floor as the rocket-propelled grenade hit the front door. The noise was ear-shattering. Glass, wood splinters, and shrapnel flew everywhere. The foyer was devastated in the blast. Hancock was severely dazed and barely conscious, but otherwise not visibly injured.

What saved the lives of everyone was the fact that all rooms off the foyer were three steps down, thereby the blast wave swept over them. Most of the shrapnel, flew over their heads. Agents Walt Lennon and Charley Matthews were momentarily stunned, but being farther away from the blast than Sgt. Hancock, could still function, if even at a reduced level.

said, "Everybody stay right here!" Susan with yelled from the top of the stairs. The agents called out something that sounded somewhat reassuring, but everyone's hearing was badly affected by the noise and over-pressure from the blast. Susan could see Hancock crawling very slowly out from under the table, apparently trying to get back into fighting position, but without much success.

"Shit!" Susan exclaimed, looking down from the second floor. Turning to Corporal Jones, she said, "Stay here at the top of the stairs." Then, cautiously going down the steps, she pointed the Uzi straight ahead and pulled the bolt back, ready to fire.

After the blast, Rachel decided that staying down the hall on the second floor wasn't helping anyone, so she low-crawled to the position Susan had just vacated. She didn't have a weapon, and didn't know much about them, but figured she had to do something to help. Ellen Hunt was about to do the same, when one senator opened his bedroom door.

Ellen turned to him and said, "I told you stay in the bedroom, damn it! Get back in there now and lock your door!" She held her position to ensure nobody else tried to leave their protected area.

As Susan reached the bottom of the stairs, she could see Hancock was in no condition to fight. Looking to the other side of the damaged foyer, she saw agents Matthews and Lennon glassy-eyed and partially covered with debris from the explosion, yet even while lying on the floor, they were pointing their weapons toward the entrance.

At that moment, two attackers ran through the open doorway! Susan blasted them both with two three-round bursts from her Uzi and they dropped like rocks. Two more attackers fired from outside the front door. She felt a sharp pain in her right bicep as a bullet penetrated it, tearing muscle and fibrous tissue. Holding the Uzi with her right-hand, Susan stumbled backwards onto the floor, managing to fire another blast at the doorway before dropping the gun from her useless arm. Her shots went low and to the right of her targets.

The two tribesmen entered the foyer and aimed at Susan's head from ten feet away. Matthews and Lennon opened fire with their pistols from the attackers' flank. Both terrorists went down, seriously wounded, never seeing where the shots came from.

Corporal Jones, at the top of the stairs, couldn't contain himself any longer. Watching Miss Witt get hit in the arm, made him realize he had to get into the fight. Charging down the stairs, shotgun at the ready, he saw one of the wounded attackers trying to get up, still clutching his AK-47. Jones fired once with his shotgun, hitting him squarely in the face.

"Take that motherfucker!" Jones screamed at the dead body.

Arshad, the fifth and most vicious attacker, the one who had beheaded Hussein Khan at Ghulam's Pharmacy, was watching the firefight from outside the Residence's front door. Now, he threw a grenade into the foyer which bounced off a wall and rolled toward Matthews and Lennon. Corporal Jones turned and hit the deck just before the grenade exploded. Susan Witt and Hancock were also in prone positions when the grenade went off.

Charley Matthews was nearest the grenade when it exploded. Shrapnel devastated his body, shredding his clothes, ripping chunks of flesh and splattering it across the room. He died without saying a word. The others' injuries from shrapnel were minor, however, they were all seriously disoriented and concussed.

Arshad moved quickly into the Residence. He had seen Susan gun down his two 'brothers'.

"You infidel she-devil!" he yelled in Urdu. Moving behind Susan, he grabbed her hair, pulled her head back and reached for his long, sharp knife to behead her.

Rachel, watching from the top of the stairs, narrowed her vision to the scene below. Her hands were shaking and sweat formed all over her body. Her mouth was so dry she could barely swallow. She felt like throwing-up but couldn't let Susan die.

Racing down the stairs at full speed, Rachel reached Arshad just as he was putting his knife to Susan's throat. She drove her shoulder into Arshad's back with such force, it took the terrorist totally off his feet, crashing him into the wall before he fell to the floor.

Arshad got up quickly and faced Rachel. His eyes looked fierce. She guessed they were about the same height, although he probably outweighed her by twenty pounds. Still holding the knife in his right hand, he screamed something in Urdu and lunged at her. Rachel parried his arm hard with a left-hand block, stepping sideways in a precision move befitting her martial arts training. Then, swiftly grabbing his wrist with her left hand, joined it with her right and holding his wrist tightly with both hands, bent it back and sideways in a movement causing excruciating pain. The knife fell to the floor. With a quick movement, she swept her left hand under his nose, finding a pressure point and hitting it hard. It tilted his head back unnaturally as he fell to the floor. She followed swiftly to get control, but he recovered and rolled out of her reach.

Regaining his footing, an evil sneer spread across his face. Rachel waited for an opening, planning to use the momentum of his next move against himself as she'd learned in her training, The knife was just out of reach for them both.

Arshad moved toward her swiftly, fists raised. Rachel deftly turned, blocking the back of his right hand at the forearm, grabbed his shoulder and clothes at his neck and smashed her right knee squarely into his solar plexis. He bent forward and moved away. The sneer gone from his face.

He rushed her, again, this time his fist making contact with the side of her head. Adrenalin level now at the max, she barely registered the impact. Rachel grabbed his extended arm with one hand and pulled him in closer, using her other arm, delivered a powerful elbow to the side of his head. Although momentarily stunned, he broke free of Rachel's grip on his arm, and unloaded a torrent of punches at Rachel's head. Most she blocked; some she didn't. But she managed to connect with a powerful hand thrust into his throat. Reflexively, he grabbed his neck and put a hand up to defend against a second strike; his face showed Rachel he was having trouble breathing.

His head piece was gone, knocked off in the scuffle. She grabbed the right side of his hair with her left hand, pulling him toward her. At the same time, she met his face with a right-handed heel strike just under his nose pushing upward, breaking it, causing copious amounts of bright red blood to spurt out.

Arshad was in pain and quickly changed tactics. He dove for the knife on the floor but failed to reach it. Rachel jumped on top of him. Wrapping her left arm around his throat, she locked her grip with her right hand, sliding it up behind his head, then bent him backward to increase the pain with added pressure. Just as she thought she had the upper-hand, Arshad hit her with a vicious rear elbow to her ribs. A second strike and he broke out of Rachel's hold.

As they continued struggling on the ground, he was now on top of her, Rachel managed to get him in a triangle choke, essentially scissoring his neck with her muscular thighs while trapping one of his arms between her legs. She squeezed her thighs with everything she had and bent his arm until she heard a loud crack as it broke. Arshad screamed in pain. Just when she thought he would pass out from the pressure of her thighs on his carotid artery, he managed to grab the knife with his free hand.

Rachel knew she had little time left to subdue him. With the second knuckle of her right hand, she found a pressure point on right temple and pushed with all her might. Arshad's movement slowed, then he stopped moving. Afraid to release her hold, she continued squeezing her thighs tightly around his neck until all movement ceased. His limp hand dropped the knife and he lay still, eyes opened, staring at the ceiling.

Totally exhausted, Rachel continued to lay on the ground with the dead terrorist trapped between her thighs; tears running down her bloody face. With adrenaline coursing through her veins, her hands trembled uncontrollably. But she was the one still alive.

CHAPTER **66**

FRIDAY AFTERNOON

The Fight Turns

Alex had no idea how many terrorists had attacked the Embassy. He only knew to count the four in the cafeteria that he and Washington had killed. Now, he tried to assess his defensive position: Henderson joined Alex and Gunny in their stairwell, he knew another Marine had joined Washington and Corporal Garner in the other. Besides these two teams of three in each stairwell on the ground floor, there were two remaining Marines at Post One on the second floor. The third-floor stairwells were being defended by the armed men and women from the CIA Station, DEA, the Defense Attaché Office, and Military Assistance Group.

"Boss, I think we need to counter-attack," Gunny said.

"I agree," Alex responded. If he had a choice, he would secure the cafeteria breach, then wait for Pakistani government reinforcements, if they would ever come. But, he desperately needed to know what was happening at the Residence. While he trusted Susan, the two DS visiting agents, Sgt. Hancock and Corporal Jones to defend the Residence with skill and courage, he was deeply worried they might not have the manpower, defensive ballistic barriers, or firepower to handle a large scale attack.

He needed to know that the senators, Ellen, Mrs. Pierce, and most of all, Rachel, were safe. Moreover, there were other Americans and Pakistani employees and American dependents, including children, scattered throughout the compound that might need help. He knew he couldn't do it all with his small force of Marines, but he had to start somewhere.

"Gunny, signal the other team that we three will assault the cafeteria, while they should hold their position as backup," Alex commanded.

As Gunny was giving hand signals to Sgt. Washington down the hall, next to the center stairwell, a grenade flew through the open cafeteria doors into the hallway. "Grenade!" Gunny yelled. Everyone jumped back into their stairwell alcoves.

The blast erupted in a deafening roar with shrapnel shredding the hallway. Mercifully, no one was hurt.

"They'll come now!" Alex yelled, referring to the terrorists. He shifted his body slightly away from the stairwell alcove and dropped to one knee, still halfway protected by the wall. Pointing his reloaded Uzi toward the cafeteria fifteen yards away, his eyes focused toward the place where cafeteria doors once hung before the RPG blast. Gunny stood over Alex aiming his Uzi in the same direction. The third Marine, Sgt. Henderson, was doing the same with his Ruger Mini-14.

Protecting the center stairwell, Corporal Garner lay prone on the floor. He and the third Marine on his team were aiming their Ruger Mini-14s at the cafeteria. Sgt. Washington was on one knee, fully exposed, pointing his shotgun toward the cafeteria doors.

Suddenly, four terrorists ran into the hallway from the cafeteria firing in both directions. Bullets crashed into the wall above Alex's head, just barely missing Gunny on the ricochet. Alex felt bits of wall hitting his chest and pelting his face. Feeling no real pain, he assumed he hadn't been shot.

Rushing toward both groups of defenders, the terrorists fired a torrent of bullets as they ran. Alex and the five Marines opened up on them. Henderson felt a bullet enter his left calf. The hit spun him to the ground. Momentarily, he yelled out in pain, quickly refocusing on the threat, managing to fire off several more rounds from his Ruger Mini-14. Next to the center stairwell, Washington felt flying splinters from the wall where the terrorist's bullets had hit. Blood ran down the side of his face. He winced but continued firing accurately, hitting the advancing men, watching them jerk from bullets hitting their bodies.

All four terrorists now lay dead in the corridor. With Sgt. Henderson wounded and needing attention, Gunny motioned to Washington for his team to counterassault. They moved toward the cafeteria.

Alex wasn't sure how many rounds he had fired. Reloading with a fresh magazine, he ran to join Washington's group, as rear cover for the team. Meanwhile, Gunny grabbed his knife and slit open Henderson's pant leg. Examining the wound, he determined the bullet likely passed through the fleshy portion of Henderson's calf. Pulling some first aid items from his gear, he started addressing the wound.

"Gunny, I can do this," Henderson said, grabbing the medical supplies from Rodriguez's hand. "The other men need you."

Alex moved with the team toward the cafeteria. Sgt. Washington stopped and knelt down next to several fallen terrorists to ensure they were dead. Another Marine turned one of the bodies over and examined him, yelling at the corpse, "You fucking asshole!"

Dropping to one knee, Alex searched another dead terrorist, hoping to find documents, maps, or a radio. The terrorist wasn't carrying anything except his weapons and ammunition. Wiping bloody hands off on his shirt and pants, he moved cautiously into the cafeteria.

It was really difficult to see. Acrid smoke and tear gas still hung in the air. But no living terrorists were in sight. While Washington provided cover with his shotgun, Corporal Garner used a fire extinguisher to spray foam on the cafeteria fires from the RPG blast. Alex was joined by Gunny Rodriquez and motioned him to follow as he was going through the breach in the outer wall.

Just then, the barrel of an AK-47 was thrust in from the outside. Four or five quick shots were blasted off. One round hit Rodriquez's body armor a glancing blow. The other rounds missed. Stunned, Rodriquez fell backward onto the floor.

Alex reacted immediately, knocking the barrel of the AK-47 upward by smashing his Uzi into it. But he lost control of his own gun as it dropped to the floor. Alex quickly snatched the AK-47 out of the hands of the attacker, grabbing the barrel with one hand and the middle of the weapon with his other, violently thrusting it up and back toward the terrorist. The weapon was ripped out of the attacker's grip. Instantly, Alex's hands were on the AK-47's trigger with the barrel pointed toward the attacker. He fired a long burst into the body.

A second attacker, outside the hole in the wall, was only two feet from Alex as he emerged. Alex saw him, tried to fire the AK-47 he had just used, but the gun jammed. Before the terrorist could react, however, Alex was on him. He deflected the attacker's own AK-47 with his left arm as the attacker fired, while connecting with a powerful right-hand punch to the attacker's jaw. The terrorist fell to the ground, dropping his weapon. Alex was so focused on the attacker that he never thought to draw his own pistol. Instead, he jumped onto the terrorist and hit him with another right-handed blow to the jaw.

Then he saw the long knife on the terrorist belt. Pulling it out of its sheath, Alex raised it above his head and plunged it full force into the attacker's chest. For good measure, he twisted the handle to inflict maximum injury. Blood bubbled up from the terrorist's open mouth as he died in excruciating pain.

Quickly looking around, Alex dropped the knife and drew his

pistol, but didn't see any targets. To his surprise, Gunny joined him.

"I thought you were hit," Alex said.

"I was, the bullet glanced off my metal insert in the body armor. It hurts like hell, but I'm all right."

"Okay, Reuben," Alex said, relieved, putting a reassuring hand on Gunny's shoulder. "Stay here and take control. I'm going up to Post One."

He picked up his Uzi from the ground and headed upstairs.

CHAPTER **67**

FRIDAY AFTERNOON

BETTER LATE THAN NEVER

Outside the perimeter wall of the Embassy compound, the Mobile Reaction Team commandos were successfully flanking the remaining four-man team of tribesmen in front of the Embassy. Within ten yards of the men, they fired, killing two and seriously wounding the others.

Looking down at the bodies of the dead and wounded, the MRT leader stared quizzically at one of the tribesmen and saw he was still breathing.

Unbelievable. I recognize this man from my own experience fighting about five years ago in Afghanistan with Pakistani Special Forces, he thought. *I don't recall his name, but he was part of a group of Mujahidin the Army trained to fight the Soviets. You just never know, do you?*

As Jim Riley and Josh Walker ran toward the smoking Embassy from several blocks away, two dark green SUVs with the SMG guard force decals on the side stopped next to them.

"Get in," Iqbal Satter yelled through his open car window.

The two men jumped in and the vehicles accelerated. "I'm damn glad to see you!" Riley said. "I thought you went back to Karachi."

"I canceled my plans yesterday when I heard a

demonstration was planned at the Embassy," Satter said. His driver pulled up across the street from the damaged Embassy building. The second SMG vehicle discharged six armed guards, all carrying AK-47s. Two more guards emerged from the back of Satter's own vehicle, equally well-armed.

Seeing Satter arrive, the Mobile Reaction Team leader, assessing the terrorists, ran up to him saluting both Satter and Riley. Satter and the team leader spoke quickly in Urdu, with both looking at one of the wounded terrorists lying on the ground. Satter shook his head sideways in apparent understanding.

Just then five lorries containing one hundred-twenty Pakistan Army troops pulled up in front of the Embassy. Satter, Riley, and Colonel Walker quickly walked over to ask who was in charge. Major Abbass, leader of the troops, was shouting orders to his platoon leaders.

One platoon rapidly cleared the area of demonstrators in front of the Embassy, threatening arrest, or worse, for anyone who resisted. The second and third platoons prepared to enter the compound through the hole in the wall. Abbass had been briefed on the phone by Lt. General Jamil before departing his barracks on the outskirts of Islamabad. Therefore, he assumed correctly that he might find Satter, Riley, and Walker on the scene.

Abbass saluted the trio as a courtesy as they approached, which they returned. "Lt. General Jamil has sent me here to clear your compound of rioters, but I can see this was much more than a riot."

Since the perimeter was now under control of the Pakistan Army, Riley turned to the SMG guard in the gatehouse and waved for the gates to be opened. One gate was too damaged to open, but the other still functioned, allowing easier access for the troops.

"I'm not familiar with your compound," Major Abbass stated.

"Follow me, Major," Riley said. He knew the State Department lawyers in Washington would later say he should've asked the Ambassador for permission to allow foreign troops onto the compound.

Fuck the lawyers, Riley thought.

About 80 troops jogged through the front gates, led by Riley, Colonel Walker, Satter and Major Abbass. They were confronted by a spectacle of several hundred demonstrators roaming the grounds. In the background was the Embassy, with blackened holes on the third and ground floors, several plumes of smoke still rising from the damaged areas. The Pakistani troops surrounded groups of demonstrators, forcing them into seated positions in various clusters on the lawn.

Arriving at Post One, Alex saw the arrival of Army troops on the camera monitor and identified Riley, Satter, and Walker as they jogged into the compound. He turned off the duck- and-cover alarm which was still wailing, then made a brief announcement on the Embassy public address system. It was hard-wired, yet Alex was amazed it still functioned.

"Attention in the Embassy, this is the RSO, Pakistan Army troops have arrived in the compound. No one should leave the third floor until told to do so by the RSO or the Marines. This is for your own safety. We believe there are no more terrorists in the building, but we have to clear each office and floor."

Leaving his Uzi at Post One, so he wouldn't be accidentally shot by a nervous Pakistani Army private, he hurried outside to meet Riley and the rest of the rescuers.

Riley was taken aback by Alex's appearance. His clothes and face were splattered with blood and dirt, his pants and shirt torn, and his bare arms were darkened with smoke, blood, and more dirt, and he reeked of tear gas.

Before Riley could speak, Alex, who had already removed his gas mask, reported the situation to the group:

"Terrorists fired at least two RPGs at the Embassy and at least eight of the terrorists penetrated through the breach on the ground floor into the cafeteria. They threw grenades at us as well. Those terrorists are all dead, as are the two outside the cafeteria that I just killed. Our communications are knocked out.

I'm not sure how many of our people were killed on the third floor by the RPG hit since we've been busy fighting the terrorists on the ground floor, but at least four communicators are dead.

"One Marine, Sgt. Henderson, was shot in the leg and needs medical attention. Others upstairs are injured, including Nancy who has a broken arm. The Marines are guarding the breach on the ground floor, and some of our armed employees are guarding the stairwells at the third floor.

"I don't know how many terrorists there were in total. I only know how many we killed in the Embassy. This was a well-organized attack by trained men. In my view, the demonstrators are a different bunch of people.

"Now, I need to go to the Residence to check on their status. Since we lost communications, I have no idea what's happened there."

As Alex was speaking, several busloads of Pakistani police arrived to assist the Army with detaining the demonstrators. Major Abbass took all this in and said, "We better clear the entire compound and look for other terrorists."

"Major, may I have some troops to accompany me to The Ambassador's residence?" Alex asked.

"Of course," Major Abbass responded. He rapidly spoke to one of his sergeants, who quickly assembled ten men to go with

Alex. Handing his gas mask to Jim Riley, Alex said, "You are going to need this when you go into the Embassy."

Riley handed Alex the British Embassy radio. "The Ambassador would like you to call him as soon as you have a status report on Mrs. Pierce and the others."

Riley watched with respect and admiration as Alex and ten Army troops rushed off to the Residence. Then, he turned and said, "Major, I'd like some of your men to join me in checking the inside of the Embassy."

Abbass shook his head from side to side, meaning yes. Then, Riley addressed Colonel Walker.

"Josh, I know you want to see how your people are doing, but I think it would be best if you could accompany the rest of the Major's men in sweeping the entire compound."

"Okay," Walker replied. He really wanted to see if his staff was all right, but trusted Riley's judgment

Major Abbass pointed to Captain Afzal and said to Walker, "The Captain will lead the compound sweep team."

"Thanks," Riley said gratefully, as he headed off with his team.

CHAPTER 68

LATE FRIDAY AFTERNOON

Reunited

As the front door of the Residence came into view, Alex fought back his emotions. The doors had been blown away and windows were shattered across the entire front. He could only imagine what the inside looked like, probably blackened and destroyed. Not knowing what to expect, Alex drew his pistol and shouted as they approached.

"Alex Boyd coming in with Pakistani Army troops!"

"It's safe to enter!" Walt Lennon, DS Special Agent, yelled back in response.

Four troopers took up defensive positions outside the front door, following direction from the Pakistani Army Sergeant, the rest accompanied Alex inside.

It was a scene from hell. Five dead bodies lay in distorted positions in the foyer; all appeared to be tribesmen, judging from their clothing. Blood was splattered everywhere, including pools of bright red blood around each of the bodies on the floor. The walls were blackened and badly damaged; furniture was lying in splinters. Alex saw Walt Lennon standing, none too steady, at the side of the foyer, pistol drawn, shirt torn, and pants covered with bloody stains. Then Alex noticed Charley Matthews quietly lying on the floor behind him, a gruesome sight. Alex looked at Walt, who shook his head, tears running from his eyes.

Holstering his pistol, Alex stood as Pakistani Army troops walked past him to search the Residence and ensure the battle was over.

Alex focused on the corner of the living room. Susan Witt was lying on a sofa, while Rachel had just finished wrapping Susan's bloody bicep with a cloth bandage. Sgt. Hancock was lying propped against the wall, looking a little dazed and unfocused, perhaps suffering from a concussion, but didn't seem to be physically wounded. He managed a small smile when he saw Alex. Corporal Jones was reclining on another sofa and appeared to have lower leg and foot injuries judging from his bloody pants and the red stain on the carpet under his legs. He was still somewhat operational and held his shotgun in a ready position.

When Rachel realized Alex was in the room, she left Susan's side and ran into his arms. They both teared-up and held each other tightly.

"When we heard the explosions, and lost communications, I thought you were dead," Rachel said, looking into his face, her voice choking up. "Are you all right? What happened?"

"I'm fine," he said, embracing her again.

She looks terrible, he thought. Her face was swollen, bruised, and bloodied; she had the beginnings of two black eyes and cuts on her face and neck. Blood covered her clothes. Squeezing Rachel tightly in his arms, he closed his eyes and thought about his long-held wish to be challenged in a deadly battle with terrorists. Now, he realized such an idea was immature, the price of that wish was too great: Some of his Embassy friends and one DS colleague were dead or seriously wounded; the Embassy and Residence were partially destroyed.

Most importantly, he had almost lost Rachel before getting to know her better or love her enough. While he would never shy away from doing his duty, neither would he ever dream again of riding to the rescue with guns blazing.

Still holding each other tightly, Rachel coughed.

"God, you stink! And you're a mess."

"It's called Essence of Tear Gas," Alex laughed. Looking at her bruises again and caressing her face, he said, "You don't look so hot yourself, but I've never seen a more beautiful sight."

"You should see the other guy." She nodded toward the dead terrorist on the floor. Rachel tried to muster a small smile, but couldn't really bring herself to do it. She started crying instead.

"No, really, are you all right?" Alex asked with concern.

"I think I'll be fine now," Rachel said as she clung to Alex, then sobbed again in his arms.

Susan smiled at the sight of Rachel and Alex embracing and raised her eyebrows in surprise.

"Clearly, there are some things going on that I wasn't aware of," she smiled.

Neither Alex nor Rachel heard her, now safely in their own world together.

The senators, their staff, the DCM, and Mrs. Pierce slowly made their way downstairs, all taking in the scene of carnage and destruction.

Alex pressed the talk button on the British radio. The Security Chief at the British Embassy responded. Then, he handed the radio to Mrs. Pierce.

"Worthington is coming on the radio in a second. When you're done, give me back the radio and I'll brief him."

The Chairman of the Senate Foreign Relations Committee spoke to Alex in a voice filled with bewilderment and shock.

"*What* in the world just happened? I wasn't looking forward to the press conference, but I never thought it would end like *this*."

Ellen Hunt looked extremely distressed. In a shaky voice, she asked: "How's the Embassy?"

"Senator, Ellen, have a seat; it's a long story," Alex replied.

Epilogue

In the aftermath of the terrorist attack on the American Embassy, the following is a list of outcomes:

Injured and Deceased:

- **Susan Witt,** along with injured Marines, **Nancy Williams and Walt Lennon,** were transported by the Pakistan Army to Rawalpindi for treatment at the Military Hospital, along with other injured employees from the RPG attack on the Embassy's third floor.
- Two days later, a U.S. Air Force medical evacuation flight arrived in Islamabad to transport the injured to the U.S. military hospital in Wiesbaden, Germany. All eventually recovered from their wounds. The flight also carried back bodies of the four dead Embassy Communicators and **DS Agent Charley Matthews.**
- **Gunny Rodriquez** refused treatment, noting he only had a deep bruise on his chest from the AK-47 round.

Evacuations:

- All official **U.S. Embassy dependents and non-official personnel** were evacuated to the United States via normal commercial flights during the week following the attack.

Insertions

- The medical evacuation flight brought into Islamabad several U.S. Air Force Communications experts, along with encrypted satellite equipment that allowed the Embassy to reconnect with Washington and other posts. The experts stayed two weeks until the State Department sent in a new team of Communicators. During the two-day wait for the arrival of the U.S. Air Force Communicators, the British Embassy assisted the Americans in sending and receiving secure telegrams to and from Washington via the British Foreign Office in London.

Disgraced:

- After being briefed by those inside the Embassy during the attack, the Ambassador told **Winston Hargrove IV** and **JC Colon** that he had lost confidence in their ability to function in Pakistan. They departed along with the other non-essential employees back to the U.S. Hargrove was reassigned to a minor desk job in Washington. Eventually realizing his career was over, he resigned and joined his father's investment banking firm on Wall Street, making a small fortune until his arrest for securities fraud years later. Colon returned to a job in Personnel, where he tried to engineer his next assignment back to Latin America.

Promotions:

- **Ambassador Pierce** and **DCM Ellen Hunt** asked **Marisol Lopez** to replace Winston Hargrove IV as Political

Counselor. She accepted and her work resulted in her promotion later that year.

- **Ambassador Pierce** asked **Rachel Smith** to stay on in Islamabad to handle the heavy demands from the world media for information on the incident. She agreed, which was especially fortuitous for the Embassy, because her designated replacement successfully argued that his assignment should be broken due to his concerns for the safety of his family. Rachel stayed for a year and was promoted, eventually taking over from her boss **Pete Lemon,** and becoming the Public Affairs Counselor.

Investigations:

- **Lt. General Jamil** led a special inquest team created by the Pakistani Army Chief of Staff to investigate those responsible for the attack. Thanks, in part, to the memory of the SMG Mobile Reaction Team leader in identifying one of the attackers, the investigation eventually focused on **Colonel Malik** and his associates in ISI who were arrested by the Pakistani military and interrogated, then simply disappeared. It was never clear to the Embassy if they had managed to flee, were executed, or were simply incarcerated into a deep, dark hole somewhere.
- As authorized by U.S. law, the F.B.I. opened a criminal investigation to find those responsible for the attack within
- the best efforts of the F.B.I. and in full partnership with DS criminal investigators, the F.B.I. received little cooperation from the Government of Pakistan.
- Two days following the attack on the Embassy, RSO Local Investigator **Mohammad Bhatti** finally had a chance to

take the fingerprints of the headless body being stored in the morgue, confirming it was indeed **Hussein Khan** from the Consular Section.

- A week after the attack on the Embassy, the Senior Consular Officer, **Sam Wentworth**, went searching for new visa application forms in the Embassy office. Upon opening Hussein Khan's locked cabinet, he found a dozen recently submitted visa applications from Pakistani citizens, none of which had been logged-in nor processed by the Consular Section. He brought his suspicions to the RSO for investigation which led to the eventual confirmation that Khan, before his death, had been involved in visa fraud. Further investigation exonerated **Vice-Consul Sheila Winters** of having any knowledge of this fraud.

- **Jim Riley** believed the suspicious death of Hussein Khan might also be linked to the attack on the Embassy. But with the lack of cooperation by the Government of Pakistan to produce those responsible for planning the attack, he had no evidence to substantiate his theory. Khan's murder remained unsolved.

Recommendations:

- **Alex Boyd, Susan Witt**, DS Special Agents **Walt Lennon,** and **Rachel Smith** each received the State Department's Award for Heroism and were promoted. **Charley Matthews** received the same award posthumously. **Nancy Williams** received a Superior Honor Award and was promoted. The U.S. Marine Corps issued a variety of medals to members of the Islamabad Marine Security Guard Detachment. All Islamabad Marines had onward assignments to any post of their choice.

- **Jim Riley** was also recognized with a Superior Honor Award for his overall leadership before, during, and after the incident. Following a further six months in Islamabad, Diplomatic Security asked him to curtail his assignment early to take over as the Director of Diplomatic Security in Washington, D.C. They, then, offered Riley's position as the Senior RSO to Alex; he accepted and spent the remainder of his tour in charge of the office.

- **The U.S. Department of State** sent in a team of engineers, construction experts, and US Navy Seabees to oversee the repair of the damaged Embassy and the Ambassador's Residence.

Outcomes:

- The **U.S. State Department**, as required by law, convened an eight-week-long Accountability Review Board to examine the incident. Despite extreme efforts of Winston Hargrove IV to turn the Board against Alex Boyd, they found the actions of all three Regional Security Officers, both before and during the attack, to be exemplary. The Review Board also noted the solid leadership of **Ambassador Pierce** and **DCM Ellen Hunt.**

- However, following submission of the Review Board's official report, the **Review Board Chairman**'s off-the-record conversations with the Secretary of State and with the Assistant Secretary for South Asian Affairs made note of the attitude and judgment of Winston Hargrove IV and JC Colon toward security as being so unacceptable that their actions could have resulted in a greater disaster. As a result of the Review Board taking testimony from Hargrove himself, the Secretary of State also complained to the President of the United States about **Benjamin Shapiro**'s instructions to Hargrove during the attack. Shapiro politically survived the incident and upon his completion of service with the National Security Council, became a frequent guest commentator on national television.

- The Board further **recommended an upgrade of weapons** issued to RSOs and to Marine Security Guards, notably replacing the Marine shotguns and RSO Uzis/Ruger Mini-14s with new M-4 Carbines of 5.56 mm.
- **Alex Boyd and Rachel Smith** continued their romance and became inseparable.

Mel Harrison

After graduating from the University of Maryland with a degree in Economics, Mel Harrison joined the US Department of State Foreign Service, spending the majority of his career serving in the Diplomatic Security Service.

Over the next 28 years, he served in American embassies as either a Special Agent/Regional Security Officer or Economic Officer in Saigon, Quito, Rome, London (twice), Islamabad, and Seoul. While in Islamabad, as the Senior Regional Security Officer, he won both the United States State Department Award for Valor, and its worldwide Regional Security Officer of the Year Award.

Following government retirement, Mel spent ten years in corporate security and consulting work with assignments often taking him throughout Latin America and the Middle East.

Mel met his wife, Irene, while both served in Quito. Irene, a Foreign Service Management Specialist, and Mel married in Rome beginning their lifelong love of travel and all things Italian.

Now, residing in Florida, Irene enjoys her genealogy interests while providing invaluable support and ideas for Mel's writing career.

Made in the USA
Monee, IL
27 January 2020